Dear Diane,

Pretty
little lies

Peace. Love. Fashion!

Jennifer Miller

Edited by: Second Gaze Editing
Cover Design: Wicked by Design
Formatted by: Kassi Cooper and JT Formatting
Photograph taken by: Anja Rohrich Photography
Cover model: Jenn Werner

ISBN-13: 9780989407403

Acknowledgements

Writing this feels very surreal. I never thought I would be here; I always dreamed that I would write my own book but just thought it was one of those dreams that are bigger than reality. I'm glad I woke up and realized that my dreams weren't going to fall into my lap, to make them come true, I had to chase them. Many of you joined me on this journey and I want to say thank you.

First, thank you to you, the reader, for picking up this book and giving it a chance. I hope this is the beginning of a beautiful friendship between us!

Georgia Cranston, our weekly writing dates were our best idea ever! The hours we've spent brain-storming, laughing and plotting have been amazing and I always look forward to each and every one. Now I only have one thing to say, "Boy! Get Georgia a new computer stat! She needs to get her ass writing!"

Jen Cola, I still don't know what possessed me to reach out to you that day, but boy am I glad that I did. I never expected to gain such a wonderful friend as a result. Thank you for believing in me.

Heidi McLaughlin, your encouragement, support and advice have been invaluable. You prove over and over again that you mean what you say and I don't even know how to find the words to thank you. Forever My Girl will always hold a special place in my heart, because it brought me to you.

Ang Corbett, I have sent you so many messages asking you questions, seeking your advice, or flat out freaking out. You never hesitate to respond to each and every one and you give the best advice. Thank you for being a true friend and we will share our love of Jax and the MC forever!

Mary Ting, you never hesitate to help me whether it is by sharing my facebook posts, or offering encouragement and advice. I appreciate it more than you know. Thanks for being my friend.

It takes a team of people to make me look good and I appreciate them all. Robin at Wicked by Design, thank you for my gorgeous book cover. You were so patient enduring my constant tweaking and trying to explain what I saw in my head. Thank you for your patience and I can't wait to work together again. Kassi Cooper, thanks for saying yes when I asked your help with formatting my paperback and Julie with JT Formatting for formatting my ebooks. Espe at Second Gaze Editing – thank you for your meticulous work, your wonderful suggestions, encouragement and for not making fun of me for my lack of commas!

Patricia, Jen J., Kim, Brandi, Heidi Mae, - you are awesome. Your love of my book, its characters, your honesty, enthusiasm and advice were invaluable to me. I can't wait to plot out book two with you. Here's to horizontal running and mermaid dancing!

Beth, I was completely honored when you asked me if you could make a trailer for my book. The time, energy and art you put into making it means so much to me and I thank you.

My family has been a constant support to me, even when I was likely very annoying at times with my never-ending book talk. Mom, thank you for being one of my biggest fans. Your love, support, advice, encouragement, editing, plotting, excitement and pure joy I've shared with you over this process, has been one of my favorite parts. I can't imagine doing this without you. Thank you for helping me work out those sexy parts too! I will never forget our desk test. Dad, Lauren and Michael – your enthusiasm, texts asking how things are going and your unfailing love and support is something that I know I can always depend on and I never take it for granted.

Hannah and Grace, thank you for helping me come up with character names and book title ideas. You two are my biggest little fans. Telling everyone, from your music teacher to random grocery store attendants about your Mommy's book in excitement, makes my heart swell. I love being your Mommy, I hope I make you both proud.

Jake, I don't know if I even have the words to express how thankful I am for you. The nights you've spent being the only parent because I was lost in Olivia's world, did not go unnoticed. I love how you want to be involved in every bit of this process with me, every step of the way. You've spent so much time encouraging me, asking how it was going, wiping my tears of frustration, telling me I was absolutely not going to give up, celebrating my victories, bragging to your friends and family and just loving me the whole way. You are the best part of me, my true soul mate and I love you more than I can ever express.

For

JAKE, HANNAH, GRACE

&

PAPA – I know you would be so proud. I miss you.

Contents

Chapter One   1
Chapter Two   10
Chapter Three   21
Chapter Four   36
Chapter Five   49
Chapter Six   61
Chapter Seven   71
Chapter Eight   83
Chapter Nine   95
Chapter Ten   105
Chapter Eleven   115
Chapter Twelve   125
Chapter Thirteen   134
Chapter Fourteen   147
Chapter Fifteen   154
Chapter Sixteen   162
Chapter Seventeen   170
Chapter Eighteen   178
Chapter Nineteen   188
Chapter Twenty   196
Chapter Twenty-One   206
Chapter Twenty-Two   215
Chapter Twenty-Three   224
Chapter Twenty-Four   233
Chapter Twenty-Five   242
Chapter Twenty-Six   250
Bonus Material   255

Chapter One

"Fashion tip: Stilettos are great when paired with a great pair of jeans, a skirt, or a dress. Not only do they make your legs look longer and give your calves a great workout but they have the added bonus of coming in handy should you need to give a cheating husband a kick in the crotch!"

I blink hard and try to bring the papers in front of me into focus. I'm almost done. I just need to sign a few more of these freaking legal documents and I can put this ridiculous mistake of a marriage behind me. When I met Deacon, I was a sophomore in college. I was vulnerable, and looking for an escape from the boring student I had become. Deacon offered me just the release I craved. The endless parties, tapped kegs, promises of hot sex, and occasionally other experimentation that I choose to forget, made getting involved with him a no-brainer. Add a side of studying and managing a fashion blog that took on a life of its own, you have my college life and relationship with Deacon in a nutshell.

My heart aches; anguish now courses through my veins just as steadily as blood. I'm really not sure at this point how or why I am still feeling pain. If I'm honest with myself, I can't really be surprised my marriage has ended this way. I mean, I got married in Vegas for god's sake; at a drive up chapel, after a drunken late night proposal that I can barely remember. Spring Break during our senior year, a bunch of us had the brilliant idea to spend the week in Vegas. One night during our stay, we did the traditional walk up and down the strip, drinking the whole way. I vaguely remember Deacon making a production on the sidewalk, getting down on one knee and asking me to marry him, a rose he had bought from a street vendor in hand. Amongst the hoots and hollers of our friends, I impulsively accepted and we flagged down a taxi cab to take us to the closest chapel.

This bizarre wedding was only the beginning of what ended up being a marriage full of questions and contradictions. I spent years wondering what I had gotten myself into and questioning why I stayed as long as I did. So the question remains, why then, am I still struggling? I've cried until I heaved from it over and over again and had nothing left. I've been so angry, that it felt like my insides were burning, and I was sure I was going to combust from the intensity of my fury. How my heart can still ache at a loss that frankly has been coming for a while, is unfathomable to me.

I stare again at the papers, and while the whole document is in the same font, the words *Dissolution of Marriage* seem to be screaming at me, taunting me with their meaning.

Dissolution of Marriage.

Divorced at twenty – five.

Single and just another statistic to add to the divorce rate.

Admitting I never thought this would happen to me is a gigantic understatement. My life wasn't supposed to go this way. At one time I had a plan, a dream, but little by little, it all fell apart.

I briefly close my eyes and see myself on my wedding day, well what I remember of it anyway. Wearing my favorite designer jeans and Madonna t-shirt, giggling, with a cocktail in my hand; and while it may have been a crazy and an impulsive thing to do, I was actually elated and excited. When I woke up the next morning and realized what I had done, I knew things would never be the same. I had a brief sense of uncertainty and I wondered how I could have been so impulsive to make such a huge, life-altering decision, but at the same time, all I could see was the life I had always envisioned, more exciting and fuller because instead of just me…there would be an *us*. I wouldn't have to be alone, vulnerable, and looking for an escape again. Maybe I could even resurrect the real me and get my life back on track. I would have a husband that would support me no matter what. Right? Any and all naysayers be damned, my life was about to start, and I would prove them all wrong. The world was mine! What a fool I was.

Now, just four years after saying I do, I realize my life is nothing but a horrible cliché. I remember the day it all came crashing down and the reality of what my marriage had become was laid out before me, refusing to be ignored.

With the eagerness of a child returning home after their long anticipated first day of school, delighted to have gotten off of work early and excited to see my husband, I exited the car. Bottle of wine in my hand and a sack of just-purchased groceries in the other arm, I intended on making Deacon a pasta dinner served by candlelight. I opened the door and walked into our apartment, immediately overcome with the stench of pot. As I walked to the kitchen and placed my packages on the counter, I saw a trail of clothing leading to the closed door of my bedroom. I froze. Doom and dread instantly ran through my body and I felt a burning from my neck to the top of my head, making me feel dizzy; sick. I knew without a doubt what I was going to find. I slowly started walking into my bedroom...

"Olivia...? Olivia?"

Blinking quickly and shaking my head, trying to rid myself of the awful picture in my mind, I look up at my attorney and attempt a smile. "I'm sorry, Clive. My mind wandered. You were saying?"

"That's okay, Olivia. I was just asking if you got everything signed? I am going to have my assistant make you a copy of the documents for your records."

Clive, whom I'm guessing is in his early 60s, has a pot belly, receding hair line and rather large ears. His kind and gentle personality never made me uncomfortable or feel stupid during this entire nightmare of a process. Once, during our conversation, he divulged he's been happily married for 30 years and has three grown children. I imagine seeing the ugly side of marriages and divorces up-close and personal has made him realize how lucky he is. I never doubted for a second that he would get my divorce done quickly and accurately.

"Thanks, Clive. That would be great," I tell him as I hand him the documents I've signed for copying.

Clive leaves his office and I'm left there with nothing but my thoughts once again. My mind flashes back to my apartment six months ago.

I picked up the articles of clothing littering my apartment floor as I walked closer to my bedroom --- a man's shirt with buttons missing, with lipstick in a shade I don't wear, on the collar. A woman's shirt in a very pale yellow, a color I didn't own. Given my skin tone, it would wash me out; my complexion is too pale to pull off such colors. Dark haired women like me should stick to bold colors.

I took a couple more steps and picked up an orange bra that must be a double D, two sizes bigger than I wear, and in a color I did not possess. An orange bra under a pale yellow shirt? Really?

I tentatively, but steadily moved closer to the door and I heard the moans coming from the other side of the door. Apparently they were much too involved...the sound of my arrival did not even phase their sexcapade in the slightest.

Opening my bedroom door, I saw more clothes trailing up to my bed, an empty wine bottle on the side table and all I can think is that it's three o'clock in the afternoon, a bit early for wine. It took my mind a few moments to catch up before I fully comprehended the scene in front of me. A naked, thin-bodied, extremely large-busted, peroxide blonde woman was in my bed, in our bed, riding the shit out of my husband. His head thrown back in apparent ecstasy, his eyes rolled back in his head. The bitch was fiercely slapping her body up and down against his. They had no idea I was standing there. None.

"WHAT THE FUCK?!" I screamed, dropping the clothing I was somehow still holding to the floor.

I stared, completely dumbfounded.

Deacon practically threw the whore off of him in reaction to my scream and she went tumbling off the side of the bed.

Our bed.

Our desecrated bed.

Deacon yelled, "Oh my God! Olivia!"

"That's right, you asshole! It's Olivia, your wife!" Before I even knew what I was doing, I stalked over to the side of the bed where I saw the blonde bitch fall, dragged her up by her hair, and bitch slapped her across the face. Deacon was standing there staring at me with his mouth open, eyes wide, and a horror-shocked expression on his face. Before he could even comprehend what I was about to do, I kicked him in the freaking balls as hard as I could.

"You bastard!" I shouted "How could you?"

With fury coursing through my veins, I was shocked at my reaction. I'm not a violent person, had never hit anyone in my life. I was completely taken over by absolute disbelief and rage at what I was seeing. In an instant, literally the span of three minutes, my life had completely changed. I was filled with absolute agony. I didn't deserve this.

After my inner bitch did her thing, I stalked out of the room and headed to the couch, where I had thrown my purse when I came home. During that time, Deacon somehow miraculously recovered from the blow to his crotch and started screaming my name while holding his hand over himself, and chased me into the living room. I snatched up my purse and headed to the front door. Before I could reach it, Deacon reached me, grabbed my shoulder and spun me around to face him.

"Olivia, wait... I can explain! It's not what you think!"

I laughed. I have no doubt it was a super creepy clown circus kind of laugh, but still I laughed in his asinine face. He is unbelievable. Of all the things he could have said to me.

"It's not what I think? Are you KIDDING ME?! I think I just saw my husband jamming his dick into some bitch that isn't his wife! Don't even try to explain yourself Deacon, there is NO excuse. There is NOTHING that you can say that could make me not walk out of here right now."

I shoved him as hard as I could and made my way to the door.

Recovering quickly, Deacon caught up to me, grabbed my arm. Hard. The real Deacon was about to make an appearance. The begging lasted all of thirty seconds. "Olivia, I said to fucking wait. You are overreacting like a damn baby. Stop being a bitch and listen to me."

I looked at him and sneered, "Screw you, Deacon."

I ripped my arm out of his grasp, knowing I would definitely have a bruise above my elbow, where his fingers dug into me hard. I opened the door, ran out, and slammed it behind me...Deacon screaming my name behind me.

I started to wait for the elevator, but when I heard my apartment door open behind me, I made a dash for the stairwell door and threw myself through the threshold, knowing that he wouldn't follow me naked down the stairwell. I ran as fast as I could down two flights of stairs, stopped, sat down on a stair and started to sob.

"Here you go Olivia. Your copies."

I jump slightly, startled by Clive's return.

"We will get these papers filed with the court, and you can expect to get your divorce decree in the mail in about two weeks."

Clive hands me my copies of the divorce documents in a manila envelope. Wow. My four-year marriage reduced to a few papers in an envelope.

"Thank you. For everything."

"You're welcome, and if you stop and see Jessica on your way out, she will give you your final invoice and make sure she has your forwarding address in our system. Best of luck to you."

I smile, give him a nod and step out of his office and walk to the reception desk to see Jessica.

After paying my bill, I take my manila envelope and walk out of the office.

The sun hits me in the face; I squint my eyes and start rooting around in my purse looking for my sunglasses. Popping them onto my face, I just stand there for a moment, take a deep breath and start walking to catch the next train. Pulling out my cell phone from the front pocket of my purse, I start dialing my best friend, Pyper.

"Hi this is Pyper! I must be treating my clients like royalty at Shimmer & Soothe Salon and Spa! You should be jealous that you aren't here yourself! Leave me a message and I will get back to you to schedule the appointment I'm sure you want to make!"

I laugh at my friend's message, as usual and wait for the beep.

"Hi, it's me. Well, it's done. I just signed the papers and left Clive's office. Why do I feel...?" I stop talking and sigh. "Honestly, I don't know how I feel. Part of me feels empty and part of me wants to host my own divorce party. With cake. A cake that has a bride on top holding a knife with the bloody groom in a pool of his own blood at the bottom. They really make those you know. Crazy right? Anyway, give me a call when you can! I'm headed home to do some more packing. Kisses!"

I press end on my phone and shove it back into the front pocket of my purse. I walk through the subway entrance, scan my link pass, and wait for the T to arrive. I start reflecting on my life here. Deacon moved out a while ago. I had to threaten to call the cops if he didn't get his ass out. But, I am leaving Boston for good. I still remember coming here seven years ago to attend the journalism program at Boston University. While it wasn't my first college choice, I will always look back, and love having lived here. In fact, once I married Deacon, I always thought I would stay here forever. Instead, I'm packing up and moving my life back to Chicago, Illinois. I'm going to move in with Pyper.

The T finally arrives and I step in looking for a seat. I take a seat towards the back and sit next to the window. Leaning my head back on the seat, watching the subway walls as they fly by, Deacon's handsome face comes to my mind. Willing to do anything to win me back, he brought me flowers over and over. He gave me sentimental cards pouring his feelings into them, telling me how sorry he was, that he made a mistake, and of course he promised that it would never happen again. He bought me jewelry, offered to move away with me to start over, told me he couldn't live without me.

7

One time, after I had kicked him out, I came home from work to find he had let himself into our old apartment, filled it up with flowers, made me dinner and once again pleaded with me not to leave him. I was so close to relenting. I can still close my eyes and remember the good times, the laughs we shared, all the times he tenderly made love to me and I felt like I was the center of his universe. As crazy as it seems, I know in his own demented way, he truly loved me. I know I loved him.

That night, I almost gave in; it wasn't because of the flowers or the dinner, it was the pure anguish I saw in his eyes and the tears that trailed down his cheeks when he begged me not to leave him. I looked in his eyes, really looked and the sight astounded me. I had never seen him cry before; but it wasn't only that. I could see the love there. I could see that he truly wanted to work things out and was pleading for me to stay. Part of me wanted to give into him. I could see myself jumping into his arms and telling him we could figure it out and try… really try to make it work. I wanted to be able to tell him that I forgave him but in the back of my mind I had realized something in our time apart. Our marriage was a sham to begin with. The fact that we had made it for four years was a freaking miracle and believe it or not, choosing to stay would have been the easy way out. Staying was easy. Choosing to move on, the hard part.

I shattered his heart that night. I looked him in the eyes and told him once again to get out of the apartment, and that I didn't want to see him again. I told him there was absolutely nothing he could do to make the situation right and that he needed to just stop. Stop trying. Stop buying me things. Stop coming over. Stop trying to fix "us," because it couldn't be done. We were broken. We were over; the marriage was over. When all of his efforts failed to work, and he felt desperate, he became mean.

Anger flashed across his face and he tried to hide it. His pleading ended up with him calling me names and storming out of the apartment. I had hurt his pride, set him off; a dangerous combination.

I know little miss blonde slut wasn't Deacon's first betrayal; I just chose to ignore the signs that were right in front of my face. I chose to believe the pretty lies he told me. The excuses ranged from working late, to stopping at the gym, or running into an old friend. When he realized the lies were becoming more frequent, he tried to bury my questions and disappointments with flowers, shopping sprees, or sex that was driven more by anger than passion. For a while, I desperately clung to the lies and the illusion that everything was fine. While his affairs mattered and of course they hurt, the simple truth was that they were only part of the problem. I didn't want to be in a marriage that only works when I played dumb and pretended to believe the lies, and allowed things to always be on his terms.

I want more.

I need more.

I deserve more.

Chapter Two

"Fashion tip – When spending several hours in a car, it makes sense to dress as comfortably as possible, but just like my mom always said, in case of an accident, make sure you at least have on some nice undies just in case someone may have to rip off your clothes to save your life!"

I take a sip of my hot mocha from *Coffee Now* and roll my eyes in ecstasy. I can feel my taste buds doing the tango of happiness. I grab a quick bite of a blueberry muffin and I'm in seventh heaven. What a perfect combination – and an ideal way to begin the two-day drive to Chicago.

I have everything set. My cell phone is plugged into the charger and the playlist created just for the drive is already streaming loudly through the speakers. My radar detector with laser jammer and GPS are mounted on the dash, and my beloved Dodge Avenger is packed to the brim with all of my worldly possessions. It is a really strange and somewhat unsettling feeling to know that the representation of one's entire life can be packed up and placed in the back of a car. There isn't much. I'm moving into Pyper's condo with her. Good thing her parents still spoil her rotten and she doesn't want for a thing. Her furniture and décor is impeccable – my stuff wouldn't have really fit in, not that she would have cared, but I didn't really want any of the apartment furnishings anyway. Too many painful memories. Deacon reclaimed the tattered belongings he had when we married, and everything else were pieces I purchased with him. Dishes we picked out together – the ones that we were finally able to agree on after looking at God knows how many patterns; the bed we selected after lying on mattress after mattress trying out, testing out and never really being able to feel the difference that the salesman insisted differentiated the various types – pillow top, plush, foam, firm, latex, innerspring. Who knew there were so many? The beat-up brown leather couch we had made love on several times. Um, no thanks. I don't want any of it. Instead, I put an ad in the newspaper and on an online selling site, sold most of it, and donated the rest. I made decent money off of everything and happily deposited it into the bank, comfortable with this decision and anxiously looking forward to starting the next chapter of my life with unblemished and unspoiled possessions.

This move still seems surreal in so many ways. Although this has been in the works for a few months, it's like I'm having an out of body experience and all of this is really happening to someone else. I still can't believe that all of this craziness is now my life. While I love my home town and can't wait to see Pyper, since it has been a while, I have so many apprehensions about going back.

I didn't ask to be cheated on, but I can't help but feel like a failure. Thinking about returning home with my tail between my legs makes my stomach churn. I've been told my recurring feelings of inadequacy and defectiveness are all normal, and are not surprising, given the fact that my husband turned to another woman – likely several women. Excellent therapy has helped me to know the truth deep down, but sometimes that truth feels far removed.

Ok...repeat...what happened was not about my insufficiency, but about Deacon and his issues. He is accountable for his behavior. That is not something I should place on my shoulders. I may have ownership, but not for his actions. I didn't do anything to warrant such behavior.

People say, of course, that a relationship takes two. And it does, but the fact is, I feel like the rug was pulled out from under me. Yes, the way Deacon behaved wasn't always healthy, but it wasn't like we fought a lot or argued about money or sex or careers or anything that should have mattered. But, what the hell was there to argue about? The man typically got his way. I avoided creating conflict, told myself that perhaps if he had what he wanted that he might change his behavior. And when that didn't happen, I made up excuses and enabled him even more. Hoping, praying that it would change him, that he would inevitably behave differently. And why did I think I could change him? Why would I marry someone I wanted to change? How does one explain this to others?

What I dread most are the possible inquiries that could come my way. While many of my old friends moved away to go to college like I did, there are still a few that remained and I know at some point, I will run into them. Including, *him,* if he's still there. I'm just not sure I can handle the judgmental looks, the insincerity wrapped in concern, the condemnation. I wish I didn't care so much about what people think about me.

My therapist told me not to be so hard on myself. She reminded me that I'm emotionally vulnerable, everything feels intense right now. I'm being too harsh on myself and likely unable to appropriately interpret others – so it is silly to delve too deep into what I think others will think, and how and why it will likely bother me. How could anyone go through such an experience and feel any other way? I just need to remember these feelings are all part of this entire process. One thing I know for sure…there is no better friend than Pyper to help me get on the other side of this abyss.

Of course, I shouldn't be surprised that I wasn't able to leave my apartment without encountering one last piece of drama. My mind drifts to our last interaction. I was putting tape on the last packing box and making sure I had everything I needed in my overnight suitcase, when there was a knock on my apartment door. I felt a shiver of dread immediately run through me from head to toe. I knew who was on the other side of the door but I opened it anyway.

"How did I know it was going to be you Deacon?"
Given his personality, why would I expect anything less? Looking at him standing there, I still felt attraction and I hated it.

After everything he put me through, the fact I still felt anything for this asshole is a mystery. He looked so dashing, standing there in his black dress pants and gray dress shirt, but considering my heart has been punched, crushed, stomped on and nearly eviscerated by him, the mere idea that a part of me still felt moved and alive just looking at him is infuriating. I know my reaction comes from my inner sex slut, because while my heartfelt stabs of pain, hurt, and intermittent rage, my libido stood up and gave him a lot more attention than he deserved. Stupid sexual urges. Granted, he doesn't instill the same reaction in me that he used to, but the slight quickening of my pulse...the warmth in my panties...it was still there. Damn him.

"What are you doing here?" I spit.

Stalking into my apartment like he has every right to be there, looking around taking in the emptiness, his eyes met mine. "I'm here to tell you, again, that you are making a huge mistake and to give you one last opportunity to come to your senses. You've gone through with this divorce without any regard for how I feel, or the fact that I've told you over and over that my indiscretion was just a stupid mistake. Now you're dumb enough to think you can go through with this stupid move. I'm telling you for the last time not to go."

I couldn't help but wonder if he was being serious. He's fought me tooth and nail on our divorce, but I couldn't have remained more resolute. Thank goodness the judge still granted the divorce despite all of his protests. He was unwilling to agree to an uncontested, irreconcilable difference-based divorce. Not guiltless, poor misunderstood Deacon. He was so confident he could stop the proceeding. Being required to go to court to hear his petitions and half-baked excuses and lies; not to mention having to relive my side of the story, was horrible-having to face the deceit and deception that had gone unknown for who knows how long. In the end, it was worth it, because it meant I could rid myself of a marriage I never should have entered. Hearing the sordid details bolstered by conviction. I refused to get caught in his melodrama. I lost myself once – never again. My libido may have been fooled by his good looks, but my heart and my head are not providing him access ever again.

"Excuse me, do you even hear yourself Deacon? I'm not about to go through this with you again, as we've been over this how many times already? Apparently you still aren't getting it, so let me tell you one last time....we are officially divorced. Not married. Not a couple, not in a relationship. Not anything. Caput. Done. Over. That means you legally have absolutely no say in what I do, where I go, or how I live my life. You have no right to tell me anything. You have no jurisdiction here. I have no desire to hear your opinion, your thoughts, or desires. You have no influence, no impact, no...anything. Now leave. I don't want you here, and you are not going to change my mind. Get out before I call the police and they make you get out."

"Olivia, just listen to me. Please."

Please. I was shocked, I admit it. I didn't even know the word please was in his vocabulary. He typically just told me what to do. He never asked me to do anything. Never inquired about what I want, or what was best for me. What would please me. I recovered from the shock quickly, because it doesn't matter. Not anymore. "No Deacon. I have nothing else to say to you. We are done. It is over. Now leave."

Deacon walked toward me with a hard and menacing look on his face. He reached out and grabbed my shoulders hard, forcing me to look up into his eyes. "Ouch, Deacon. You're hurting me. Stop!"

He didn't let go, if anything his grip became firmer. "This is far from over, Olivia. It doesn't matter how far away from me you run, princess. You can't get rid of me that easily. I did not want the divorce, do not want this separation, and I know once you get the chance to think this over, you will realize that you don't want a life without me either. If you need space, fine, I will give you some. For now."

I'm stunned. Amazingly, my hands were not shaking with the unsteadiness and alarm, even near panic, that engulfed me. I don't understand why he is making this so hard. I tried to shake his grasp off my shoulders but he didn't budge.

"Hear me now Olivia, this isn't over."

"Are you threatening me, Deacon?" Infuriated, tears filled my eyes. It wasn't only the physical pain that caused this hurt, *but the continued dread and terror he can still invoke. I'm angry at myself for having a moment of pause and regret, for opening the stupid door, for all of it. I just want him to go, to be gone. I don't want to waste any more tears or emotions on him. I promised myself right there, while looking in his intimidating, incensed eyes that, that would be the last time I cried over him.*

Before he could answer there was a knock at the door. "Olivia? It's Mrs. Mooney from next door. Are you there honey?"

That time, when I pulled away from his grasp, he dropped his hands. I hastily turned to open the door for my neighbor, and so he could get the hell out. As he slipped by me, he whispered in my ear, "See you soon princess."

The sound of Home by Philip Phillips loudly resonates through my car, snapping me back to the here and now and I shudder at the memory of Deacon's last promise to me. Trying to brush off the disturbing feeling, I look down at my phone and I smile, seeing my best friend, the gorgeous, red-headed Pyper blowing me kisses in the picture, alerting me to her calls. I turn down my radio and happily answer her call. "Hey sexy lady!"

I hear her unrestrained laugh and it makes me smile. "Hey yourself, beautiful best friend of mine! I was just calling to make sure you got out on time and that your gorgeous ass is on its way home!"

She makes me laugh out loud. Her friendship and love is just the balm I need for my wounds. "My car is packed to the brim and I am already on my way. Homeward bound as we speak!"

"I'm so glad that you got off okay. I'm still angry that you wouldn't let me fly out and make the drive with you, or let me ship your things so you could have jumped on a plane and been here already."

"Pyper," I sigh, "there was no need for you to do that. I'm more than capable of driving myself out there and the time to be, well, in transition and by myself, will be good for me."

"It isn't about being capable. You will have more than enough time to be by yourself while I'm at work. It's about you letting me be there for you right now."

15

"You will be…soon enough. And you are already doing plenty."

Sighing at me so she knows I'm still aware of her displeasure, she decides to move the conversation along. "I am so excited to see you! I can't wait for you to get here. I have so many things I want us to do. I can't wait to get you all settled in and unpacked. The spare bedroom is all set and just waiting for you to make it your own. When you get here, I think we should start out with you visiting my spa, because I'm sure you are going to need a massage after that long drive."

I can't keep up with her; she is talking a mile a minute. I laugh and say, "Sure, a massage sounds great. I'm sure you're right; I'm going to need it. I can't wait to get there too. Thanks again for everything. I don't know what I would do without you."

"Not another word. This is what friends do. And what you would do without me? Well, you will never have to find out."

"Thank God for that."

She laughs and asks, "How are you doing? Any problems before you left?"

I swear, it's like she has a sixth sense about these things. Or maybe she just has Deacon's personality down pat. I'm not sure if that makes her extremely intuitive, slightly scary, or a combination of the two. I don't know how she does it, but I suppose that is one of the many reasons she's my best friend. I don't always have to say the words to her, she's the other half of my brain, and she just knows. I proceed to tell her about Deacon's last hurrah, how he basically tried to order me not to leave, and his comment that we aren't over.

"Oh Olivia, I'm so sorry. What a jerk! Like you really needed one more round before you got out of there. Good thing is, you are on your way and you won't have to deal with that anymore. You are coming back home where you belong and where you should have been all along. Just like we planned."

I should have known she wouldn't be able to resist slipping that in there. "I know. You are right, as always." I smile.

"Don't you forget it babe! Well, I'm going to let you go so you can concentrate on driving. Please call me if you have any trouble and call me when you take a break, and again when you stop for the night."

"Okay, okay, calm down. I will call you, I promise."

"Hey! I'm serious! You'd better. I want to know you are okay, alright? And Olivia, I really can't wait to see you."

"I can't wait to see you too. I will call you soon. I promise. Love ya!"

"Love ya back, lady!"

When we hang up, my mind immediately goes back to the day Pyper and I first became friends. We were in the 2nd grade and assigned to the same class. Our teacher was Miss Montez, and bless her heart, she had the patience of a saint. One day, during recess, I was standing by the monkey bars, so excited to get on them because I had finally mastered swinging all the way across -a very huge deal when you are eight years old! I stepped up to the ladder and started to ascend to the step that would take me to the top rung, when Joey, a skinny kid with a severe booger problem, stepped in front of me, and exclaimed that I wasn't allowed to get on the monkey bars because of the new rule that refused access to people with four eyes. It was my first day wearing the dark-rimmed, slightly cat-eyed glasses, and already being a bit nervous about my new look, felt the emotions I had suppressed all morning rising rapidly to the surface. Balling my hands into fists, tears gathering in my eyes and being too shy to speak or certainly to fight back, even to booger boy, I started to come back down the stairs. Suddenly, a red-headed spitfire, carrying all sixty or so pounds of herself, with authority that any child could see, marched up, kicked Joey in the shin, and told him to get lost! As Joey ran off crying to the teacher, Pyper turned to me without a care in the world, completely oblivious to the fact she was about to get yet another lecture on bullying, and said, "Well, go on; what are you waiting for?"

We've been inseparable ever since.

Pyper has been by my side through everything. First pimple, first bra, when I started my period, she started hers merely days after mine. We attended our first boy/girl party together and had our first kiss on the same night, in eighth grade when we played Spin The Bottle at a friend's birthday party. She cheered me on when I took my driving test, and held my hand when I got my first eyebrow wax. She helped me get ready for my first date, giggled and swooned with me when I fell in love, and later, she was there for me to wipe my tears when that first love…the one I thought I would be with forever…broke my heart. Even after I moved away, and she opened Shimmer & Soothe, yet another gift from her Dad, after graduating from beauty school, she was still there for me. Always.

My parents are no different and I smile to myself thinking about them too. Now retired, as soon as they found out about Deacon and I divorcing, they told me I was more than welcome to move to Arizona and stay with them. But I just can't do it. I need my independence and they also need theirs. I love them even more for offering me sanctuary and I know without a doubt they will always be available for–and supportive of me. I know how lucky I am, despite the fact that, at times, I feel like I've been nothing but a disappointment to them. Alright, perhaps that's a bit dramatic, but still how I feel at times, nonetheless.

The only disappointing thing I did was marry quickly and had a wedding that they couldn't attend. They supported my decision to go to Boston University, even though it was a last minute decision, having chosen not to attend journalism school at Loyola University in Chicago after months of planning. Getting your heart broken can change your plans quickly. It's not like I settled for Boston. Both universities had always been my top two choices. While they were sad to see me go so far away, they understood my need to do so. They supported me all through school, even after I was married to Deacon and were confused and unsure about the decision I had made. While they would voice their concerns for me, and at rare times for our relationship, they never tried to run my life, and I love them for it. They are very happily married and their marriage has been a wonderful example to me of what it means to truly be soul mates. Given that, one might wonder why I made the Deacon mistake, but I think I was just so desperate to be loved again, that I jumped at the first guy – well, the first great looking guy - that showed me attention in college. Plus, I admit to being intrigued by the fact that he was a couple of years older than me. Not only was he good looking, but he was an upper classman who was interested in me. At least, that's what I think happened.

Even though my parents were concerned about the divorce and its impact on me, I think part of them couldn't be more relieved. They met Deacon, of course, and he was always on his best behavior while they were around, but I think they had a feeling that things were not exactly as they appeared and that I wasn't as happy as either they had hoped me to be or I had wanted to be.

Fortunately, as a journalist, I can work from anywhere, so relocating was a non-issue, as far as my job was concerned. I have a few style magazines that consistently print my fashion articles, and another one that has a "What's Hot Now?" column to which I regularly contribute. I love my work, and it pays me well, which is crazy considering it started out as a crazy fluke. I've always wanted to be a journalist, but my success came quickly after I started a fashion blog for an assignment, and to my surprise, it completely took off. Hundreds of followers on my blog quickly became thousands, and to my utter astonishment, hundreds of thousands. As if that wasn't crazy enough, businesses started contacting me about advertising opportunities. Then, magazines contacted me about interning for their companies and asking me to write articles for them based on my blog style. I couldn't believe my good luck. To this day, I have no idea how my blog, "Pink Sugar Couture" became so popular, but it has been an amazing ride so far, and I love the flexibility freelance writing provides. One of the best parts is that I constantly get sent up-and-coming products or clothing to try out, in the hopes that I will feature them in my articles. It's a definite bonus, even if I had to donate a lot of those awesome items before I left Boston so I could fit everything in my car. While I love writing, fashion is a second love, so being able to combine the two is complete nirvana. I am currently working on an article titled "What trend did you follow that you wish you hadn't? Tell me about your fashion embarrassments!" We've all been there! What's not to love about this so-called job?

I'm really hoping to line up some local magazine work when I'm back in Chicago. A few magazines focus on the nuances of the city, and I would love to contribute to them. Perhaps a weekly feature about locally owned businesses that everyone should visit and support. I would love to do that! Or perhaps I could visit different restaurants or boutiques and feature them in articles. That would be a blast, and I know Pyper would love to help me with that. She never passes up a chance to do a little shopping!

So, while this is not at all the journey I thought I would be taking at this point in my life, and even though the last few months have been extremely difficult, a part of me is positively giddy about what lies before me.

Before I know it, I press down on the accelerator a little bit harder, anxious to get to my destination, the distinct bass of a song now playing through my speakers creating a lively, rhythmical pounding in my ears, and I'm feeling energized in a way I haven't felt for quite some time.

Chapter Three

"Fashion tip: You can run but you can't hide! Wearing oversized clothes in an attempt to conceal one's true size is ineffective. They actually only make you look larger. No matter your size, wear clothes that properly fit your body. Wear oversized clothes when sleeping or driving in a car for two days!"

I carefully try to navigate my car down East Ontario Street, wondering how the hell people do this all the time. Nothing like stop and go driving, avoiding opening doors and hitting the rear ends of the cars making sudden stops. I forgot what driving in the big city of Chicago was like! The streets are so busy – were there always so many restaurants located along this road? And, of course, Pyper's condo is in Streeterville, a very popular and ritzy high rise building on the extreme lake front. Her condo attracts so many well-known, affluent individuals. It wouldn't surprise me if I ran into Oprah in the lobby. Driving thru the ornate gate, and meticulously maintained Cyprus tree-lined entrance, the doorman comes out to greet me. Giving a slight bow, he kindly navigates me to the underground parking garage and advises me to park in the northwest space near the freight elevator to make unloading my car easy. I see his name tag says 'Henry' and I thank him. God bless Pyper for having planned ahead. I barely pull in to what I now understand to have been a parking spot reserved just for me, and suddenly several people swarm my car, ready to help me unload and transport everything into Pyper's condo. I have no idea who these people are or where they came from, I'm just elated and thankful for the help.

The last five hours of my drive seemed to drag on forever. I'm a physical and emotional contradiction. On one hand, I'm physically spent, weary and wiped out, with notable shoulder and back stiffness and soreness, and relieved that the drive is over. Yet, a pleasurable tingling-like sensation from each nerve ending permeates me with an anticipatory excitement and exhilaration. I'm happy to be here; to be home.

Before I can even completely step out of my car, or greet what I quickly decide to interpret as my own personal welcoming committee, I hear feet slapping against the pavement in a fast run and a high-pitched squealing sound. I barely have time for my mind to make sense of the screech and the flash of red before I'm tackled by a very excited and barely coherent red-head, her pounce so fierce that it nearly knocks me down. I think she might be a little happy to see me. I jump up and down in her arms, squealing unintelligibly in response. Our mutual happiness and excitement is unleashed.

"YOU MADE IT! Oh my gosh, I'm so thrilled you are here Olivia. Let me get a good look at you." She holds me at arm's length like my Grandmother would do, then slowly and intently looks me up and down taking an inventory. "You look so good honey, just a bit tired and you have shadows around your eyes, nothing cool cucumbers, a good shower, some pampering at the spa, a great concealer, and hanging out with your best friend while drinking a few cocktails can't cure!"

Pyper's good mood is infectious, and I laugh at her and squeeze her again, in spite of her assessment and the lengthy list of remedies she has just prescribed. "That all sounds amazing Pyper! What do you say we make sure all my boxes get taken inside? I would really like to take that shower before heading out or doing anything else. I do feel kind of tired and a little gross from being in my car so long."

"Of course, follow me."

I grab my overnight bag out of the back seat and head toward the elevator, trusting that the unpacking crew - aka welcome committee - will do their job without incident.

I've visited Pyper's condo a few times. She was over the moon when her Father surprised her with this gift. He may spoil her, and she may lack for nothing, but the thing I love about Pyper is that while her Daddy definitely takes care of her and ensures she has the best of everything, she isn't snotty or uppity about it. She's laid-back, kind, easy going, and definitely knows how to have fun. Maybe it's because she doesn't have the same stresses and worries that some of us do regarding money, I don't know, but she's great and not at all how you would expect the daughter of Mr. Lexington, the owner of one of the top grossing mobile phone companies in the country, to be. She also works hard, has a great head on her shoulders, and doesn't seem to take it all for granted. She's amazing and I'm so happy she's my best friend.

I hop in the elevator and Pyper punches the number for the seventeenth floor. Inside the elevator, I look at myself in the mirror and see that Pyper was just being kind. I look as exhausted as I feel, with tired looking, washed-out skin, dark circled eyes, and droopy hair. If only my blog readers could see me now. Oh the horror! Oh well, nothing a shower, change of clothes, and laughter with my best friend won't fix.

"Once we get inside, don't worry about a thing. You know which room is yours. Head in and do what you need to do. I'll handle the movers and make sure they get all of your belongings and place them inside. Then, once you're refreshed and ready to go, I have the whole works scheduled for us at Shimmer & Soothe. Massages, facials, manicures and pedicures. It will be the perfect girl's day to celebrate our first day as roomies!"

"That sounds wonderful Pyper, and I would love to do all of those treatments with you before long, but maybe for today we can just do the massage? I'm pretty exhausted from my drive, but a massage sounds absolutely divine."

"Of course! I'm so sorry, I wasn't thinking about how tired you would be. I'm just so happy to see you and I went a little crazy. I'm sorry for being selfish."

"You could never be selfish Pyper. I know you're just taking care of me and I love you for it."

Pyper smiles, "I love that you are here, so I have the opportunity to do so! Now go on and get your shower."

The elevator dings, we walk off and head to the right down the hallway, until we reach 17E, Pyper's condo. Unlocking the door, she enters with me right on her heels. We proceed down the small hallway, past the hall closet, where we enter the kitchen. The kitchen is striking, all dark wood and gray marble, with an octagon-shaped eat-in nook area. Equipped with Viking appliances that include a double oven, full of stainless steel appliances, pots and pans strategically positioned over the island, dazzling track and drop lights, and all the appliances and gadgets one could want and many one definitely doesn't need – it's a cook's dream. The ample built-in wine cabinet and over-sized beverage refrigerator across from the large pantry and pub counter with high-back leather padded bar stools, only further add to the allure. Pyper heads to the French door refrigerator and grabs a bottle of water. "Want one?"

"Sure, thanks!"

She gently tosses it to me and amazingly, I catch it.

I walk to the spacious living room and dining room area, located just off the kitchen, to admire the rooms. I take in the dual wood/electric fireplace, Brazilian cherry hardwood floors, gorgeous area rugs adorned with a cream leather couch, love seat, easy chair, and ottoman, each filled to the brim with coordinating plum and silver throw pillows. A black coffee table, end tables holding large silver candlesticks, table lamps and various mosaic pieces that pick up Pyper's color scheme add to the beauty. The dining room table is a large black wooden table that seats six. The chair back carving adds a bit of softness, even femininity to the space. In the center of the table is a huge silver vase holding an enormous arrangement of flowers. It's just as I remember. All very much Pyper; exquisite, well-done, but not over the top. Meticulous and well-organized, but not off-putting; rather, comfortable, warm, and inviting. And there it is---one wall that is nothing but glass, with an amazing view of the magnificent mile, Navy Pier, and the best part - an unobstructed, nearly panoramic view of Lake Michigan. This room and this view is my favorite part of Pyper's condo. It is totally captivating! At night, when the whole city is lit up, it's absolutely gorgeous – the lights shimmering, nearly dancing as they reflect off Lake Michigan – mesmerizing. I can't wait to see it tonight. And with that thought, I feel my shoulders relax a little.

I make my way down the hallway to the left, past Pyper's home office to the guest bedroom, located on the right. I remember that the hallway half-bath looms just slightly down the hall on the opposite side, and that Pyper's bedroom is at the end of the corridor. Standing in the entryway to the room, I peek in and once again think that the architect who designed this floor plan should have received some award – not only did she maximize every square inch, provide more storage space than most houses, but crafted it so that the bedrooms are actually two grand master suites – both abundantly sized with two huge walk-in closets, bathrooms that are larger than my prior bedroom, built of lovely travertine and stone with milk – glass windowed snail showers, and garden spa tubs, along with granite topped double vanities, and a small private room merely for the toilet. Incredible!

I begin to wheel my suitcase into the room and pause, staring at the room. I can feel Pyper at my back. The guest room that was once decorated so beautifully in a sea green and contained only a nice pull out couch and chair is now completely redone with glossy white walls and brand new bedroom furniture. The couch and chair are gone, replaced with a gorgeous four poster canopy bedroom set in rich mahogany, with side tables, and a matching chest of drawers. In addition, there is a lovely media armoire, a coordinating mahogany desk and padded office chair, as well as an area set up to serve as a reading nook, with a lovely overstuffed chair, a storage ottoman, and goose-neck lamp. I turn open mouthed to Pyper.

"Wow Pyper! This room – the furniture — it's all amazing! When did you get this room redone?"

With a look on her face revealing both pride and happiness with my reaction, she said, "I had it repainted and refurnished once we finalized plans and I knew you were going to come live with me."

I turn to Pyper with tears in my eyes, "What? Pyper! Why would you do that? You know I was perfectly fine sleeping on a pull out. I told you I didn't want you to go to any trouble for me. You already won't let me help with rent. This is too much." I am overwhelmed with her generosity.

"Look, I want you to be comfortable here and I knew you would love this bedroom set. I had the walls repainted because I want you to choose what color you want and have this space reflect you. If you don't want to paint the walls, you don't have to. This is a new start for you, a new beginning. I knew you got rid of all the stuff that reminded you of Deacon, and I sure as hell wasn't going to let you sleep on a damn pull out couch. Don't even get me started on the rent thing because we've been over that. I don't even pay rent on this place. My Dad can more than take care of it, so we will let him. Don't bring it up again. My parents can't wait to see you by the way!"

"I promise to take the best care of everything while I am here, and I can't thank you enough. I really missed you. I love you."

"I love you too, chica! Now get that sweet ass in the shower, because we have massages to enjoy. While we are out, we should stop by a store so you can pick out the comforter, sheets and blankets you want! If you're up for it, I know just the place."

"Sounds perfect."

Throwing another smile at me over her shoulder, Pyper turns and scurries down the hallway to her room. Smiling to myself, I walk into my room, already thinking about what color I want to paint the walls. I set my suitcase on the bed, open it, grab my bathroom items and head to the shower. So far, things are off to a great start.

Stepping out of Pyper's Mercedes and striding the short distance to the entrance, I feel renewed by the shower. With thoughts of how to personalize this newly claimed space, recently unknown energy seizes me, and I can't help but smile. I'm looking forward to my massage, and again feel grateful to Pyper for having the forethought to arrange it. Shimmer & Soothe is really quite magnificent. Entering through the large glass doors, I immediately notice that to the left of the reception desk there is now a small gift shop that appears to sell many of the products used by the spa and its professional staff: luxurious robes, slippers like those in the women's lounge area, and the various facial, massage, body, hair and makeup products.

I follow Pyper to the reception desk, which is located front and center when you walk inside. Behind the reception desk is an impressive and eye-catching wall-mounted fountain. It is made of three large, slate panels suspended between beautiful metal fixtures with accent lighting in an overhead valance that highlights the water sheeting over the natural stone. Beautiful.

I can't help but notice that the girl working behind the desk visibly straightens when she sees her boss walk in. Young, no older than nineteen, with blonde hair and dark brown eyes, she is adorable, with a sweet voice to match. "Hi Miss Lexington. How are you?"

"I'm doing fine Caroline, how are you? Keeping things running nice and smooth up here I hope? Appointments keeping pace with projections?" Pyper catches my eye and winks, "Did the delivery come for the Longevity facial supplies as planned?"

"Everything is going well, we've gotten a lot of bookings today, and yes, the products arrived about an hour ago. Margo and Hannah are in the back, unpacking the boxes and placing the price labels on them."

"Excellent. Caroline, this is my best friend in the whole world, Olivia Brooks! She's just moved back to Chicago and you will see her often, so remember her face. Olivia, meet Caroline."

I smile, "Hi Caroline, nice to meet you."

"Hi Ms. Brooks! It is so nice to finally meet you. Miss Lexington has been talking about your arrival a lot, and I've been anxious to meet you."

"Well I'm happy to be here, thank you, and please call me Olivia."

27

"Caroline, Olivia and I were to have a full schedule, but instead we've elected to just get massages for today."

Before she finishes, I interrupt, "Actually Pyper, I'm fine with keeping what you had originally scheduled. I'm feeling great so, if it's still okay, let's proceed as planned."

"Are you sure?" I nod and so Pyper continues, "Okay, great! Never mind Caroline, please go ahead and let Kelly and Stephanie know we are here. Ask them to give us ten minutes to change and then they can meet us in the lounge to take us back for our facials, which I believe is first on the schedule."

"You are correct. I will tell them now, Miss Lexington."

I can't help but grin at the proper way Caroline keeps speaking to my friend. Pyper motions to me and we head off to the right of the reception desk which is where the women's lounge is located. The male clients' lounge entrance is located to the left of the reception desk. On the backside of the wall with the fountain is a spacious sitting area with strategically placed tables and chairs for clients to enjoy a beverage, chat, or read. If they choose, they can order lunch from the hotel restaurant across the street, known for its health-conscious, yet luscious fare that provides a modest discount to spa patrons. There is an ornamental serving table set up against one wall, providing complimentary coffee (decaf and regular), hot water with various herbal and non-herbal tea bags, iced tea, lemonade, a cold water cooler, and a juice and protein shake bar across the room against the opposite wall. Glass doors lead out to the large indoor Olympic size swimming pool, which is surrounded by plush lounge chairs, each containing a fluffy towel.

Having entered the women's lounge, we proceed to a desk where we are assigned a locker, given a card with the locker number on it, and told to place our clothing and belongings in and set the four digit combination to any number of our choosing. I follow Pyper back to the women's locker room, open the locker, and find a velvet-soft robe and medium sized spa shoes, which are really just flip flops. Removing all of my clothes except for my off-white, lace bikini undies, I put on my robe and spa shoes and go with Pyper to the waiting area, where we relax in comfortable chaise lounges and pick up a recent gossip magazine to browse while we wait for our estheticians. I notice, and can't help but take a peek at the newest *Pose* magazine to see if my article appears as a cover headline. Doesn't look like it, but a quick scan of the index shows it is on page 11. 'Hot Trends Coming This Spring.' I smile, seeing my name below the title. I don't think I will ever get used to that.

I lean back in my white plush chair and take in my surroundings. Across from the waiting area are the women's restrooms and across from the restrooms is a full style vanity that contains every single product and beauty tool a woman would need to get ready to go out after leaving the spa. Further down the hallway are the women's showers, a sauna, and a steam room. Pyper really does have excellent taste. The whole area is done in various shades of gold, brown, and white. It couldn't be more classy and trendy, yet infuses a relaxing and renewing ambiance at the same time. This isn't the first time I've seen the spa, but she's made some changes since I was here last.

"Pyper everything looks amazing. This place has really come together. You must be so proud of yourself!"

"I don't know if I would say that, but I do really love this place, and I'm thrilled that S&S is doing so well."

We aren't waiting long before our estheticians arrive, halting our conversation. We are taken through a door at the back of the room that has us exiting toward the pool. There is an enclosed walkway that leads us to another building that houses all the treatment rooms. Walking through the ornate wood door, I pause, momentarily transfixed by the effortless beauty - the large Zen garden in the center – simple plants and flowers arranged in an appropriate feng shui style, a rake set to the side apparently for rearranging the soil – a calming exercise for the mind - I have heard - and the treatment rooms outlying the perimeter situated in a large square. The mood is calm and serene, and I can hear the trickle of water from the fountain at the Zen garden's center. We are escorted to the last door on the left, which has a plaque beside the door, indicating that it is a couple's treatment room. I snicker. I briefly consider the interesting rumors that Pyper and I could generate and snicker again! But, eagerness to begin my facial envelopes me and I quickly take my place on one of the treatment tables. It's going to feel amazing.

An hour later, having received my facial, I'm lying on my stomach with my eyes closed, listening to very soft music with the pleasant aroma of lavender oil infiltrating my pores. Hands move swiftly, but firmly, working out all the knots in my neck, back and shoulders that I received from driving the Avenger for twenty-six long hours. I feel the tension of the drive – and the last few months - melting away. I am in pure heaven. With great effort, I turn my head slightly to the side and glance at Pyper who is receiving her massage on the table next to mine and our eyes connect. She was obviously staring at me. It's unnerving when we do that, I swear we really do share a brain. We grin at each other and resume the position.

"This was the best idea ever," I somehow manage to vocalize.

"I know. I expect payment in alcohol."

I can't help but laugh. Oh well – so much for the healthy benefit of releasing our nasty toxins. Here's to new, yet-to-be-discovered contaminants! "You got it!"

"So what do you want to do tonight? Want to get dressed up and hit the town? Any old friends you want me to call up and invite out with us? What should we do for your first night home?"

I laugh at her, "Dressed up and hit the town? After this? No way. I'm going to be ready for a nap. Honestly, I would just love to stay in and drink some good wine, enjoy the gorgeous view from your condo and order takeout pizza from Gino's East. After this pampering, I'm not going to feel like moving a muscle. Does that sound okay to you?"

"Your wish is my command. Today and tonight is all about you."

"Well in that case, I say we get the aforementioned wine, takeout and maybe a chick flick. I just want to enjoy a night in with my best friend. I haven't seen you in way too long, and would just like a quiet evening in, where I can talk with you without having to share you with anyone or yell over loud music!"

"Like I said, babe…whatever you want. That sounds like the perfect evening."

As my masseuse starts massaging down the back of my legs and her hands make their way to my feet I know I made the right decision. My body is going to feel like rubber after this.

Several hours later, feeling completely refreshed, relaxed, primped, plucked and pampered, Pyper and I return to her – now our - condo, giggling, our arms full of packages. We are loaded down with new bed linens, spa products I just had to have, a large pizza, the movie *Pitch Perfect,* and of course, both red and white wine. We are ready for our girls night in!

Pyper starts grabbing plates and wine glasses out of the kitchen cupboard, and I head back to my room to drop off my purchases. Returning to the kitchen, I accept the plate with a slice of the best pizza in Chicago, and a large glass of slightly fruity smelling red wine. We head to the living room and settle ourselves on the couch and I take my first bite of heaven. Who needs anything else – this is orgasmic!

"Ohh myyy gaawwwd. Wow I have missed this stuff. No one does pizza like Chicago. All of those places in Boston that boast Chicago Style on their signs ought to be arrested for false advertising…it is nothing like the real thing. They can never get it just right."

Pyper giggles, "You sound like you are enjoying that pizza a little too much!"

"Go ahead and laugh it up bitch! If you had gone as long without a man and sex as I have, you would take pleasure in anything you could too," I say laughing with her.

"Who needs a man when you can just use a vibrator? Come on, tell me you have one!"

"Of course I have one. After my divorce, I ordered the mother of all vibes! It undulates, vibrates, pulsates, massages and even tells me how beautiful I am."

Pyper chokes and almost spits her wine all over the place, while I giggle uncontrollably like I'm a sixteen year old girl. "I obviously need to upgrade to whatever version you have!"

"Seriously, it has been ages. You don't appreciate what you're missing until you don't have it at your beck and call anymore. There may have been a lot of other things wrong with Deacon and me, but we didn't lack sexual chemistry. He could always rock my world; problem was it wasn't only my world he was rockin'.""

Pyper snorts, "Better you found out when you did, as opposed to a few years down the line when you could have had kids!"

"I absolutely agree. Not that it made it any easier."

"I know Livvie." I smile at the use of my nickname, "I'm not trying to make light of it. Please don't think that. I'm just trying to look at the positive side."

"Sometimes I still can't believe this has happened and I wonder if I did the right thing. I wonder if I should have been willing to give him another chance, or if I should have gone to couple's counseling instead of just individually, but I think I always knew deep down that it was very likely our marriage was going to end up in divorce. I mean, I'd always had a plan, a path in life. You know me…I was the straight-A student through high school, class president, head cheerleader. I had a plan for college; I was always determined and motivated. Then, when plans fell through, I was so heartbroken and everything changed so fast. I wondered what it all meant. Why did I think any of it had been important? I felt tricked and silly. I rebelled from all of it, went nuts in college, drank, experimented, married Deacon, and by the time I woke up and started taking control of my life again, I was already in so deep. I felt stuck. I wanted to make something meaningful from all of the stupid actions and decisions, wanted to prove something. I felt I needed to own up to my actions by making it work with him. So I tolerated a lot; turned my head, made excuses. Then, when I walked in on him, it was like I was back in the very same place again. And it was the last straw; I had had it. That was it. Pretty pathetic huh?"

"No, it's not pathetic and no one has the right to tell you what you could have or should have done, or what they would have done. Don't let others place their expectations on you. Everyone has an opinion about what they would do if their man ever cheated on them. Some say they'd stay at all costs, while others say they wouldn't put up with it and would leave. Others say they would hear him out, get incredible effective counseling, because staying is easier than leaving. And then, of course, others swear they would kick their spouse's ass and leave immediately. But the fact is, no one really knows. It's an opinion at best, an assumption. The honest truth is that unless someone actually confronts that reality, they don't know how they would react. How could they? There are so many variables. Being confronted with the actuality of an event is completely different than talking about what one might do IF it happened. You did what you needed to do for you. And so what?! So you lost your way for a little while, many people do at some point. The important thing is you found it again."

"You're right Pyper." I smile at her gratefully. I'm so glad I can tell her my deepest thoughts and bare my heart to her, and know without a doubt it's safe; I am safe. "That is definitely something I've learned from this, too. I will never judge someone that finds themselves in a difficult situation, whether I have similar experience or not, projecting my own judgments or opinions onto them isn't right. Aside from the fact that Deacon cheated on me, there were so many other issues. As awful as it sounds, my finding him in the act of cheating on me was almost a blessing, it made me step back and take a look at the entirety of my marriage and examine it for what it really was, and unfortunately Deacon's infidelity was far from the only problem."

Taking a deep breath I admitted, "I don't think I've ever felt so suffocated, so controlled in my life. When you're in the middle of it, it's hard to appreciate what is occurring, how stifling and limiting the other person is. Deacon never wanted me to do anything without him, have any interests that did not include him or have any life, really, outside of him. I rarely ever just had time to myself or girl time with just my friends. He was too possessive, manipulative, and dominating to allow for that and it is partially my fault because I let him. I rarely experienced anything that was truly mine – that added dimension to our relationship, to me. And work – he was jealous and angry about my work life as well, except for the income, though he embraced the fact that I didn't need to work outside of the home. I allowed

Deacon to be my whole life and included in everything I did. I didn't have any unique contribution to make to our marriage, which only added to the isolation and claustrophobia."

Pyper just sits listening to me, drinking her wine, and refilling my glass as the words pour. Even though we had conversations on the phone almost every day since I began divorce proceedings, it was like a water faucet spewing after being shut off for so long, emotional words and sentiments gushing forth, but mostly focused on Deacon's cheating bastard ways. This was the first time I'd been able to reveal to her so many of these well-hidden truths, my ugly little secrets, and some of the realities and the self-discoveries that I'd made along the way.

"The thing is Pyper, even though I got back on track with my career and what I wanted in life, I still lost myself in my marriage. I was so caught up in being how Deacon wanted me to be and acting how he wanted me to act, even wearing what he wanted me to wear, that I forgot what I liked, who I am and what matters to me. I was running from home trying to escape the pain I was feeling from the betrayal of Luke, and even though I didn't know it at the time, I was willing to get lost in anything and anyone to bury and diminish the intensity of the pain and loss, and even shame I felt. Deacon's behavior made all that very easy. I was easily able to lose myself in our so-called relationship. I feel like I've spent part of my life living it for and as someone else. I forgot that I have needs – let alone what they are - and that I matter too. I'm just glad I came to my senses."

"It's understandable, Olivia, that after what happened with you and Luke that you would have felt that way. I feel partly responsible because I knew you were running when you decided to go away to school and when you got together with Deacon. I was afraid that you were jumping into something much too quickly as a way to escape the hurt. I should have said something."

I shake my head in disagreement, "I wouldn't have listened. I was lost in the numbness that partying, drinking, and my crazy rebellious activities were granting me. I was too determined to forget. I would have heard you say the words, but they wouldn't have resonated at the time, so don't give that another thought. And now that's enough of that, I don't want to talk about Luke or Deacon anymore tonight."

Pyper gave me a look that I knew meant she wasn't going to listen to my request for a moment; she was not going to allow me to change the topic. "Have you thought about the fact that since you are back in Chicago, it's likely that you are going to hear about Luke? I don't know if he is still here, but it is a definite possibility and if so, you aren't going to be able to hide forever."

"Yes I've thought about it, how could I not? But I still don't want to talk about it! Not right now! I will deal with that when and if the time comes. Plus, before I can even think about that, I need to get back into the swing of things. Given that my marriage with Deacon was over long before I walked in on him and blonde bitch girl, I've been thinking about what it would be like to move forward for a long time. I know some might think it too soon, but I need to have life on my terms for a while. I want to have fun, flirt, and date again. I want to feel my age and try to be a bit more lighthearted. I need to get to know myself again - remember who I am, what I like, and regain confidence in making my own decisions, living without someone telling me what I can and can't do! I'm a grown ass woman and I want to finally start acting like it. I'm taking back my life!"

"Then let's find you again, Olivia. Let's get you back out there. Let's rediscover the girl that is the best friend a girl could ever ask for! You are a remarkable, talented, smart and funny girl – with great taste – especially in friends! So, first things first, let's get you settled in. Then, once things calm down a bit, I have a PERFECT idea on just where to start!"

Okay - I'm not going to lie, that comment made me nervous. It could have been the gleam in her eye as she made that statement or possibly the maniacal laugh she let out after saying it. I was aware that I had opened a potential Pandora's box.

Oh boy.

35

Chapter Four

"Fashion tip: Ladies, I love low rise jeans as much as the next girl, but there is such a thing as jeans that fit too low. When you try on a pair, sit down, bend over, act like you are picking something up off the floor, even bend your knees all the way and touch the ground. Stretch up toward the ceiling. If you feel a draft behind you, yes, that IS your butt hanging out the back. It may well be gorgeous, but most of us really do not want to see it. Please for the love of denim, try on a different pair."

A few weeks later, Pyper and I are hanging out in her living room, drinking wine and talking. I anxiously wait for Pyper to reveal her big idea regarding how I can get my old self back. I know I need to put myself out there and start having fun again, especially since I'm finally feeling more settled in. I have painted my new room a pretty aqua color on one wall that reminds me of the ocean. It's gorgeous and is the perfect accent to the comforter and shams. And how lovely does that tone look with the mahogany colored furniture? I have a few other accents in mind as well. Oops, I digress. What was she saying?

Pyper is looking at me, smiling, eager for my response. What did she say? Something about online dating and dating profiles? Did I shake my head yes and say 'uh huh'? I hold my breath and she repeats "So, let's create dating profiles on Date Me! Ready?"

I just stare at her blankly for a minute, and then laugh. "Are you joking?"

"Nope! I think it will be fun!"

"I don't know about that. Not to sound pompous, but do we need to use a dating site to get dates? Isn't that for people that can't get a man on their own? Eager people? Desperate people? Hopeless, bleak, miserable people? Is that who I am? Is that who you think I am? Do I really need to resort to that?"

Pyper rolls her eyes at me, "This is *the* thing to do in the dating world. Think about it, how else are you – I mean we - going to meet a man? We don't attend church often, and I'm not really sure I'd want to go to church to pick up a guy anyway. Something tells me God wouldn't look on that favorably."

"I think you are right about that, plus that would be weird. Hi, so my name is Olivia and I saw you praying over there and thought I could be the answer to some of your requests, so maybe you'd like to go out and we could uh, worship, together? I don't think so."

Laughing, Pyper continues, "Exactly. Picking guys up at bars only gets you trouble. There are only so many grocery stores and produce departments. We don't belong to any kind of social club, civic organization, or hobby group or whatever where we can meet someone. You work from home and not too many men come to the spa – and those that do are likely not looking for a relationship with gals like us. This is the way to do it. Look at it like this…you research a car before you buy it right?"

Snorting softly I reply, "I don't think I'm ready to 'buy' it yet Pyper. And what do I say? Hi, I'm Olivia, I just got divorced, and I'm eager and desperate to find someone. People will think I'm a loser and a whore!"

"First of all, you have been living in Boston for the last seven years, and other than me, you've not really kept in touch with anyone here. No one will know anything unless you tell them; unless it's something you want them to know. It isn't like you are looking to get married. You need to have fun. And besides, it's been a long time since you dated. You need to get back out there again. Look at it like an amusing diversion. Besides, you're the one who said that your marriage with Deacon was over long before you actually signed those papers and you've been wondering what singlehood would be like again. Well, it's time you find out. As your best friend, I'm not taking no for an answer on this. Let's at least look! Come on Olivia, jump."

I can't deny that she's making some good points. I do want to have some enjoyment, get out and meet people and feel like a normal twenty-five year old woman. I mean, all work and no play makes Olivia a dull girl, right? In truth, I have always liked dating. Getting dressed up, the stimulation of getting to know someone new, the thrill of having a good time and the exhilaration of feeling attractive – all great feelings. The idea of making a new friend, or the potential thought of experiencing butterflies again is certainly appealing. Where would the harm be in looking at the site? I doubt anything will really come from it anyway.

"Okay. I'll jump. But only if we do this in tandem - you hold my hand and we jump together. I mean what are best friends for? I can't enjoy the delight or humiliation alone you know!"

Pyper smiles at me. "Well duh! You think I'm going to let you have all the fun without me? Not a chance! This is going to be so fun! Let's grab our laptops."

Pyper heads to her office to grab her laptop and I snatch mine out of my bedroom. Meeting Pyper back in the living room, I top off our glasses of wine, only to realize that we've just about gone through one bottle – so quickly, hmmm - so I proceed to the wine fridge – I still can't believe she has one of those - and grab another bottle of chilled Riesling, our favorite. We set our laptops up on the coffee table side by side and sit on the floor in front of them.

For a minute, we just stare at each other and giggle. Yep, we are definitely starting to feel the wine, I'm not sure if this is going to be a good thing or not! Oh well! If we're doing this, then I'm going all in. We both pull up the dating site called Date Me and realize we have to register before we can even browse through any profiles. We each quickly enter a username and password and, then annoyingly, realize that we also have to provide our email address, birth date and tell them how we heard about their website. I just type the word 'Pyper' and giggle to myself. Once that information is entered, we start entering information into our individual profiles, but we realize we can now browse the site, so decide to first look around at some of the men's profiles a short time – for motivation and ideas. At least that's what I tell myself.

On the main page there are a few featured profiles with brief information showing the person's screen name, age, what city they live in, and an answer to a random question. The questions vary and immediately a few catch our eyes.

"Oh my gosh, Pyper look at this guy" I turn my computer to show her a man whose name is WayneH and it says he is thirty-three. He's got light brown hair, a goatee and has remarkable green eyes. It is only a head shot but his looks don't really hold my attention. I mean he's not bad looking, average, but my eyes are glued to his question and answer. "Look here, it says 'The Most Private Thing I'm Willing to Admit is…I am sterile. I just have a fun gun'." And he has signed that little tidbit of awesomeness with a smiley face.

We completely bust out laughing like crazy girls. "My Grandmother used to always say it takes all types to make the world go round. That woman was smart!" Pyper states through her laughter.

"I can't breathe!" I gasp, "A fun gun! Hilarious!"

We see several others that make us laugh until we snort.

At one point, Pyper again turns her computer to show me a full body shot of a guy that says he is twenty-nine. He's dressed in a black suit, with a white dress shirt peeking from under the suit coat, with one too many buttons undone. One hand is placed in his pants pocket, the other on his hip. He has dark brown hair with a receding hair line and is wearing dark sunglasses. He's obviously trying to look suave and sophisticated, but comes off looking like a gigolo.

I take in his appearance and look at Pyper questioningly. Reading the look on my face she says, "Check out his photo caption."

I look under the photo, "At my best friend's funeral. RIP Shawn." Again we crack up. "Why, oh why would anyone put that? I mean, I'm sorry about your friend but dude, so not cool!"

"Oh man… I wonder what his best friend would think?"

"Pyper I'm telling you right now, if you think you look hot at my funeral someday and want to use your photo to try and get guys on a dating site...I totally approve."

Pyper chokes on her wine and we just lose control yet again. Oh, my stomach is starting to hurt from laughing so hard.

"Pyper wait! I think I have a winner! I think the prize goes to SurferBoy, who is twenty-three years old." I show her SB's photo. He is quite attractive with blonde hair, blue eyes and sexy messy hair. His muscular arms and legs and rippled abs are accented by the board shorts and white polo shirt. Flip flops finish his look. He definitely has the surfer look going for him. Pyper checks him out, "He is cute – and he has a nice body too."

"Yes I agree. Check out his question and answer!"

I see her eyes moving to the information I told her to look at, "I'm really good at..." and he inserted "liberating your pleasure wave."

We giggle uncontrollably yet again until we both collapse. We have tears rolling down our cheeks.

"Some of these people are crazy Pyper! What women do they think they are going to attract by saying these things? I don't get it! Does this stuff actually work for some women? "

"Wait... what are you saying? You aren't totally turned on right now?"

Giggling I reply, "Oh you caught me. I just didn't want to admit it. I'm totally going to need a date with my vibrator after this guy's profile! He can liberate my pleasure wave?! Ohhhh baby!"

We top off our wine and keep giggling.

"Okay, so come on, Olivia, all the crazies aside, look at this guy." This time she turns her computer to show me a twenty-seven year old, drop dead gorgeous prospect. His eyes almost look gray, and he has the five o'clock look going on - stubble along his chin that is just asking to be touched. His nose is slightly crooked, but he could seriously be a model. He's identified himself as Ethan.

"Woah, he's cute."

"And look, his answer to the featured question is actually normal."

"What am I doing with my life? His answer is 'I'm an attorney that stays very busy with work but I'm looking for a special someone to share my spare time with. She would understand that I'm driven in my career but that I also enjoy an active lifestyle. I enjoy rock climbing, playing basketball and going to the movies.' Very nice. Now this is the kind of profile that I can get on board with. He doesn't appear to be a lunatic... Or talk about pleasure waves."

"Me too. Good answer from Ethan. Okay Olivia, we have to fill out our profiles now!"

I laugh. "You still want to do this?"

"Of course! You aren't scared off by just a couple loony tunes are you?"

"Okay, why not? I doubt anyone will even pay attention to my profile. Look, it shows they have over 3 million users worldwide. That's insane!" I realize there's a buzz in the sound system or something. Or perhaps, it's the wine. No biggie. This is a really good idea. Why didn't I do this before? Pyper has such excellent ideas and I need to take her advice more. She's such a good friend. In fact, if she suggested that I dance naked around the living room right now, I would...no hesitation...

We start filling out all the required information. Our zip code, then if we are interested in a male or female. I hesitate and then enter male. Our name, age and birth date is already pre-filled after filling out the username and password previously, so we only need to write a mini bio about ourselves and the type of man we are looking for. Then we can add answers to all kinds of questions, but quickly discuss that option and decide to just complete the bio for now. Keep it simple.

"Pyper I have no clue what to put here!"

"I have an idea! How about we write each other's profiles? Then we exchange and have to approve them before we post them; okay?"

"I think that is a great idea! You know me better than I know myself! I'll go first." I take Pyper's computer from her and speak out loud as I type, "I'm not interested in most guys, I'm not one to fall for just anyone and so it makes those that I do connect with all the more special. I'm a fiery redhead that isn't afraid to share her opinion. I'm not offended by a dirty joke and can dish out plenty of my own. I have a tendency to curse like a sailor when really angry, and while I'm not a feminist, I am definitely independent. I own a spa and am completely capable of taking care of myself. I'm not looking for some guy to come in and sweep me off my feet, but instead want a partner that I can share my life with and isn't threatened by an intelligent woman. Sarcasm is the spice of life, so bring it on! I hope to meet you, but if you can't handle any of the above description, don't bother!"

"What do you think?"

Pyper doesn't even hesitate before she says, "I like it! It's me, for sure. Okay, my turn."

She grabs my computer and starts typing, "Happy, healthy, fun-loving, I'm looking for a great guy. I love laughing, writing, my kindle, honesty, music, foodgasms, handbags, kisses, coffee, road trips and kindness. Lots of kindness. I dislike calories, bugs, dishonesty, tomatoes, doing laundry, poor grammar, and alarm clocks. I like to walk with no destination in mind and love the sun on my face. I would do anything for my friends and family, think way too much about the order of my Netflix queue, and believe in kismet. You should message me if you are likely to be as happy spending a Sunday lazing away in bed as you would going outdoors and being active, if you like breakfast foods, believe in romance, and are a handsome, ambitious and courageous guy who keeps his commitments."

"Well… how's that?"

"Perfect! Like I said… you know me well!"

"Okay so next up, we have to post pictures. Let's take snap shots of each other!" We pull out our phones and begin to snap pictures of each other smiling and laughing like we are models on a photo shoot. We plug our phones into the computer and begin uploading them so we can turn around and post them to our profiles. I took a really good one of Pyper mid laugh and another one of her smiling while looking straight at me. Her eyes are shining and she looks happy. I see that Pyper captured a good one of me with my head slightly turned to the side, laughing, and another, where I'm looking straight at her. My cheeks are slightly flushed from the wine and my eyes may be slightly glassy, but all in all, the pictures are fine. We decide on our monthly payment plan, upload our pictures, set our notification preferences, and voila! We are now officially on a dating site.

"I can't believe we actually did this! I have to admit it was a lot of fun. I guess the worst that can happen is that I get a free dinner right?"

"Right!" Pyper readily agrees. "It says our profile will be active in a couple hours. I can't wait to see what kind of response we get."

I just smile at her. "So, tomorrow is Sunday, do you have to go into the spa at all tomorrow?"

"Yes, I should drop in briefly. I need to make sure the remainder of the product display was set up in the gift shop. My parents are expecting us for a late lunch. That's still okay with you, right? They are really anxious to see you."

I smile, thinking of Pyper's parents. Her dad, Ted, is a great guy who loves to spoil his only child. Nothing is too much or out of reach when it comes to her. Pyper learned long ago to indulge him because he's going to do what he wants, no matter what. Pyper's mom, May, is actually her step-mom, but they married when Pyper was so young, she considers May her mother. Pyper's mother, Audrey, died from cancer when Pyper was five years old, so she doesn't really remember her. I've seen pictures of her though, and Pyper looks just like her; the same red hair and blue eyes. May has been a wonderful mother to Pyper, and they adore one another. They both are like my adoptive parents and Pyper is my sister in every way, except without the fighting and sibling rivalry. I spent just as much time at Pyper's house growing up as she did mine.

"Of course! I can't wait to see them too. It has been so long. I need to work on my article for *Style Incorporated* tomorrow, and do a blog post on 'Pink Sugar Couture' as well. I'm going to organize my closet a little better, too. I unpacked in a hurry so I could paint, so I want to fix the mess I made. I will be ready when you are though."

Pyper smiles at me knowingly and then laughs. "Anal Olivia," she sing songs, "making sure the closet is perfect," she giggles. Apparently she is feeling the wine as well.

"Shut up. There is nothing wrong with making sure all the things are...with the right things...." I laugh at the fact that I'm having trouble putting the right words together.

Pyper snorts, "Yes, all the things should be together. So tell me, miss fashion blogger extraordinaire, what articles are you working on for the magazine and blog?"

"Marc Jacobs just had his style show for his fall catalogue so I'm doing a write-up about it for the magazine and my blog post is going to be a bunch of different fashion tips. My followers love them, so I try to do one every few months or so."

"Oooh I love those posts too! Fun! I bet I could come up with some good ones for you."

"No doubt about it, let's hear one," I challenge.

Pyper takes a moment to think about it and says, "Umm, how about, don't wear rompers unless you want to look like a baby wearing a onesie." Pyper lifts her chin up at the end of her statement showing how proud she is of her advice.

"Nice. I'm impressed. Can I steal that one?"

"But of course, my dear. I aim to please."

My response to that is a very lady-like snort.

"I still can't believe how your blog just took off, it's so exciting," Pyper says with a wink.

"Yes, very exciting. I love it! Well, I am off to get changed and get my butt in bed before I drink anymore of this wine and become incoherent and am unable to function tomorrow."

"Okay, I will text you tomorrow when I'm leaving the spa," Pyper tells me through a yawn. No doubt she's on her way to bed as well.

"Sounds good. I know I've said this a lot the past few weeks, but I'm really happy to be here. Thanks again."

"No thanking me. I am beyond happy to have you here."

We hug each another and I head to my room.

After I change my clothes for bed, I cuddle up in my crisp, new sheets and grin at the cool sensation of my pillow cases. I love my new white down comforter; it looks like one continuous ruffle. It was quite expensive, but is so pretty. I complemented the white with aqua and royal blue throw pillows, and a throw blanket. I love it all. I know I'm in Chicago, but it looks beachy. I snuggle down in bed but can't fall asleep. Somewhere in between being awake and not yet quite asleep, my subconscious resurrects long-forgotten memories. As the reel begins to run, another part of my mind questions if being in Illinois again is making these memories surface.

I can't wait to see him. I am going to miss him so much while he's in California on vacation with his family. I wish they could have gone earlier, rather than the last couple weeks of summer. There's so much to do before we head off to college together. Oh well. Let's enjoy the moment. We have a romantic day planned. We're going to bask in the presence of each other before he leaves me tomorrow for two weeks. Two weeks that will feel like a lifetime. It will be okay; we have the whole year planned—I'm so eager to begin this next part of our relationship. Two weeks is nothing. Instead, I'll concentrate on the picnic I'm packing for us to enjoy by our favorite tree...our special tree.

One night, not long after we started dating we went for a walk around my neighborhood. At the end of a dead end street is a field, and in the middle of the field all by itself stood a tall oak tree. It looked completely out of place yet, exactly perfect at the same time. Like it had been previously rehearsed, without speaking a word, we walked to the tree and sat and talked for hours. Now, going there and chatting is a favorite pastime; a good habit. It's our tree. Luke even carved our initials in it. 'L loves O.' I smile, thinking of the day he carved that little love note and spent hours kissing me senseless up against the tree. Luke's kisses set me on fire from head to toe. Once he started, I never wanted him to stop. And a few times we hadn't stopped.

I smile secretly to myself, thinking about the tree and those intimate occasions. I have no regrets. That boy is everything to me. I want him to know how much I love him, how he makes me feel, and how I want to be with him, always. He has branded himself on every part of me, heart, body, and soul. I can't imagine myself without him and I don't ever want to. He's the other part of me.

As I'm finishing packing our picnic lunch, my phone beeps, letting me know I've just gotten a text message.

Luke – Babe, something came up at home. Running late. Will leave here in the next 20 minutes or so!

I wonder what came up, but don't think twice about it. I'm just anxious to see him. I grab the picnic basket, head to my car, and start driving the fifteen minutes to Luke's place. He can't come get me yet, no worries, I will just go there and wait for him, pick him up. No sense in making him waste time driving. I want each and every minute we can squeeze in together. I pull up to his home, drive up the driveway, and park. I practically skip to the front door, knock. Pearl, the housekeeper opens the door. "Hi dear. Come on in."

"Thanks Pearl." Pearl has worked for the Easton family a long time. She's used to seeing me come and go, and has always been very kind to me. Once I'm inside, I start to head up the stairs to Luke's room, assuming he's there, but Pearl tells me she thinks he's in the kitchen. I retreat back down the few steps I had taken and walk down the long hallway, aware of voices – intense, louder than normal conversation. I look behind me, but Pearl is no longer there. I think I hear Luke's voice and start to enter into the kitchen but just as I've cracked the door, the louder voice stops me in my tracks. It's Luke's mom.

"Luke, I know you are serious about this girl and I don't like it one bit. You are far too young to be in a committed relationship already. You have your whole life ahead of you, and I'm not about to let you settle for the first girl you had a crush on. I get that she seemed like enough while you were in high school, but you are going to college soon."

"Mom, it isn't like that."

"Don't lie to me, Luke Xavier Easton. I see the way you look at her. I already told your dad that instead of going to Loyola University just because that girl is going there, you should go to Northwestern University, like we had talked about at one time. I don't think it is a good idea at all that the two of you go to the same school. She'll drag you down; keep you from realizing your

potential, interfere with your studies. I'm not going to allow you to let some girl get in the way of your future."

"Mom, I told you that you have it all wrong. Olivia and I aren't serious. She's a great girl, don't get me wrong, but she's been a fun distraction. She has been a cool person to be around and scratch that itch for me while getting through high school, but once we get to college, I plan on cutting her loose. I am not about to rest my future on the first girl I've ever dated."

The tears begin streaming down my face. His words cut through me like a knife. And my heart. Oh my God, my chest hurts. It's like I can literally feel it breaking inside my chest. I don't even realize that I'm clutching my chest, holding my hands over my heart like I can keep it from breaking out of my body. Like I'm holding it in. The pain is unbearable. I can't believe what I heard. I'm just a distraction? He's going to cut me loose?

I suddenly realize that I had stepped through the doorway – that I was further into the room than I thought. I'm just about to turn around and run away when Luke looks up and sees me standing there. He takes in my tear streaked face, my hand over my heart, and his face instantly pales and a look of horror crosses his face.

He realizes he's been caught, that I heard what he said.

Without another thought, I turn around and flee down the hallway. I run out the door, and nearly run down Pearl, who was walking toward the kitchen, in my haste to get out of there. I can't breathe. It hurts to breathe.

I hear Luke yelling, "OLIVIA!" But I don't stop. I feel almost other-worldly. Out of my body. Before I know it, I've started my car and accelerating as fast as I can, I race out of the driveway and out into the street. I don't know where I'm going. I can't think. I can't breathe. My chest. It hurts so much. I just drive.

I hear my phone ringing – playing My Love by Justin Timberlake. Then it starts beeping alerting me to not only phone calls but text messages coming in as well. I ignore it all, I don't understand why he is calling me. Because I know his secret? What else is there to say? Is he wanting to try and offer some explanation? Does he feel guilty that I overheard the truth, and that he didn't have the guts or heart to tell me face-to-face? And when was he going to do that? Today before he left at our tree? With an ear-piercing, heart-wrenching moan and uncontrollable weeping, the reality of what I just heard comes crashing down. I mean nothing to him. He doesn't really love me. It was all just words...a game. I keep driving. I just need to keep driving.

After all of this time, it amazes me that that my heart can still hurt from the memories of something that happened so long ago. Eventually I fall into a restless sleep.

Waking up with a jolt, I wonder what has woken me up. I gaze around the room and see the bright warm sun coming in through the windows, casting square lights on the floor. Oh, that must be it. I forgot to shut the drapes before I fell asleep.

Beep Beep......Beep Beep.......Beep Beep....

Oh. My phone is beeping. That must be what woke me. I grab it and my eyeglasses off the bedside table, hastily put my glasses on, having disposed of my recent pair of extended wear contact lenses before bed, and glance at the clock. Nine o'clock. I slept in, and it feels nice. Stretching, my mind begins to spin with what I'd like to accomplish today. I am finally able to focus on my cell phone's screen and realize that the beeps were alerting me to new emails. I tap the envelope icon and open my email.

My inbox is full of emails all from the same sender. 'Date Me.'

I rapidly scroll through them. There has to be at least 50.

Holy. Hell.

Chapter Five

"Fashion tip: If you're riding a magic carpet with a guy who's named Aladdin and a monkey named Abu, then I can see why you may have a need for harem pants. Otherwise, unless you are a washed-out rapper, or a genie in a bottle, I would recommend staying away from this horrid fashion trend!"

efore I can even begin to contemplate how many emails I may have received, I get out of bed, go to my closet to grab a change of clothes and head to the bathroom. I leisurely remove my clothes and start the shower. While waiting for the water to warm up, I grab my toothbrush and toothpaste and start brushing my teeth, while simultaneously checking myself out in the bathroom mirror.

I've lost weight since my divorce, but I don't look gaunt by any means. My stomach still has a tiny pooch, which I'm convinced is never going to go away, no matter how many sit-ups I do, but my face does look a little thinner. The dark circles under my eyes are prominent as ever, without makeup to cover them up. My hair seems to have lost a bit of sheen too. Can stress do that? Maybe it just needs a good, deep conditioning. I lean closer to the mirror and look deep into my green eyes. I see the beginning of a glimmer there, like a hint of a secret waiting to be revealed. The corners of my mouth rise a little at the thought. I know without a doubt, little by little, the real me will shine through. The insecure broken girl I became will keep fading away. I feel better than I have in a long time, which considering everything, may seem somewhat strange, but quickly reaffirms that getting out of Boston was good for me.

I also can't discount Pyper's influence. Friendship really does help heal the soul. I'm lucky to have Pyper. She's a loyal and authentic friend. And she knows how to look beyond appearances and what I may say to what is actually in my heart and soul. Such that if I were to attempt to delude her by saying with a straight face that I'm moving on and doing just fine, she would walk to me with a slight smile, give me a hug and yet, know without a doubt that I'm not really doing okay. She would continue to encourage and support me, standing right by my side, for however long necessary. She cuts right through the bullshit and sees the truth; sometimes even when I don't see it myself. It really is true what they say; *a true friend will see the tears pouring down your face, while the others believe the smile you're faking.*

Setting my toothbrush down, I turn and walk to the shower, grab a soft blue towel out of the linen closet beside the shower, hang it on the hook and step in. Once inside with the warm therapeutic shower spray nurturing my entire body, I start thinking about the day ahead. I need to organize my closet, throw some laundry in the wash, work on my blog post, and my Marc Jacobs fashion show write up. I also need to draft my newest article about harem pants. Apparently they are making a comeback. Ugh. Just the thought makes me shudder. Then later, I will be off to lunch with Pyper's parents. My mind wanders to the memory that seemed to come out of nowhere last night. Luke. I have no doubt that being back in Illinois again ignited that memory. When I considered coming back here I knew this was a possibility, and though I tried to play the "what if" game to prepare myself, it doesn't make it any easier. As if thinking about him was just asking for another memory, one assaults me before I can stop it.

It's a beautiful spring day outside and we are sitting underneath "our" tree. I'm on a blanket with the smell of grass and dirt beneath me, and the smell of sunshine and flowers blooming in the air. I'm lying on my left side, facing Luke, who is lying on his back with his arms thrown above his head, eyes closed. I'm watching the sunlight trickle over his face and body in dancing patterns made from the light shining through the leaves hanging from the tree's branches. I can't stop looking at him. He's beautiful. His dark hair - short on the sides and spiked on top, in the popular style guys are wearing right now – that he somehow seems to pull off better than all the others. He has a strong straight nose, high cheekbones that make me swoon, and a strong jaw with a slight dimple in his chin. He has one dimple on the right side of his mouth that deepens when he gives me a full blown grin, and it just begs me to explore it with my tongue. His best feature is hidden underneath his closed eyelids. His eyes are the most striking blue. Like the sky on a cloudless day. His full eyebrows and long dark lashes that any girl would envy only make them more breathtaking. His lips are full and kissable, and when he is thinking hard about something he presses them together. Sometimes he sticks his tongue between his lips and holds it there when he's concentrating, which always makes me smile. My favorite thing about that soft mouth of his - besides his kisses - is when he raises one corner to smirk at me. When he gives me that sexy smirk, I would do almost anything he asks, which is why I will do anything to make sure he never knows it.

Once my eyes leave his face, they trail down his strong neck, to his chest. His grey t-shirt is just snug enough that I can see his muscular chest underneath. The bottom of his shirt has risen up slightly, giving me a look at the hair dusting his stomach and the tease of his hip lines. Football keeps him in excellent shape. Everything about him is perfection.

Before I can get much further, movement distracts me and I look back at his face. I see those beautiful lips curve up into a smile at the corners. "You're staring again," he says.

He doesn't fool me. I know he knew I was staring the entire time, and he allowed me because he silently enjoyed it. But, I decide to play along. "I don't know what you're talking about."

"Okay but turnaround is fair play."

He opens his eyes and I inhale quietly at the sight. I'm thankful it was soft enough that he doesn't hear. I feel silly sometimes at the way he makes me feel; the way he can make my body feel with just one look. Like I'm the most exquisite thing he has ever seen. His looks could make me a believer. He just stares at me for a moment and I look right back. I can't look away; why would I want to?

"You're beautiful, Olivia. I'm the one that should be doing the staring. The way your hair is blowing in the wind, the light from the sun is dancing on your face, your cheeks are slightly flushed, your lips are pink...you take my breath away."

Now I'm staring at him in wonder. "Oh Luke, don't you get it? If I'm beautiful at all, it's because of you. The way you look at me, the way you make me feel, it's like nothing else matters but the two of us right here, right now. When I'm with you, all the insecurities go away because for some reason you don't see them. You make me perfectly imperfect."

"I don't think so, Olivia, there's nothing imperfect about you." Then he leans in, and I know he's about to kiss me and the butterflies in my stomach start doing somersaults. His lips meet mine and my whole body comes alive. He moves closer and our chests are touching, then he rolls me to my back and places part of his body on top of mine. He looks down at me, cups the side of my face and traces his tongue along my bottom lip, seeking entrance. When I give it to him and his tongue meets mine, my body becomes like an inferno. He consumes me. My heart, my soul, every thought, and every wish belong to him. He makes my soul sing.

As he takes his lips away from mine, his thumb brushes across my cheekbone and he looks deep into my eyes. I swear in that moment, his eyes are reflecting my thoughts and feelings.

Snapping myself out of that painful memory, I'm angry with myself. It wasn't real. Maybe it seemed to be and maybe he said it was at one time, but he changed his mind. He changed; his feelings changed. I don't know, but he clearly didn't feel that way after all. When I fled his house that day, I purposely didn't answer his calls the entire night. I don't even remember where I went, but I know I drove around for hours. My parents were beside themselves by the time I got home. My Mom told me that Luke had been there but I refused to talk to them about it right then. I knew Luke was leaving for vacation the next morning for two weeks, so all I had to do was avoid his calls overnight.

Once I knew he was gone, I had two weeks before he returned to figure out what I was going to do. So, I begged my parents to help me rearrange my plans and attend Boston U, instead of Loyola. With a bit of work and a little luck, I knew that by the time he returned, it would be just in time for classes to begin and I could already be gone and moved into my dorm room. Thank goodness for Pyper's dad and his connections to the BU board of trustees. Without him, I would never have been able to pull it off. I heard that Luke tried to reach me, but I switched my phone number and forbid Pyper or my parents to give it to him, or anyone else who might betray me. I also told them that I did not, under any circumstances, want them to tell him where I was. I felt bad for putting them in the middle, but my parents saw how hurt I was, and they were willing to do anything for me at that point. Pyper's parents would just defer any questions to my parents or to Pyper…and she could handle herself and anyone else. She was just as angry at his betrayal as I was, and I knew I didn't have to worry about him getting to me through her.

I haven't seen or heard from him since that day at his home. I made sure I didn't have to deal with the inevitable break up and the pain of hearing him tell me he was moving on and wanted to experience all that college life had to offer him, because I cut him loose first. I did the dirty work for him.

Shaking my head as if it would make the sad and painful memories immediately disappear, I step out of the shower and begin drying off. I wrap my wet hair in the towel and get dressed. Before I dry my hair, I decide to search for Pyper. I want to see if she woke up to the same insane amount of emails that I did. I search the condo, but Pyper is not to be found. I find the note she has left on the kitchen counter.

"Hey hot stuff! I peeked in to tell you I was off, but you were still sleeping peacefully. I even heard you snore! Just kidding! Maybe.

53

Anyway, I'm off to work for a bit. Be ready at 1:00, I will be back by then to grab you so we can head to my parents place! And yes, I received some emails from Date Me too. Stop freaking out! We'll check them out together! Kisses! Pyper"

I smile and help myself to a cup of coffee from the pot she already had brewed, bless her heart, and add some milk and three sugars. I like my coffee sweet. I head back into my room and begin tackling my to-do list!

A few hours later, I'm feeling rather accomplished. I've finished my fashion show article and sent it off to the magazine editor, I uploaded my new blog post for 'Pink Sugar Couture' and responded to my comments from previous blog posts. I've made good headway in organizing my closet, and unpacked a couple of boxes I still had left in the back. I've gotten ready for lunch and am waiting for Pyper to get home so we can head out the door together. I'm wearing my straight leg distressed jeans, with a plain, white wife-beater tank top, with tons of chain necklaces in gold. I've readied my leopard print Dolce & Gabanna tote bag I received as a gift from 'Your Style' magazine, will wear my heeled black suede ankle boots, and my black knitted cardigan that has frills along the edges. I'm set. It may be just lunch with Pyper's parents, but May always dresses to impress, even for a simple lunch, so if I were to show up in jeans and a t-shirt, I would feel underdressed, not that May would likely care.

A few minutes after I sit down and start browsing through the latest issue of Cosmo, Pyper comes through the front door like a firestorm. "Hi! I'm here! Just give me a minute and I'll be ready to take off!" She says as she goes flying by me. I don't even have a chance to respond.

She comes out two minutes later, "Sorry I'm running a few minutes late! I should not have had that last coffee. I had to pee so badly on the drive home. I was afraid I wasn't going to make it in time." She smiles at me.

I look her over. She looks amazing in straight leg jeans, a white t-shirt with a grey sequined scarf, grey sweater that has a slight shimmer to it, light pink ballet flats, and a light pink tote bag that matches her shoes. I love that she has as much fun with fashion as I do.

"No worries at all. How was everything at the spa?"

"Thanks, and the spa was really good. I probably didn't need to go in, to be honest. The display looked perfect and Caroline had everything completely under control up front. It was busy, which was nice to see."

"Plus I'm sure it doesn't hurt for the boss lady to make an appearance! I'm so glad your business is flourishing Pyper. And so are you! Success agrees with you! You look great!"

She smiles at me and says, "Back at ya babe. We should take a picture of you in that outfit for one of your 'Outfit Shares of the Week' posts."

"Oh, great idea! Would you mind?"

"Not at all," Pyper says already holding her hand out for my cell phone. She snaps the photo and says, "Let's hit the road."

"Okay, and thanks! Your car or mine?"

"Mine." We walk down and get into her Mercedes, pull out of the underground parking and start making our way to Pyper's parent's home. Pyper's Dad owns the high rise building where we live, but instead of living there, they have a massive home in Lincoln Park, a northern suburb of Chicago. It's only about 20 minutes away. We will be there in no time.

"So I was woken up by my phone beeping like crazy this morning. From your note I'm assuming you had the same little wakeup call?"

"Well I wasn't woken up because I had my phone on silent, but let me guess…you freaked out didn't you?"

"Maybe just a little, but then I decided not to dwell on it and tackled some other things I needed to get done. I got like 50 emails! In one night. That's insane! I haven't even looked at them other than to see where all the emails came from. I can't bring myself to peek. I can't even believe it. It has to be some kind of weird fluke."

"You haven't looked at them? Girl please! I've already gone through mine and deleted a ton of rejects that won't have the pleasure of even a minute of my time. There are a few possibilities though," she says with a grin. "We can check out yours when we get back from my parent's place."

"Okay, sounds good. Although, maybe I should just delete them? I'm seriously second guessing this whole thing."

"Don't you dare, Olivia! We are getting you back, remember?! End of discussion."

I can't help but grin at her when she gets all bossy at me. "Yes ma'am."

"Oh, I love this song!" Pyper turns up the radio and Kelly Clarkson blares through the speakers singing 'Stronger'.

I love the song too, but it makes me think of Deacon. And Luke. While going through the stress of both break ups, blasting woman empowerment music over and over makes me feel better.

I can't help but sing along to the words.

Pyper looks at me and smiles, I grin back. We sing louder.

Before long, we arrive at her parents' house and park out front. We begin making our way to the front of their impressive, massive house, and even before we can reach the door, it opens, and May comes flying out, completely bypasses Pyper, and enfolds me into her arms. Her hugs are amazing. "Hi honey! Oh I'm so happy to see you! I'm so happy you are home. Don't you worry about a thing, you are here now, and we love you and you are away from that horrible man. You never should have left, but we won't even think about that, you are back now, and I'm so glad."

I don't think she even stopped to breathe through any of that. I squeeze her back really hard, "It is so good to see you too, May! It's been too long since I've been home."

May looks lovely. Black slacks, a cream blouse with a skinny belt around the waist, and 3-inch heeled dress boots. Simple, but attractive, jewelry adds just the right amount of accent to her outfit. She doesn't look her age of forty-nine at all. I only hope I age as well as she does. Or that I have a great plastic surgeon.

"What the hell? Don't worry about saying hello to me! I'm just your daughter, no big deal!"

May immediately lets go of me and with a smile, pulls Pyper into a hug as well. "Hush with that mouth now, dear. You know I'm happy to see you too."

"I know. I just couldn't resist giving you a hard time."

May links arms with both Pyper and me, and we stride in through the entrance. I look up from her smiling face and see Pyper's dad, Ted, standing there with a smile on his face, while looking at his wife. The look that passes between them is so full of love. It just pours out of their eyes in a way that almost makes me want to look away from the intensity. He looks to me and smiles, his eyes sparkling.

"Olivia, it's so good to see you. It has been far too long, my dear." He hugs me as well, then turns to his daughter and hugs her too. "Hi, sweetheart. How's business?"

Pyper let's go of her mother, gives her dad a hug too, and says, "It's great daddy, I was just there this morning and the place was hopping!"

"Come on in girls. We have everything ready. I hope you're hungry!" May leads us through the house to the kitchen.

We walk inside the front double doors and enter the foyer. There is a glass table directly in front of us, and a huge chandelier hanging overhead. The floor tiles glisten and are so sparkly, I'm sure you could eat off of them. To the left of the front doors is a curving staircase with black iron railings on either side of the stairs in a beautiful scrolling pattern that lead to the upper floor. Maneuvering around the table and passing the staircase, we walk straight ahead and come to the living room, but take a right and start walking through their chef's caliber kitchen until we get to the dining room. The dining room is beautiful. Decorated in a dark blue and white, there is a large oak table smack in the middle of the room that seats no less than twelve people. One wall is nothing but glass windows with double doors that lead out to the garden. We walk toward that end of the table and take a seat.

We are barely seated before Mrs. B, who has worked for the Lexington's forever, but still manages to look exactly the same age, comes out of the kitchen carrying our salads and drinks. She kisses me on the head as she sets my salad in front of me and whispers, "Good to see you dear."

I smile at her and say, "You too," and start digging in. I'm famished!

After we finish our salads, we are served broccoli quiche, with fresh fruit, and rolls that Mrs. B no doubt made that morning. My favorite part is the honey butter she makes to go with the rolls. To. Die. For. Everything tastes wonderful, and I'm having a great time catching up, filling them in on the Deacon drama, most of which they already know from Pyper, when May says, "Guess who I ran into the other day?"

"No idea mom. The possibilities are endless." Pyper smiles slightly at her mother but looks at me and rolls her eyes.

I smile to myself until May says, "I saw Luke Easton when I was coming out of Water Tower Plaza. He looks marvelous. I told him about your return Olivia and he seemed very interested! Do you plan to see him since you're back?"

I choke on my lemonade. Pyper starts pounding my back in assistance, sending me a look that oozes with apologies. The food in my belly suddenly feels sour. May knows of my history with Luke, why would she think I would want to see him? Do I want to see him? NO! I don't want to see him. Right? Dammit!

"MOM! Why would you ask her that? Of course Olivia doesn't want to see Luke."

"Oh dear, I'm sorry. It's just that so much time has passed, I figured maybe things have changed. It's water under the bridge. I just remember how he tried desperately to find out where you had gone all those years ago, and...oh I don't know...it would be nice if you two could reconnect and maybe work things out."

"That is a nice thought, May, but I'm not interested in taking steps backward. Luke and I..." I feel kind of choked up and I don't know why. Man. May's revelation is really doing a number on my emotions. Pyper is staring at me and I know I'm going to be asked some questions later. I can just feel it. "Well, what I mean to say is that Luke and I were a long time ago, a lot has changed. I know I'm a different person now, and I'm sure he is too. I'm not interested in reconnecting."

May just smiles at me, and Ted changes the subject by asking me about the magazines I'm writing for right now. Have I mentioned Ted is awesome?

Except for the unexpected, and momentarily uncomfortable conversation at the table, we had a nice time visiting, and before we know it, we are out the door with containers full of leftover food from May and Mrs. B, with promises that we will be back again soon to visit.

"It was really great to see them. It makes me miss my own parents, though. I hope you don't mind if I just borrow yours until I see mine again!"

"Are you kidding? They would love that." Pyper hesitates and then she says, "So, about what my mom said..."

I interrupt her before she can continue, "There's nothing to talk about. You know that was all a long time ago."

"I know it was, but there is something you aren't telling me. I saw your face. You were surprised by her running into Luke, obviously, but at the same time, you weren't shocked. I can't explain what I saw in your face, exactly, but I know you well enough to know something is going on there. So what gives? What aren't you telling me?"

Sometimes I wish she didn't know me so well. I sigh. "It's just since I've been back here Luke has crossed my mind a lot. I'm sure that being back has allowed all the thoughts and feelings I suppressed to reemerge. I don't think you ever forget your first love, or the person you thought was going to be your lifemate, you know what I mean? I know you don't ever forget your first heartbreak either. I still remember it all, Pyper. I remember his face, his kisses, his touch, how he made me feel like I couldn't breathe, because I was so overwhelmed by the mere existence of him. He was all consuming. I know some would say I was so young, and what do I really know about that, but it was real. I felt it. It mattered."

Tears start gathering in my eyes. Shit. "I guess what I don't understand is why it still hurts. It's painful, and I think that is what bothers me. It has been seven years, Pyper. Seven years! Why does it still hurt? Why do I still remember it in such vivid detail? I can't help but wonder what the hell is wrong with me!"

"Nothing is wrong with you, Olivia. It makes sense that you would think about him, especially with you being back here. You've rarely visited Chicago since the day you left seven years ago. Other than the time you came and visited me for the spa grand opening, you've only been here a handful of other times. Don't be so hard on yourself."

"It isn't just that. I mean, what is wrong with me when it comes to men? The two men I've had serious relationships with in my life, both broke my heart. The sad thing is, I was married to Deacon, yet thinking about Luke, and what happened between us hurts more. I guess I should just be happy that I quit being blind where Deacon was concerned, and be grateful I divorced his ass for his complete douche-baggery."

"Douche-baggery?"

"Yep. Douche-baggery. Own it. Use it. Love it."

Pyper laughs at my comment but turns serious again as she says, "There isn't anything wrong with you. The problem is with them. Luke is the one that is to blame for your break up. Not you. All you are guilty of is giving him your heart and loving him. As far as Deacon goes, he's a controlling asshole that couldn't keep his dick in his pants. You didn't do anything wrong there either. Don't take on their 'douche-baggery'. Make them own it. The problem is all theirs."

"You are right, but while the problem is theirs, the fact is, the effects touch me, and I'm still feeling it all again and again, although I wish I wasn't."

"Well I know just the thing to help with that you know! The answer is right in your grasp. "

I just look at her and she nods towards my phone that I didn't even realize I was holding in my hand. "As soon as we get home, time to pull up those messages! Time for you to go on a date."

Chapter Six

"Fashion tip: When wanting to look sexy on a date, remember that looking truly sexy involves knowing what to bare, and what to keep under wraps. Choose one- only one- body part and show it off! If you share a little cleavage, cover your legs, if you show off those gorgeous gams, keep it covered on top! If, however, you choose to expose a little extra on top for a blind date, I recommend keeping a scarf in your purse should eye contact become an issue. Or perhaps, a small can of pepper spray."

Pyper and I have barely stepped inside the front door of the condo before she instructs, "Go grab your laptop."

When I walk inside my bedroom to grab my laptop, I take a minute to kick off my boots and put my handbag down before joining Pyper in the living room. I join her on the floor, side by side, with our computers propped on the coffee table once again.

I pull up my email program and just stare at the screen full of unread emails from 'Date Me' and blink.

I bite my bottom lip, "I'm pretty sure I've gotten even more responses since the last time I looked. I'm feeling overwhelmed. I'm just not sure about this."

"Oh chill out, it's okay. Let me take a look." Pyper grabs my computer and starts going through each one and I hear her mumbling to herself, "No. No. Oh, hell no. Hmm. Maybe. Cute. Oh! Nice."

I can't help but giggle at her. This is crazy.

Whatever she's doing takes time, so I admire the magnificent view outside the window while I'm waiting for her. After several moments, she turns my computer back towards me. "Okay, out of all those emails you had a welcome email from 'Date Me', another one reminding you of their rules and guidelines, a few asking you to answer various questions that can be posted on your profile, and then there were several emails notifying you that you received a kiss."

"A kiss?"

"Yes, a kiss. If someone views your profile and likes it, he can send you a kiss."

"Okay. That's interesting. How do you even know about these virtual kisses?"

"Because unlike you, after we completed our profiles, I took some time to read about how it all works." She rolls her eyes at me. "Anyway," she sounds a bit exasperated with me. "I left ten profiles for guys that sent messages to you that I think look promising. Take a look at their messages and their profiles, and narrow it down. Whomever you think you might be interested in, message them back! That's what I'm going to do too."

I'm skeptical about this whole thing, but I will humor her. I read their messages and then pull up their profiles and read through them, taking note of their likes and dislikes and what they tell me about their personalities in general. I delete one because he's a smoker, and I'm not a fan. I delete another because he's a big horror movie fan, and I'm way too much of a wimp for that, even previews on TV for horror movies freak me out. A few guys have horrible quotes on their pages that just make them look like they are trying way too hard. No thanks. That leaves five promising possibilities.

"Oh. Pyper. Umm. Look at this one." A gorgeous blond-haired, blue-eyed man is smiling at me from his profile picture. "His profile name is NoahA and he is beautiful."

Pyper laughs at me. "What else does it say?"

I laugh. "I don't care. Does it really matter? He's beautiful."

Pyper laughs again, "Yes it matters and you know it!"

"I could just go on a date with him and stare at him the whole time and be happy."

Pyper sighs this time and turns my computer towards her, "Well his likes are reading, playing flag football, painting and it says his occupation is a landscape architect. Hmm interesting combination, he's artsy and athletic. Well, message him back and ask him about getting together."

"Aye, aye cap'n" and when I salute her she laughs.

I message him back and over the next few hours Pyper and I laugh as we go through our matches and read our messages. I've narrowed it down to four men that I am interested in and message them back. Aside from NoahA, I also reply to a JaketheSnake, Ethan, the man I saw when we made our profiles, and another named DanielCubsFan. I've chosen them based on their interests and some of the questions they've answered. It appears that we could be good matches. And they're pretty to look at. I admit it. Lame screen name for Jake aside.

"Okay, how many do you have it narrowed down to, Pyper? I've sent responses to three that I would consider meeting if they get back to me."

"I have five that I've responded to. Their profile names are Dale90, JayH, BlakeE, SethBearsFan1, and Cooper88."

I admit, I'm surprised because Pyper is damn picky! Feeling accomplished and pretty proud of myself for taking the leap back into the dating world, I prepare to shut down my computer. Before I get far into the shutting down process, a blinking on the far left side of the screen catches my eye. Looking closer, next to my profile avatar, I see that a blinking light notifying me that I have a new message. I click on it, and find a response from DanielCubsFan.

"I got a response!" I squeal slightly in my excitement. Aw hell. What is wrong with me? I may have to admit that I'm actually enjoying this and even a bit excited.

"Well, open it!" I feel somewhat better about my reaction when I hear the same excitement in Pyper's voice.

I open the message and read out loud, "Hi Olivia. I'm so glad you responded to my message. I would love to meet you. Perhaps we could save time and meet in person instead of spending unneeded hours on the phone. Would you be available to go out to dinner some night this week or next? If so, please message me your phone number and we can make arrangements. I look forward to hearing from you."

Pyper, who is looking over my shoulder points to my screen, "Look, it shows that he is active right now, which means he is online. Click this button and you can chat with him right now to make plans."

"What? No! I'll just message him again!"

"No way, Olivia! You are not going to chicken out on me! Live chat!"

"Damn you, Pyper Lexington!"

I click the button that allows me to private message Daniel and I start typing, 'Hi I just got your message. I would love to arrange a day and time to meet; my calendar is pretty open, as my work allows for a flexible schedule. What night works best for you?'

"How's that Pyper?"

"Good! Send it."

I push the button that reads send, and within seconds I get a response. Ah, I'm giddy!

"He says, 'Hi Olivia. I'm so glad to hear from you again. How about this Thursday night at seven o'clock?' What do I say?" I ask Pyper, my voice sounding high pitched due to my nervousness.

Pyper laughs at me! "Tell him you are game."

I start typing a response, "Sure, Thursday night would be perfect. Do you have a specific place in mind you'd like to meet?"

We message back and forth a couple more times, making arrangements to meet at Maggiano's, an Italian restaurant in Little Italy that is one of my favorites, and exchange phone numbers.

"OH MY GOD, PYPER!! I HAVE A DATE ON THURSDAY NIGHT! WHAT THE HELL AM I GONNA WEAR?!" I screech.

Pyper laughs really hard at my reaction, which only serves to aggravate me. "Don't laugh at me! Can you not see I'm freaking out and panicking here?!"

"You have plenty of amazing outfits you can wear. We will get it all figured out!"

I just sit and stare at my computer for a little bit. Once I'm over the original shock of having a date so soon, I tell Pyper, "Okay, now let's get a date scheduled for you too!" And just as I say this, Pyper is chattering excitedly because she has received a response. Admittedly, I'm distracted.

Holy hell. I have a date.

Thursday night has arrived and I am REALLY nervous. There are butterflies on steroids in my stomach. I mean, why did I let Pyper talk me into this? Can I plead temporary insanity? Peer pressure? But then, I think about standing Daniel up or cancelling last minute and I know I can't do that. I'm sure once I get there, I will be fine. I just wish the nervous feeling in my stomach would go away. I feel like I could be sick.

I look at myself in my floor-length mirror. Maggiano's is a very nice place, so I am dressed up to suit the atmosphere. I'm wearing my cranberry, silk, sleeveless dress by Marc Jacobs that I bought at an off-the-rack department store last year. It has a full skirt, a sweet bow on the front on the left side and a round neckline that shows just a hint of cleavage but is still rather chaste. I have a black, cropped cardigan with embellished roses around the collar to go over it, and my black satin peep toe heels to match the cardigan. My makeup is done nicely, with a smoky eye, cheeks that look barely flushed and a nude gloss on my lips. My long, dark hair is down, flat ironed, and is laying nice and smooth down my back.

I look pretty, I think. I'd want to date me.

I walk into my bedroom, grab my leopard bag, and quickly pull everything out and place it on my bed, grabbing only what I need for the evening and stuff it into my black Kate Spade handbag, a gift from my mother. As I'm doing this, Pyper knocks on the door and I tell her to come in.

"Hey, can I borrow...." She stops speaking when she gets a good look at my appearance, "Wow, you look great!"

I look at Pyper and smile, checking her out in return, because she has a date tonight too. Cooper is taking her to Ambria, an amazing French restaurant. I wish we were going to the same place and could make it a double. That would help with my nerves tremendously, but I'm not a baby, I don't need my hand held. I think.

"You look gorgeous, Pyper. Cooper will not be able to take his eyes off of you!" I mean it. She looks eye-popping in a lace three-quarter sleeve dress that is emphasizing all of her curves. Her lips are a gorgeous red, while the rest of her makeup is subtle. Her fiery red hair is shoulder length, with choppy ends and side swept bangs. If she were blonde, she would look like Reese Witherspoon, but with green eyes. She has a cute, pert nose, but it is the sharp chin and jaw line that make her resemble Reese.

"Thanks! I see you are switching bags. I was hoping that was the case, can I borrow your leopard bag? I'm going to wear my leopard print heels and your bag would look fantastic with them."

I pull out the last of the items that were left in the bag - a chapstick, a quarter and old receipt that fell to the bottom and hand the bag to Pyper. "It's yours, here you go."

Her smile and calm demeanor helps to relax me a bit. "I'm nervous. I keep going back and forth on whether or not I can do this."

"You will be fine. All you are doing is having conversation with someone over dinner. That's it. You know, I only want you to be happy and if you really don't think you're ready, then we can call it all off right now. You don't have to do this, though I do think it will be good for you. Get your first date out of the way. But, there's no pressure here. If you're not ready, you're not ready. I know I tease you and get a little bossy at times, but it is all meant in love. I just want you to find happiness again, but how and when you decide to look for it is always on your terms."

"I know that Pyper, and you're right, this will be good for me. I said I wanted to date again and feel my age. I admit I'm nervous, yes, but I'm excited too. It's just that the fear of the unknown is overshadowing the excitement a bit."

Pyper walks over and hugs me. "Regardless of how Daniel is or isn't, you are amazing. Remember that. Have fun, and I can't wait to talk to you when we both get back and compare our evenings!"

"You have fun, too. Remember though, if anything goes wrong, call me immediately and I will be there as soon as I can get there. No questions asked."

"You got it, same goes for you okay?"

"You bet! Okay. Well, I have to head out, or I'm going to be late."

"Me too! I need to hurry! Bye, Olivia, it will be great! You'll see!"

An hour later, I'm sitting at a table across from Daniel with a glass of white wine, and a plate of four cheese ravioli in front of me that is so fabulous I would marry it if I could. Seriously, it is melting in my mouth. The service is impeccable and the lights are dimmed low to create an intimate ambiance. I can see people at the tables closest to us, but the people sitting at the tables further away look like moving shadows. The candle on the table makes light dance across Daniel's face. He really is attractive, and I have enjoyed looking at him, but his beauty does not make up for the fact that he is incredibly arrogant and proud of it.

"I was the best baseball player on our team in college. My batting average was an amazing three ninety-six. Other players were close, but no one could outdo me. I would have definitely gone to the pros too if I hadn't ripped a tendon in my shoulder."

When he started this story he was just finding his love of baseball in junior high. Yes, it has gone on that long. Aside from the fact he loves to talk about himself and I've barely gotten a word in, this whole conversation is happening between him and my boobs. Not once has he made eye contact with me. Not. Once. Even when he introduced himself, he was looking at my chest. I wonder if he thinks they are going to start talking back to him.

"Tell me about what you do for a living." I try to steer the conversation in a different direction.

"I'm getting there," he says brushing me off. "So after I hurt my shoulder, I tried to continue playing ball, but it didn't take long for me to realize that my baseball career was over...." I'm barely listening to him. I just nod and make humming noises where it seems appropriate, while inhaling my tasty pasta. I briefly hope I'm not looking like a pig in front of him, but then I realize he doesn't even notice - he's still staring at my boobs. I wonder if I shake them in a shimmy, if his face would move quickly back and forth in time with my breasts. It could be amusing to test that theory.

I sigh to myself. I guess I have only myself to blame. I mean after we were seated I did ask him to tell me about himself. I just didn't know that he would go on and on and on. He hasn't asked one thing about me. At least I know why the man is still single.

"Are you finished, Miss?" The waiter is standing next to me and I didn't even notice him appear, given my inner monologue. I look down to realize I am finished.

"Oh, um, yes, thank you very much."

He looks to Daniel, "Sir?"

"Yes, I'm finished too," he tells the waiter while still looking at my breasts. I can't help it, I shake them just a little and holy hell! His head does move side to side a bit. Oh man, just wait until I tell Pyper about this. She's going to tease me for days about how my boobs have magical mesmerizing abilities.

Before the waiter walks away, he places the bill on the table.

Daniel grabs the bill looks at it for a moment and I don't believe my ears when he says, "Okay so your glass of wine was nine dollars, and your plate of pasta is fourteen dollars, so your total is going to be twenty-three dollars." I'm pretty sure my mouth is hanging open but he doesn't notice. "He was a good waiter too, so I'd recommend you tip him fifteen to twenty percent."

I'm shocked into speechlessness. It isn't that I mind paying for my own dinner, but I admit, I assumed he would pick up the tab. To me, that is just a gentlemanly thing to do. It shows that the man has an innate need to take care of a woman and, admittedly, I find that attractive.

Taking my wallet out of my purse, I grab a twenty and ten dollar bill and set it in the tray the waiter provided to collect the money. "Here you go."

Daniel glances at what I've left and says, "I will tell him you need change."

"No it's fine. I don't want change."

"That is much more than twenty percent Olivia, he really doesn't need that much."

"Daniel, I'm perfectly aware it is more than twenty percent. Please leave it as it is. Thank you." Talk about a tight wad. Ugh. Just get me out of here already.

He sighs at me. He SIGHS AT ME! I would love to smack him and then get the hell out of here.

When he places his money on the tray with mine, I stand and grab my jacket and purse. He stands and waits for me to put my jacket on, never once offering to help me get it over my shoulders. We are making our way towards the entrance to the restaurant when I feel him grab my ass. Before I can whirl around he whispers in my ear, "I got us a room that we can use for a few hours or all night. I suggest we see how it goes. Of course, if we only use it a few hours, then it will be cheaper for us than if we stay for the whole night."

I stop. I literally stop and blink. Did he just say that? I feel anger start rising in my chest and progressively moving upwards, heating my face and neck. I slowly turn to him and since my jacket isn't buttoned up the front yet, he of course is looking at my breasts. Again.

I reach out and push his chin up until his eyes meet my angry ones. "My eyes are right here, asshole. If you were hoping my boobs were going to start speaking to you, that's not going to happen. It is clear that you are your own number one fan, and aside from the fact it's insulting that you assume I would be intimate with you after the first date, if you are anything in bed like you are out of it, I'm not interested. I don't doubt for a second that sex with you would bore me to tears, not to mention that you would likely talk about yourself the whole time during your...uh, performance. I can assure you, that while you would no doubt think you were fantastic, I would find you lacking. I am not going anywhere with you. Don't contact me again."

With that, I storm past the tables and head towards the exit, not even caring if anyone heard me. As I make my way to the door, I just keep my head down, looking at the ground, because I know my face is flushed in anger, and I just want to get home and forget this date ever happened. Just as I step out the door and the cold air hits me, I slightly bump into someone. "Oh, sorry," I mumble. I hear a gasp. I hope I didn't hurt whomever I bumped into, but I don't stop and ask. I'm practically running to my car.

Once safely buckled in, I start the car and I can't get out of there fast enough. I can't believe I just had the date from hell. As tears of frustration and anger build in my eyes, I wonder why I even attempted to do this.

Wait. I know why.

Pyper.

I laugh out loud. That read headed bitch isn't going to know what hit her when I get home!

Chapter Seven

"Fashion tip: Guys this tip is for you! You only get one chance to make a first impression. And let's be honest, girls like clothes and care about what they wear. We practically make an event out of selecting just the right outfit. What does this have to do with you? Well, most girls want their guys to look as good as they do. So, make an effort. It won't kill you to wear a nice dress shirt and dress shoes on a first date. Don't show up wearing your favorite college hoodie and stinky sneakers with your favorite smelly socks. It likely won't go well if you do."

She's a voodoo priestess and she has worked some kind of voodoo magic on me. That has to be what it is. How else can I explain the fact that I'm dressed for what will likely be another dating nightmare of torturous proportions? Am I being dramatic? Absolutely. I'm prone to drama in situations like this.

Somehow, Pyper has managed to talk me off the ledge from my awful date with Daniel. After she finished laughing about what an ass Daniel turned out to be, she told me the horrible story of her own date.

"I'm serious, Olivia, the guy's laugh resembled a horse's whinny. He had a long face and slight buck teeth, and every time he uttered a word or laughed, I kept waiting for him to neigh or snort. I swear, his head morphed into a horse moment by moment – at least in my mind. I kept wanting to yell YEE-HAW."

"Pyper, come on. It couldn't have been that bad."

"Believe me, it was. It definitely explains why he only has a side profile picture and he is smiling with his mouth closed."

I just shook my head at her. She said he had other personality deficits that made him unattractive to her, but I admit I wonder if the laugh and buck teeth were really the off-putting characteristics. I love Pyper, but she is very picky when it comes to men. Someone's nose could be a little crooked, or they could have what she calls "girly hands" and that's it...she's done! After Pyper's retelling of her date, the two of us laughed so much that the bad date vibes with Daniel started wearing off. And that's when she dropped the bomb. She'd signed us up for speed dating. Oh Lord.

Now, here I am, standing in my bathroom, drinking some liquid courage, wondering how she managed to talk me into this.

I look at myself in the mirror one more time, checking out the outfit I've chosen. Pyper said the dress code is casual, so I've decided to be comfortable in dark wash jeans, paired with a black sweater. I tied an abstract print colored scarf – mustard yellow, black and white - around my neck, and my shoes are simple, but cute black ballet flats that have a slight shimmer to them. I'm wearing my hair down and my makeup is minimal. I don't want to look like I'm trying too hard.

Sighing, I walk out of my bathroom into my room and drain the last drops from my wine glass, while heading to my jewelry chest to get my diamond stud earrings. I place them in, and after tucking my hair behind my ear, take a quick peek in the mirror on my jewelry chest. It's as good as it's going to get tonight. Picking up my wine glass once again, I head out of my room, grabbing my black Coach bag.

I hear Pyper walk up behind me as I'm placing my empty wine glass into the sink. Turning around, I take in my friend. She's standing with her hands on her hips, posing, waiting for me to comment. Looking her up and down, I begin to laugh when I read her shirt. She's wearing jeans and a grey cardigan with silver flats, but the white t-shirt under the cardigan says *Yes, I Am Single. You're Gonna Have To Be Amazing To Change That.* Man, I love my best friend. Only she could get away with wearing a shirt like that to speed date.

Smiling, Pyper takes her hands off her hips and pulls her cardigan into place. She looks at me innocently, "What?"

"Nice shirt."

She just shrugs. "You ready to do this?"

"No."

"Oh come on Olivia! This is going to be great! I've always wanted to do this and now I get to do it with you instead of being lame and going by myself."

"Pyper, this is madness. Need I remind you about the date from hell I just had not two weeks ago?"

"Oh big deal, Olivia, so you had one bad date, mine wasn't great either. Should I remind you of his laugh again?" and then she imitates it and I have to say, I probably would have walked away from a guy that sounded like that too. It's rather horrifying.

"Okay, okay. Let's go before I change my mind."

When we reach the parking garage, I ask Pyper, "Your car or mine?" while checking out my lip gloss in the elevator mirror.

"Yours."

"Okay."

We start walking to my car. Aside from Pyper's car, there are only a handful of others here. Everyone has plans tonight I guess. We pass a white, four-door Chevy Malibu and it's parked like someone was in a hurry, taking up two spaces. I hate it when people do that. Unlocking the doors to my car, we jump in and start making our way to the hotel that is hosting the speed date event.

Upon arriving at the hotel, we enter through the main doors that open into the lobby. A few feet from the doors is a large sign directing individuals attending speed dating to go to the ballroom located down the hall, third door on the left. Pyper and I make our way there and my stomach starts doing flip flops. I'm so nervous. I can't believe I'm doing this. I look over at Pyper and she has a huge smile on her face. How does this stuff not faze her?

Once we walk into the ballroom, there are at least 20 or more people inside. A blonde girl sitting at a table to the right of the entry immediately greets us with a big smile. "Hello! We are so glad you made it tonight. What are your names, please?"

Pyper smiles at her in return. "Olivia Brooks and Pyper Lexington."

The blonde, whose nametag reads 'Nikki,' looks for our names and checks them off the list. She hands us nametags with our names printed on them. "Here are your nametags, ladies, and this piece of paper here is called your speeding ticket. You will use your speeding ticket to rank your dates and make notes as you meet each of your dates tonight." She hands us each a pen and a piece of paper that says *Speeding Ticket* in bold on the top, along with the picture of a traffic light. There is a column on the left side that has a bunch of names, and under each name is a bit of space, apparently for note taking. Obviously, this list is of names represents the men attending this evening. Next to the column of names there is a column in red that says 'No' at the top, next to the red column is another in yellow that says 'Maybe,' and a column in green at the end that says 'Yes'. Each of the columns have boxes in them across from each name for placing check marks. It appears that after meeting each person the intent is to check whether or not they are a No, Yes, or Maybe. Oh, man. I can't help but giggle a little.

Nikki smiles at me knowingly. "Go ahead and help yourselves to drinks and appetizers if you'd like, and in about," she looks at her watch, "five minutes we will get started."

"Thank you." Pyper and I say together.

I immediately make a beeline for the bar they have set up. Another glass of wine sounds like just what I need.

"Take it easy, Olivia, you already had some wine at home. We both know you are a bit of a lightweight, you don't want to overdo it."

"Pyper, I could drink ten glasses of wine and I'm not sure it would be enough to get me through this."

Pyper just rolls her eyes at me. "Okay, so it is kind of crazy, but if we hate it, we never have to do this again. We can at least try it, right?"

"We are. We're here! Just know I'm here under protest."

"Noted. Now look pretty and smile! Time will fly by, we will be through this in no time, and you'll be thanking me!"

After I have a glass of Riesling in hand, and Pyper has a glass of Merlot, we stand together taking in the room. It looks like a junior high dance, with the guys on one side and girls on the other. You can see the guys blatantly checking out the girls, while the girls try to look like they don't care. The girls are standing around talking to each other, but they slyly check out the men out of the corner of their eyes. Everyone is 13 all over again.

In a circle around the room are small tables that have one chair on each side, facing one another, and on top of the table are bells attached to a clock and numbers. I hear someone tap a microphone, and I look to the front the room. "Hello, everyone. My name is Abby and we are just about ready to begin. Thank you all for joining us tonight. For those of you attending for your first time, let me give you a brief run down."

I snort. Whispering to Pyper I ask, "Did she say rub down?" Okay, immature, I know, but everything seems funny right now.

"Ha. Ha. Olivia. Listen!"

"On your name tag you will find a number. This number indicates the table you will start at tonight." I look at my name tag and my number is ten and I glance at Pyper's and hers says nine. "There are fifteen tables and thirty people here tonight. Once you all go to your assigned table and I tell you to begin, one of you will press the bell on your table. This begins the timer that is attached. You will then begin your five-minute date. After the time is up, there will be sixty seconds in between each date so you can make brief notes, if necessary, on your speeding ticket. Men, please step away from the table to write your notes, ladies stay seated. After the sixty seconds are up, men you will be told to move clock wise to the next table. Ladies, again, you will remain seated, and will stay seated throughout your fifteen dates."

I giggle at that. Fifteen dates. That's hilarious. I'm having fifteen dates in one night! I'm a total date slut! I notice Pyper look at me with exasperation. Oh, come on! How does she not find that funny?

"If you look on the bottom of your speeding ticket, you will see our website. Tomorrow you can go to the site and log in with the number on the bottom of your sheet. Your name will appear and you will be prompted to click the names of those individuals you feel you made a connection with tonight. If the person you list also selects your name as well, you each will receive an email with the contact information for the other person, so you can pursue your relationship. Anyone have any questions?" Abby asks.

No one says anything. It was easy enough to follow. I quickly do the math in my head. Five minutes with fifteen guys, with one minute in between each date means almost ninety minutes of dating. Piece of cake. I can handle ninety minutes.

"Okay, since no one has any questions we will begin in approximately five minutes. If you don't have a drink and would like one, get one now to have at your table, if you'd like. Once we begin, we will not stop for a break, other than the sixty seconds in between each date."

I look at my glass of wine. Yep, time for a refill. I quickly drink what's left in my glass and head to the bar to grab another glass to take to my table with me. While I'm waiting in line behind other people who obviously have the same idea as me, Pyper comes up next to me just as I am ordering another glass of Riesling, and she looks at me disapprovingly. I think she's going to say something, but she doesn't. I feel fine, relaxed even. And okay, things are suddenly pretty hilarious, but I don't know what her problem is. She wanted me to have a good time, didn't she?

"Okay, everyone, please head to your assigned tables so we may begin."

"Good luck!" I say with a cheery wave and big smile to Pyper. This time, when she looks at me, I see concern briefly register on her face, but I just keep smiling as I head to my table.

As I approach, there is someone sitting at my table already, his name tag reads 'Sam.' He has light brown hair, glasses, and is dressed in khaki pants and a white dress shirt. I'm rather surprised I don't see a pocket protector in his shirt pocket. Nothing about him really stands out at me, to be honest. I don't feel an immediate connection or anything when our eyes meet. Bummer. Too bad I can't just yell out "NEXT!"

"Hello!" I say. I think I may have been kind of loud. Oops.

He startles, and somewhat shyly says, "Hello."

I set my speeding ticket and pen on the table, set my handbag at my feet and take a seat. I smile broadly at Sam. He seems a bit taken back. Hmm, I kind of feel like maybe my smile is reminiscent of the Joker, but I'm sure I'm imagining it. I'm just nervous.

Abby is at the podium again, "Okay everyone on the count of one please press your bell to start the timer. Three…two….one." Sam and I both reach out to press the bell at the same time. I push his hand out of the way and slam my hand on the top. "And go!" I say.

He smiles at me again somewhat hesitantly and asks, "So how long have you lived in Chicago? Were you born here, or did you move here?"

"Oh, well, I grew up here, and after I got my heart broken by someone I thought loved me, I ran away to Boston to attend college where I lived for five years. Then after I went through a nasty divorce to a guy I shouldn't have married to begin with, I came back here to live with my best friend, Pyper. She's over there." I tell him, making a halfhearted attempt to wave behind me. Then I take another swallow of my wine.

"Oh, well. How…nice, I guess." He mutters.

I snort at him. Nice? Not hardly.

"How about you, Sam?" I ask and I'm pretty sure I hissed the 'S' like a snake.

"I was born and raised in Chicago. I went to college for website design, and right after I graduated I got a job with Websites R Us and enjoy creating websites for several clients. It keeps me busy."

"Oh, so you're a techy geek huh?"

"Umm, I prefer the title internet designer."

"I'm sure you do." I think this is going well. This is easy. "What do you like to do in your spare time?"

He clears his throat, "Well, I enjoy taking walks in the park with my dog. I have a yellow lab named Goldie."

I interrupt, "Wow, that's original." I say, deadpanned. Okay, kind of rude on my part, but really? Lame name.

"Well, actually, my six-year-old niece named her."

"Oh. Well that's awesome!" Way to go Olivia! You just insulted his niece. You rock at this. "How many nieces and nephews do you have?"

"I have four. Two nieces and two nephews. Do you have any?"

"Nope. I'm an only child."

"Oh." We just stare at each other for a few seconds. Then a few seconds more. And a few more. Wow. This is awkward. Maybe I should get up and sing and dance?

He clears his throat again and just as he's about to ask me another question a bell rings signaling the end of our date. Thank God.

"Well Olivia, it was umm interesting meeting you."

"Hey, you too, Sam. You have a good night, and good luck or whatever!"

He stands and steps away from the table. Turning to my speeding ticket, taking full advantage of the sixty seconds, I check STOP next to Sam's name. I'm not gonna lie. Sam was boring and I don't really have a website I need designed, so I don't see an advantage here. I'm sure Sam thinks that went well though. I'm sure I at least got a MAYBE from him. Go me! I've totally got this. I am an amazing speed dater. I should get a button. Or a medal.

I look back at Pyper, catch her eye and give her two thumbs up. Before she can respond I turn back around.

"Please head to your next table, men," Abby says. Walking towards me with a swagger that shows his confidence, this guy has blond hair, blue eyes and is wearing jeans and a light pink polo shirt. He looks like he is well-built. His arms are muscular, and I can see the definition of his chest through his shirt. Nice. The man has to be comfortable with himself to wear that color. His nametag reads Kip.

"Hi Olivia," He says while looking at my name tag a bit too long, or is he looking at my boobs? Oh no, not again. Been there done that with Daniel.

"Hello Kip, nice to meet ya."

"Okay everyone, let's get ready. Three....two...one."

I let Kip ring the bell, beginning our five minutes.

"So tell me about yourself, Olivia."

"Okay, sure." I'm good at this part! "Hi, my name is Olivia Brooks. I'm twenty-five years-old and I am a journalist. Don't let that fool you though, the only hard hitting topics I cover are whether or not harem pants are coming back in style, and if eyelash curlers really work. But I love it." I smile. I really do love it. "I divorced my asshat of a husband when I came home and found him screwing some blonde whore in our bed. What a day that was! Despite his begging, I moved back here to live with my best friend so I can try to get some semblance of a life back." Suddenly I feel a little choked up. "She's a really great friend. I don't know what I would do without her." I sniffle and take another large swallow of my wine. What is wrong with me? Why did I just tell him all of that? Oh well, I'm sharing… this is good. Right?

"Do you happen to have a tissue, Kip?"

"Uh, no, sorry, I can see if I can get you one."

"No that's okay." I wipe my nose on my hand and sniffle again. Sexy.

"Wow, okay so that's quite a lot to take in there, Olivia."

"Don't I know it, Kip. What about you? What's your story?"

"Well I'm afraid mine isn't as interesting as yours Olivia. I moved here when I was accepted to Northwestern University, where I went to study engineering. I have never been married and I really enjoy my job as an engineer. I work a lot, but in my spare time I enjoy playing racquetball at my gym to keep in shape, doing the crossword puzzle in the Sunday paper, and eating good food."

"Cool."

He just laughs at me.

I can't help but ask, "Tell me then, why are you here? Can't you get a date without coming to one of these things? I'm here because my so-called best friend roped me into coming."

"Outside of work, I'm not involved in many things that allow me to meet other women. I've already dated the single possibilities employed at my work place, and they didn't work out. I'm tired of my friends trying to set me up, too. I thought this would be a perfect meat market, if you know what I mean." He winks at me. For real. You can't make this shit up.

"Meat market?"

He just shrugs and grins at me, his eyes piercing mine. Is he kidding me?

I take another drink of my wine. I'm ready to be done with this now. This is stupid. I wonder how Pyper is getting along. I hear her laugh from time to time.

"Well Kip, it sure was nice meeting you. Best of luck to you on your dating endeavors." I lift up my wine glass and say a toast, "May you find your lucky lady here tonight, and never have to come to another one of these ridiculous things again."

He laughs, "Thanks, Olivia. You too."

A bell rings. I have the best timing. I am so amazing with this speed dating stuff. End of date two. I grab my paper and next to Kip's name check the STOP box. I also put a brief description, *engineer, blonde, asshole, meat market.* Brilliant note taking on my speeding ticket.

My next several speed dates are unremarkable. I'm pretty sure I mentioned Deacon more times than I care to admit. I remember at some point, someone did manage to track down a Kleenex for me, and I'm pretty sure I even told an embarrassing story about a wet t-shirt contest I was in once, and about making out with a girl in college on a dare. I continue to rock this speed dating thing. If they gave out grades, I would get an A+ for sure.

A man named Adam is sitting at my table now. He's a really good looking guy. He has dark hair, dark eyes, and dark glasses. The glasses make him look hot. I think he knows it though, so that takes him down a few notches in my book.

"What is your favorite color?" I'm surprised by his question.

"Pink," I answer. "And yours?"

"Yellow." I like that answer. Yellow is a good color. Bright. Cheerful. Sunny.

My turn, "Favorite movie?"

"Die Hard."

"Ugh. That is such a guy movie."

Laughing at my response he asks me, "What is your favorite movie?"

"*The Princess Bride,*" I answer. That movie is hilarious. I can watch it over and over again.

He smirks. Something about him makes me uneasy, but I don't know what it is. He reminds me of something. Or someone. "What is an important quality you look for in a man?"

"That's easy. I want him to not be a cheating bastard liar." Am I slurring slightly? "Are you a cheating bastard liar, Adam? Because I have to be honest, I'm pretty sure that all men are. Very few have any redeeming qualities. They make promises and don't follow through. That's my experience with men, Adam. Is that how you are, Adam? Hmm? How many women's hearts have you broken? How many women have you lied to?"

Again with the smirk. "I've never done that, princess. What would make you think I would ever break a woman's heart? I'm just here looking for someone that has interests similar to mine and wants to hang out." He smiles. It's a smarmy smile. It seems like he's just saying the words but doesn't mean them. I lose it. I don't know if it is the endearment 'princess' or his attitude that is to blame, but I snap just the same.

"You've never done that? That's what they all say." I stand up, grab my wine glass, and drain it. "THAT'S WHAT THEY ALL SAY!" I yell. I start yelling loud enough for everyone in the room to hear. "All you men are the same! You say whatever you think a woman wants to hear, until you get us right where you want us. Like a spider, you trap us in your web, then you keep the manipulations coming, wrapping us in your silk with your pretty little lies. You tell us we are beautiful, that you want to be with us forever, you tell us we are your everything, you say all you want is to spend your life loving us, BUT YOU LIE. YOU ALL LIE." I hear glass shattering. I think I dropped my wine glass.

Pyper rushes to my side and tries to speak urgently in my ear, but I brush her off. I'm not finished.

"Run while you can ladies. Do you hear me? Run. Don't let them fool you with their suave moves, nice words, and what you think are their good intentions, because you will be hurt. You will be hurt over and over again, and they will take everything from you. They will steal your heart, your soul, and your mind until you feel like you can't breathe from the pain of it. Just when you think their work is done, that they can't possibly take anything else, you realize the pure devastating confusion that comes from feeling like you can't live without them. Even after what they've done. Even when they've left you broken, a shell of the person you used to be. PROTECT YOURSELF LADIES!"

Pyper is pulling on my arm now, and I'm pretty sure I hear her apologize. I'm too busy looking at the faces around me. Some are staring at me, wide eyed, others are smirking at me, some are giggling to themselves. Why aren't they listening?

"WHY AREN'T YOU LISTENING?" I begin to sob, wiping my face on my sleeve.

"Come on, Livvie. It's okay. I'm listening to you. You're right. Let's go, honey, okay? It's okay. It's over. Whatever set you off babe, it's over. Let's go." She talks to me soothingly over and over like I'm a child.

"You believe me don't you Pyper? Men will just hurt you. They'll make your soul bleed."

"I know Olivia. Come on, let's go home. I'm sorry, I'm so sorry."

I take her arm, "Don't apologize Pyper, you didn't do anything."

"I'm just sorry you're hurting."

She walks me out of the room, down the hall, and to the front doors. Pyper leads me towards my car, helps me in, and even buckles my seatbelt. I think I see a tear fall from the corner of her eye.

Chapter Eight

"Fashion tip: I'm not sure where the misconception comes from that cause some women to think "club-wear" means "show all of your lady parts-wear." Trust me, you can be hot and sexy without wearing dresses that are so tight they are a second skin. If you have an amazing body, go ahead, show it off, but do it with class. As long as your clothes fit properly, you will look great and feel fabulous. And if you forget everything else I've said here, remember this - wearing spandex is a privilege, not a right."

I wake up to the smell of coffee. I crack my eyes open and I'm pretty sure the light in the room is going to render me blind. Dammit! I didn't close the drapes again. As I start to wake more fully, the events of last night start to become clearer. Unfortunately. I remember breaking down after being called princess by a cocky asshole, and needing Pyper's help to get home and into bed. Pyper was amazing as always, she helped me get undressed, made me drink some water, and even tucked me in. I owe her. Big.

I open my eyes in a squint and see Pyper standing next to my bed, coffee in one hand and a bottle of ibuprofen in the other.

"I figured you were going to need both of these this morning."

I sit up and it feels like my head is going to explode. "You are a saint." The pain is so intense, I'm expecting my brain to start seeping out through my ears. Taking the bottle from Pyper's hands, I open it, pop four tablets into my mouth, and take a sip of my coffee. I swallow the pills and wince.

Pyper laughs softly, "It's got a splash of vodka in there to help with the hangover."

"Thanks, Pyper. You are being way too nice to me after the way I acted last night. I am so sorry. I'm sorry I ruined your night, I'm sorry I drank too much, I'm sorry for embarrassing you."

"Olivia, first of all, I'm the one that is sorry. I shouldn't have pushed you into doing something you didn't want to do. Secondly, it is impossible for you to embarrass me. I didn't know any of those people, and they mean nothing to me; you are everything to me, so screw them and their judgments."

She's amazing. My best friend is unbelievable. I hope I'm as good to her as she is to me. I plan on making it my mission.

"Olivia, if you don't want to date, then you should have adamantly told me you didn't want to do this. I know I've been pushing you, but I would never want you to feel forced and be angry with me. Your friendship and trust is more important to me than anything else."

I can't help but sigh with the weight of my feelings. How do I explain this to her? "It's not that I'm feeling really bad and I think this dating thing, even though it has been awful so far, is just what I need." Pyper opens her mouth to comment, but I raise my hand silently asking her to wait a moment, "Pyper, I haven't let myself just feel. Not once. Not with Luke, not with Deacon...I just keep pushing through every time. I've never just let it all out. With Luke, I ran as fast as I could and sure, I cried, but I never really let go. I never really let myself grieve over the loss of him in my life. I never allowed myself to feel sad or angry. Instead, I reacted. I left, threw myself into school and partying, and tried to make it all disappear by marrying Deacon. And now with Deacon, I'm doing the same thing again. I just dealt with the business of ending my marriage and am determined to accept its finality. Sure, I saw a therapist, but only because I knew I should – it was the right thing to do. But then, I just focused on getting out of there. I've never truly allowed myself to react, to be angry, to just feel the pain and the loss."

I look at Pyper with tears in my eyes and see her own filling up. "Deacon has made me distrustful of men, but it's more than that. I made such a bad decision by throwing myself into a marriage with him, that I can't trust myself right now either. Sometimes Pyper, the reality of what I allowed my life to become is hard to swallow. It isn't that I am still feeling pain from the ending of my relationship with Deacon. I don't miss him or regret leaving, but I feel anger at myself for giving him power. He can't *make* me feel anything, but I'm giving him power by letting his manipulations get to me."

Pyper reaches out and catches the tear I didn't even realize was falling. "My therapist actually told me that this would happen eventually. She said I couldn't suppress my feelings forever, and letting them out is part of the healing process and would allow me to move forward. Last night, even with all the wine, suddenly I had a moment of complete clarity. I saw very clearly what Deacon did to me. Adam was sitting at my table smirking at me like a complete douche, and when he called me 'princess' just like Deacon, I came unglued. I allowed myself to *feel*. Finally. The insecurity, the feelings of inadequacy, the fear that all men are the same, the anger I feel at myself, it all took on a life of its own. I think the atmosphere, the cocky guy at my table, and no doubt the wine made those feelings manifest and explode. Regardless, I think dating and meeting new people is exactly what I need. It's good for me to be reminded that not everyone is like Deacon. I need to keep moving forward."

I take a deep breath and admit, "The other part is that being here... back in Chicago... is just...I..."

Pyper puts her arms around me. "I know. It's Luke memories. Say no more. I get it."

I nod, letting her know she hit the nail on the head, "I'm lucky to have you, Pyper. Thanks for loving me. I don't know what I would do without you. And on a side note, I hope to God I never see anyone that was there last night ever again!"

Pyper laughs at me. "I hope you never see anyone from there either. No doubt you left quite the impression. And I'm the lucky one. Now come on, get up, I'm going to make you some breakfast. You need to put some food in your stomach to help soak up the left over alcohol in there."

"I am the luckiest girl in the world."

"Yes, you are! Now get moving!" She smacks me on the thigh, emphasizing her words.

I wince. I think while she may say I don't have to be sorry, she's making me pay just a little.

Several weeks have passed since my epic breakdown at speed dating and I'm feeling much better. Finally, Chicago is starting to feel like home again. Pyper and I have settled into a routine, taking turns making coffee in the morning, she goes off to work at the spa, while I write like mad for the magazines that employ me and the blog that started it all. The condo now feels more like ours instead of just hers. I've even been on another date since the never-to-be-forgotten speed dating. Noah contacted me through 'Date Me' and he and I went to an Imagine Dragons concert. We had a really great time and I wouldn't mind seeing him again.

I flip another page in the magazine I'm browsing through at Shimmer & Soothe while waiting for my manicurist Bridget to begin. Pyper planned a relaxing girl's day after a long week for the both of us, and it was just what we both needed. It is really awesome to have a best friend that owns a spa and constantly hooks me up. I'm not ashamed to admit it.

I have been massaged, exfoliated, cleansed, and slathered. After a body wrap to remove the toxins from my body, an amazing smelling skin softening cream was applied. It smells like lavender, my favorite. I feel fabulous.

Pyper and I just put our feet in warm water to begin our pedicures and our backs are being massaged by the vibrating chairs we are sitting in. I set my magazine down when Bridget places small bowls on either side of my chair and gestures for me to place my fingers in the water, to begin soaking my nails. My whole body feels like jello. Ahh, this is the life.

I really love spending time like this with Pyper, just enjoying time with one another. Our hair isn't done, we have no makeup on, no cell phones, no computers - just the two of us and conversation. It's a connection on a whole different level. We've been looking at magazines, talking about the articles, asking each other silly survey questions from Cosmo, all just very girly things. It's perfect.

Flipping to the next page in her magazine, Pyper looks up at me, "Do you think you would be up for going out tonight? We can go to a club, have a couple cocktails, flirt and get our dance on!"

"That sounds fun! We haven't had a girl's night like that in ages! I think it would be fun to get dressed up, go out, and get our groove on." I laugh at the thought of us shaking our booties on the dance floor. We are way overdue for some fun.

"Great! I was thinking we could go to a new club Caroline just told me about, on Hubbard Street called Zero Gravity. She said she heard it's amazing and I'd love to check it out."

"Sounds perfect, I'm game!"

Several hours later, Pyper and I are ready. We've really done ourselves up for our night out. I'm wearing low-rise, silver coated skinny jeans with a black sequin tank, and black heels so high that I will likely pay for wearing them later. My hair is flat ironed straight and is flowing down my back. I've done my makeup heavy with dark eyes and a nude lip. Simple stud earrings complete my look, as I've got enough bling going on with the tank and pants. My license, lip gloss, and debit card are in my pocket, leaving my hands free. I don't like having to worry about carrying around a bag or clutch in a dance club.

Pyper looks amazing in a strapless, grey and black leopard print mini-dress. She's curled her hair in waves so it barely touches her shoulders. Her makeup is opposite of mine. Hers is light on the eyes and cheeks so it showcases her bright red lips. She's also wearing high heels that are black sequined and quite fabulous.

She smiles at me, "Look at you!"

"No, look at you!"

She laughs. "I want to be someone else so I can look at both of us!"

I laugh too.

Looking at Pyper's dress it occurs to me, "You don't have pockets, do you need me to hold anything for you?"

"Nope I've got it covered," then proceeds to reach into her bra and shows me her license and cash, "I'm good to go!"

I giggle again, shaking my head at her. We are going to have fun. I'm really looking forward to a great night. "Alright then, let's go! We'll go to the front and have Henry the doorman grab us a cab!"

When we walk inside the nightclub, my mouth falls open. I look at Pyper and she has the same look on her face. Zero Gravity is amazing. The club is a huge rectangle. Chandeliers hang from the ceiling; the color palette of the club is white, light blue, dark blue, and silver, which creates a very sophisticated look. White leather couches surround the outside of the dance floor with light blue and dark blue pillows thrown on them for added comfort. Sporadically placed around the room are tall, white tables without chairs, so people can use them to stand on or lean against while chatting and they offer somewhere for people to rest their drinks. On top of the tables are large white flower arrangements and flameless candles, which cast shadows on the faces of people standing nearby.

The dance floor in the center of the room is already full of writhing bodies dancing to the music thumping from the sound system. I'm no audio guru, but the strong bass and balanced treble leads me to believe the equipment is top of the line. On the other side of the room from the entrance, there is a stage. There is a DJ up there tonight, but I'm guessing Zero Gravity has its share of live bands as well. There are bars set up on both sides of the room, comprised of large white squares with frosted glass blocks on the inside of each square. Eight of them align to create one long counter for people to lean against as they are waiting for the bartenders to get their drink of choice. In addition to the bars and gorgeous bartenders – male and female - there are waitresses walking from couch to couch and table to table, taking orders. All of the waitresses are wearing dark blue pants or form-fitting, not too short skirts with white collared, slim fit, button down shirts with a silver bow tie. The pocket of the shirt displays the club's logo, clearly identifying them as employees.

On either side of the stage are spiraling metal staircases that lead up to a second level. One side is clearly a VIP area with couches and tables set up and various areas roped off. The couches are set up in u-shapes facing the dance floor below. I wonder if there is a bar up there too? On the other side, there is one wall that is all glass and doors sporadically placed down the wall. There is a rope prohibiting access to that side with a man that must be a bouncer protecting the blocked entrance.

"How about we start with a drink?" Pyper motions to the bar at our left.

"Definitely!"

We maneuver through several bodies, making our way to the bar. It amazes me what some girls will wear to a club. I pass one girl wearing a dress so tight it looks like it's painted on her body. The mini-dress is red and the material looks plastic. It's molded to her large breasts, making the fact she isn't wearing a bra painfully obvious. I can practically see her areolas through the material. The skirt is so short I wouldn't be surprised if her ass and lady bits show when she bends over. To complete her outfit of awesome, she's wearing heels that are so high she almost hobbles when she walks. She looks ridiculous, so of course, I discreetly take a picture of her with my cell phone so I can use it as inspiration for writing a blog post later about keeping it classy.

Another girl is wearing a halter dress that ties behind her neck and at the center of her back like a swimsuit. Two pieces of fabric come from the back of her neck to cover her breasts, meeting a crystal buckle at her navel. The dress is completely backless and the skirt is a mini. How her breasts keep from being exposed is a mystery. Oh my gosh – maybe they don't!

To each their own, I suppose, but I can't help but shake my head. How about leaving a little something to the imagination? Geesh!

I look at Pyper and she rolls her eyes, having seen the same women. I smile.

Pyper and I reach the bar and she orders us each a vodka cranberry.

"This club is amazing!" I can't keep from looking around, trying to take it all in. "How long did you say it has been open?"

"Not long, maybe a couple weeks now." Pyper speaks loudly into my ear to be heard over the loud thump of the bass, "There was an article in the social section of the Tribune talking about the opening I guess, but I didn't see it. A restaurant that closed down a while ago was here and the owner did a complete renovation, it seems. Caroline was talking about it at the spa the other day."

"Well I'm really impressed, it's fabulous. I'm glad we came."

The bartender hands us our drinks and Pyper pulls bills out of her bra and slaps them on the counter. The bartender grins slyly at her, but Pyper turns and we start making our way to look for seats. With perfect timing, a few girls have just vacated a couch, so we snag their places before someone else beats us to it.

Pyper turns to me, takes a sip of her drink and then asks, "What article are you working on right now?"

"Funny you should ask, because I thought I would ask for your help on this one. I'm working on an article for *Martini* magazine. Each month, their magazine is comprised of a lot of sex related articles, along with the usual fashion fluff and celebrity interview." I take a sip of my drink and continue, "The article I'm working on is *Things You Should Never Say to a Guy*. Want to weigh in?"

Pyper immediately smiles devilishly at me, "Absolutely. What do you have so far?"

"Well of course the worst thing you can say to a guy is, 'Is it in yet?'"

Pyper laughs loudly, almost spitting out her drink in the process, "Yes! Definitely not a good thing to say! You may as well kill him instead. Less painful!"

Her reaction has me laughing too, "True. That would certainly be more humane! I don't think I could ever do that to a poor guy! Next is the ever popular, 'It's not you, it's me.'"

Pyper laughs and then admits, "I may or may not have used that line once or twice myself."

"Why does this not surprise me, Pyper?"

"Hi ladies, excuse the interruption, but can I get you another drink?" A very petite blonde-haired waitress asks us, interrupting our conversation. Pyper answers, "That would be great! We are drinking vodka cranberries. Thanks!"

"Sure. Be right back."

"Okay Olivia, what else have you got?"

"How about 'Does this make me look fat?'"

"Oh! There are sixteen thousand possible answers to that question and any one a guy would mutter would be incorrect."

"Exactly!" I laugh.

"How about 'Size really *does* matter!'" Pyper suggests.

I snort at that one! "Yes, that or, 'That's it?'"

Pyper and I laugh so hard we can barely breathe!

While we are trying to catch our breath, a couple of guys walk up and stand in front of us. We look up into their smiling faces to see one guy has blonde hair and blue eyes, while the other has brown hair and brown eyes. They aren't bad looking and they seem friendly. "Hi ladies, my name is Dylan and this is my buddy Ken. We couldn't help but see you two laughing over here and we thought we would come over to see if we could be let in on the joke," says blondie.

"Yeah. What are you two hot girls laughing so hard about?" says Ken. I really want to ask him where Barbie is. That would be rude though, and cheesy.

Pyper looks at me with a smirk. "Actually, I bet you boys would be able to contribute to our conversation. My friend Olivia here is writing an article for *Martini* magazine about the things a woman should never say to a guy. Care to weigh in?"

They both take seats, a little too closely, one on either side of us and we proudly tell them the answers we already have.

"Well you forgot, 'You remind me of my Dad,'" Dylan suggests.

"Ewww! Don't tell me you've actually heard that before!" Pyper gasps while wrinkling her nose in disgust.

Dylan just shrugs in answer, and Pyper and I giggle in response.

Ken says, "Oh my personal favorite, 'Oh my God, thank you for the drink! I can't believe the bouncer fell for my fake ID.'"

91

We all break into hysterics. I can't help but ask, "Oh my gosh! What did you do?"

Ken looks at me like that is a crazy question, "Well I ran, of course."

We all laugh harder, the alcohol we've consumed adding to the humor.

"Good contributions guys, thanks for being such good sports." I definitely have some good material for my article.

While we've been chatting, the waitress returned with our replacement drinks we ordered, plus Ken and Dylan bought an additional round as well, slippery nipple shots for all of us. I'm definitely starting to feel more than just a buzz. I'm slightly nauseated and realize I haven't eaten anything since we had a light lunch of a salad at the spa. Not good.

"So tell us ladies, how good of friends are you?" Ken asks raising his brows at us.

"We are best friends, pretty much sisters," Pyper says. "Why do you ask?"

Ken looks at Dylan and the look they exchange makes me feel uneasy. "We were just wondering if maybe we could interest you in a foursome. You are both gorgeous, and with the way you two were laughing and talking with us, I know you find us attractive too, so what do you say the four of us get out of here and go make some fun of our own?" Dylan asks.

Pyper and I look at each other, totally grossed out and speechless.

"Hell to the no." I tell them.

Before they can utter a response, Pyper tugs on my arm, "Come on, let's go get our dance on!"

I smile and nod at her, words seem beyond my ability at the moment.

Pyper grabs my hand, tows me to the dance floor, and keeps going until we are in the middle of the moving mass of bodies, safely escaping the two creepers we left sitting on the couch. The speakers are blaring techno music and it feels like it's echoing inside and outside my head. I close my eyes, trying to center myself and end up losing myself to the music. I raise my arms above my head and move my body to the beat. Pyper links her fingers with mine so we can make sure we stay together and not get pushed apart. I squeeze her hands gently and keep dancing.

I feel a body come up behind me, pressing flush against mine and it startles me. I open my eyes just in time to see Pyper being pushed flush against the front of my body because Ken is behind her pressing himself against her, which means the asshole at my back is Dylan. "What the hell?" Pyper asks.

"Dance with me baby," Dylan slurs into my ear.

Dylan grabs my hips and slams his pelvis into my ass. I can feel his erection against me, and I am immediately uncomfortable and pissed off. "Pyper...let's go."

"Guys, we don't want to dance, we are going to head home," Pyper tries reasoning with them.

"I don't think so," says Ken. "You ladies have been teasing us all night, we know you want us, now let's dance." Ken smashes his hips into Pyper's ass, making her slam against me again. Her head smacks into my mouth and I taste blood almost immediately. I cry out and cup my mouth with my hand. I can feel the inside of my mouth where my tooth just cut it starting to swell.

"Oh God, Olivia, I'm so sorry! BACK OFF YOU FUCKING ASSHOLES," I hear Pyper start screaming, trying to get us away from Dylan and Ken, but they just won't listen. People around us start to realize there's a problem and finally, I see someone pull Ken away from Pyper. He's a big guy and I hope he is a bouncer. I'm still struggling to get away from Dylan when I hear, "Get the fuck off her."

I freeze.

I can't move.

I know that voice.

It haunts my dreams and my memories.

I am still cupping my mouth and I look over at Pyper, eyes wide to see her eyes matching my own while she's looking at the person standing behind me.

I feel Dylan get pulled away from me and the voice I could never forget says, "Ian, escort both of them the hell out of here. They are not to return again, ever."

I very slowly begin to turn around and look right into the eyes of Luke Easton. The first boy I ever truly loved. The first boy that ever broke my heart. My high school sweetheart. The boy that I've never been able to forget. The boy that was supposed to love me forever.

That boy is now a man and he takes my breath away, his blue eyes as mesmerizing as I remember.

I sucked in a breath. I feel sick.

"Hello, Olivia."

I remove my hand from my mouth, open it to respond...

And throw up on his feet.

Chapter Nine

"Fashion tip: There is nothing wrong with your sleepwear consisting of cotton shorts and t-shirts if that is what you prefer, but don't discount cute matching sleep sets! You never know when you may wake up happy that when you went to bed the night before, instead of wearing your holey Beatles shirt you've had since you were fifteen, you chose a super cute tank and short set instead! You'll have to trust me on this!"

"Olivia! Olivia! Wake up! Wake up right now!" Pyper is whisper yelling at me.

"Ughhh," I moan and struggle to open one eye and stare at her. My head hurts, plus my mouth feels like sandpaper, rough and dry, and the inside of my lip hurts for some reason. I glance through the same, now barely-open eye at the clock next to my bed and see it is only eight thirty in the morning. What the hell is she doing waking me up this early? She knows I'm the world's worst morning person until I've had coffee. And why does my head hurt so much?

I open my other eye and see Pyper running around my room like a crazed lunatic flailing her arms like a muppet. I can't help but smirk a bit because she looks ridiculous. When she disappears into my closet, I wonder what the hell she's doing, but decide I really don't care and close my eyes again.

"Olivia, I said get up right now," she hisses at me. I crack my eyes open again and see her approaching my bed. She's carrying a pile of my clothes in her arms that she ends up throwing on my bed.

"Do we have an appointment or something that you didn't tell me about?"

She sighs and rips the blankets off of me. I sit up and glare at her fully, "What the hell? What is going on?"

Putting her hands on her hips she snaps, "Well excuse me for being a good friend! I just thought you might want to make yourself presentable. You have a guest."

It should be against the law for someone to be this snippy and sassy first thing in the morning. Does she think I have mind reading capabilities? How should I have known someone was here?

"A guest?" I ask, confused.

"Yes. That's what I said! Now get the hell up, Olivia. Luke's here!"

"WHAT?!" I shriek.

"Shhhh!" Pyper holds her finger over her mouth shushing me while rolling her eyes.

"What do you mean Luke is here? Why is he here?" I'm panicking. Why is he HERE?

Then it hits me. Last night. Parts of the evening are fuzzy, but I do remember Pyper and I getting dolled up for a girl's night out. We decided to go to the new club, Zero Gravity, and we had fun. We drank too much, laughed, danced. Thinking about dancing makes me remember Dylan and Ken from last night. I still can't believe those two jerks accosted us on the dance floor. Then I remember more.

Luke.

Oh God, Luke.

At the nightclub.

He ripped Dylan off of me. My bloody lip. I remember hearing his voice and freezing. Turning to him and then...oh no.

"Pyper?"

Pyper has been watching my face. I know she saw my confusion turn into clarity, because she raises an eyebrow at me, "Yes, Olivia?" I hear sarcasm in those two words.

"Please tell me I have finally lost my mind. That all the stress in my life has made me bat shit crazy and I'm hallucinating that I saw Luke last night."

"Oh honey, you more than saw Luke last night."

"Oh God, Pyper, please tell me that I did not throw up on him."

"Not only did you toss your cookies on Luke, my sweets, but he assisted us to a cab while you were pretty much out of it. You were dealing with the combination of alcohol and shock, so you may not remember that Luke made sure we got home safely. I wasn't thinking and when he asked the address for the cab driver I gave it to him. That is how he knows where we are, and is the reason he is currently sitting in our living room."

"And you let him in? Why couldn't you have called security? What if I don't want to see him?"

"He repeatedly knocked on the door, refusing to go away until I let him in to see you. He said if I ignored him he would just keep coming back every morning again and again. He made it clear he is not taking no for an answer. I figured you would rather see him on your own turf, than be confronted by him somewhere else because he is obviously on a mission. Now, you should get up and hop in the shower real quick and get dressed so you look presentable when you see him again. Right now, you're sporting an awesome semi-death look."

"No. No way. Tell him I don't want to see him. I have nothing to say to him."

"Olivia, I just told you he isn't going to take no for…"

Before Pyper can even finish her sentence my bedroom door is pushed open and Luke is standing in the doorway. I'm struck stupid looking at him. My heart starts pounding and I can't look away. I hate that he is able to still take my breath away after so many years. And those seven years, well they've been kind to him. He's absolutely gorgeous. He's wearing jeans, a black t-shirt, black boots and a black leather jacket that is unzipped. His dark hair is longer on top, and styled with a carelessness that looks like he just shoved his hair every which way. He's sporting a very sexy five o'clock shadow and his blue eyes look intense and are red-rimmed, like he didn't get much sleep.

That brings me to his body and oh boy, it has filled out. Where he was lean at eighteen, he's downright built, and no doubt sculpted, making him all man and downright sexy at twenty-five. His shirt is pulling across his chest and as if he sees me looking he crosses his arms over it drawing my attention back to his eyes.

"Umm... I'll just... yeah... ummm... yeah I'm going to go." Pyper stammers.

I don't even acknowledge her or watch her go. I'll deal with that traitor later. I can't believe she let him in here.

He just stands there at first, his eyes locked on mine. I hear him clear his throat and he finally breaks the silence, his lips lift slightly in a grin, "So...you're back."

I can't speak. I just nod stiffly.

He lets loose a full blown grin at me and it takes my breath away. I remember that smile with gut wrenching clarity. Girls used to be rendered speechless at that smile, willing to do anything to make it appear again, as if he was bestowing a great blessing upon anyone he revealed it to. Despite trying or thinking I am, I can't look away from him.

Taking a step further inside my room he says, "There have been many times over the years when I've imagined what it would be like to see you again. I have to say, I didn't imagine the encounter would include puke."

I feel heat rise in my cheeks and I know they are pink. I'm so mortified. I also feel self-conscious with him standing and me still sitting in bed. I stand quickly in my haste to put us at an even level, and he immediately takes me in from head to toe. I swear I see his eyes heat a little. I look down at myself and say a quick prayer of thanks that I'm wearing my cute navy blue, eyelet lace cami and boyshort set from Victoria's Secret. Then I get angry at myself when I realize what I'm thinking and I stalk to my closet so I can grab my robe that's hanging on the back of the door. I feel his eyes follow me the whole way.

I step into the closet, grab my robe, and shove my arms inside. I temporarily mourn the fact there isn't a mirror in my closet, wishing I could check my hair, which is no doubt morning crazed and wish I could brush my teeth too. Once I realize that I even care a little, it just makes me stop. I'm not trying to impress him. At least I think I deserve points for trying to convince myself of that.

I walk out of my closet and come up short when I realize he's come all the way in my room and was waiting outside the door to my closet. I close my robe and cinch the belt tightly. We just stare at one another for a minute. Silence has never felt so loud.

"Olivia..."

I interrupt him, "What are you doing here, Luke? Do you want an apology? Okay fine, I'm sorry I threw up on you."

"No. No of course that's not why I'm here," he takes another step towards me and when I back up a step, he stops. "I came here because I need to see you, to talk to you. I want to know how you are, how you've been the last seven years. I want to look at you, to hear your voice. To see that you really are here, that you're real and really back. I want to know that I didn't just imagine you or think I saw you like I've done so many times before."

I gasp slightly and my heart twists. I don't know what I expected him to say but that definitely was not it.

"I don't understand Luke. Tell me why. Why do you care?"

Luke shoves his hand into his hair. It's a gesture I remember well. It's his tell-tale sign that he's nervous or feeling frustrated about something.

"Olivia, I have so much I want to say, so much I need to tell you, so much I want to ask you."

"Well, I don't have anything to say to you. I heard everything I needed to seven years ago. I want you to leave. Now."

I begin to slide past him to go to my bedroom door, with the intent of holding it open, emphasizing my point. I want him to leave.

I think, right?

Yes. Definitely.

Luke reaches out and grabs my arm gently as I start to walk by him. Startled, my eyes meet his. He's touching me, and that fact makes me lose my breath. Being this close to him makes my brain scramble and my cheeks flush again. I hate that my stupid cheeks always give away how I'm feeling. I press my lips together as a way to try and help me hold my emotions inside.

His eyes look to my lips, then back to my eyes and he says, "Don't. Please. Just, give me five minutes, Livvie. Just hear me out."

Maybe it's the use of his nickname for me only used by him, and the rare occasions when Pyper is displaying extreme affection, since she knows how it affects me. Or maybe it is the look in his eyes, but I find myself nodding in agreement and saying, "Fine. Five minutes."

He loosens his grasp on my arm, trailing his fingertips down towards my wrist and lingering there. Even though I have my robe on, his touch feels like fire blazing down my arm and I feel every inch of the gesture, as though we are skin to skin. He hesitates, like he doesn't like removing his fingers from touching me, or maybe he's just afraid I will walk away from him again if he's not holding onto me.

"Wow. I..." he swallows hard and I see a quick flash of something in his eyes. Confusion? Pain? Uncertainty? I'm not sure. "It's hard to know where to start. I have dreamed of having this chance with you. To talk to you, to try and explain and now that you're here, I feel like I've forgotten everything I wanted to say."

My heart starts to soften, but I give myself a mental slap and make myself remember the pain this man caused me when I heard him tell his mother I was just a distraction. I feel my body stiffen and my eyes harden, "You now have four minutes."

Suddenly his words start coming at me so fast it's like a verbal avalanche. "Olivia, what if I told you that what you heard me tell my mom that day seven years ago was not what you thought it was? You walked in at an awful time."

I grunt at this comment. I can't help it.

He continues like he didn't hear me, "What you heard me saying to my mom was my attempt at getting her off my case by telling her what she wanted to hear. I was so sick of her always bad mouthing us and putting her two cents in about us all the time. That day was hardly the first time I heard her opinion about my relationship with you; her assumptions about what you meant and what was going to happen if we stayed together. She didn't like it or want it for me. She was worried I was getting too serious, too fast and that my studies would suffer. As you know, I was leaving the next day for a family vacation for the last couple weeks of summer and you and I were going to spend that day together before I left. My mom saw me getting ready to head out and asked me where I was going. When I told her I was meeting you, she started in on me again. Right there and then, I had a plan. I just wanted the subject of us dropped so I could get to you as quickly as possible and spend as much time with you as I could, but I was also determined to try and make peace in the only way I knew how. I didn't want to go on vacation with my parents and have her bitch at me the whole time. It would cause my parents to fight, impose unneeded anger and drama, so I gave in. I played her game and told her what she wanted to hear, so I could get out of there, leave the next day, and maybe actually have a good time with my mom and dad for once."

He pauses and runs his fingers through his hair again. He looks away for a moment, "I told her…"

"I heard what you told her. You told her I was a distraction you were planning on cutting loose, that I meant nothing to you other than a good time."

"Yes, that is what I told her. It was the worst mistake I've ever made. I told her those lies, even though they couldn't have been further from the truth. I just wanted to pacify her. Nothing mattered to me more than starting college with you and finally getting to live our own lives. I was finally going to be out of the house and away from her constant judgment. I just had to get through two more weeks. The plans you and I made were everything to me. You…you were everything to me. I hate that I made you doubt that."

I just stare at him. I don't know whether I should believe him or not. The rational part of me knows that if what he's saying isn't true, he wouldn't be here. Why would he bother? The stubborn part of me isn't convinced.

"I'm so sorry. God, I'm so sorry Olivia. I tried reasoning with her before that day. I told her how much I loved you and wanted to be with you, but she just wouldn't hear me. She refused to believe my feelings were real, telling me I was far too young to feel that way. She told me I couldn't possibly know what true love was at only eighteen years old. Eventually, I realized I would just have to play along to get her to leave me, and you, alone. If I had any idea you would have heard me, or that you would leave me..." he whispers the last part trailing off.

After a moment he clears his throat and continues, "Olivia, when I saw you in my club,"

It takes a second for what he just said to register, "Wait. What do you mean your club?" I ask, shocked.

"Oh. I'm the owner of Zero Gravity. It's a new development, and no one really knows about it because I was able to keep my name out of the paper when an article was written about the new club. I bought the space and renovated it quickly. It hasn't been open for very long."

I'm amazed that the club I was admiring last night was his doing. I can't believe that out of all the clubs we could have gone to last night, we go to one that Luke owns.

Without thinking it through I admit, "The club is amazing."

He smirks at me and I see a little of the old Luke in that look, "Thank you." Then he continues our previous conversation. "As I was saying, when I saw you last night, I just knew this was my second chance. Our second chance. Fate brought you to my club."

"Second chance? Fate? I don't know about that, Luke. I think you are reading too much into this. I appreciate you telling me what really occurred that day, but it doesn't change anything. It still happened and I'm a different person now. I'm not the same Olivia I was seven years ago, and I'm sure you aren't the same Luke I knew either. At one time, I wondered if I ever really knew you at all. Maybe we saw each other again last night so it would allow us to have closure."

Luke grabs my left hand and looks at it then asks, "Olivia...are you...are you involved with someone?"

I hesitate before answering. "Well no, not right now."

His brow furrows and he lets go of my hand so that he can cup my face instead. He looks at my mouth and brushes his thumb over my sore, slightly swollen lip. I just stare at him dumbfounded, once again affected by his touch and the tender look in his eyes. When his eyes meet mine again, he says, "I believe you walked into my club last night for a reason Olivia. I don't believe in coincidence. I know we were put back into one another's paths again for a reason. I refuse to let you just walk away from me again. I want you to let me in on everything about you, Livvie, leaving nothing out. I want you to tell me everything I've missed. I want you to tell me everything I should have been there for. I want you to fill me in on every moment of the last seven years, and I want more than anything to know you again and have you know me in return. I know you are angry, and I know you have doubts, but let's work through them. You are right, I *am* a different person now. I'm sure you are too, but I've never forgotten you, Olivia. Never. I can't let you go again. Don't ask me to."

My eyes fill with tears. He seems sincere and my heart is aching. He is right, I'm still angry and I do have doubts. I can't help it. Even if what he said is the truth, the day he broke my heart was pivotal in my life. To have it explained away so simply, makes me feel such angst.

Aside from those feelings and thoughts, I want this. My heart, my mind, my body remember Luke. Like a magnetic pull, I'm drawn to him. I feel a need for him, but I'm afraid. I can't take anymore hurt; I know I wouldn't be able to handle it. To let him in again, knowing that I could just be setting myself up for failure seems unwise. I've already been through enough, I can't handle much more. Part of me wants to hide and run away. Being a grown up sucks ass sometimes.

Pulling away from Luke with much more internal effort than I hope is apparent, I look away and say, "I don't know, Luke. I'm sorry, I just don't know if I can do this. I don't know if I can give you access to me, to my heart, and risk getting hurt all over again."

Luke grabs my upper arms, not in a cruel or mean way, but in a firm, loving gesture to make his point and I marvel that with Luke, I feel fire at his touch; with Deacon, this same gesture always meant pain was forthcoming. The realization that a part of me instinctively still trusts Luke, despite everything, says something. His touch makes me feel alive again for the first time in months. He waits for my eyes to meet his again and when they do, I'm lost. "We can take it slow, Livvie. Let's be friends again. See what happens. Just…just give it a chance. Give me a chance."

I swallow. Can I really say no? Would I really be able to just let him walk away? Do I want him to? No. I would rather have him be in my life again for a little while, than not at all.

Before I can think it through anymore, I nod my head, "Okay Luke, friends. We can try being friends."

Luke takes me in his arms and I can't resist putting my arms around his waist and hugging him back. I hear him breathe in deep and I think he's smelling my hair, which for a moment worries me because I have morning hair! Then I hear him whisper, "Thank you," and it makes all thoughts of my hair leave my mind.

I inhale and take in his spicy scent, and I hope I'm confident in my decision-making.

I'm putting my heart out there again.

I just hope he doesn't break it into pieces again.

Chapter Ten

"Fashion tip: Always check out the back view in a full length mirror before leaving the house. Don't like what you see? Then don't leave until you do. Every single angle matters. Trust me."

uke pulls away from me and holds me at arm's length. A pleading look appears on his face and he says, "Let me take you to breakfast. I would really like to spend some time with you, catching up. Do you have plans? Would that be okay?"

I take a moment to think about it. I know I said we could give this a shot as friends, but I'm uncomfortable and nervous. Saying and doing are two different things. Am I ready right now? Can I really do this? Go out with him? Alone? Forcing myself to stop, I shake my head at myself and answer, "Um, okay sure."

He smiles his knock-out grin at me and I see his dimple on the right side of his face wink at me. I suppress a groan. That smile is going to be the death of me.

"Great. That's great. I'm going to buy you the biggest breakfast ever! Thank you." He just stares at me with that smile on his face, and I wonder if the awkwardness I feel will ever go away. Every word, every look, every gesture feels far too orchestrated. Spending more time together is the only cure, I know that, but the very thought makes me feel somewhat ill. Stupid nerves.

I gesture to the bathroom behind me, "Okay, I just want to hop in the shower real quick and I'll be ready to go."

"Oh, yeah. Of course. I will just go wait for you in the living room."

"Okay," I give him a slight smile, "I'll be quick."

He starts backing up towards my door, "Take your time." He keeps looking at me and doesn't realize he's reached the door, before I can warn him he runs into the closed door. He grins sheepishly at me and I try to stifle a laugh. He turns to open the door, takes one more look back at me, then walks out, softly closing the door behind him.

I collapse right where I'm standing straight to the floor. My mind is spinning, and the tears I was holding in while all the revelations from Luke were coming, now fall freely from my eyes. None of this even feels real, I was in Luke's arms again, staring into his eyes. All my uncertainties assault me like bullets. Quick, rapid firing, one after another. Is he telling the truth? Was he just trying to get his mom to leave him alone? Is it possible to just be friends? Can I let the past go and really try to move forward? A huge part of me feels like a piece of my heart has been returned to me, but I also feel trepidation, because another part of me, and I'm not sure how much, is still angry at him.

Deciding to explore these thoughts and feelings later, I try to gather myself so I can take a shower. Before I stand up, I hear a soft knock on my door and Pyper peeks her head in. As soon as she sees me, she comes in and closes the door behind her. When she reaches me, she sinks down on the floor right next to me and takes me in her arms. I grab on to her tightly and soak up all her love and support.

"Are you okay?"

"Yes and no. That's a really difficult question to answer." I laugh half-heartedly.

"Tell me what happened."

She doesn't say please, she doesn't tell me I can talk to her if I want to, she just knows I need to. Knows I need her. There isn't even a doubt or a question. "Okay, but he's taking me to breakfast and I'm supposed to be getting ready. Keep me company while I get ready, so I can tell you at the same time?"

"Of course." Pyper stands up, reaches down to me and I grab her hand so she can pull me up. I follow her into the bathroom and begin repeating my conversation with Luke, leaving nothing out, while simultaneously starting the water in the shower. While it is warming up, I quickly brush my teeth. When finished, I take a towel out of the linen closet, hang it on the hook, and then disrobe. I throw my pajamas to the floor to put in the hamper when I'm finished, but hang my robe on the hook with my towel.

Pyper whistles low, "Wow, so it was all a big misunderstanding? He was just trying to tell his mom what she wanted to hear?"

"That's what he said and I don't believe he would lie about it. I certainly questioned it at first, but given all the time that has lapsed, why would he be dishonest and why even bother with me if there wasn't validity to what he's saying? Why make contact with me at all? That wouldn't make sense. And, Luke could never look me in the eyes and lie – not before, and I don't think even now. Even when he teased me, he always had this certain look in his eyes---sort of a gleam. And I didn't see a hint of it." I furiously scrub my hair while thinking it over, "I can't really wrap my mind around it completely right now, though. To think about everything that has happened, how that one conversation set so many things in motion…it's more than I can really deal with right now. I'm going to need time to let it digest."

"When he came out of your bedroom he asked if it was okay to sit on the couch in the living room and apologized for pounding on the door, but thanked me for letting him in."

"This feels so strange. I mean, it's Luke. I never thought…I can't…" my eyes start to tear up again and I duck my head under the water, rinsing out the shampoo.

"I think this is great."

"Excuse me? What did you just say?" I can't keep the surprise out of my tone and I'm sure she hears it.

"You heard me. It's Luke, Olivia. Sure, a lot of time has passed, but Luke is still Luke at his core, just like you are still the same Olivia you've always been. You've grown up, and things have affected and helped shape the woman you've become, but I don't believe the core of who we are changes. You still have a huge heart, you are funny, kind, generous…all the things you've been from the first day I met you. I think having him in your life again is a positive thing. You guys ran into each other again for a reason. He's right for you – always has been, so just go with it. Stop overthinking it and take a chance. We are working on getting the real you back again, remember? Jump, Livvie. You can do it."

While I quickly run a razor over my legs, I reply, "I do think you are right about there being a reason, I don't believe in coincidence. I mean, of all the clubs we could have gone to last night, we end up at the one Luke just bought. That's crazy!"

"I can't believe it either, but hey! I bet we can get free drinks now and access to the VIP section and maybe we can even have parties there…"

Leave it to Pyper to already be thinking about how we can benefit from this latest development. I can't help but laugh at her. After I rinse all the body wash from my body, I turn the shower off, grab my towel from under my robe, and start drying off. "I'm going to jump, but I'm scared to death. I'm going to need you every step of the way. I'm not too proud to admit it. I know I'm the annoying, needy friend right now, but please bear with me."

"Not another word. I mean it. How many times do I have to tell you? That's what…"

I interrupt her, "friends are for. I know. It just seems like I am the one constantly needing the support. Just remember, if you ever need me, I'm here for you too."

"I know that, without a doubt. It's you and me babe. Forever. That much I can count on in this life."

"Me too, Pyper, me too. On a completely different note, I have NO idea what the hell to wear!!!" I wrap my hair in my towel, pull my robe off the hook, shove my arms in and wrap it around me pulling the belt tight. Once I'm decent, I step out from the shower and look at Pyper with a look of panic on my face.

Pyper laughs, "I have a feeling you could walk out wearing a paper bag and Luke wouldn't care. You start blow drying your hair and I will go through your closet and find you something. Cool?"

"Definitely cool. Thanks."

Pyper smiles at me as she walks out of my bathroom and makes her way to my closet.

I begin blow drying my hair while trying to apply makeup at the same time. Taking a deep breath I try and calm myself down when I realize this is not going to end well. I'll look like an electrocuted clown if I keep this up.

Pyper walks back into my bathroom after several minutes, steps over to me, and takes the hair dryer from my hand. She gestures to me to sit at the vanity and starts drying my hair so I can have my hands free to do my makeup. Best. Friend. Ever.

"I've got your outfit all laid out on your bed. I chose a pair of your jeans, a grey t-shirt and a red skinny belt to go over it. Then, I paired that with your red cardigan with the white stripes to throw on if you need to, and your red ballet flats. I even grabbed your cute, grey tote bag and changed it out for you real quick. You look great in red and I thought it would be perfect. Plus, it's an adorable outfit, not too dressy, just casual enough."

"You're the best. I'm so nervous. What am I going to talk to him about? My stomach has so many butterflies right now. And is turning cartwheels. And my intestines are in my throat. I hate this feeling, it's that I'm-going-to-throw-up-any-second feeling and Pyper, if I throw up on him again, I will die. Once was enough, thank you very much."

Laughing at me, Pyper turns off my blow dryer and picks up my flat iron that I had heating up. She starts running it through my hair, making it look sleek and smooth. "Calm down. You have plenty to talk about. Seven years of life to talk about, that's a lot! I seriously doubt you will struggle for conversation."

"Yeah, you're right. I need to chill out. We are going to breakfast, it isn't a big deal. We are going to be friends. It's cool. I'm cool. It's all cool." I'm totally handling this. Of course, just as I'm getting some confidence, a flashback assaults me...I'm speed dating...and I thought I was handling that just fine too. Crap.

"Yes, you are the epitome of cool. There," she smoothes my hair one more time with my flat iron, "all done."

My hair looks nice and I have finished my makeup as well. I've done a grey smoky eye, pink cheeks and a light lip gloss.

"Okay, I just need to get dressed and I'm ready."

Pyper leads the way out of my bathroom, "Okay, go ahead. I will tell Luke you are just about ready to go."

"Awesome, thank you."

As Pyper heads to my door and walks out, I head to my bed and start putting on my clothes. She even laid out a bra and panties for me. In red too, which makes me smile. I'm going to be very coordinated. My hands shake slightly as I step in my panties and I force myself not to let my mind wander. Once I'm dressed I walk to the full length mirror and take a look. I look nice. Casual, but chic. I care about how I look and it shows, but I'm not over the top either. I turn around and check out the back view, making sure everything is in place.

I head to my jewelry chest and open it. I open drawers and start going through my boxes of jewelry, I still store lots of it in the boxes I received them in. As I'm opening the top of each box looking for the red tear drop earrings I want, I happen to catch sight of a dark blue box on the bottom that holds some of my old jewelry. Taking the box out of the drawer, I open it. Inside, is a gold baby ring, my senior class ring from high school, an antique opal ring that used to be my great grandmothers, and a ring that Luke gave me when we were dating in high school. My breath catches. I didn't exactly forget that I had it, but I haven't opened this box in a long time. Pulling the ring out, I stare at it, remembering when Luke gave it to me

.

I have been cheering my butt off. My voice is strained, and my arm and leg muscles are nearing the point of exhaustion. It's been such a close game between our high school and our biggest rival, Highland High. I'm not sure why they elected to schedule a game against the Rockets on homecoming weekend, because if we lose, all the guys on the team will be in foul moods all weekend. Girls wearing lovely dresses, sexy shoes, special up-dos, and carrying amazing bouquets, being escorted by pouting dates does not a terrific homecoming celebration make.

We have the ball, are down by five, with just under one minute remaining in the game. We are only forty yards away from scoring a go-ahead touchdown and securing a win. If we time it right, run down the clock just enough, then score a touchdown, we will win by one. The cheering squad has been huddling shoulder to shoulder, clutching hands, holding our breath. It is too intense to say a cheer. We watch in silence as the clock winds down.

I gasp when the ball is passed to Luke. He catches it, protectively snuggles it closely to his body, and starts running. Fast. Really fast. Ten yards…twenty yards….thirty yards… forty yards… "TOUCHDOWN" we all scream as the time expires.

I jump up and down, screaming uncontrollably. That's my man! I can hear the announcers screaming "THE KNIGHTS WIN!" over and over. All the girls on my squad hug me and we jump up and down, squealing like excited preschool children. I'm so excited for Luke. We all storm the field in excitement. I make my way through, highly electrified, screaming players and fans and search for Luke. I can't wait to hug him and give him a congratulatory kiss. Players keep passing by me and I don't see him. I search the backs of everyone, looking for his telltale number ten. Finally, our eyes meet.

We break out into huge grins and run to each other the best we can through the crowd. "Olivia!"

"Luke!"

I see some people try and stop Luke to congratulate him but he pushes past them, one destination in mind. When we reach one another, Luke picks me up and I wrap my legs around his waist. He twirls me around and around, laughing.

"We did it!" he yells in excitement.

"You did it!" I correct him, "I'm so proud of you Luke!"

He pulls back from me and smiles that sexy smile I love. I lean in and our lips meet. I don't waste time, I immediately sweep his mouth with my tongue tightening my arms around his back, then trailing my hands up into his hair and clutching handfuls. Luke responds and pulls me tighter too.

"Luke! Olivia!"

We break apart to see Pyper coming towards us, yelling our names in excitement. Luke gives me another light kiss on my lips, then sets me down. When Pyper reaches us he asks, "Do you have it?" I lower my brows in confusion, I'm not sure what he's talking about.

Pyper smiles, "Of course!" She reaches into her pocket and pulls out a small box, handing it to Luke.

Luke takes it from her and turns to me. I feel my eyes widen as I look from his eyes, to the box he is holding and back again. "I wanted to wait until the dance tomorrow night to give this to you. As excited as I am right now because we won, and as much as I feel on top of the world because of this game, it doesn't compare to the way I feel about you. So, to prove it, this seems like the perfect moment to give you this." He hands me a box and says, "Open it."

I take the box from him, my breath catching in excitement. I take the lid off the top and sitting inside is a silver ring with an open heart. I smile. The ring is beautiful in its simplicity. Luke has never given me jewelry before. "Luke, it's beautiful, I love it."

He takes the ring out of the box and places it on my right ring finger, "You have my heart, angel, completely. I just wanted you to have a reminder in case you ever need it, but I hope you never do. Never doubt how I feel about you."

I look at the ring on my finger and dream that someday, he will be placing a different one on my other hand, "I love you Luke Easton."

"I love you too, Livvie."

He cups my cheek and leans in to place a kiss on my lips.

Blinking as an attempt to clear the memory from my mind, I remember how I contemplated tossing the ring away after he broke my heart and realized the emptiness of the promise made that day. But, I couldn't bring myself to go through with it. Instead, I kept it buried in the bottom of my drawer. I get a little choked up looking at it. I place it back inside the box, put the lid on, and keep searching for my red earrings. Giving up, I just grab some silver hoops and place them in my ears. I walk towards my bed, grab my bag, once again silently thanking Pyper for having the forethought to do this for me.

Just as I'm starting to walk out my bedroom door, I feel my cell phone buzzing in my bag. I fish it out and look at the screen. The number is unknown. I answer it anyway, "Hello?" I hear silence. "Hello?" I say again. Still silence. I look at my phone and see the call is still connected. Weird. Shrugging my shoulders, I hang up and tuck the phone back in my bag.

When I'm just outside the living room entrance, I see Luke and Pyper looking like they are in a serious conversation, but they immediately quit talking when I walk in. Luke stands up and smiles at me, but Pyper raises one eyebrow - a talent I envy- and gives me a smirk. I wonder what they were talking about, but I make a mental note to ask her later.

I smile a little at Luke in return. "I'm ready to go. I tried not to take too long." I feel uncertain and shy.

"I would wait for you as long as it takes." I admit that makes me melt a little and I smile a bit bigger at his words.

Pretending what he said didn't make my stomach jump, I head to the front door, assuming he would follow. "Bye, Pyper, see you later."

"Bye. I may not be here when you get back, I'm going to the spa to work for a little while."

"Okay."

"Bye, Luke." Pyper says looking at him intently.

"Bye, Pyper," Luke says, "and thanks again."

Pyper doesn't reply and we walk out the door and close it behind us. Luke places a hand at the small of my back as we walk to the elevator. We are silent, staring at the elevator door – or at least I am - the entire ride down to the parking garage, but I can see portions of Luke's reflection despite the elevator's design, and realize that Luke keeps looking over at me. The butterflies in my stomach are going crazy again.

When the elevator reaches its destination, we step out into the garage. Once again, Luke's hand presses on my back and he gestures with his hand to the right, "My car is this way."

As we approach a black car, he walks to the passenger door and opens it for me. Looking at him I ask, "What kind of car is this? It's very nice."

He grins, "It's an Audi R8; she's my baby."

I grin back, "She? Your baby?"

"That's right."

I start to sit in the seat but I pause when I see a single yellow rose lying in its middle. I look back at him curiously and he smiles. "For you." He reaches down, grabs the rose and hands it to me, "Did you know a yellow rose not only means friendship, but it stands for new beginnings?"

I take the rose from him, "No I didn't know that. Thank you."

He nods, waits for me to sit in the passenger seat, and closes the door. I raise the rose to my nose to take in its tantalizing scent as he walks around to the driver's side. Opening the door and getting in, he looks over at me smelling my rose, buckles his seat belt, and smiles again.

"Can I ask you a question?" I ask while buckling my own seatbelt.

"Of course."

"The rose. How did you know I would be in your car and you would give it to me?"

He places the key in the ignition and starts his car. It lets out a soft purr as *she* starts up. "I didn't know...but I hoped. I sure as hell hoped."

Chapter Eleven

"Fashion tip: I know it is very cold in some places in the United States, I'm from Illinois after all. I get cold, I understand it. Don't even get me started on the brutal Chicago wind, but unless you're an Eskimo, or an out of touch reality star, super furry boots just won't work. And please, if you insist on wearing them, does it have to be with shorts? No, no it doesn't."

"Where would you like to go for breakfast? Any place in particular? Have a taste for anything specific?" Luke asks.

"I'm not picky. I love breakfast food, so I will find something I like to eat anywhere we go."

Luke places his arm on the top of my seat to look over his shoulder as he backs out of the parking space, bringing him a little closer to me. My skin tingles at his nearness and my breath catches. He's so close to me, I can almost feel the heat off of his hand at my neck. I feel ridiculous for my reaction, but at the same time, I love the way it makes me feel.

"I remember you used to have mad love for French toast, is that still the case?"

"Absolutely. A love like that doesn't fade," I tell him seriously.

He laughs low at that and my tingly skin breaks out into goose bumps, "I know just the place then."

Luke takes a left out of the parking lot, and we are on our way. I take a second to digest the fact that I am in a car with Luke, on my way to breakfast. Wow. This feels surreal. I put my rose to my nose again and take a deep breath. For some reason, this calms me a little.

Luke glances at me from the corner of his eye, "I have a confession to make."

Lifting my eyebrows, I look at him, rose still at my nose, and wonder what he's about to say. It sounds ominous. "Oh?"

"I knew you were back in town. I ran into Pyper's mom a while back and she told me, but one night as I was getting ready to walk into Maggiano's for dinner, you bumped into me on your way out. I was so surprised to see you, I just stood there in shock. I had hoped to run into you, and I even tried to find out where you were staying after I saw Pyper's mom, but I didn't expect to literally run into you."

I'm shocked. Maggiano's restaurant? I vaguely remember bumping into someone in my haste to get away from boob-lovin' Daniel. I just stare at him, not sure how to reply.

He talks quickly, unsure of my reaction. "By the time I gathered myself enough to run after you, you were already pulling out of the parking lot."

I decide to just be honest. "I umm, had actually been there on a date," I say glancing at him. He frowns. "It did not go well and I was in a hurry to get away from him."

This time when I look over at him, I see a smile teasing at the corner of his mouth. I'm not sure what to make of that.

"How could a date with you not go well, angel?"

His term of endearment sends a shiver down my spine. "Well, obviously I wasn't the problem," I tease. "Daniel, that was his name, well let's just say he liked himself a lot, he never once asked a question about me, and he...well...he pretty much had a conversation with my breasts the whole night."

Luke looks at me, eyes widening as he glances down towards my chest then back up at my face. He quickly turns back toward the road and I'm pretty sure I see his cheeks pink a little, "What?" he chokes.

I can't help but laugh at his reaction, "Well, when he would talk to me, he never made eye contact, he just stared at my breasts the whole time. Then, as we were leaving, he had the audacity to tell me he made arrangements for a room and we could see how it went before we decided if we wanted to pay for it by the hour or for the night."

Luke's jaw tightens. "I think it's a good thing I don't know where to find Daniel. Please tell me you punched him in the balls."

I smirk, "No, but I handled myself just fine. I told him off and got the hell out of there. Although, come to think of it, he did deserve a punch to the balls."

"Well, that explains your hurry. I'd like to say I'm sorry your date didn't go well, but I'm not."

I elect not to read into that comment, "Well, at least I got a great dinner out of it. I missed Maggiano's. We didn't have one in Boston."

"We? Boston? Is that where you were living?"

"Yes. That's where I've been for the last seven years. I attended Boston University and stayed there after I graduated." I completely ignore his other question.

Luke runs his hand through his hair, "I didn't know where you went. It was like you disappeared without a trace. No one would tell me anything. You had your phone number changed and I couldn't find you. I was limited in what I could do, my parents wouldn't help me and made sure I didn't have the money to hire someone that could. They told me to respect your wishes and what your parents told me you wanted." He sighs and continues admitting, "I didn't want to listen and was very angry for a long time. I wanted to find you, Olivia. I tried to find you any way I could within my means. I *never* forgot you, I couldn't."

My eyes tear up at the emotion in his voice and I try hard to keep them from escaping and falling down my cheeks. I clear my throat, collecting myself. "I never forgot about you either, Luke. I tried like hell to force you out of my mind and refused to think about you. Sometimes it would work well for a while, but there

117

were moments when thoughts of you would make it through the walls I built around my mind and heart." I tell him shyly.

His head turns toward me at my words, and I know he's seeking my eyes, but I avoid them and look out the window at my side, embarrassed by my confession. We are both quiet and I know this is only the tip of the iceberg. We have so much that has gone unsaid, and I know the journey of working through it all will be necessary if we are going to have any relationship whatsoever. However, in between all the imminent revelations, I really hope to be able to just enjoy spending time with him again. He wasn't only my boyfriend and the boy I thought was going to be my future, he was also my best friend - next to Pyper - and I missed him.

We come up to West End Café and I smile. I love this little café. It's been a longtime favorite. They have always had the best French toast. Luke sees me smiling and a smirk of self-satisfaction appears on his face. He knows I'm pleased.

Once he parks, we walk up to the restaurant and Luke opens the door for me. I walk up to the hostess and Luke comes up beside me. When we have her attention she asks, "How many?" and Luke answers, "Two please."

The hostess is young, maybe nineteen-years-old at most, and I can't help but giggle when I see her gawk at Luke. Luke looks at me, eyebrows raised and I just smile and shake my head. I remember how he has always seemed oblivious to the effect he has on women. I can't blame the girl, Luke is very attractive. It's not only his gorgeous face, or the way his shirt pulls just right across his chest, displaying his muscle tone underneath. It isn't just the way his jeans fit him perfectly, or how he completely owns the black leather jacket he's wearing. It's also the confidence that bleeds from his very being, and the swagger he has when he moves. He was always very comfortable in his own skin and it made people stop and take notice. I'm not at all surprised that this hasn't changed.

Leading us to a table in the far corner, the hostess hands us our menus. "I'd love to take your drink order, what would you like?" She brushes her fingertips on Luke's arm when she asks and looks only at him while waiting patiently for his answer.

"What would you like to drink, angel?" Luke asks completely ignoring her.

"I'll take a coffee please." The waitress nods, but her eyes still don't leave Luke. He doesn't look at her when he says, "I will have the same please."

She looks a bit crestfallen. "Okay, coming right up."

I have to admit, I like that he didn't flirt back with her. Whenever Deacon and I would go out to eat somewhere, he always flirted with the waitresses and it always made me uncomfortable. I usually felt like I may as well have been invisible. With Luke, it was like the waitress was the invisible one. It's a nice change and makes me feel good.

Luke looks at me and I stare back. "I feel like we have so much to talk about, yet I have no idea where to start."

I let out a breath, "I'm glad you said that because I feel the same way. I have no idea where to begin either. There is so much to share and so many things I want to ask. This feels awkward and familiar at the same time."

"Should we start from the day everything changed? When you were," he looks down at his lap as if the words are hard to say, then looks back at me again, "when you were at my house?"

Before I can respond, our hostess reappears with our coffees. She sets down the sweeteners and bowl of individual creamers on the table then looks at Luke, "Your waitress will be with you shortly."

Luke just nods but doesn't look at her, his attention on the sugar packets. Before I can grab one he reaches out and touches my hand not letting me grab any packets. "Do you still take three artificial sweeteners and a vanilla creamer?"

I smile and nod. "I can't believe you remember that!"

He holds my eyes, "I remember everything, Olivia."

I look down, feeling flush. That was a loaded comment if I ever heard one. My mind instantly goes to our more intimate moments, lips touching, chests pressed together, hands exploring, and I can feel my cheeks heat even more. It is safe to say I remember everything too. Luke hands me the Splenda and creamer; I put them in my coffee, stir, then take a sip before I look back at him.

Luke takes pity on me and doesn't comment on my red cheeks, "Back to what I was saying before we were interrupted, do you want to start our conversation from the day you overheard me talking to my mother?"

"Luke, let's just start with something simple; catch up on the frivolous things. Our conversation will get there on its own. I know we need to talk about that day, and many days since then, and I know you are curious because I am too. But, we just reconnected and seeing you again, well that's a lot to take in on its own. Let's just take things slow and let the conversation go where it may."

Luke nods his head, "That sounds good to me." He leans back in his seat and looks at me intently, "I just want to say that I don't want any secrets between us and no lies. Lies are what tore us apart to begin with and I don't want that to happen again."

"I agree. No lies."

He smiles, "How about we start with your parents, tell me how they're doing."

Just as I open my mouth to reply we are interrupted by our waitress. "Hi, my name is Cassandra and I will be your waitress, I see Sarah already brought you something to drink, are you both ready to order?"

Luke and I look at one another and we both nod. We're ready. "Go ahead, angel."

I look at our waitress and smile, happy to see she's looking at me too. "I'd like the cinnamon and vanilla French toast, please, with a side of bacon." I tell her, then hand her my menu.

She nods to me and turns to Luke, "For you, sir?"

He smiles and looks at his menu as he places his order, "I would like your bacado omelet please, with hollandaise sauce on the side, and a side of hash browns."

"You betcha, coming right up!" She takes Luke's menu from him and leaves our table to put in our order with the cook.

I smile and continue our conversation like we were never interrupted, "My parents are wonderful, they're retired and living in Arizona. They really love it there and have no intention of ever leaving. I think they may try to be snow birds at some point, which means they will stay in Arizona during the winter and go somewhere else during the summer. I wouldn't be surprised if they decide to spend the summer in Chicago, since I'm living here again. They tried to convince me to move there with them, but I politely declined. I'm really not interested in living with my parents again."

Luke chuckles, "I can understand that. I'm glad to see you and Pyper are still such great friends, though I'm not surprised."

"Pyper has been my rock. I can't imagine her not being in my life. Her friendship means everything to me."

"Have you kept in touch with anyone else from high school?"

"No, not a soul. Only Pyper. How about you? Did you graduate from Loyola University then?"

"No I didn't. I stayed there for the first year and then transferred out."

I'm surprised, "Oh, really? You were so excited about attending Loyola, that surprises me."

Luke smiles sadly, "That was always our dream, and without you, it wasn't much of a dream anymore. Getting through the first year without you was tough. Before the year was over I had already applied and been accepted to the University of Illinois and I transferred there the following year."

I am shocked and moved by his admission.

"I ended up graduating from U of I with a business degree and began working for my father in the family beer distribution business. I learned a lot and quickly proved myself, moving up the ranks. I like the fact I wasn't an automatic shoo-in with my dad just because it's a family business. He made me prove myself, and I did. My father decided to expand the business and not only supply beer to bars and stores, but to open a chain of clubs as an LLC attached to Easton Distributing Company."

"A chain? Wow. So Zero Gravity isn't the only club you own?"

"Zero Gravity is the only club that belongs to me and my company exclusively. For my first solo assignment my father sent me to California to assist with opening a club called Storm. The club did so well that my father made a deal with me. He would let me choose the next place we opened a club, if that club did as well as the first, he would give me a percentage of the profits, which would enable me to open a third club at a place of my choosing. While this club would still be operated under the EDC name, the management, salary, hiring, design, and profits would be exclusively mine to handle."

Luke pauses and takes a sip of his coffee before continuing, "The second location I chose was Miami. Miami is a big party city in Florida and I knew any new club would do well there. We opened Club Bailar about a year ago and it, as you can imagine, was a raging success. The location is perfect and we had lines to get in from the day it opened. My father stayed true to his word and I received a large amount of money to open my own club. Several months ago I started looking into various locations."

I'm intrigued, listening to him tell me about what he's been doing. It makes me feel content hearing him tell me about his life. In quiet secret moments over the years, when I would allow myself thoughts of Luke, I wondered what happened to him, where he was, what he was doing, and who he was with. I don't have to wonder anymore. A part of me feels more complete than I have in a long time, with those thoughts no longer being questions, but answers.

"So why did you choose Chicago for your third location?"

We are interrupted by the waitress placing our food on the table before Luke can answer my question . My French toast looks so good and I can't wait to take a bite! "Can I get you anything else?"

"Olivia, do you need anything?" Luke asks me.

"No thank you, I'm fine. This looks great, thank you."

"Thanks." Luke tells our waitress and then turns to his food, unwraps his silverware and cuts out a big piece of his omelet, taking a bite. I like watching his lips and jaw move while he chews. When he swallows and licks his lips, I realize I'm staring and turn to my own plate of food. Covering my French toast with syrup, I unwrap my own silverware, place the napkin on my lap, cut a bite and put it into my mouth.

"Mmmmm," I moan, it tastes wonderful. I look up at Luke to see him staring at my lips. I can't help the small smirk that plays on my lips at seeing him doing the exact same thing I was just doing to him. I turn my attention back to my food and take another bite.

I hear Luke clear his throat, "How's the French toast?"

"So good. How's your omelet?"

"Very good."

"Now finish telling me, why did you end up choosing Chicago as the location for your club?"

He finishes chewing and then swallows and takes a drink of his coffee before replying, "Well, I guess for a couple reasons. First of all, Illinois is home. While we didn't grow up in the city, it's still home and I missed it. The other reason," Luke hesitates and his brows furrow, making me think he's unsure about sharing whatever he's about to say. "Well my mom," he doesn't have to say more than that and I felt myself flinch slightly at the reference to his mother. I know it has been a long time, but the fact that she hated me still resonates. "Well my Mom is sick."

"Sick?"

"Yes, she has cancer."

"Oh my gosh, Luke, I'm so sorry!" Regardless of how I feel about her and that I believe she is partly responsible for what happened between Luke and me, I would never wish something like this on her.

"Thanks. It started with a mole on her leg, she got it checked out, they sent her for a biopsy, and we found out she has melanoma. She's undergoing treatment and we're hopeful for a full recovery, but the chemotherapy treatments have been rough. I decided to come back home and be closer to her and my dad so I can help out."

"Oh, wow. Well of course you wanted to. I would want to be close to my parents as well if one of mine were sick."

Changing the subject from his mom, Luke says, "Tell me, what brought you back to Chicago, angel?"

I knew this question would come up at some point. Did I want to get into it now? I wanted to keep things light, but is that really possible? I suppose now is as good a time as any. Deacon was not going to be an easy conversation to have, no matter when it happens.

I sigh deeply, look up into Luke's eyes and say, "Well, Pyper asked me to come and live with her so I could, shall we say, start over," I see the question in his eyes, so I finish with, "because I just went through a nasty divorce."

Luke chokes on his food.

Aw, damn.

Good thing I know the Heimlich maneuver.

Chapter Twelve

"Fashion tip: When you don't know what to wear – pick black. If you're a woman, throw on a black dress and you're good to go. If you're a guy, put on jeans, a black t-shirt, and black boots, then you're done and in style. Black is easy. Look at it like a get out of jail free card in a game of fashion Monopoly."

I'm glad I don't end up needing the Heimlich maneuver after all. It was touch and go for a moment, but just as I get up to slide in next to Luke to offer assistance, he held his finger up to me, indicating he was fine and to give him a minute. I wait patiently as he gets himself under control.

Maybe I should have made sure he wasn't drinking or eating anything before I dropped that bomb on him, "Are you okay?"

He nods his head yes but it takes him another few minutes to regain his composure. He uses his napkin to wipe the tears from his eyes, evidence that he was truly choking and he looks up at me and slightly stutters, "You're married?" His voice sounds gravelly.

"No. I *was* married. I am now divorced."

"Sorry. That's what I meant to ask."

It is quiet and awkward between us for a few minutes, neither of us quite knowing how to continue. Luke finally asks, "How long were you married?"

"Four years."

"How...when...do you...I mean, are you...," sighing and running his hand through his hair he finally gets out, "Dammit to hell, what I'm trying to say is that I didn't know. I had no idea you were married."

I decide a bit of levity is necessary, "Yeah, I kind of gathered that based on your reaction. No worries, how could you have known?"

"I'm sorry. I'm just shocked. Wow, four years huh?" His eyes look sad but determined and his jaw keeps clenching and unclenching. "I'm guessing you met someone when you were in college?"

"To your first comment, it's okay, I'm doing fine. And we said no lies, so it seemed that divulging my marriage was the right thing to do. The fact that I was married is a part of my life that I can't change and I'm not going to lie about it. And to your last question, yes, I met Deacon in college."

He flinches when I say Deacon's name as if stating it made it more real. "I don't want you to lie. I'm glad you told me. So that would mean your last name isn't Summerton any longer, is it?"

"No, it's not. Initially, I wanted to keep my maiden name because with my career I thought it might be smart, but when I suggested it to Deacon, he insisted I change it. I did, so now I'm Olivia Brooks."

"Brooks," he repeats to himself. "Well it makes sense why I couldn't find you on any social media site or when I tried to Google you."

"It does."

"So, what happened? Why the divorce? If it's okay to ask..." he trails off, a question in his voice.

I smile at him because I know he is trying to let me keep my privacy if I choose, but that he's curious too. "It's okay to ask, but it really isn't an easy story to share." I take a swallow of my coffee because my throat feels dry "I'm sure you want to know more about what happened."

"Honestly? Yes and no."

I wasn't expecting him to say that, but I understand what he means. If our roles were reversed, I'm not sure I would be interested in hearing the details about how Luke, the former love of my life, met, fell in love with, married and then divorced someone else. Curiosity would without doubt win in the end because my imagination would only make things worse, but initially, I would probably just want to throw up at the thought.

"Olivia, I meant it when I said I want to know everything about every minute and every day we spent apart from one another. I don't expect that it is all going to be easy to hear, but that doesn't change the fact that I still want to know." He reaches for my hand and I hesitate, not sure I want to let him hold it. We are supposed to be trying our luck at friends, but this feels intimate. "Everything that has happened in your life since you left matters, and it ended up bringing you right back here, with me. So yes, I do want to talk to you about this and learn more. That is, if you want to talk about it with me."

I squeeze his hand and pull away, "I will tell you about it, but not here. Would you mind having this conversation another time? I'd prefer to have more privacy than this when I share that part of my life."

"Of course. Sure. I'm sorry."

"Thanks." I smile back at him and ask, "So tell me, when you aren't busy running your club, what do you like to do for fun? Still a big sports fanatic? ESPN obsessed?" I purposefully change the subject to something lighter and easier.

Putting his elbows on the table and clasping his hands under his chin Luke answers, "Well I still love sports, and yes, you are correct. ESPN pretty much runs on a constant reel on the TV when I'm at home. Before I moved back here, I was involved in a football league and I'm really hoping to find one I can join here. I miss it sometimes since I haven't played much since college. Of course, I enjoy going to the gym, I'm still a movie lover, and actually when I was in Miami I did a little bit of modeling from time to time."

It's my turn to choke. Did I hear that correctly? Luke laughs at me. "Telling you that was so worth your reaction. Pay back is a bitch."

I ignore that because I'm only focused on one thing, "I'm sorry, did you say modeling?"

I swear he blushes a bit at the top of his cheeks. It's really endearing and makes me lean in closer to him to hear more. Stupid table in the way. Wait. What am I thinking? It's good the table is in the way! "Yes, modeling. One of my good friends from college, Sienna, works at an agency and she suckered me into coming in once when she was in charge of a shoot and the model was a no-show. To my surprise, I actually had fun, the photos turned out great, and one thing led to another. Before I knew it, I was sent on some auditions where you basically stand there and let them look at you, and I booked a few well-paying jobs. She told me there would likely even be opportunities here in Chicago, if I'm interested." Luke says, shrugging his shoulders.

"Wow, I'm speechless." Holy hell, Luke is a model. Speechless doesn't even begin to cover it. Just thinking about him modeling makes me tingle from head to toe.

He grins at me, "Maybe I will show you a few pictures some time."

Oh God yes, please do! "You have a portfolio you can share with me?" I so kept my cool with that question. Go me.

"Yes I do, and I've even kept every ad that I've been in." His cheeks deepen in color a bit more with his admission.

"I would love to see them all," I tell him honestly. I wonder what he's modeling in the photos. David Beckham in his underwear flashes across my mind. Woah. I wonder if Luke models briefs. Suddenly it feels very warm in here. I clear my throat and remove my sweater. I try to concentrate on the other comment he made about looking for a new football league before I embarrass myself by being visibly flushed at the mere thought of Luke and that body of his on display. Clearing my throat, I change the subject, "Before you came back to Chicago, where were you living? In Miami? I know that's where you said you opened your last club."

"Yes. When I left here and went to California to open the first club, I lived there for a year. Then, I went to Florida, where I stayed until I came back here to open Zero Gravity."

"Did you like living there? I've never been to Florida. I'd like to go some time actually, but it's because I want to go to Disney World." I admit to him, laughing at my childish secret.

"Disney World, huh?"

"Well, for some reason, we never went as a family when I was a kid. I'm not sure why, but I've always wanted to go."

"Maybe someday I can take you. I can take you to the club there too. Even if it would mean a bit longer vacation, given that they are miles apart."

I just smile at him shyly, not making any promises. My heart stutters a bit at his suggestion, but I'm not even allowing myself to go there.

"What about you? What do you like to do in your spare time and what about your job? I know you haven't been here too long yet, but what do you or did you do for a living?"

"Even though I didn't attend Loyola as planned," he looks away when I say that, "I still went to school for and graduated with a degree in journalism from BU. In all honesty, I started out my college days with some heavy partying." I have his attention again and his jaw has dropped at my comment. Okay yes, geesh, I was always a goody goody, but he should know things change. "Then, a professor gave us an assignment to start a blog. I started a fashion blog, thinking no one would really read it, but I had fun with it. To my surprise, it really took off and it landed me an internship at a local magazine in Boston. Once they started publishing my articles more and more, I started to get braver and more confident with my writing and started submitting for freelance journalist positions at various magazines. Plus, several even contacted me through my blog asking me to write for them as well. I've been very lucky to have a couple that religiously print my articles and request new ones. I even have my own column in one and I freelance for others. I really love it." I can't help but smile because that is the truth. I really do love my job and interacting with my followers on Pink Sugar Couture is probably my favorite part.

"That's really great, and I'm not surprised at all that your blog and column is popular. You always loved writing." Luke seems genuinely thrilled for me. It's nice.

"I really love it, actually. While I'm here in Chicago, I would love to write for a local magazine. I have some great ideas

129

about what I would like to contribute, so eventually I'm going to look into contacting them and see what happens."

Luke clears his throat and attempts a smile, "I'm glad that after," he stops and begins again, "well given what happened with us...well I'm glad that you still pursued your dream."

I smile at him to relieve his discomfort, "Me too. As far as what I like to do, I love to read, of course, order and watch movies from Netflix, listen to music, try new products, shop for shoes and handbags, and lately get spoiled at Pyper's spa," I tell him, grinning.

Before he can respond, our waitress comes by and leaves our check on the table. I start to make a grab for it, but Luke beats me to it. "Not a chance," he tells me. "Are you ready?"

I take one more sip of my coffee and nod. "Yes."

We head up to the cash register and Luke pays the bill. Then we walk to the doors which Luke opens for me and walk towards his car. I feel a bit sad. I'm not really ready for Luke to bring me home, but at the same time I'm emotionally exhausted from just an hour together at breakfast and our conversation at the condo before coming here.

When we reach Luke's car he opens the door for me and closes it once I'm tucked inside with my now somewhat wilted rose on my lap. He walks around the front of the car and I can't help but watch him make his way. He still has a nice ass. I smirk to myself. I can't help it. I'm divorced, not dead.

Once he's sitting in the car, Luke puts his key in the ignition, starts buckling his seatbelt, then turns to face me. "Olivia?"

I turn toward him too. "Yes?"

"Do you have anything else planned right now?"

I don't, but I don't want to admit that to him. Maybe I'm being immature, but I don't want him to know that my schedule is wide open, so I avoid. "Umm...why?"

"Well, I was wondering if maybe you want to go see a movie or something?" I can see the hope in his eyes. He doesn't want me to tell him no and I'm not sure that I have the willpower to do so anyway. Before I can respond, he leans a little closer to me, "Look the truth is, I'm not ready to bring you home."

That does it. I couldn't say no now, even if I wanted to, but at the same time I have to admit part of me doesn't want to make this easy for him. I can admit to myself that I am happy to have him back in my life again. I'm conflicted – that's for sure. On one hand, I'm still angry with him, but on the other hand, a big part of me knows that I need to let that go if I'm really going to be able to move on and be friends with Luke and have him in my life again, "Okay, sure. That sounds good."

Luke's responding grin is magnificent, and it makes that dimple of his I love peek at me. "Great! How about we catch comedy?"

"That sounds perfect."

"There's a new one out right now that I think is more stupid than funny, but I think it's right up our alley. What do ya say?"

"I'm game."

He lets out a deep sigh of relief. I wonder if he was nervous that I would say no. Funny, I was no more ready to end our non-date than he was. Non-date. Does that make it an outing? A meet up? A shindig? I can't help but chuckle to myself.

Luke glances at me curiously, raising a brow. I just shake my head at him.

It isn't long before we are pulling up to the movie theatre, getting out of the car and walking side by side into the entrance. We head up to the ticket booth and I start taking my wallet out of my purse, "No way," Luke replies seeing what I'm doing and then proceeds to purchase and pay for both of our tickets.

"Fine, but I'm buying the popcorn then. And the drinks."

"Popcorn? But we just ate!"

"Doesn't matter. Who can watch a movie at the theatre without popcorn? That's like peanut butter without jelly. Like Turner without Hooch. Like Danny without Sandy."

Luke laughs, "Okay, okay I get it, I get it."

Smiling, I head to the counter and order a popcorn and two drinks. Handing Luke his drink he says, "What kind of drink did you get me?"

I blush to myself realizing what I've done. "Oh. I'm sorry. I got you a Dr. Pepper, I remember that was your favorite. Well, at least it used to be. I should have asked you and not assumed."

Luke laughs at my expression, "I like that you remember. I still love Dr. Pepper, this is perfect."

It's nice to know some things don't change; it's comforting. I admit satisfaction at my actions as well. Even with all the time that has passed, it's nice to know that some things are consistent, dependable. Some things are still easy and natural.

We make our way to theatre 10, where our movie is playing. Luke turns to me, "Do you still like front row in the top section so you can put your feet up on the bars?"

"Sure do!"

Luke leads the way and I follow him up the couple of stairs and we head towards the middle of the front row in the top section. Once we take our seats, I place the popcorn between us.

We may have just eaten but that doesn't keep us from shoveling the popcorn in our mouths. I watch Luke lick butter off his lips so I'm looking at his mouth when he starts talking to me. I look into his eyes, hoping he didn't notice my staring. "So, angel, are you up for a game of twenty questions while we're waiting for the movie to start? I want to see if some of the things I remember about you are still the same."

"Okay me first! Favorite color?"

"Blue. Yours?"

"Teal. Favorite movie?"

"The Shining. Is yours still Beauty and the Beast?"

"Of course. I'm a sucker for a happy ending and Disney."

He smiles and asks, "Favorite food?"

"Pizza. Is yours still steak?"

"You got it. Meat and potatoes all the way baby," he rubs his flat tummy. I can't help but look down and wish I could see under that shirt. I need to stop with this, what is up with me? Slutty much? "Ocean or mountains?"

"Ocean," he replies immediately. "Besides Disneyworld in Florida, where is a place you've always wanted to visit?"

"Hmmm… that's a tough one because there are so many, but Paris comes to mind first. How about you?"

"I would love to visit Ireland one day. I've heard it is beautiful, plus drinking ale at an Irish pub would be pretty cool."

"Okay I have a good one," I tell him, "If you suddenly found yourself turned into a woman for a day, how would you spend the day?"

"Well that depends. Am I a beautiful woman? Where would I be living? Would I have a nice body? Do I have a boyfriend?"

I laugh at him, "Why does any of that matter?"

He smiles, "It doesn't. Honestly I would spend the day at home exploring the equipment."

I laugh hard and loud at his comment. "Nice."

"Hey, I'm just being honest. Here's one for you. If you won a million dollars tomorrow what is the first frivolous thing you would buy?"

"Oh that's easy, a black leather Chanel bag with chain straps that are silver and has the silver c's in the front. It would have a magnetic closure and cell phone pocket on the inside."

Luke cracks up laughing, "Why does that not surprise me?"

"Don't knock my handbag obsession. There are worse things I could be addicted to!"

"If you say so!"

The movie is supposed to start in only a couple more minutes so we won't get to twenty questions but this has been fun. "One more question for you. If you could have any super power, what would it be?"

Luke smirks and I see his eyes brush over my body from head to toe then looks me in the eye and I see a subtle simmer beginning in his eyes. My face and body heat in reaction. "Well, the 16-year-old boy in me wants to say x-ray vision and the twenty-five-year-old that I am now, well, he has to agree."

With perfect timing, the lights in the auditorium lower, and I am grateful; after his comment, I'm sure my face has to be bright red. I can feel it burning, but I can't fight the slight smile that I feel on my lips.

As we both reach for popcorn, our hands brush against each other making tingles shoot all the way up my arm and even straight between my legs. I've seen him all of one day and already he has me wanting him. I hope I can keep a lid on these desires, but I think it is safe to say being around him is not going to make it easy.

Chapter Thirteen

"Fashion tip: Did you know that one in three women wear the wrong bra size? Bras that either gape because they are too large or those too small that squeeze one's chest, creating unnatural bulges, are equally unattractive. Get fitted properly! Move around in it – bend over, raise your arms over your head. Do they go off by themselves? If so, you need a different size. Adjust the clasp and ensure the cup and brand are well-fitting. Adjust the straps so they sit naturally on the chest. If your breasts are flowing out the sides or over the top of the cups, the bra is too small. Your bra should lie flush against your skin. The absolute best thing you can do for yourself if you still aren't sure, is get fitted! (Those living in the Chicago area – I can make a great suggestion – message me if you are interested!) Make sure you are supporting your girls properly! You never know when your bra is going to be seen! *wink, wink*"

Back in the car on our way to my condo after the movie, Luke and I are quiet. The movie was funny, just the right amount of humor combined with stupid – which made it perfect.

I can't help but wonder what is going to happen when Luke drops me off. Will he kiss me? Will he want to? Do I want him to? It seems too soon for that. We just reconnected again, and while my mind is telling me to take things slow and to remember that I have walls up for a reason, my heart remembers this - remembers him. He made an imprint on my heart long ago, and it hasn't forgotten, it's begging for me to let him in again. And my body – well it refuses to be left out of the equation. His nearness and brief touches still set my body on fire. I feel like a live wire, ready to sizzle at the slightest touch. I both love and hate the feeling.

We pull into the parking garage and I turn my head towards Luke, "You don't have to park or anything, you can just let me out and then you can take off."

He looks at me like I'm crazy, "Now that wouldn't be very gentlemanly, would it? I'm going to ride up the elevator with you and take you to your front door."

I nod my head in a manner that says sure, if you insist, then that's fine with me. The tension between us in the elevator is palpable; the uneasiness and slight giddiness make the corners of my mouth slightly turn up, even though I'm trying not to show that I'm affected. I'm looking at Luke out of the corner of my eye, I can see him looking at me in turn, with a soft smile playing at the corners of his mouth when he realizes we are both checking the other out.

When the elevator reaches my floor, Luke saunters uncharacteristically slow to the door of my condo – as if to savor every last second. I turn to look at him, and part of me really wants to ask him if he would like to come in for a cup of coffee or a beer; but it has been a long day and the other part of me just wants some time alone now. I'm looking forward to getting into comfortable pajama pants and reflecting on everything that's happened.

"Thanks for breakfast and the movie, Luke."

"You're welcome. I'm glad you came out with me. I know the last thing you expected was for me to storm in on you this morning. After seeing you last night, I couldn't wait another minute to try and talk to you to make things right between us. Thank you for giving me a chance to be in your life again. Whatever you do, please don't change your mind. I've missed you."

I get a little choked up at his comment, so I just nod. I start to put my key into the lock, knowing that Pyper may be home. But I'm not going to check first. If she sees us standing here she will invite him in. I'm not ready for that. Before I can get the key in all the way Luke stops me by asking, "When can I see you again?"

I freeze, and my brain starts turning. It isn't that I don't want to see him again, and I'm not surprised he asks to see me again, but I'm startled because I don't know what to say. I want to see him again, but by immediately agreeing, does that make me seem way too eager and available? I also just want time to digest everything before I decide.

Luke, seeing my hesitation takes another step towards me, causing me to look at him. With sincerity in his eyes, he cups my face between both of his hands, "I want to see you again. Soon. Can I see you tomorrow or in a couple days?"

I get lost in his eyes for a moment. They're full of hope, eagerness, sadness, and something else that I don't want to think about right now. Just the thought makes me tremble. He notices the fact that I'm lost in him for a minute, because a knowing smirk appears on his face, which snaps me out of the moment. He may be sexy as hell, but I still want to wipe that look off his beautiful face. I pull away from his hands, "I'm sorry, I'm not really sure what the rest of the week is going to look like for me. I'm supposed to go on a date with Noah this week, but we haven't nailed down an actual day and time yet, so I can't commit to anything right now."

Luke takes a step back from me and his eyes narrow slightly and I've accomplished my goal, because that arrogant look that was on his face has disappeared. "A date?"

"Yes. A date."

"You're dating?"

"Yes. I'm dating. I've *been* dating. That's what people, adult people do, right?"

Luke sucks his bottom lip into his mouth and is quiet - the wheels turning in his head I'm sure. I can't believe I mentioned Noah and my potential date with him, but why not? Luke and I may have reconnected, but that doesn't automatically make me his. I don't belong to anyone. I'm not property.

"Well, where are you going with this guy Noah?"

"Excuse me?"

"I asked you where you plan to go."

"I heard what you said, why do you want to know?"

"Well, how did you meet this guy? How do you know he's a good guy? Has Pyper met him yet? How serious is this?"

I'm taken back by his questions. "Not that it is any of your business, but he is a good guy, I've been out with him before. I…well, I like him. And no, Pyper has not met him yet, not that it matters."

He just stares into my eyes for a moment and I wonder what he's thinking. Before I can ask him he asks, "May I please have your phone?"

I wasn't expecting that, "My phone? What for?"

"I'd like to put my phone number in it so you can contact me when you know your schedule."

"Oh, okay. Sure." I start digging around in my purse looking for my phone; I find it and swipe the screen so I can enter my password before handing it over to Luke. Once I give it to him, he starts tapping at the screen, adding his information to my contacts. I hear a chiming sound after a moment and Luke pulls his phone out of his pocket and glances at the screen.

"There. Now I have your number too."

I smile at him when he hands my phone back to me and notice that he is not smiling at me in return. He has a serious look on his face.

"Olivia, I'm not going to let you run and hide from me. I had a great time with you today, and I know you had a good time too. I finally found you again, and I'm not about to let you go." He reaches his hand towards my face again and brushes his thumb across my cheekbone. He leans in and places a kiss on my forehead, his lips lingering there for a moment, making my breath catch and my eyes flutter close.

Luke pulls away from me and when I open my eyes I see that damn sexy smirk is back on his face again. "Goodbye, Olivia. I'll be seeing you soon." Then he gives me one of his dazzling full blown smiles, his dimple winks at me and makes me want to place my lips there. Damn these hormones.

I clear my throat, "Goodbye. Thank you again for today."

He winks at me, "You're welcome," and starts walking back to the elevator.

I stand and stare at him for a moment, not able to move my body. He looks back at me, "Go on in so I know you are safely inside."

Fumbling with my key again, I roll my eyes because really, what could happen? I have been going into buildings at my own leisure without needing oversight for quite some time, but I indulge him and push my key the rest of the way into the lock, turn it, and open the door. As I start to close it behind me, I hear his soft chuckle.

I'm barely through the door before Pyper pounces on me. "How did it go? Are you okay? Did you have a good time? What did you do? Did you guys kiss? Tell me *everything!*"

"Geesh, calm down and give me a minute to breathe here!"

"Not a chance, I didn't think you would ever get back. I've been dying here. I need information!"

"Okay, okay, let me just go change really quick."

Pyper sighs at me like I'm the biggest pain in the ass. She's so impatient when she's about to get good gossip. "Oh, alright."

I head to my room, walk in, throw my purse on the bed, and head to my dresser. I decide to go for comfortable and take out some yoga pants and my favorite Madonna t-shirt, then go to my bathroom to change. Once I'm feeling relaxed, I decide to pull my hair to the top of my head into a messy bun and wash my face really quick. When I'm done, I head out to the living room, where I know Pyper will be impatiently waiting for me.

"Oh my gosh, it is about time! I about died from the waiting in here!"

Rolling my eyes I tell her, "Don't be so dramatic, Pyper."

She sighs and holds a wine glass out to me. "Here is a glass of wine, just get on with it already!"

"It isn't even five o'clock yet."

"Who cares? Now spill!"

I take the glass of wine from Pyper and share the details of my day, leaving nothing out. Everything from what I ate and what Luke ate, to the hostess that couldn't keep her eyes off of him, to his hand at my back, the question and answer game, the movie, and then his insistence that he drop me off at the door.

Pyper is leaning in towards me as I'm talking, as if she'll miss a word if she doesn't. "Are you going to see him again?"

"Yes, I think so." I know I don't sound convinced and Pyper hears it in my voice.

"Why didn't that sound more believable? Do you want to see him again?"

"I do want to see him again, that's the problem."

Pyper scrunches her nose at me, "I don't understand."

I take a sip of my wine, then try to explain, "I want to see him so much that it scares me. But then, when we were standing at the door and he was holding my face in his hands, I started to lose myself in him and he stared back at me for a moment and then that confident *I've got her right where I want her* look appeared on his face, and suddenly I didn't want to make things so easy for him. Plus, I don't want to jump into a relationship with him. I may know the truth now, but that doesn't mean we should pick up right where we left off. It also doesn't mean that things are going to be easy."

Pyper frowns, "What do you mean?"

"Well, first of all, I don't want to seem pathetic because I'm instantly available when he wants me to be. I know I don't have a demanding social life or anything, but making it seem like I would do anything, say anything and drop anything to be with him tomorrow is not a vulnerability I want to show him."

"Well that is understandable. Playing a little hard to get isn't going to kill him."

"I know, you're right, but it's more than that. I may have agreed to give him another chance and to let him into my life again – as a friend - but my life doesn't revolve around him. First, I've been there done that with Deacon. No thanks. I'm not making the same mistake twice. Second, while being with Luke feels…"

I struggle to find the words and Pyper knowing me well, just waits patiently for me to continue.

"Being with him feels kind of like coming home. It's hard to put into words but I instinctively remember him. Not only do I remember things about him, like the soda he drinks, or how he sucks his bottom lip in when he's thinking hard about something, but my heart remembers him too. I feel content with him. I mean, sure, I'm also nervous as hell but at the same time, I feel like I can be myself with him more than anyone."

"Well that's good. Some spouses can spend years together and never feel that way. I think that's amazing. And the fact that you remember him and feel that familiarity in your heart makes sense. You share a history together. It makes sense that in some ways, you would instinctively gravitate to what you know. Even resort to what was habitual behaviors and well-known territory."

I pull my legs up under me on the couch, "Yes, you're right. I wish I could just go with it and not read into every thought and every emotion, just let my instincts take over, but I can't do that. Luke apologized, and I do forgive him, but I haven't forgotten that the lie he told his mom spun my world out of control and sent me careening straight into the clutches of Deacon. I mean sure, I know intellectually that I am the only one that can be held responsible for my choices because they were mine and mine alone, but there is a part of me that feels like Luke is at least, in part responsible, and I haven't forgiven him for that. I know that's crazy."

Pyper reaches out and grabs hold of my hand, offering me comfort, "No, that is not crazy. It makes complete sense."

"I just think it is going to take time for me to get over that. Seeing him and hanging out like we did today I know will help, but again, I know it may be a pride thing, but I don't want to appear too eager. He really wants to see me tomorrow or the following day, but I told him I have a date with Noah this week and so I can't give him a firm day or time right now. At least not until my plans with Noah are solidified."

Pyper's eyes widen and then she bursts out into laughter, "You told him you were going out with Noah?"

Pyper's reaction makes me laugh too. "Yes. I can't believe it. He was looking at me with cocky confidence in his eyes and a smile on his lips that makes me want to simultaneously smack and jump him. It made me pissed that I felt that way, so I used words to wipe it off instead. I admit it; I wanted to knock him down a few pegs."

Pyper is holding her stomach because she is laughing so hard, "That's just freaking perfect. It's good for him."

"Well, by the time he left, it didn't seem to faze him much. He winked at me," I frown remembering the look on his face, "Cocky bastard. Sexy cocky bastard, though. Damn him."

Pyper giggles at me. "So do you and Noah really have something going on this week?"

"Yeah, we do. We talked about meeting at Water Tower Place to grab a bite to eat and shop around a bit. I just need to check my email to see what day and time he chose. I told him I'm pretty flexible, and to just let me know when it works for him."

"Well, why don't you go check your messages while I make myself a quick salad for dinner. Are you hungry?"

I groan and pat my still full belly, "No, I had a ton of popcorn at the theatre."

"Okay, be right back and then we can talk about our date this week."

"Our date?"

Pyper tosses a grin at me over her shoulder as she heads to the kitchen, "Yep. It's called retail therapy."

The next afternoon Pyper and I are at the mall shopping. My date with Noah is in a couple of days and I decided a new top is in order. I'm in the dressing room at Nordstrom trying a few that caught my attention - and hopefully that of others - and showing Pyper after I try each one on to get her opinion.

I walk out wearing the one I think is a keeper, Pyper looks up, "I love that! " I turn around so she can see the back and she whistles, "Ohhh sexy!"

"I feel sexy. It's a perfect combination of sweet and sexy." I look down at the pink and white vertical stripe top and admire how the front has a slight oval neckline while the mirror reveals that the back forms a deep v. At the bottom of the v, there's a bow that has ruffles cascading down from underneath it. It makes me grin; even feel happy. "This will look great with a pair of jeans and maybe my pink wedges."

"You have to get it. If you don't, I will."

As I walk back into the dressing room to change back into my own top, I hear my phone chime. Pulling it out of my bag, it says I have a new text message from "Luke – Love of my Life." Way to be subtle. Opening it, I read his message, "I woke up smiling today because I finally found you again." My face warms at his message and my heart jerks in my chest. I decide not to respond and instead let it sink in. I lock the screen and start to tuck it back into my purse, when it chimes again. Luke has sent me another message. I realize I'm smiling before I even read it. "I love your smile." My grin becomes wider.

Heading to the register to purchase the top, I smile at all of the bags in Pyper's hands. She's an expert shopper. She's bought a new Coach bag and sunglasses, as well as a gorgeous new blouse from White House Black Market. Once I have my new top in hand, Pyper grabs my elbow and starts pulling me out of the store. "Let's go to Victoria's Secret next!"

"Okay." As we approach the store, I admire the gorgeous lingerie in the windows and am quickly transported somewhere, watching the expression on Luke's face as he longingly gapes at me, wearing the lacey black bra and panty set. Thinking of his gorgeous eyes smoldering at the sight of me makes me excited.

"Come on, Olivia. Now that you are back in the dating world, it is time to buy some beautiful things for your imminent sexy times."

I laugh, "Imminent huh? Thank God. I could use some sexy times. It sure as hell has been a while. I contemplated sitting on the dryer the other day just for a change. How sad is that?"

Pyper laughs and I giggle; and we begin browsing through the lacey bras and barely there panties and lingerie. I start looking for my size in a sexy black number, and before I realize it, my hands are full of items for me to try on. I look at Pyper and see she has several items too.

"I'm going to go try these on, Pyper."

Pyper starts heading to the dressing room area with me, "Me too."

Upon reaching the dressing room, we pause as the attendant who has her back to us, helps unlock a room for another customer. Pyper looks at a display next to us while we wait. When the attendant turns toward us, I gasp. Pyper comes quickly to my side, no doubt having heard my gasp. It's Kim Anderson, a girl from high school that I never liked.

"Well, well, well…look what the cat dragged in. Olivia Summerton, it sure has been a long time since I've seen you." I don't bother to correct her when she calls me by my maiden name.

"Kim Anderson. Wow. Long time no see. How are you?"

"Actually, it is Kim Chadwick now."

I'm not surprised to hear her last name. She dated Kyle Chadwick throughout high school. Good for them, I guess. Kim is a classic over-achiever. She was very competitive in high school, always trying to one-up me in everything. I tried out for cheerleading, so did she. I would raise my hand to ask a question, so would she. Anything Luke and I did, she and Kyle would try to do better. I remember when Luke and I were voted "Class Couple" she threw a tantrum because she thought they should have been chosen. She was my constant, annoying shadow in school. Pyper being ever protective of me, could never stand her.

"Good for you, Kim. I assume that means you and Kyle got married?" Pyper makes an attempt to be nice, and I'm impressed.

Kim sneers at Pyper, not returning the sentiment. "Yes. We did."

Kim does not like Pyper on account of this one little kiss Pyper and Kyle shared our senior year. It was during a time when Kim and Kyle were off in their on-again, off-again relationship, and Pyper and Kyle had both had a little too much to drink at a party. The punch was spiked, fun was had, kisses were exchanged. It wouldn't have been a big deal – because Pyper wasn't interested in dating Kyle or anything – except Kim's friends that witnessed it reported the sordid details to Kim.

I decide to change the subject before Pyper takes the opportunity to tell Kim off for her attitude, "We'd each like a dressing room please."

Stomping over to the dressing rooms, Kim unlocks two doors side by side. "Here. So what ever happened to you Olivia? Last I heard, Luke finally dumped you and you took off."

Pyper takes a step towards Kim and I grab her hand, stopping her. "I moved to Boston to attend college and now I'm a journalist for a living. I'm doing great. Thanks for asking."

I pull Pyper towards our dressing rooms, we exchange a look, and go in to try on our respective potential purchases. Inside, I stand there for a moment, allowing myself to make the facial expressions and say – if even to myself – some of what I really was thinking. I dread having run into someone from my past, and my stomach burns from Kim's comment, but I decide that I handled it just fine. I remove my clothes and try one of the bras I've brought in with me. Standing there, checking out the sheer lavender bra in the mirror, I notice a sign stating that the dressing rooms are monitored. I can't help but cringe. I sure hope I'm not on candid camera, giving someone a show.

"Excuse me, ma'am," I hear someone from another dressing room call out.

"Yes?" I hear Kim reply.

"Could you please come in here? None of these tit contraptions are fitting me and I think I need someone to come in here and measure me so I know what the hell size I should be wearing."

My mouth drops open and I hear Pyper snort in the dressing room next to me. I slap my hand over my mouth to try not to let a giggle escape.

It's quiet for a moment, but then I hear Kim answer, "Sure." A door creaks open and then, "Oh my gosh, ma'am! You do not have to be completely naked in order for me to take your measurements! Please put your bottoms on and let me know when you've done so."

I hear the door creak again - Kim must have stepped out. I slap my other hand over my mouth because I'm going to lose it. I hear a thump in the room next to mine and wonder what Pyper is doing to try to contain her giggles as well.

I hurriedly try on the rest of the sets I brought in the room with me. I really like the black lacey set I was first attracted to when we walked into the store and also an electric blue set that is sheer and leaves nothing to the imagination. I also select a fuchsia set that is very simple, but elegant.

When I walk out of the dressing room, Pyper has a few sets in her hands and while she has a straight face, I can see the merriment jumping around in her eyes. We walk to the registers together. Once we are waiting in line, we look at each other and burst into laughter.

I wipe off the tears on my cheeks, "Oh man, Kim is still such a bitch. Serves her right."

"So true." Pyper wipes off her eyes too, "That just made my freaking week."

Still giggling a little as we walk out of the store, I happen to look over to my right. I'm not sure what makes me look that way, but I catch sight of someone and instantly freeze. I feel the blood drain from my face and fear trickle down my back. Walking away from me, going the other way, is Deacon. What the hell is he doing here? Without a word to Pyper, I take off after him.

"Olivia? Olivia? Where are you going?"

I don't even think - I just move. Just as I am about to catch up to him, a huge group of people walk right towards me and I have to weave in and out of them. One of them accidentally bumps into me and knocks my packages out of my hand.

"Shit!" I bend over to start picking them up.

"I'm so sorry!" the boy that made me drop them is mortified and helps me retrieve the packages from the ground. I thank him and stand up, ready to continue on my warpath, but I come to a complete stop. I've lost sight of him. I stand there and look around, turning in every direction. Nothing.

"Olivia!"

I turn towards the sound of Pyper's call and see her running after me, all her bags swinging in her arms, hair flying behind her as she tries to make her way towards me. I didn't realize I had gotten that far from her.

"What the hell was that about?"

"I'm so sorry, but I swear I saw Deacon. Here. At the mall."

"Deacon?"

"Yes. We walked out of Victoria's Secret and for some reason I looked to my right, and I saw him walking in the other direction. At least, I think I saw him."

"Olivia, that doesn't even make sense. Why would Deacon be in Chicago?"

"I don't know, Pyper, you tell me." I don't mean to sound so irritated, but the thought of Deacon here makes fear stir in my belly and chest.

"Olivia, you need to stop thinking about him. Let him go. He's a dick and he doesn't deserve anymore of your thoughts or energy. Keep him in the past where he belongs, and just keep moving forward."

"Yeah, you're right. I just swear..." I sigh. "I guess I'm seeing things. I'm sorry I took off like that."

"It's okay. I was just scared. I didn't know what was happening."

"I'm sorry again. Any other stores you want to hit?"

Pyper smiles, "No, I think I've done enough damage."

I return her smile, "Me too. What do you say we get some take out and head on home?"

"Sounds fabulous."

I shake my head a bit trying to brush off what just happened. Deacon here in Chicago is a horrifying thought. I can't help but feel uneasy as Pyper and I make our way to the exit, heading toward my car.

Chapter Fourteen

"Fashion Tip: A scarf is the perfect accessory! Whether worn with a jacket when it is cold outside or with your favorite t-shirt, you can dress up an outfit in the time it takes to make a knot! Don't be afraid to play with color. Keep one stashed in your purse for a quick transformation!"

I'm standing in front of the mirror, getting ready for my date with Noah. Instead of going to Water Tower Place like he had originally suggested, we decided to go ice skating. I love ice skating. I'm wearing the cute top Pyper and I bought when we went shopping together, with jeans as planned, but instead of wedges, I have on a cute pair of gray knee high boots. Even though the rink is indoors, it will still be cold. I've pulled my hair back into a ponytail so that it stays out of my way while I'm skating, and my makeup is light.

Pyper walks into my room and checks me out, I see her behind me in the mirror, "You look great! Getting ready to go on your date with Noah?"

"Yes. My hair looks okay pulled back right? I just want it out of my way."

"Absolutely, you look amazing. Where are you guys going again?"

"Well, our plans changed. We were going to go to Water Tower Place, but instead we are going ice skating."

"Oh that will be fun! Are you guys headed to an indoor rink or outdoor?"

"Indoor, the one on California Avenue. I know it will still be cold though."

I head to my closet so I can grab my gray, wool pea coat that will match my suede boots and a soft cream and gray scarf. I check the pockets of my coat to see if I have a pair of gloves inside. When I can't find them in a drawer, they are almost always in the pockets of my coats. Sure enough, I pull out a pair of teal ones. They will do.

I walk out of my closet and see Pyper is still standing there, "What's up? Everything okay?"

"Oh yeah. Everything is fine. I just wanted to make sure I knew where you were going. You know our rule."

"Yep. Always tell the other where we will be and who we are with...just in case."

"Exactly. That way I can tell the cops if you turn up missing."

I scrunch my nose at her, "That is such a pleasant thought."

"I know, but a necessary one."

"You're right."

She smiles and says, "Don't worry, I'll pick a great picture for the milk carton."

"Ha. Ha. Very funny."

"Is Noah picking you up here?"

"No, we are meeting at the rink."

I put my jacket on, wrap my scarf around my neck and I'm ready. I take out only the necessities I will need from my purse and place them in my pockets so I don't have to worry about dealing with a purse while I'm trying to skate. I pull out my license, debit card, the little bit of cash I have, and a lip gloss. I head to my bedside table where my phone is charging, pull it off the plug and put it in my back jeans pocket.

Turning towards Pyper I tell her, "Well, that's everything. I'm ready. What are you doing today, love?"

"Oh, my friend Kate called and she and I are going to meet for lunch. I haven't seen her in a while."

I know that is code for she probably hasn't seen her much since I moved in. "Pyper, just because I'm here doesn't mean you can't go out with your other friends. I know I've have had moments of craziness, but I'm doing fine. Really. It is okay to leave me, you know."

"I know that, silly, but you are my girl. It had been forever since we hung out, and for a while I just wanted it to be you and me in our own little bubble, reconnecting and hanging out. I needed it just as much as you did. So no worries about that, okay?"

"Alright then, just making sure you are clear on how I feel about that. I hope you have a great time with Kate!"

"Thanks, Livvie, you too! I'm sure your date will be…one to remember."

I look at her and shrug my shoulders. "I'm not sure what you mean by that, but I'm sure it will be a good time. I really enjoyed my last date with Noah!"

I make my way to the front door with Pyper trailing me. Grabbing my car keys out of the bowl we keep on the table by the front door, I'm set. "See ya later."

Pyper walks to the door and grabs it to close after I head out. "See ya!"

While waiting for the elevator to reach my floor, I feel my butt start to vibrate and it startles me. I pull my phone out of my back pocket and check the screen, number unknown. I push talk at the same time the elevator reaches my floor. "Hello?"

I walk into the elevator, press the button to the parking garage and the doors close. I don't hear anyone on the other end of the line.

"Hello? Anyone there?"

No one replies and there is static on the line.

"Hello?" I say one more time.

No one there. The elevator opens to the parking garage and I press the end button on my phone as I walk to my car. I'm sure whoever it was couldn't hear me because I was in the elevator and they will call back.

When I arrive at the skating rink, I see Noah almost immediately standing there, watching people as they enter and obviously looking for me. He sees me, smiles and walks toward me. Tall and lean, with dirty blonde hair and blue eyes, he is definitely easy on the eyes.

He reaches me and gives me a hug, "Olivia hi, you made it."

"Hi, yes I made it! I hope you weren't waiting long."

"No, not at all! I would have gotten your skates for you but I'm not sure what size you need so I decided to wait until you arrived."

"Oh! No worries!"

We make our way over to the counter so we can pay for entry into the rink and get our skates. There is a young girl behind the counter who looks like she would rather be anywhere but here. She looks up as we approach, "Hi, what size skates please?"

Noah looks at me, "An eight please."

"I will remember that for next time," he promises. "I will take a size 11 please."

The girl hands us our skates and tells us our fee for admission. Noah doesn't hesitate, whipping out his card and paying for us both. Once he signs the receipt, we head toward a bench and start taking our shoes off and replacing them with ice skates. We stand, walk over to the cubbies, place our shoes in the same one and unsteadily make our way to the rink. I should have thought about how walking in skates in front of a date is awkward. I feel like I look like a complete dork. The good thing is, he is doing the same thing so we look like dorks together, I guess.

When we reach the ice, Noah looks to me in question, "So I know you told me you've ice skated plenty of times, but do we need to take it slow or will you be fine? I don't want to get you hurt or anything."

Instead of replying, I take his hand in mine and step onto the ice. We effortlessly make our way around the rink, holding hands and smiling. It may have been a while since I last ice skated but it is always something I've done well.

"Well that answers that question! You are good at this!"

I laugh, "It has been a while but it's like riding a bike."

He laughs in return, "Yes it is. I know you told me on our first date that you moved back to Chicago a few months ago now. Did you live here long when you were here before?"

"I was born here, actually. My mom is a nurse and my dad a doctor. They met at Northwestern Hospital in the emergency room."

"In the emergency room?" Noah asks, smiling at me, "Sounds like that could be an interesting story."

"Well, I think it's a great story. They met literally over the butt of a patient in the emergency room." I giggle, making Noah laugh too. "My mom assisted my dad with the removal of a pencil from, you guessed it, someone's butt. Apparently, the patient didn't see the pencil sticking out of the cushion in the back of their chair and they sat right on it. I guess the damn thing entered the body like a knife."

The thought makes me shudder, "I like to tease them about it. Their eyes met and they started to fall for one another over someone's butt. Come on! It doesn't get better than that! I like to tell them they are ass-tastic and ass-mazing. They just roll their eyes at me now, but I pretty much think I'm hilarious."

Noah laughs, "You are pretty funny. You have a great sense of humor."

I look at Noah and smile. "Thanks. My parents are still going strong. They are still happy in their marriage, retired a couple of years ago and moved to Arizona. They are only in their early fifties and they are loving life. I'm really proud of them. They still volunteer at a hospital there from time to time, I think they'll continue to do so as long as they can. They love their work and helping others."

"They sound really great. Do you see them often?"

"Oh, a few times a year or more. I love heading out to visit them in the winter when the weather there is phenomenal."

"Oh, I bet. A great time to get away from the snow."

"Exactly. What about you? Do you see your parents often?"

"Well it's just my Mom. My dad left when my brother and I were little. My mom raised us as a single mother. I have no idea where my dad is, and honestly if he had come back then or even now, I have no interest in having a relationship with him."

"Oh wow, I'm so sorry."

"Don't be. It's all water under the bridge now. My mom is an amazing woman that did the best she could with what she had. I know things were hard, but my brother and I didn't know it because she sacrificed her own needs constantly to be able to provide for us. Now that I'm older I, of course, know what she gave up for us, but back then I had no idea."

"She sounds amazing."

"She really is. She lives with me, so I see her every day."

"Oh? She lives with you?"

"Yes. I'm very over protective of her and really don't want her living on her own, so I insisted she stay with me. My place is more than adequate for the two of us."

"Wow. Does that make privacy difficult?"

"Not really. She stays out of my business, for the most part. Frankly, my brother and I spoil her. We feel like it is our turn to take care of her, after she took care of us alone for so long. She tries to brush us off and doesn't want it, but we don't listen."

Okay so I'm trying not to judge. It's no big deal that he still lives with his mom right? "Does your brother live with you too?"

"Oh no. He's married with a family of his own, so it's just my mommy and me."

Oh Lord. Mommy? I swear I can hear Pyper in my head screaming RED FLAG! RED FLAG! I say the only thing I can, "I bet she secretly loves her sons doting on her!"

"I'm sure you're right."

"How many children does your brother and his wife have?"

"Two. One girl and one boy so far. Renee and Jack."

"So far?"

"Yes, definitely. I have no doubt those two will have a brood."

"I'm jealous. I would love to have a niece or nephew to spoil. That is one of the bad things about being an only child."

"Yes, I love those kids. I spoil them rotten."

"I love it. I bet they love their Uncle Noah."

I look at Noah and he looks at me. He really is nice looking. Maybe I can see past the whole living with his mother thing. We hold eye contact for a while, which is great until someone cuts me off and I almost fall. Noah grabs me around the waist, preventing me from face planting in the ice, and we come to a stop on the side of the rink.

"Thanks. Sorry about that."

"No problem." He is looking at me and I'm looking back at him, he starts moving his face close to mine and I'm sure he's going to kiss me, but then…SLAM! Next thing I know, I'm in a heap on the ice.

It takes me a minute to realize what's happened. I was knocked over on accident when Noah was bumped from behind and accidentally knocked into me.

"Olivia, are you okay?"

"I'm fine. That just surprised me, are you okay? What happened?"

"Some jackass bumped into me."

I hear a voice say, "Sorry about that."

I freeze and my head snaps over in the direction of the voice I would recognize anywhere.

Luke is standing there, in skates, staring at me with one eyebrow raised. I stare back at him, my mouth open in surprise.

"Hello, Olivia, I'm so sorry about that. I'm not sure what happened." The fact that he says this with a smile on his face and a mischievous look in his eyes tells me that he knows exactly what happened. He totally did it on purpose to prevent Noah from kissing me!

Luke is here! While I'm on a date with someone else!

Noah looks from Luke to me and back again. "You two know each other?"

"No." I say at the same time Luke says, "Yes."

I look at him and he is looking back at me clearly amused.

Damn him.

Chapter Fifteen

"Fashion tip: People, the fanny pack went out of style way back in the 80s. I don't care if it's a Louis Vuitton; it's still a fanny pack. If you wear one, you not only look like you are on vacation in 1982, but it shows you have no idea what's in fashion – whether you consider yourself style savvy or not. So get rid of it and replace it with a small fashionable purse with a long strap. You'll thank me later. Trust me."

Poor Noah looks so confused, I don't blame him. I turn to him, trying to put my back to Luke, but Luke just moves over so that he is standing next to me, "Noah, yes, I do know Luke, he's an old *friend* of mine." I turn towards Luke, "What are you doing here, Luke? I didn't know you liked to ice skate." I look past him to see if he's alone, "Are you here with a friend or something?"

"Oh, I'm here with someone that is much more than a *friend*." He stares into my eyes as he speaks and I feel myself blush, his intimation clear.

Noah does not have a clue what is transpiring between Luke and I, "That's great. You and your girlfriend should join Olivia and me if you'd like."

With a devilish look on his face, Luke doesn't look away from me, "Oh no, that's okay. She won't be staying here much longer."

I raise my eyebrows at him in challenge. "Well that's too bad *you* are leaving then. It was nice to see you, Luke. Have a good rest of your day. Bye." I totally give him the brush off, he needs to go.

I see humor dancing in his eyes when he looks at me, and in that moment I realize he has no intention of leaving me here with Noah at all. Shit. How the hell am I going to handle this? "Noah, I scraped my hand when I fell, would you mind getting me a band-aid from the desk attendant?"

Noah looks from Luke to me and back again in confusion, unsure about leaving me with Luke. I smile at him reassuringly, "I would really appreciate it. It's bleeding a little." That's all it takes to spring Noah into action and I'm grateful, because I just want a minute alone with Luke.

"Oh no. Of course. I'll go get one right now. I'll be right back." Noah takes off, skating toward the exit to go to the attendant station, which I can see has a ridiculously long line, so I turn my attention towards Luke.

I can't help the scowl that appears on my face. "What are you doing here?"

Before answering, he comes toward me and takes my hand in his, looking it over. He brushes his finger against the scrape on my finger and before I can say a word he has my finger in his mouth, sucking on the scrape. I suck in a quiet breath. Oh. My. God. He did not just do that. I start to flush. Everywhere. Pulling my finger out of his mouth, he looks at it again. "Are you okay? Does it hurt?"

"Uh…" How the hell does he expect me to be able to speak after that? When I can find my voice I answer, "It's uh fine, it's just a scrape."

He brushes his fingers over it and tingles shoot all the way up my arm. It's unnerving what his touch can do to me. I've never felt this with anyone else before. Ever. I gently pull my hand from his and ask again, "What are you doing here?"

"Well, what does it look like I'm doing here? I'm skating." I can hear the amusement in his voice.

I narrow my eyes at him, "By yourself?"

"Well sure, why not?"

"Did you follow me here?"

He scoffs, "No, of course I didn't follow you here."

I look into his eyes, trying to tell if he's being dishonest with me, "Need I remind you that we promised each other no lies?"

"No reminder necessary, angel, because I'm not lying to you. I did not need to follow you to know you would be here."

"If you didn't follow me here, then how then did you know I would be here?" Before he can even reply, I answer my own question. There's only one other person who knew where I would be this afternoon. "I should have known she was up to something with all those questions. Milk carton prevention my ass."

"Mmm, what about your fine ass?" Luke asks huskily.

I make a gesture blowing his question off, too angry at Pyper, "Damn that red-headed bitch. She's in so much trouble! Why would she do this?"

"Oh, don't be too mad at Pyper. I can be pretty persuasive when I want something, and make no mistake. I want something."

I feel a thrill shoot through me, but I ignore it, "What did you do? Bribe her with chocolate?"

"Close, next best thing."

"Shoes? You bought her shoes?! Oh my god! Does she have no shame?"

He just laughs, not the least bit ashamed at his actions, "I didn't buy her shoes, just waved a gift card around in front of her face. She's easy to bribe."

"She is so dead. I can't believe a pair of freaking shoes mean more to her than my privacy. She is going to rue the day!" I even laugh at myself with that comment because I catch myself shaking my fist too. I might be irritated with Pyper, but I admit I find her amusing too. I know she didn't have any ill intentions with revealing my date plans to Luke.

His laughter fading, a stern look appears on Luke's face and I see his jaw tighten before he asks, "So, is that Noah?"

I glance over to where Noah is still standing in line at the counter, waiting for the attendant to finish with the people in

156

front of him. I'm pretty sure I sense a bit of sarcasm in Luke's voice at that question. "Yes, that is Noah."

"And you actually like that guy?" he asks sounding indignant.

"Yes, I do." Except for the whole living–with-his-mommy thing, but Luke doesn't need to know that.

He scoffs at my comment. "Oh, please."

"What do you mean 'oh please'? He's a really nice guy. He's also sweet, goal oriented, good looking," Luke's eyes narrow at that but I continue, "and we have a lot in common."

Luke scoffs at my comments and if I wasn't so annoyed with him, I would laugh at his obvious jealousy, "Oh give me a break, angel, he's boring as hell and you know it."

My turn for indignant, "What?! He's not boring! He's anything but boring!" I tell him adamantly.

Luke and I are still standing on the side of the rink and I'm surprised no one has yelled at us to get off the ice since we're just standing here. Normally they don't want you in the way of other skaters. I look over to the rink attendant and see the teenager in charge blatantly checking out some girl's ass as she skates by his chair, while he talks to yet another female standing next to his chair. Obviously, he is focused on other things right now.

"Oh please, you know you would be having much more fun if you were out on a date with me right now."

I'm dumbfounded; I don't even know what to say. We are supposed to be starting over as friends, but he just said date. Friends don't date. Forget the fact that my hearing him say the word date made a thrill run through my body. Before I can even acknowledge his assumption, Noah has skated back to my side.

"Finally! I'm sorry it took so long. The people in front of me took forever," he hands me the band-aid, "here you go."

I smile at Noah, and when I reach out to take it from him he takes my hand in his instead and looks over my scrape just as Luke had done before him. Bringing it to his mouth he kisses it, "I'm sorry you got hurt, I tried to take the brunt of the impact."

"It's okay," I murmur, purposefully keeping my eyes from Luke's face.

Noah proceeds to unwrap the band-aid and while he's focused on that, I stupidly chance a glance over at Luke and see his lips pressed together in aggravation.

"There," Noah says, "all better."

I shiver a little because the fact that Luke is jealous right now is totally turning me on. I know it's wrong. Here Noah is being so sweet, but my whole body is tuned in to Luke and his reaction. It's distracting. Noah misunderstands my shiver and wraps his arm around me, "Are you cold?"

I open my mouth to answer but Luke, who's frowning even deeper now while scowling at Noah's arm around me, snaps, "Of course she's cold, she fell on the freezing ice. The least you could have done was bring her a cup of hot chocolate to warm her up."

Noah's mouth falls open and his face flushes slightly, "I'm so sorry, Olivia, he's right. I didn't even think about getting you a warm drink. I guess because we aren't allowed to bring food or drink out here on the ice, and I was so consumed with getting you a band-aid, it didn't occur to me."

"That wouldn't have stopped me." Luke says looking rather proud of himself. The ass.

"It's okay, Noah. I don't need a drink, I'm fine. Really."

"No, it isn't fine. I'll go get you something right now."

Poor Noah turns and makes his way back to the exit to get me something to drink. I turn toward Luke and shoot daggers at him with my eyes, making my anger evident. He's being an ass and it is pissing me off, "What the hell? That was mean."

"Oh, please. He should at least know how to treat a woman."

"How do you know he doesn't? Maybe he treats me just fine, Luke. Maybe he treats me *just right*." I don't know what is wrong with me. Noah and I haven't even kissed, but I'm making an innuendo all the same, making Luke think that we've done more, much more, than that because I know it will make him mad.

Luke's eyes harden and he grabs hold of my arm. He tows me towards the rink's exit.

"What are you doing?"

Ignoring me, he doesn't let go of my arm and instead, hauls me toward the back of the rink where there is a hallway that's hidden off to the side, leading to an employee area, restrooms and a back door. Walking isn't easy in these blasted ice skates. I'm glad Luke has a firm grip or I would have fallen already.

"Luke, what are you doing?" I ask again, "Where are we going? I'm on a date, you can't do this."

He doesn't listen; he just keeps on walking, not paying any attention to what I'm saying, dragging me along behind him. He isn't hurting me, he's just being insistent. He heads out the back door and before I know it, we are standing outside.

"What the hell are you doing?" I ask him yet again. I'm standing on the pavement trying to stay upright without letting my ankles twist in my skates, waiting for him to answer me.

He responds to my question by pressing me against the brick wall as soon as the door closes behind us, and before I can even take a second to process what he's about to do, he crushes his lips against mine. He traces his tongue along the seam of my lips, begging for entry. When he moves closer to me, pressing his body flush against mine, a moan escapes my mouth, making my lips part. Taking full advantage, Luke explores my mouth with his tongue, stroking my mouth over and over. He's not being gentle. One of his hands is at my waist, fingers digging into my side, while the other is fisted in my hair, tugging my head back, giving him easier access to my mouth. His hips repeatedly push into mine, making a slow heat start in my belly and head south.

When he pulls away from me after a moment, both of us are breathing hard. I couldn't hide the fact that his kiss affected me even if I wanted to. It's obvious, in the need that is no doubt in my eyes, the flush that's bleeding into my cheeks, and the embarrassing groan of unhappiness I made when he pulled away from me.

"Leave with me, Olivia. Right now."

"What?" I feel disoriented. For a moment, I completely forgot where I was, but the fog is lifting and complete mortification is taking its place. "Oh my god, I can't leave with you. I'm here on a date! I have to get back in there. He's probably wondering where I am."

"No. Don't go back in there. Come with me. We can go anywhere and do whatever you want. Just don't go back inside."

"Luke, you know me better than that. I'm not going to just leave him here. That is not me at all and I won't do it."

"Angel, don't make me beg."

"I'm not standing him up like that. He doesn't deserve that."

"Fine, but I'm not going anywhere. I'm going to be here the whole time."

I groan. "What the hell is this? You and I are supposed to be trying our relationship again as friends. This...this..." I gesture between the two of us at a loss for words. "Whatever just happened between us is not a good idea."

"You're wrong, Olivia. What happened between us couldn't be more right. The last time I felt that complete, was the last time I held you in my arms. You own me in every way. Do not even try to tell me that you didn't feel something too. No lies remember?"

I look down at the ground, take a deep breath, feel my heart pounding double time in my chest, and think to myself, *no lies*. "I'm not trying to tell you that I didn't feel something too," I say softly, "but that doesn't change the fact that this should not have happened. We are working on being friends. Plus, standing up Noah is not okay and I won't do it."

"Okay fine, I get the standing up Noah thing, but angel, in case that kiss didn't make it clear, hear me now. You and I will never be able to be just friends. We are the other half of each other's heart and soul. I cannot apologize enough for what happened between us. I will never forgive myself for losing you, and I will spend every day the rest of my life working on making it up to you, if that is what it takes. But the fact is, I don't give a flying fuck if Noah or anyone else is freaking prince charming in the flesh, I want you back and I will fight anyone and do anything I have to in order to make that happen. The worst day of my life was the day you ran away from me, and I have spent countless moments since wondering about you, missing you, comparing every woman I've ever been with to the fucking ghost of you. It is not an option for me to let you get away again or to just be your friend."

Luke steps towards me again. He places his hand under my chin and stares into my eyes for a few beats before he says, "Olivia, listen closely please. I want to make sure you hear me. I. Want. You. Back," he says very slowly, "Make no mistake of what my intentions are here. I will *not* lose you again. I wouldn't survive it a second time. Maybe that makes me an asshole…I don't know, but what I'm trying to be is a guy that will do anything because he desperately wants his girl back."

I'm speechless and his declaration leaves me breathless. He's being forceful, but yet he's so different from Deacon in every way. He isn't hurting me, ridiculing me, yelling at me. His fire comes from passion, not anger. I realize that I want him to fight for me too. I desperately want the other half of me back too, but what I can't admit to him is that this feeling scares me. I don't trust him yet; I don't trust myself anymore either.

I nod my head so that he knows I heard everything he said to me, but I don't reply because aside from not being sure I can find my voice, I also need time to digest his words. He removes his hand from my chin, brushes the back of his fingers on my cheek and then backs away from me just a little. "Go ahead and do what you have to do and date who you have to date. Get it out of your system if that's what you need to do, but know that I'm not going to make it easy for you. I'm going to be there every time you turn around, reminding you of what we had and what we will have again. When you finally admit to yourself that you want that too, I will be here with open arms. I'm going to be waiting for you to come back to me."

My mind is reeling. He takes another step back from me, his eyes full of heat locked on mine.

My heart wants me to stay but the fear takes over and it takes everything in me to turn away from him and go back inside looking for Noah.

Chapter Sixteen

"Fashion tip: Just as you would never get between a fashionista and a sale at Bloomies, the same should be said for women that appreciate fashion via the perfect pair of shoes or handbag. Even jewelry plays an important role in fashion and some can obsess over the perfect pair of earrings or a necklace. That being said, never try to get between a woman and her fashion obsession no matter what it is. Just don't do it, you won't win."

To say that things are awkward when I return to the ice skating rink is an understatement. Fortunately, it isn't because Noah is walking around like mad trying to find out where I had gone off to. I lucked out because he waited in line long enough that he had just begun to notice I was missing by the time I returned. When I walk up to him he says, "There you are!" I tell him I had been in the restroom. I didn't promise him not to lie. He doesn't question me, which makes me feel guilty, but I'm admittedly relieved at the same time.

The rest of our date is uneventful; Luke keeps his word and doesn't leave. When Noah and I return to the rink to skate some more and talk, Luke sits at a table drinking coffee, eyes on me while I go round and round the rink. I finally decide I've had enough, I'm cold and tired, not to mention uncomfortable with Luke sitting and staring at me. Noah and I make our way to remove our skates and return them to the person manning the skate rental counter. While there, I notice Luke out of the corner of my eye, leaning against a counter, still watching me. How Noah doesn't notice him, I have no idea.

I don't think it can get more awkward, but I'm wrong. While walking me to my car, Noah turns to me so we can say our goodbyes. He leans in for a hug, "Thanks for a great date. I really enjoy spending time with you."

Noah is so tall that when I hug him I place my head on his chest turning it to the side. Within my line of sight, I see Luke leaning against his car watching me. He has his hands crossed over his chest and a scowl on his face.

Noah pulls away from me and leans in. I feel dread enter my belly. If I thought a hug was uncomfortable, a kiss is going to make me throw up knowing Luke is watching. I feel my eyes widen just before Noah places a brief kiss on my lips, then he pulls back and looks at me questioningly. I know he would like more but I have a horrifying vision of Mr. Peeping Tom stalking over here and ripping Noah's lips from mine should I give in. The truth is, I pull away from Noah and smile because I feel nothing for him. He's a nice guy and damn fine looking, but there's no chemistry.

I try my best to forget about the man watching us from the back of the parking lot, "I had a nice time with you too."

"I would really like to see you again. I will give you a call this week and maybe we can go out again?" he seems shy when he asks me, and I am angry with myself a second later when I realize that before answering, I subtlety looked over at Luke.

Feeling unsure about seeing him again I don't make any promises, "I will talk to you later." I may have said that rather loudly hoping my voice would carry a bit.

"Okay, great. I will see you later, I told my Mom I would be home in time for dinner."

I swear I hear a laugh carry on the wind. "Okay, bye, Noah."

"Bye, Olivia."

I watch him walk away for a moment, then glance again in Luke's direction and see he hasn't moved. I sigh and since I was standing on the passenger side of my car, I walk around the front to the driver's side, pressing the unlock button on my remote.

When I reach for the handle to open my car door, I see a pink rose pushed through the handle of the door waiting for me. An automatic smile comes to my face and I put the rose to my nose, smelling its sweetness.

Attached to the stem is a note.

"I always want to give you a reason to smile."

I smile wider, I can't help it, my mouth has a mind of its own. I look over at Luke in question and he's staring at me. When our eyes connect he smiles back at me, giving me a small nod of his head and a sexy wink. I look away, get in my car, buckle my seatbelt, turn the key in the ignition, and begin making my way back to my condo with a smile on my face the whole way.

Once I arrive home, I throw my keys in the bowl on the table by the door and prepare to give Pyper a hard time about the fact she divulged the location of my date to Luke. Instead the condo is quiet and still; Pyper isn't home.

My first stop is the kitchen. I reach up to the cupboard above the refrigerator and grab a bud vase, filling it with water and place my rose inside. Taking it with me to my bedroom, I place it on my bedside table and decide a bubble bath is in order. I'm wound up pretty tight and feel emotionally exhausted from the day, but I'm also still feeling chilled from the cold radiating off the ice at the rink. A bath will be a perfect way to warm up, relax, and let my mind wander and reflect on everything Luke said to me. I'm still reeling from his speech and I just want a nice and quiet space to let my mind relive his words. I want to hear them again in my mind and think about how they make me feel.

In my bathroom, I turn on the water in the large garden tub so it begins to warm up then take everything out of my pockets and set it all on the counter. After removing my clothes, I take a moment to examine myself in the mirror trying to see what it is about me that Luke still wants. My eyes look better every day, the dark circles continuing to fade. Instead of the frown that's been glued to my face for nearly a year – my lips are slightly turning up once again. My breasts are full, but high, my tummy flat and my thighs are a little fuller. I can't deny I've got some junk in my trunk, but I like said trunk. I definitely have curves, which can make clothes shopping difficult at times, but I would rather have them than look anorexic. I don't think my body is the only reason Luke is interested in me, but I have to admit, it isn't bad.

I turn away from the mirror and flip the lever under the faucet to close the drain, so the tub begins filling up. While I wait, I take my glass jar of lavender bath salts off the side of the tub and sprinkle some into the water. While the amazing smell of lavender begins permeating the bathroom, I quickly use the toilet, wash my hands and finally step in and ease myself down into the warm water. I sigh and lean against the tub, closing my eyes and reveling in the feel of the warm water against my skin, chasing away the chill.

I begin hearing Luke's words over and over in my mind like a mantra.

"Do what you need to do, date whomever you have to, but I won't make it easy."

"…desperately wants his girl back."

"I'm waiting for you to come back to me."

I am so tempted, so *very* tempted to call him and to give in. I want to run into his arms the next time I see him, but I know I can't. At least, not yet. He still has no idea what I've been through, no idea that in a small way, I feel like he's responsible for my marriage to Deacon. I can tell that my anger at him has simmered some, and I think that it will diminish completely, but it isn't completely extinguished yet. I know what Luke said about not making this easy for me, but am I ready to commit to him yet? Do I want to start dating him and just him? Not yet, but I know I could get there. I can't help but hope that perhaps together we can chase the last of my anger away. But for now, I still need a bit more time.

I grab my shampoo and start scrubbing my hair and massaging my scalp. I love baths and scalp massages. Luke flashes across my mind again and as I grab the shower head and start rinsing the shampoo from my hair, I remember another time when Luke was giving me a scalp massage in the tub and the activity that preceded the massage. Our first time having sex.

I remember how rebellious Luke and I felt. Each of us lying to our parents, telling them we were staying at a friend's house was not something we were proud of. Remembering that fact instills a bit of guilt and remorse, even after all of these years, when I picture my parents' trusting faces as I lied to them. At the time, assuaging the guilt was easy while lying in the arms of the boy I loved. Luke had put cash aside he was earning by helping out at his dad's office on the weekends. He surprised me with what was definitely a pricey room at a nice hotel in the city. We had spent considerable time talking about what we wanted for the first time we chose to make love and how we wanted the night to be memorable, not just some quick episode in the back of a car or trying to do it at our homes while worrying when our parents might return. I smile, remembering the effort Luke went through, making sure it was a night I would never forget. Closing my eyes, I see the vast number of candles placed around the room, pink flower petals strewn everywhere and even sparkling cider chilling bedside. I thought it was so sweet; he had checked in ahead of time in order to surprise me when I walked into the room. We were both very nervous and while the night was everything I had hoped for, sex for the first time was not like it is portrayed in the movies. We weren't flawless or perfectly choreographed. I remember the pain at entry, how awkward we were, and the fact I didn't climax. Yet, all of that was overshadowed by the fact that I was with Luke, the boy I loved. I knew we would figure it all out with time and even giggled to myself when I knew practice would make perfect.

My tummy tingles, even now when I remember how nervous, yet excited we were when we saw each other naked for the first time. We had let our hands roam somewhat freely before, had touched and felt one another. But that night was the first time we were completely naked together. He was beautiful, lean and muscular from playing football, and I was sure - absolutely perfect. I remember my eyes widening when I looked down and saw how large he was and it made me nervous. I felt

166

embarrassed when his eyes roamed my body, stopping on my breasts and proceeding south, but when his eyes came back to meet mine and I saw the pure need and want in them, combined with his whispered, "I love you so much, Olivia," I believed I would always be safe in his arms. He made me feel beautiful in every way. I was desperate to be with him and show him how much I loved him too.

My memories include the two of us afterwards, lying together, catching our breath, and reveling in what we had just done. Luke suggested we take a bath together, my other surprise was that he obtained a room with a large jet tub that had more than enough room for two. I readily agreed, not so much because I briefly acknowledged that the warm water would feel great in all the places where I felt sore, but the idea of taking a bath with Luke was intriguing, to say the least. Once in the tub, Luke and I washed each other's hair. He massaged my scalp while I groaned in pleasure. What started out as playfully washing of one another resulted in us groaning in pleasure in other ways, as we started exploring each other's bodies again. That time we seemed to be more relaxed and I got a taste of how amazing sex could be.

Our first time was beautiful, albeit awkward, but perfect in the pureness of our love for one another.

I can't help but compare the Luke from seven years ago to the Luke I see now. He's still got the same swagger when he walks, although now it's with more confidence. His hand and facial gestures when he talks are so familiar that it makes me smile to myself; he still smirks and grins exactly the same. His body, though, is now all man, and I can't deny I want to see what he has hidden under his clothes. Desperately. The lean and slightly muscular boy has now filled out, with broad shoulders and defined biceps that his t-shirts do little to hide. When he pressed me against the wall and kissed me today, I had a crazed need to rip his shirt off so I can stop trying to picture what's underneath and instead, explore the concealed secrets, progressing from theory to fact. I'm betting on strong pectoral muscles and well-defined abs. I wonder if his hip bones form a sexy v that points south. Just thinking about seeing Luke in all his glory makes me ache between my legs. I want him. My body remembers his and I want to explore it with my hands, lips and tongue again.

I feel like I'm on fire, the warm water only adding to the intensity of sensations. I remove the shower head, turn it back on and turn it to a stronger power and start moving it slowly over my body. I tickle my breasts, roam over my stomach and then reach the spot that's begging for release between my legs.

Once I get out of the bath, I put my hair up in a towel and wrap a robe around my body. As I'm tying the belt, I hear what sounds like something clatter to the floor. Pyper must be home; I wonder what she knocked over.

I walk out of my bedroom and head down the hall toward the kitchen, where I believe I heard the noise, but when I reach it, I don't see Pyper anywhere. However, the bowl that holds my keys on the table by the condo door is on the floor with my keys a few inches away. Huh. I wonder how that happened. It must have been teetering on the edge of the table when I got home earlier and I just threw my keys in it, not even noticing. I don't know what the thing is made of, but it must be strong because it isn't broken. I'm bending down to pick it up, when little miss traitor herself walks through the front door.

She freezes for a moment when she sees me and before she smoothes it away, I see the guilty look cross over her face, "Hi."

"Hello." I place the bowl back on the table.

I set the bowl back in its place on the table, placing my keys inside, and turn to Pyper, hands on hips and give her my most annoyed look. She smiles nervously at me. "So, how was your date with Noah?"

"Really? You are going to pretend like you don't already know how interesting my date was with Noah?"

That's all it takes and the flood gate that is Pyper's mouth opens, "Look, I'm really sorry, but the man offered me a deal I couldn't refuse."

"Is that right?" I ask, raising my eyebrows at her, "and what exactly was this deal you couldn't refuse? What was too good to pass up that it was worth what happened to me today when Luke just happened to show up at the same place I was with Noah? Hmmm?"

168

A guilty look crosses her face again, "Well um, he showed up here this morning looking for you. He said he was going to see if he could take you out. When I told him you weren't here, he persistently asked me where you were. So much so that he really started to get on my nerves, and I was willing to do anything to get him to go away."

"Uh-huh, sure. I'm on to you, Pyper Elizabeth Lexington. Don't even try to fool me because I know you! All he had to do was wave around a puny little gift card using the temptation of your favorite shoes or handbag and you were a goner. Forget the fact that you can go to the store any time you want and buy whatever you want. I totally don't get you, Pyper."

"Don't try to get me or middle name me, Olivia Grace Brooks. I'm a slave to fashion. I'm so sorry! It's an addiction. When he offered me... "

"Nope," I hold up a hand to stop her, "I changed my mind, I don't even want to know. That way, whenever you wear whatever it is you buy with your traitor money, I won't have the desire to take it and burn it, since it obviously means more to you than loyalty to your best friend!"

Okay, at this point, I am kind of egging it on and giving her a hard time, but she deserves it! Sisters before misters and all that.

"Okay fine, I won't tell you, but you're missing out! They are going to be totally awesome," she gushes.

I sigh at her enthusiasm, "Just promise me you won't do it again."

"Was it that bad? I'm really sorry," but I notice the soft curve at the edges of her mouth she is trying to keep hidden.

"Are you? Are you really? Why don't I believe you?"

"Maybe because you know if he comes knocking again with another pair of..."

"NO!" I yell at her.

Pyper laughs, "Fine. What I meant to say is that if he comes bribing me again and it's as good as the first offer, then I can't make any promises. Slave to fashion, remember?"

"You're impossible."

"That's why you love me."

Chapter Seventeen

"Fashion tip: Just say no to scrunchies! Bows and ribbons tied in your hair are also in the same category as scrunchies, unless you are a seventh grade cheerleader or younger. There is nothing a scrunchie can do that an elastic hair band can't. There are also these other great inventions called bobby pins, headbands, clips, even hair scarves or a hat. Use them."

'm feeling lazy and I don't want to get out of bed. I dreamt all night long about random things that I can't even recall now, but when they awoke me during the night, they seemed significant. I'm comfortable all snuggled in my bed and I am seriously considering just staying here all day, but I need to write an article for *Trend* magazine, do a blog post, and get ready for a date that I'm kind of regretting having agreed to.

On the table next to my bed, my phone chimes; I pick it up and notice that the time is nine o'clock. I slept in and it feels great, but I could seriously go back to sleep for a while. Looking at my screen I see I have a text from Luke already.

"Good Morning, beautiful, are you awake yet?'

I tap the screen to reply, "Morning. I just woke up."

His reply is quick, "What? No good before morning? It isn't a good morning?''

I smile, "Ugh. What's good about it? Please refer to the previous message."

"I like knowing some things never change. You're still not a morning person, huh?"

My reply, "Mornings suck," is straight, honest and to-the-point.

His reply of, "I left you something at your front door. Maybe you will have a good morning after all," makes me jump out of bed. Crap! I wonder if he is at the front door. I run to the bathroom to brush my teeth, and pull my hair up in a bun. I throw on a pair of somewhat threadbare sweat pants, but they will do, considering I was previously just wearing a t-shirt and panties. Plus, they are really comfy and I don't care if he thinks I look ridiculous. I didn't ask him to come over at the crack of dawn. Okay, so it is nine in the morning, but close enough!

I walk out of my bedroom, down the hall and start approaching the front door with trepidation. I'm being stealthy like a ninja because if he is on the other side of the door I don't want him to hear me. If he's standing there, I'm not sure I want to answer yet. Once I get to the door, I put my eye to the peephole and see the hallway, but nothing else. No one is standing right in front of the door at least.

My phone chiming again makes me jump, almost making me pee my pants. It's Luke again. "Did you get it yet?"

I look out the peephole one more time and still, there's nothing there. I guess if he has to ask me if I got "it" then hopefully that means he isn't hiding outside of my view from the peephole. I unlock the door and open it slowly. When it is at a small crack, I peek through. I see something on the ground in front of the door, so I open the door all the way to see what it is.

Two pink roses and a large cup of coffee from Starbucks are sitting there. Before reaching down to pick them up, I turn my head and look down one side of the hallway and then the other and it confirms no one is there. He must have just dropped the items off. I bend down and pick up the roses and I'm pleasantly surprised to feel the coffee is still warm when my hand wraps around it.

Walking back inside the condo and closing the door behind me, with the roses already at my nose, I go back to my bedroom. The other pink rose Luke left me in my car door is wilting a little bit, but I add the other two to the same vase, set my coffee and phone down, then pick up the vase and take it to the bathroom to fill it from the tap.

Sitting back in bed, I grab my coffee and take a sip - it's so good. I really love that he knows just how to make my coffee. It's sweet. I set it back down on the table and reach for my phone so I can return his text message.

I type out a reply, "You didn't have to do this, but I'm so glad you did. The coffee tastes fabulous and the roses smell wonderful. It is definitely verging on a good morning now."

He replies, "I know I didn't have to, but I woke up thinking about you and I wanted to. I'm taking care of my girl, whether she likes it or not. What is your answer?"

My heart warms at his words, they give me a thrill. Thinking about me and taking care of me? I like that. A lot. I'm not sure what he's referring to about wanting an answer though, "An answer for what?"

"Take a closer look at one of the roses I left you. Specifically the petals."

I scoot over on my bed so I can reach the vase and take it off the table. Staring down at the flowers, I notice a small piece of paper that is folded into the petals. I pull it out and open it up. In his tiny handwriting, Luke has scrawled a question, *"Have lunch with me?"*

Now, more than ever, I'm regretting the date I agreed to today. I would really love to go to lunch with Luke, but I can't just bail after agreeing to go. I admit, part of me may be playing a little bit hard to get, but the truth is that aside from Luke and Deacon, I've never really dated a whole lot of people. Before I jump back into…well whatever it would be with Luke, I want to experience this. I want to be sure.

Knowing I need to answer Luke's question, I start typing out a response, "Luke, I'm really sorry, I already have lunch plans. Rain check?"

While waiting for his reply, I drink more of my coffee, its warmth feels wonderful going down my throat, warming me from head to toe. It takes a few minutes for his reply to come, "Have dinner with me then."

172

Wow, he's persistent, I'll give him that. At this point, it may be easier to just call him but I kind of like texting back and forth, "Don't you have to work at your club tonight?"

"That's the nice thing about being the boss, you pay people to handle things for you."

I sigh. Good point. I'm not sure about going out tonight. I quickly start thinking about the pros and cons. First of all I'm not sure how long my date this afternoon is going to last, and I may be tired afterwards since we are meeting at the park for a little bit of exercise and sunshine. Who am I kidding? I'm just nervous about saying yes, so I don't. Yet.

"Let me think about it alright? I'm not sure how long my other plans may keep me tangled up today."

I smile when he replies with, "Cancel them."

I laugh out loud. That comment is so Luke. "I can't. Sorry."

"Well it was worth a shot. I will be eagerly awaiting your answer. Enjoy your coffee and the roses, angel." I picture his sultry voice saying "angel" and I get instant butterflies. I'm doomed. Fighting my feelings for him is next to impossible.

Setting my phone aside and picking up my coffee, I head to my desk so I can work on my articles.

I'm out of the shower, hair dry, minimal makeup on and standing in my closet in a sports bra and panties, when I hear Pyper knock on my door and open it, "Olivia?"

"In here," I call out from the depths of my closet. I'm sorting through my clothes and looking for my Juicy sweat suit to wear on my date today. I'm actually looking forward to going to the park. I was surprised when I checked my dating profile a few nights ago and saw I had a message from a man named Jason. We exchanged a few messages back and forth and he's made me laugh a few times. We have a lot of books and movies in common and he seems genuinely nice. I wasn't surprised when he asked to meet in person, since we seem to have hit it off.

173

Jason suggested we meet at a local park that he said he frequents for some laps around the trails, and I immediately agreed to the date location because I love the idea. The weather outside is cool, but not cold, and if nothing else, at least I will enjoy the scenery. The fact that it is in a public location too - just in case - is a bonus.

Pyper sticks her head in my closet, "Hi love! What are you up to?"

I finally see my pink suit and grab it off the hanger and head out of the closet. I smile at Pyper as she steps back, letting me out of the closet and I walk over to my bed. Throwing my clothes down, I turn around and head to my dresser, open a drawer and start digging through it looking for a t-shirt. "Hey!" I finally reply, "I didn't know you were home. I walked out of my room earlier to grab a delivery and didn't see you around."

"A delivery?" Pyper asks.

I shyly say, "Yes. Luke texted me first thing this morning telling me to check the front door."

A huge grin appears on Pyper's face, "What was at the door?"

I gesture to the table next to the bed, "Two pink roses and some coffee."

"Well, that was sweet. Wasn't that sweet?"

Raising my eyebrows at her I say, "Yes, it was very sweet of him. He asked me to go to lunch, but I can't. I, um, have a date. I'm getting ready for it right now." I tell her tentatively. I haven't forgotten what happened the last time she knew I was going out on a date. I'm not about to fall into another trap by this crazy redhead.

Her smile fades. "You have a date? How did I not know this?"

"Yes, I do and I didn't tell you, that's why." I finally find just a plain v-neck white t-shirt to go with my sweat suit, and pull it out of my drawer, being careful that I don't unfold everything else on top of it as I pull. Shutting the drawer, I turn to Pyper and pull the shirt over my head while waiting for her response.

"Are you seeing Noah again?"

"No, not Noah." Noah had called like he said he would and left me a message asking me out again. I haven't returned the call. Cowardly, I know, but I'm not looking forward to telling him I don't want to see him again.

I should have known only telling Pyper that much and nothing else wouldn't fly. Pushing her lower lip into a pout Pyper reminds me, "You have to tell me who you are seeing and where you are going. It's for your own safety remember? What if something happened to you, I would have no idea what to tell the police."

I roll my eyes at her, "You are being dramatic. I'm not going to disappear, nor am I going to fall for that again."

Her pout is gone and a look of irritation replaces it. "Olivia, I'm serious. If you don't tell me, I will just get into your dating profile myself and see what I can find out."

"You wouldn't dare. Besides, you don't know my password."

"Oh, you underestimate me." I scoff at her until she says, "Mr. Bunny05." I gasp and my mouth falls open.

"What the hell? How did you know that?"

"We've been friends forever, duh. Besides, you use that password for everything. It's the name of your first pet and the age you were when you got him. Give me some credit! I do know my best friend."

I know her too, but I'm not about to tell her that I have no clue what she uses for her passwords. Apparently I need to start paying closer attention. Turning back to my bed, I grab my pants and step into them, "Fine. His name is Jason Pine and we are meeting at a local park. That is all I'm saying, so don't even try asking me anything else."

"Well, that at least explains your choice of clothing."

"Hey! What's wrong with this outfit?" I ask her as I go back to my dresser so I can get a pair of socks.

"Nothing is wrong with it, you look great, nice ass in those pants. I just meant because it isn't what one would typically wear on a first date."

"Well, alright then. I was going to have to kung fu your ass. And for your information, I like the fact this is going to be a low-key date."

Pyper starts playing with the ends of her hair. I forgot my tennis shoes when I grabbed my clothes from the closet. Putting my jacket on that matches my pants, I go to my closet to get my shoes. Raising her voice so I can hear her in the closet, Pyper says, "Well, if you aren't going to tell me where you are meeting, at least tell me about this Jason Pine guy."

Grabbing my favorite pair of tennis shoes off the shelf in my closet, I walk back out and sit on the chest at the end of my bed and start putting them on. "He seems nice. I wouldn't mind getting to know him better, which is why I agreed to see him. It appears we have a lot in common and I've really enjoyed talking to him online. He asked me to meet him in person and I agreed. I was feeling lazy when I woke up and was regretting my plans, but I think it will be nice to meet him."

"Well, he sounds promising. What are you..."Pyper is interrupted mid-sentence by her phone beeping. She pulls it out of her pocket and looks at the screen. She hastily types something and puts it back in her pocket.

"Who was that?"

"Oh, just spa business, sorry about that. I was going to ask you what you are doing after your date?"

"I'm not sure. Luke asked me to have dinner with him tonight, but I'm on the fence."

"Why?"

Avoiding Pyper's eyes I reply, "I'm not sure how long my date will last, and I have an article to finish."

"Why else?"

"That's all."

"Do I have to play the best friend card again? I know you, so spill. Why else?"

Freaking best friend radar. "Okay, fine. Because my feelings for Luke make me feel nervous. Who am I kidding, even being around him makes me nervous. I know that he and I...well...we feel inevitable and that scares me so much." Pyper steps forward and takes my hand in support. "He hurt me, Pyper. I hate that he has managed to worm his way back into my heart again with a few interactions and pretty words. Part of me wants to run into his arms and never look back, but the other wants to run away again. I just don't want to make the same mistake again. I was wrong about him before. I was wrong about Deacon. I just don't trust myself or these stupid feelings."

"Olivia, I understand. I do. But there comes a time when you just have to have faith. Stop living by what if and stop letting your over-thinking mind talk you out of what your heart is telling you. Promise me that sometime soon you will take a moment to stop, be silent in your mind, and listen to your heart. Trust yourself and let your heart lead you to the place you want to go."

Her words make my eyes burn like I'm fighting back tears I didn't even know I needed to cry. I give her hand a tight squeeze, "I promise."

"Good! Now go and have fun on your date and stop spending time trying to anticipate what is going to happen next, that takes the thrill out of living. Expect the unexpected, Olivia."

I nod my head at her, but I can't help but think I should just buy her a damn Team Luke t-shirt.

Chapter Eighteen

"Fashion tip: Wearing clothes in several sizes too small DOES NOT make you look thinner. It makes you look like a big zit straining to pop. Also, pea green is not a good color. On anyone. Ever."

I pull into the parking lot that's right next to the entrance of Potterhill Park. I quickly find a parking spot facing the park entrance. Once I shift my car to park, I look around to see if anyone resembles Jason. His photo on 'Date Me' is somewhat grainy, but I'm positive that won't be a hindrance, I still have his word description to go by. I catch sight of a man standing alone inside the entrance to the park and he resembles Jason's picture. Average height and build, blonde hair, wearing a sweat suit like Jason told me he would be sporting, and while I can't see his eye color from this distance, it does appear to be him.

I turn the key in the ignition, shutting my car off, undo my seatbelt, and step out. I straighten my jacket that became twisted around my waist while I was driving, and put my car keys and cell phone in my jacket pocket after closing and locking my car door. I catch a glimpse of myself in the car window, and use it to quickly check my appearance. I run my tongue along my teeth, smooth my hair a bit and call it good. Not much more I can do at this point anyway.

I start making my way to the park entrance. There is a large gate to walk through to gain entrance. Use of the park is free, so

I'm not sure why there is a need for a gate, other than for looks. As I get closer, I push my sunglasses to the top of my head and make eye contact with the man standing alone. A smile appears on his lips. I smile in return and ask, "Jason?"

A look of confusion crosses his face and my eyebrows scrunch up in response. Maybe he didn't hear me. I take a few steps closer and try again, "Hi Jason, it's me, Olivia."

Now with a look in his eye that gives me the creeps he says, "Honey, I'm not Jason, but you say the word and I can be. I will be anyone you want me to be." I look at him feeling very confused, debating how to respond when I feel a tap on my shoulder.

Turning around, I meet the blue-eyed stare and smile of a man just like Jason's profile description, but that is where the similarities end. The man before me is bald, short, and must be at least fifty to sixty pounds heavier than he looks in his profile picture. He has something white in the corner of his mouth, toothpaste possibly? He appears to be a little out-of-breath and when I look down, I immediately look back to his face again. He is wearing a pea green sweat suit that looks at least two-to-three sizes too small. Some things you can't unsee and the image of his stomach and nuts being hugged in pea soup green is now embedded in my brain. He looks like a green pea on steroids. The color of his clothes, combined with my confusion makes me blink repeatedly at him as if that will make what I see in front of me change. I even cock my head to the side like a bird and stare.

"Hi, Olivia? I'm Jason," he says to me and I see a slight pink brushing his cheeks. It makes me feel like an ass.

Quickly trying to cover my surprise, I put my hand out to shake his. "Hi, Jason. It's nice to finally meet you in person." I can hear the gentleman I originally mistook for Jason trying to mask his chuckle behind me. I ignore him.

Jason smiles a little and says, "It's nice to finally meet you too, Olivia. Are you ready to walk the trails?"

"Absolutely. Let's go."

As we turn around, I see the not-Jason dude still smiling crudely. I give him a dirty look as we pass, walking side-by-side next to real Jason that doesn't look like the real Jason should. Oh man.

I would be lying if I didn't admit I am curious as to why he would put a profile picture up on 'Date Me' that looks absolutely nothing like him. I'm guessing the picture has to be *at least* a few years old and it isn't like I can bring it up in conversation. *So Jason, what's up with your profile picture being a complete false representation of what you really look like?* Um no. That's not going to happen. I would like to tell myself I'm not hung up on things such as looks, but I'm not going to lie because looks do matter in a sense. It's often the first thing you notice about someone and while I'm not so superficial that I can't appreciate Jason for his fun personality, you still have to have chemistry. I fear I'm not physically attracted to this man walking next to me, and it isn't just the sweat suit he's wearing, in a hideous color that makes me want to throw up either. Instead of reading too much into it right now, I decide to just see how the date goes.

As we walk, I can't help but admire the beautiful sights all around us. There are trees as far as the eye can see, in varying shades, starting the metamorphosis from summer to fall. The sunshine, while high in the sky, still manages to hit the trees just right because of their height, and makes them appear to glow. I feel like I'm in the middle of a gorgeous painting. It's breathtaking. "This park is really beautiful," I say by way of making conversation, "fall is my favorite time of year. I love how beautiful the trees are when the leaves start to change."

"Yes, I agree. It really is a beautiful time of year, although people think I'm pretty crazy because winter is actually my favorite time of year."

"Really?" I'm surprised. Usually Chicagoans endure the winters, we don't love them. "Sorry, but I would have to say crazy is right. How can you look forward to winter? You actually like the snow, bitter wind and freezing temperatures? Oh and the shoveling! I hate shoveling snow! Someday, I would love to be a snow bird. Maybe live here in the summer and somewhere warmer in the winter."

"I've loved winter since I was a child, I can't really explain it. I'm sure it has a lot to do with Christmas being my favorite holiday."

We are walking at a fairly brisk pace. I tend to start walking faster when I'm talking. "Oh, I love Christmas too. I love everything about the holiday. Trimming the tree, buying presents, wrapping gifts, I love it all. I still get just as excited Christmas morning as I did when I was a child. It's a great holiday."

I notice when Jason answers he's slightly out of breath. "Yes...those are things...I love too. I think my favorite...part though is all the..." he trails off, trying to catch his breath and I realize I'd better slow my pace. I didn't realize how fast I was walking. Once he seems more in control he says, "Christmas lights. I like to see...everyone's houses lit up."

"I like to see the lights too. Do you have a favorite decoration you put in your yard or a certain color of lights you always decorate with? A favorite tradition?" I glance at him out of the corner of my eye to make sure he is okay. I notice he has a bit of sweat above his brow.

"I have..." before he can finish his response, we pass a couple on the sidewalk and they recognize Jason.

"Jason Pine, is that you? Long time no see, buddy! How are ya?"

I stop and look to Jason and see he's stopped too, although he looks like he wanted to just pretend he hadn't heard them and keep going. "Hello, Denise," nodding his head he says, "Aidan."

"Jason, man," Aidan says, "We haven't seen you out here in a really long time! Great to see you here exercising again."

"Err, thanks. I'll see you guys later." After that comment, Jason walks away. I flash Denise and Aidan a small smile, shrug in apology, then hurry after Jason, wondering what that was all about.

"Friends of yours?"

"Sort of. There are a lot of regulars that come to the park and I know quite a few of them from when I used to come here more frequently."

"Used to?" I can't help it, I'm curious.

"Yes, I used to come here more often, but the last year or so I haven't come around as often."

"Oh, well that happens to all of us. Things come up and work can keep us busy."

He nods, but doesn't comment, and we continue walking in a somewhat awkward silence. The trail starts curving to the right and a steep incline is just ahead. I start evening my steps, preparing for the workout my calves and thighs are about to receive.

About half way through, I start hearing Jason huffing, and each exhalation sounds like a slight wheeze. I look over at him and feel my eyes widen in surprise. Jason is pumping his arms like they will help him move faster, his mouth is open as he is gasping in and out, seeming to struggle for each breath, and sweat is pouring down his face. The front of his jacket is unzipped to the middle of his chest and his white t-shirt underneath is soaked through.

"Jason, are you okay? Do you need to take a break?"

"Urg."

Umm.

"Jason, maybe you should nod your head yes or no?"

Before he can answer, we begin to get closer to a woman coming from the opposite direction. I can see on her face that she recognizes Jason before she opens her mouth to utter a word. Closer now, she says, "Jason! It's so great to see you out here again!"

"Blarg," is what I hear come out of Jason's mouth. Okay, obviously this is too much for him. He can't even speak coherent words, let alone sentences. Why would he think this would be an ideal place for a date? I'm so confused by his choice.

We finally make it to the top of the incline and are about to go under a part of the path that looks like a tunnel due to the side by side trees along either side of the walkway. There are a few benches along the side, so again, I decide to ask Jason if he would like to take a minute to catch his breath.

"Why don't we take a seat and relax for a few moments. My feet and calves are a little sore after that incline." Really, I'm okay and could keep going, but he is clearly not fine.

Panting, his eyes turn towards me, his mouth now in a grim line. In lieu of answering me, his head bobs up and down in a quick nod.

We sit down side by side on the bench and Jason tries to get control of his breathing. He leans over, elbows on his knees and keeps huffing and puffing. I wonder if I should rub circles on his back in a soothing motion, but decide that is more personal than I'm willing to get with someone I barely know. After several minutes, Jason's breathing is under control. He takes a final deep breath, sits up and turns to me smiling. "I hope you are having a nice time."

Is he serious? We've barely spoken, and I'm worried that I'm going to end up having to call nine-one-one because he has a heart attack. Oh my gosh, if that happened, that's it. I am done with this dating crap. At this point, I just want to get this date over with. I want to go home.

I don't respond to his comment and instead say, "Are you ready to keep going? I think if we head through this tunnel and to the right it will just end up being a large circle leading us back to the parking lot." There, that was subtle right?

"You are correct, that is the way to go."

We each stand up and start making our way along the path once again. Jason seems to be more in control, so I'm hoping reinitiating conversation is safe. "Do you have any hobbies that you enjoy?" I'm really not sure what else to say. Conversation that was easy on the phone before feels more awkward today.

Before he can answer, I almost stop walking in shock. I'm looking straight ahead anxious to reach the destination of the parking lot, when I see someone that looks just like Luke. What the hell would he be doing here? I have to be seeing things. The man is still quite a ways away, but the closer we get, I have no doubt that is Luke headed this way. I would recognize that swagger anywhere.

I grab my sunglasses from the top of my head and put them on my face. A giggle escapes me because I realize I had hoped in doing this, it would somehow hide me. They aren't invisibility sunglasses unfortunately. Dammit.

Luke is just about upon us now, and I can see a tell-tale smile on his face. He was here looking for me. Damn Pyper. I don't know how she managed this but, I just know she's somehow responsible. Again.

"Olivia! Fancy meeting you here."

Oh that grin. It simultaneously infuriates me and turns me on. "Luke," I spit through my gritted teeth, "what are you doing here?"

"Well it's a beautiful day, and I thought coming to the park would be a great way to enjoy the beautiful weather, plus this park has a great view."

Of course, he is looking me up and down as he says that and when his eyes reach mine once again they are a combination of mischievous and smoldering. He looks between Jason and me expectantly. Sighing I say, "Jason, I'd like you to meet Luke," yep his eyes are definitely amused, "Luke, this is Jason."

Luke reaches out his hand to shake Jason's. "Nice to meet you man."

"You too."

"You guys mind if I walk with you?" asks Luke.

"Yes," I say at the same time Jason says, "No."

Completely ignoring me, Luke turns and starts heading back in the direction he just came from walking along side me. "So, what were you two talking about?" Luke asks.

Well, isn't this comfortable I think to myself, "I was just asking Jason if he had any hobbies he enjoys."

"Oh, cool," says Luke, "what do you like to do, Jason?"

"Well, remember a few years back when beanie pets were really popular?"

"Yeah, sure, I remember," I reply. "Those little stuffed toy animal things right?"

His laugh sounds somewhat mocking, "Oh Olivia, they are much more than just stuffed animals. When I was about five-years-old they were released by a toy company called Kidlets. The original beanie friends were Skippy the Frog, Porkers the Pig, Whiskers the Cat, Moo the Cow, Crabby the Crab, Hoppers the Rabbit, Rainbow the Fish, Pokey the Porcupine, Bananas the Monkey, and Henrietta the Hippo. The toy company stopped producing the product in 1998, but the demand became so high they decided to initiate a comeback with new and different pets for the line, never again reproducing the first nine. So far, I've managed to track down six of the nine original beanie pets. I have made it my mission to find the other three."

Oh. My. God.

This cannot be happening.

I hear Luke smother a laugh behind his hand. I feel a flush begin in my cheeks at the fact Luke is witnessing pea soup's revelation. Jason is looking at me expectantly, "Oh, wow. Well that is an um, different hobby you have there Jason. Are they worth a lot of money?"

"Not yet, but I fully expect they will be. They are already worth a few dollars more than purchase price. I expect this to go up. I have them all in glass cases, displayed on a shelf in my house, keeping them in pristine condition for when they are ready to re-sell. Maybe I can show you some time."

I hear Luke laugh again - the ass. Jason seems to be completely oblivious and I pretty much want the ground to swallow me up, but I'm also smiling just a bit too. I look at Luke out of the corner of my eye and see that he is also looking at me. He starts to smile wider and I have to quickly look away before I start laughing out loud.

"Well, that's cool man. Good luck with your hobby. I hope you end up finding the other three bean guy things." Luke says.

"Beanie pets," Jason corrects, "Thanks. I'm sure I will, the key is patience and I have plenty."

I'm relieved when I see the parking lot just up ahead and I feel my shoulders relax a little, knowing that this crazy date is almost over. Not wanting to delay the inevitable, I say, "Well, Jason, it was nice to meet you. As Luke said, good luck with your beanie friends and it has been nice getting to know you."

"Thanks, Olivia. Would you like to go get some dinner or something?"

"Uhhh…." Before I can even think about how I am going to back out graciously, I'm saved by Luke.

"Oh Olivia, I was hoping to steal you for a bit, I would love to get your feedback on some design changes for the club."

"Oh, okay. Sure, Luke. Sorry Jason, but thanks for the offer."

"Okay. Well, I will talk to you later. Bye, Olivia." He proceeds to give me an awkward hug, made even more uncomfortable by the fact he is still drenched in sweat. I pat him gently on the back and discreetly wipe my hand on my pant leg. "Bye."

I watch as Jason walks to his car, and then turn to Luke eyebrows raised, "Just out enjoying the weather, huh?"

"Look, angel, I told you I wasn't going to make this easy, and I meant it. I didn't want you to get so caught up in your date with this Jason guy that you forgot about me, but I see now that I needn't have worried about that."

"Well aren't you arrogant! Maybe I really liked Jason."

Luke is smart and chooses not to laugh hysterically at that comment. "I'm not arrogant, I just know you, and I know that guy is not the kind of guy you are attracted to."

"Oh, really? Then what kind of guy am I attracted to?"

In answer, Luke slowly walks towards me, making me back up. When my back comes into contact with the side of my car, he takes advantage of the fact that I can't go anywhere and I feel the curve of his body pushing against mine. He leans in until his lips are just a breath away from mine, "Me." Oh holy hell. "It's okay to admit it, Livvie. I know you are attracted to me, even if you are trying to tell yourself you aren't."

He leans in and instead of kissing me, he turns his head to the side and starts trailing his nose along the side of my neck and I'm lost in him. I can't help but tilt my head to the side giving him easier access. Everything about him…his smell, his lips, his body, it's intoxicating. I want him.

I'm a complete goner. He lifts his face up from the side of my neck and makes eye contact with me. He begins moving his lips towards mine. My eyes look from his eyes to his mouth, back to his eyes, and then his mouth again. My lips part and I start moving my lips toward his like they are a magnet seeking its source. Why do I keep fighting this? I want him, I've missed him, and I never thought I would have this opportunity again, so what am I waiting for? I just need to give in, trust him and believe what he says; believe in second chances.

186

I'm startled from my thoughts when my phone rings. "Shit," Luke says, it scared him too, or maybe he's just mad that our almost kiss was interrupted. He steps away from me and I smile at him apologetically, taking my phone from my pocket. The screen shows 'Unknown Caller,' so I assume it's just going to be a hang up call again, but I answer it anyway.

"Hello?"

"Hello, princess."

Fear crawls up my spine. It's Deacon.

Chapter Nineteen

"Fashion tip: Only buy a bargain if you love it. Just because something is on sale for $29, doesn't mean it is a must have. Save your money for something you really want and will definitely wear. Immediate gratification is not all it's cracked up to be!"

My mouth falls open, I start breathing a little harder, and I freeze. Just the sound of his voice makes my skin crawl. I don't know if it is the separation that has given me clarity and a realistic look at the man that used to be my husband, or if it is the simple fact that I know a phone call from him isn't going to result in anything positive.

Luke, sensing my unease, lifts his eyebrows in curiosity and tilts his head to the side in concern.

"Olivia. Are you there?"

"I'm here," I whisper and let out a slight shudder at the sound of his voice.

"It's so good to hear your voice, princess."

I stay silent because I can't return the sentiment. I see Luke look off to the side, his brows are furrowed and I can tell he's wondering why I'm behaving differently – edgy, higher pitched, abbreviated speech, a slightly irritable tone. I can also tell he's wrestling with whether he should stay right where he is or walk away and give me privacy. I can see the indecision on his face.

"Where are you right now? What are you doing?"

Returning my attention to the man on the phone, I do my best to shake off the fear and start to get to the bottom of why Deacon would be calling me. "It's none of your business, Deacon," at his name Luke's head turns back to me and his eyes snap to my face.

"I was only trying to make conversation. I'm curious to know how you are and to see how your day is going. I want to know how all of your days have been since you left me," his voice sounds angry at that part, but I can tell he makes an effort to soften it and adds, "I miss you so much, princess," making it come off sounding so much more gentle.

I'm not buying it, "Don't call me that."

"Why? You know you're my princess. You always have been and you always will be."

"No, Deacon. I'm not your anything. Not anymore." Luke takes a step towards me and places a hand on my shoulder, still looking into my eyes. I'm thankful for his silent support and I draw strength from him, "What do you want?"

"I'm calling because it's time you quit this."

"Quit this? What are you talking about?" I should just hang up the phone, but I know if I do, he will just continue to call me over and over until I listen to him. I know how he operates and I'd rather just get this over with.

"It's time you stop trying to make this pathetic attempt at a life without me. I let you leave, Olivia. I gave you your space and now I'm done with this. Your little vacation is over. I'm not about to stand back and let you think you are going to move on without me. It is time you come home. Now."

I flinch. He's using the tone that usually makes me cringe in dread. It means he's not going to take no for an answer, and if I don't listen to him I'm going to regret it. His tone brings back the many times I've heard him speak to me this way before – bringing back memories of him in front of me with his fingers digging into my flesh, yelling into my face telling me what to do.

At my flinch, Luke comes even closer almost listening at my ear. I see the concern all over his face and he is not happy. "No. You can't control me anymore. You have no say in anything regarding my life. This is not some vacation. This is not me being difficult. This is me living my life, without you. How dare you call me and think you can tell me what to do? Hear me now, I am not yours."

His voice becomes so loud that I know without a doubt Luke can hear him. "Listen here, you bitch. You are mine. Do you hear me? You are MINE. It doesn't matter what some fucking piece of paper says, you belong to me. I fucking own you. Now get your ass back to Boston. Do you hear me? If you don't, you'll regret it."

I'm stunned speechless by his words and before I can even attempt to come up with a reply to his delusional command, Luke takes the phone from my hand. His whole body radiates anger, but his touch on my shoulder is still gentle. He practically yells into the phone, "Who the hell do you think you are? Don't you dare talk to her like that, you son of a bitch. You think you're some tough guy talking to a woman like that?"

That is sure to piss Deacon off right and proper. I can hear him yell, "Who the FUCK is this?"

"I'm the guy that's not going to let some asshole prick talk to my girl that way." Oh god, that's going to put Deacon over the edge, "I don't know what your problem is, but you had better leave Olivia alone, or *you* will regret it. I will personally make sure of it. If you call her again and continue to harass her, we will call the police."

Before Deacon can even attempt a response, Luke hangs up the phone and hands it back to me. I'm not mad he took control, I'm grateful, but I would be lying if I didn't say I'm scared too. I know Deacon, and that is not going to go over well. I have no doubt he will be calling me again. I shudder again, just thinking about it. Luke puts his arms around me and I let him, I need the comfort. Deacon's phone call has shaken me to the core. "Are you okay?" Luke asks.

He knows I'm not. I'm sure he can tell by my shaking. I'm shocked and angry, and I hate the fact that Luke is witnessing this nightmare. I don't know how to answer his question, so I just nod my head once.

Rubbing my back Luke, says quietly, "I think it's time you tell me about Deacon."

My eyes meet Luke's and I nod my head again in agreement.

Luke talks me into leaving my car at the park, telling me he will have someone take care of it – whatever that means - and drives me to his home. I am not surprised to find out Luke lives in the West Loop. A trendy neighborhood, full of spacious lofts, cozy cafes and popular nightspots; this screams Luke and reflects his personality.

When I walk in his loft, it's as impressive as I expected it would be. Immediately inside the door there is a small foyer. A large light fixture hangs directly above us and there is a closet to our left. A few feet in front of us, on the left side is a staircase leading to the loft above. Walking straight ahead, I enter a room that is a large square that makes up the space for the living room, dining room, and kitchen. On the right is Luke's living room area. He has a black leather couch that faces the wall and is flanked by black end tables, and also has a coffee table in front of the couch. Next to the couch there is also one oversized leather chair and ottoman. The wall has a large flat screen TV hanging from it. Below the TV is a mantle. I see a few pictures, but can't make them out from where I'm standing, and below the mantle is a gas fireplace.

Behind the couch, in the middle of the room is a large dining room table that is black wood. It is surrounded by six chairs and I'm surprised to see a large silver vase full of pink roses sitting in the center. Seeing the roses makes me smile. To the left of the room is the kitchen. Painted hunter green with cherry wood cabinets and black appliances, it also has a long counter acting as a breakfast bar, with three black wooden stools underneath. The center of the kitchen has an island with a bowl of fruit sitting atop it.

The first floor has wood floors throughout, so in front of the black leather couch is an attractive rug with a hunter green, black and beige design. He also has another matching rug under his kitchen table. It all looks very nice, and is the epitome of a bachelor pad. There are very few wall hangings and the place still feels somewhat sterile.

I walk to the doors leading out to his balcony. Stepping closer, I see that his view is beautiful - tall buildings and blue sky as far as the eye can see. He even has a wrought iron table and chair set out on his patio. A perfect place to eat a meal or drink a cup of coffee, weather permitting.

"This is home sweet home. I'm still working on making it homier, but it's comfortable."

"I think it's really nice. Your view is amazing. Even though it is a one-bedroom, I'm assuming?" Luke nods his head yes, "It is very spacious. You've done a great job decorating it so far and making great use of your space. I really like it but yes, it could use a few more homier touches as you said. It's very much a bachelor pad." I tease, smiling at him.

"Well, I hope to change that someday soon." He returns my smile, but there is no teasing in his tone. He's very serious and he's directing that thought right at me.

I feel my face flush with warmth at his insinuation. Still smiling, Luke grabs my hand and at the moment of contact, a thrill runs through me. How does he do that? Does it happen to him too? "Come on, why don't you sit on the couch. Take your shoes off, if you want to relax. Can I get you something to drink? We should order some take out or something too. You've got to be hungry, I know I am. There is a great Chinese delivery place close by, does that sound okay?"

"I would love a bottle of water, if you have one, and Chinese food sounds great."

"Okay, just a second." Luke disappears into his kitchen and I hear him open the refrigerator and a second later the beeping of a phone sounds.

I take the opportunity to look around the room a little and just as I begin to sit down, those framed pictures on his fireplace catch my attention again. I walk over to look at them, the curiosity too much to ignore. The first picture, sitting in a hunter green frame, is of Luke's parents. His dad is standing behind his mother and he has his arms wrapped around her waist. She's leaning against him and they are smiling into the camera. It's a lovely photo, they both look happy and I think the photo is a recent one. Luke's mother looks a little bit older than I remember, although she's aged extremely well. Her body looks frail and her face thin, but her blue eyes - so like Luke's - are shimmering in happiness. Luke's father is an older version of Luke. Very attractive, his stature emanates confidence and wealth.

The second picture is of Luke. Set in a black frame, Luke is looking back at me and is wearing a cap and gown, holding a diploma in his hands. His smile is so wide, his dimple is showing. My stomach clenches at the image. I should have been standing next to him. Seeing him standing there alone makes me sad. Things could have and should have been different. Did he think of me then? Had he wondered if I was having a graduation of my own around the same time? The thoughts are upsetting, and I feel a bit of panic set in. Why am I here? I should leave. I'm not ready to be here. I don't want to deal with these emotions.

Moving my eyes to the last picture, I gasp and pick up the heavy silver frame. Holding it in my hand in disbelief, I stare at the picture of Luke and I in caps and gowns at our high school graduation. My hair is even longer than it is now, and I'm smiling a big smile, but not at the person taking the picture. No. I'm smiling up at Luke. I remember that day and know I have nothing but pure love shining in my eyes as I look at him. Luke is looking at the camera. He has a big smile on his face too and his eyes are shining, displaying his joy. The look on our faces makes me ache and wish we could go back to that day. I long to once again feel the happiness I see reflected in my eyes. I'm tired of every emotion I feel lately being laced with pain and loss. We look so young – our lives just getting ready to begin.

After I left Luke, I boxed up all of my pictures with the two of us together and have never really thought of them again. I think my parents have them stored somewhere, because they wouldn't have thrown them out. I left them at my old house because I couldn't bear to burn them or throw them away. This picture feels like it was a lifetime ago.

I hear the floor creak behind me and I turn around, facing Luke. Looking at him with what I'm sure is pure disbelief on my face I whisper, "You still have this?"

Looking in my eyes, he replies, "I still have them all."

"But why? Why would you have this up on your mantle?"

"When I ran into you again at Maggiano's restaurant - when you didn't even know I was there – I became even more determined to find you. I knew you were here, I actually saw you, and my desire to talk to you and to be able to look into your eyes again, to explain…was overwhelming. I didn't think I would ever see you again, let alone that you would walk into my club one day. The next day I went to my parents' house. My old room is almost exactly like it was when I lived there, it's actually a little embarrassing to tell you the truth. I went to the top of my closet and pulled down the box I had stored there that held all of our pictures and gifts you had given me…just remembering. I came across that photo and I couldn't stop staring at it. I started to feel hope. I brought it here and placed it on the mantle as a reminder to me not to give up. I knew it wouldn't be easy, but when I look at that picture, and remember us, it comforts me and reminds me to be understanding and patient because in the end, it will be worth it. You're worth it, angel."

I shake my head in disbelief, "I don't know what to say."

"You don't have to say anything. You asked, and I just wanted to tell you the truth," he grins, "No lies."

"I still have the ring you gave me," I whisper to him, as though I'm revealing a deep dark secret.

That grin of his becomes magnificent and his dimple winks at me. I feel my heart leap in my chest and a feeling of warmth travels from the top of my head all the way down to my toes, completely enveloping me. I tingle in my chest, my belly and between my legs at his beauty. "You do?" he asks, surprised.

"Yes." My voice sounds gravelly from my emotions, "I was looking for a pair of earrings a while back and came across it. I could never bring myself to get rid of it. I've kept it in a box with my other jewelry all these years."

"I'm going to get you to wear that ring again someday." I look at the ground in response not, sure how to respond. "Here's your water, love."

I can feel my resolve start to melt a little at his endearment. There is a warm feeling in my heart that isn't going away. "Thank you."

"Why don't we sit down?" He gestures to his couch and the two of us take a seat and I twist the cap of my water off and take a few swallows. I didn't realize how thirsty I am. Luke places his hand on my knee, "Tell me about Deacon."

I take a deep breath and look him in the eye, "I'm not sure I even know where to start."

"Start at the beginning. I want to know it all. From the day you met him."

I nod my head and take a deep breath.

Chapter Twenty

"Fashion tip: Don't be afraid to add an element of surprise! Whether it is a large statement necklace with a white tee, a bright colored belt or bag to bring color to an outfit, or even a pair of bright red stilettos with your everyday black dress, go for it. A touch of contrast makes for a great look!"

I begin to think back to six years ago when Deacon and I met. "Sometimes I wish I'd never gone to the party where I met him. My roommate, Abigail, had begged me to go to a party off campus with her. She told me how much fun it would be and teased me for all my studying and told me I deserved a break. She was right, it felt like I had been studying non-stop the moment I arrived in Boston. Never taking a break or having fun." I look right at Luke, "I was determined to do everything I could to just throw myself into my schooling. I wanted to forget. I wanted to forget you. I wanted to try to forget my broken heart and move on the only way I knew how."

Luke squeezes his eyes closed for a moment at my words, but then opens them and nods his head at me to continue. I feel awful, I'm not trying to hurt him, but I'm not going to hold back either. If he wants to know, then he will be told everything.

I laugh a little at the memory of my roommate, "I remember Abigail whining and hopping from one foot to the other, waiting for me to agree with her. How could I say no?" I shrug. "I agreed and told her I would go with her, but if the party got too rowdy and out of control, then I wanted her to promise me we would leave. That kind of thing wasn't my scene. Not yet anyway."

Luke's eyes widen at my words because that doesn't sound like the girl he once knew. He's quiet, though, and just listens to me, looking at me intently.

"I don't even know if she heard me ask her to make that promise because the second I agreed to go with her, she started squealing and tearing through our closets, picking out clothes she deemed worthy of getting us 'some hot action'. I decided if I was going to go, I was going to do it up right and I threw myself into getting ready. More than anything, I just wanted to fit in."

I think back, remembering every detail of that night, even applying my makeup. Heavy eyes in lavender that made my green eyes pop, just enough blush to make my cheeks look flush and a nude lip completed the look. I flat ironed my hair stick straight and parted it in the middle. It curled at the ends nicely and I put way too much hair spray in it so it would keep its sleek look. I wore a short, sleeveless, studded black mini dress. The front of the dress had gold studs that went in a vertical line down the front on either side, another row which curved around the neckline, and two rows of studs that crisscrossed over the top of my breasts, meeting the vertical rows on each side, emphasizing my hourglass shape. My dress was short, but I knew it was downright modest compared to what other girls would be wearing. I had a gold cuff around my wrist, gold hoops in my ears, and high black stilettos on my feet. I was going to regret them later, I knew, but at the time, I didn't care.

Abigail looked great too, in a bright red mini that had short sleeves and dipped so low in the front that if her boobs were any bigger, it would've been indecent. Somehow, she completely pulled it off, the whole look came together with nude stilettos, simple diamond studs in her ears and natural makeup.

Snapping myself out of those memories, I continue. "When we finally arrived at the party, which took a little bit of time because everyone takes the T everywhere, we could feel the vibration from the music outside the house. People were milling around the front yard, and the house was lit up like a Christmas tree. I remember being surprised that they weren't worried about angry neighbors or policemen coming and making them turn the music down."

"We were giggling in anticipation as we entered the house and I admit, I was excited. It was my first college party and I just wanted to start having some fun. I was so tired of feeling sorry for myself, so tired of missing you, and feeling like nothing was making the thought of you disappear." Luke nods in understanding, pain filling his eyes, but he still doesn't speak. "The music was so loud when we walked in that I had to practically scream at Abigail just to be heard. Drinks were immediately thrust into our hands, and people right and left were greeting Abigail. It was blaringly obvious, to me at least, just how secluded I had kept myself because I didn't know anyone."

"Abigail pulled me onto the dance floor and I was all too eager. I started dancing and quickly lost myself to the music. A few beers, and a couple hours later I was feeling pretty damn relaxed and more comfortable with myself. I didn't even feel concerned that I had no clue where Abigail had gone off to. The last time I had seen her, she was practically getting molested on the dance floor by some frat boy, and I assumed she was making the most of that situation. Feeling warm, I decided to make my way outside to get some air. I strolled toward the back of the house, weaving in and out of bodies, and finally stepped outside."

I don't even see Luke in front of me anymore. I'm looking through him and I can see the party playing out before me, like a movie. I even see myself breathe in deeply and take a moment to look up at the sky. The moon was huge in the sky that night and the stars seemed to shine extra bright. I thought they were beautiful.

"I was standing there, just enjoying the feel of the cool air on my skin and the view, drinking a beer when some drunken idiot stumbled into me from behind so hard, he almost knocked me over and caused me to spill my beer. I said, 'Excuse you, asshole' to him and the guy turned to look at me. He looked incredibly mean. I could see anger in his eyes, his face was pinched, hands fisted and his eyes roamed over my body. When he finished getting his fill, he looked me in the eyes and sneered. He said, 'Hey baby, if you were words on a page, you'd be what they call fine print.'"

Luke's lips lift slightly at the ridiculous come on and I smile a little in return. "My mouth dropped open in surprise because I couldn't believe how lame this guy was and then…and then I just started laughing. I was laughing at him so hard I could barely breathe. He didn't like my laughing at him much. I don't know if he really thought that line would work for him, or what. He reached for me and tried to grab me in anger but before he could, a guy stepped in front of me, his back facing me and told Mr. Lame Pick Up Line Guy that he had had enough to drink and to walk away from me or he would make him."

"Mr. Lame Pick Up Guy – whom I found out was named Steve - walked away, and the guy that had been my hero turned to face me."

I stop talking for a second and take a drink of my water, remembering seeing Deacon for the first time. My breath had caught, and I thought his blue eyes were pretty. He was tall, with blond hair and a tan that seemed out of place in Boston. He had been wearing jeans, a white t-shirt which was tight over his lean chest, and he held my attention.

Before I can continue, there is a knock on Luke's door. Luke and I both startle at the sound. He was so caught up in my story, and me in my thoughts, that the knock sounded louder than it actually was. "That would be our dinner. I'll be right back." He heads to the door, I hear it open, his voice murmuring as he talks to the delivery person and then the door closes again. Luke reappears, carrying our food. "Let's move to the bar or dining room table."

"The bar works. Can I get the plates?"

"No plates needed, angel, let's just be casual and eat out of the cartons. Okay with you?"

"Low-key, I like it. What did you get?"

"I got you your favorite, beef and broccoli." Luke stops and looks at me, "Well at least that used to be your favorite. Shit, I just ordered and I didn't even ask you."

199

"It's okay, you did good. I still love beef and broccoli, that's perfect." I couldn't mean it more, my stomach actually growled as soon as he said beef and broccoli. "And did you get yourself chicken fried rice or has that changed for you?"

He grins, "You got it. I love that you still remember." I smile, pleased that I still remembered as well.

He hands me my carton of food and chopsticks. I open it, rip the chopsticks apart, and take a bite, "Mmmm... so good."

I feel Luke's eyes on me; when I look up, he's staring at my mouth. I involuntarily lick them in response. I clear my throat and he shakes his head, looks away, then takes a bite of his rice. "So continue. The last thing you said was that the hero guy turned around to look at you."

"Yes, you're right. He turned to face me and told me he had seen Steve starting to harass me and thought he would give me a hand. I thanked him but told him I could have handled it fine on my own." Luke smiles a bit at this.

"He said to me, 'I'm sure you could have, princess, but I thought I'd rescue you because your feet look tired since you've been running through my mind all day.' He gave me that one liner with a straight look on his face until he couldn't hold it in any longer and then he broke out in a huge grin that made me smile at him in return and start laughing. I held out my hand and introduced myself; he told me his name was Deacon."

I take another bite of my food and as I chew, my eyes move to Luke's face. I see his lips are in a grim line reminding me that this is hard for him to hear, but part of me doesn't care. It didn't have to be this way, he is responsible for that. He looks at me, encouragement on his face and sadness still lingering in his eyes and I realize that Luke knows that too. I don't need to place blame on him anymore because he already carries it on his own.

"That party ended up being the first of many. Deacon and I started dating and hanging out almost constantly after that. I drank heavily, experimented a lot, and deep down I convinced myself he was everything I could ever want and I was sure I was madly in love with him." I can hear Luke's teeth grind at that statement, but I ignore it. I take another bite of my food and after I swallow, I continue.

"I realize now all the lies I told myself. He was allowed to hang out with his friends whenever he wanted, but the second he couldn't get ahold of me, he would flip out. I lost most of my friends because of him, but it was okay because I told myself Deacon was just being over-protective and he just didn't want to share me. It was okay that Deacon could wear his tight jeans and shirts and then dictate to me what I was allowed to wear and what I was not allowed to wear because that just meant he was possessive and didn't want anyone seeing what was his. It was okay that he drank a little too much because he was just having fun. It was okay that he proposed to me in Vegas while he was drunk and wanted to take me immediately to seal the deal because that just meant he wanted me so desperately. It was okay if he would squeeze me a little too tight and leave bruises because that just meant he was passionate."

Luke throws down his food on the table and stands, up knocking his chair over. His eyes are furious, his hands are balled into fists, and his posture is tense. He is gritting his teeth so hard I can hear them grinding together. "He hit you?" he spits.

"No. He never struck me. He would grab me a lot, hard, when he was angry, and sometimes his grip would leave bruises."

"That isn't any better, Olivia. That is not okay. Not ever. Tell me you know that. Tell me you got out right away and that you didn't endure that over and over."

I smile a soft smile at Luke, trying to calm him down, "Sit down, Luke."

It takes him a minute, he closes his eyes and takes a deep breath, then picks his chair up off the floor, sits back down, and starts cleaning up the rice that fell out of his container when he threw it on the table. "I didn't leave right away, no. But I did eventually and that is what matters."

Luke closes his eyes briefly again and rubs his temples, "The way he spoke to you on the phone, does he always talk to you like that? What was the last straw that made you finally get out? What changed?"

I sigh. I'm embarrassed. I know this isn't a reflection on me, but that doesn't mean it is easy to confess or that it didn't take me a while to reach that conclusion through time and therapy. "He would speak to me like that when he got angry. He would start out in a pleading and nice tone, but if I wouldn't comply – and comply quickly- his tone changed. As far as the last straw...well..." I tense up and close my eyes. I feel Luke place his hand on mine and squeeze.

"You're scaring me, Livvie," he whispers. "Please tell me he didn't hurt you."

I look up into his eyes and take a deep breath, "I started having a feeling he was cheating on me. He would have crazy excuses for being home late and he wouldn't always answer when I'd call. Sometimes he would cancel our plans at the last minute and tell me he had to work late or that everyone at work decided to go to dinner and he couldn't get out of it. One time I called his office when he was supposed to be working late, but there was no answer. Of course he had a reason for that too, though I don't remember what it was now. What really made the light bulb finally go on for me though was when he accused me of cheating on him. A few times, he would confront me and want to know if I was seeing someone else for one ridiculous reason or another. I never did cheat on him, but somewhere inside, I knew he was asking and acting paranoid because he was projecting his own guilt onto me. I didn't know for sure, I had no proof. Until the day I came home early and found him screwing another woman in our bed," Luke squeezes my hand so hard it hurts, "that was almost a year ago now."

"What did you do?"

"What I'd like to think every woman would do in that situation. I walked into my bedroom, screamed at him; bitch slapped the girl, and kicked Deacon in the balls. He ran after me, begging at first, then eventually the real him came shining through like always, with threats and mean words. I left, kicked him out of the house with police assistance, filed for divorce, and I've never regretted it once."

Luke whispers, "That's my girl," and it makes me smile, even though the subject matter should make me want to do anything but.

202

We sit in silence after I finish telling Luke about Deacon. I can tell he is letting everything I told him resonate before commenting. I just let him be, not wishing to disturb his thoughts, and finish my food.

After a few more moments, Luke stands up, takes our empty Chinese food containers and throws them away in the kitchen. He comes back to the breakfast bar and holds his hand out to me. I take it, and he waits for me to stand and then he leads me back to his couch. We sit down and face one another.

"I don't even know how to say what I want to say to you." Luke reveals.

I am silent while I wait for him to work it out.

Luke looks down into his lap as he speaks, "I hate that you were married to a man like that dick head. I hate even more that it was because of me that you were married to him. I don't even know how or where to begin to tell you that I'm sorry for everything, Olivia. I want more than anything for you to be able to forgive me, but now, knowing even part of what you've been through, I feel like an asshole for even asking your forgiveness."

"Luke, I realized something when I was talking to you. I've already forgiven you. I look in your eyes and I see the sadness there. I see that you are torturing yourself much more than I ever could. Hanging on to my anger would only hurt both of us, and I don't want to hold onto it anymore. Besides, while what happened between us may have led me to Boston, I'm the only one responsible for the choices I made. Not you. Not what you said to your mother. Me."

Luke finally looks up and reaches out, touching my face, "Things should have been different for us, Livvie. I used to wish I could go back to that day and do things differently. I still do. I would spend hours sometimes daydreaming about going back into the past and changing the events of that day. Ridiculous, I know."

"It's not ridiculous. I wish we could change it too, but in some ways I'm glad we can't. It may be hard to believe, but it wasn't all bad. I had some great times with Deacon and made some good memories in college; and while I may have gotten a bit off track for a while, I'm really proud of the career I've made for myself. I love it. Those things, I wouldn't want to change."

"I'm proud of you, angel. What you've been through, what you've made of yourself, you *should* be proud. You sitting before me now," he looks in my eyes, "I dreamed about it so many times, but I can honestly say the reality is so much better than the dream. You are more beautiful today than you were seven years ago."

I smile and take a minute to gather the courage to ask, "What about you? I know about your career, but what about you personally? No wives you haven't told me about? No girlfriends?"

He chuckles a little, "No, no wives. I've had girlfriends here and there, and one relationship that lasted longer than the others. Rebecca and I were together for a couple years and even lived together for a little while, but we broke up."

The thought of Rebecca makes my stomach sour. Jealousy is a bitch. "What happened?"

"I told you, angel, I compared everyone to you. That wasn't just some stupid ass line. There was something missing with Rebecca and me. She wanted a commitment and I didn't. We broke up for good when I came back to Chicago to open the club, and to be closer to my mom, so I can help out if she needs me."

"Oh. Wow. So that wasn't too long ago then."

"It feels like forever ago. Our relationship had ended long before that. Rebecca and I were just going through the motions. I think she hoped I would change my mind, but I didn't."

"I'm sorry that it didn't work out for you," I lie. I'm not really sorry at all, but what am I supposed to say?

His eyebrow raises at my comment and a smirk appears on his lips. He holds my gaze and says, "Are you? Because I'm not sorry at all. I always knew I was holding out for something much better."

I stare back and we hold each other's gazes for a few moments, the heat between us thick and building.

"Olivia?" He pauses and seems to struggle with getting out whatever it is he's about to say.

"Hmm?" I ask feeling breathless, I'm lost in his gaze. I want him to kiss me. So much. I want to feel his soft lips against my own, his tongue stroking mine. I want his need for me to be evident in the way his hands hold me close, trying to make me a part of him. I don't want there to be any space between us. I want to explore his body with my hands.

Interrupting my thoughts, Luke starts speaking and it takes a minute for my brain to process his words. "I'm going to ask you to go out on a date with me some time soon. Not right this minute. But it's coming. Will you consider saying yes?"

I can't help but smile at his obvious nervousness. It's sweet. "I will consider it," I give him a big smile so he knows my answer will be yes.

He smiles back at me, "Good, I just thought I would be a gentleman and give you a heads up," then his face turns serious. "Do you think," he stops and swallows to clear his throat. Just as he's about to speak again, he shakes his head. "Spend the rest of the day with me," he blurts, "I don't want you to leave. Let's watch a movie, or something. I will make popcorn," he promises with a smile.

I look at him, positive that he changed his mind and whatever he was going to say to me, he decided not to. The moment now broken, I respond knowing there is nothing else I can say right now, "I would love to spend the rest of the day with you." I tell him honestly.

Luke's grin is magnificent. He leans towards me and my breath catches. He places a small kiss on the tip of my nose, and then he stands and gestures to the cabinet across the room, "My DVDs are in there. Go ahead and pick something out. I'll make us some popcorn." With that, he heads to the kitchen to do just that.

I sigh to myself and wonder again what he was really going to say to me before he changed his mind. Maybe eventually he will ask me. In the meantime, I'm anxious for when he will ask me on a date. I already know my answer will be yes.

Chapter Twenty-One

*"Fashion tip: For some fashionistas, putting the final touches on an
outfit can mean something as simple as spraying yourself with your
favorite perfume; tying your whole look together. A great trick I learned
is to spray your favorite perfume onto the bristles of your brush. Run your
brush through your hair from root to end and your hair will smell fantastic
throughout your day!"*

I open my eyes and sigh deep and long. I don't know
why, but I'm feeling different this morning. I don't feel
stressed or tense. My body feels relaxed all the way into
my bones like I just had an amazing massage. I haven't felt this
content in a long time; I didn't even know I was missing this
feeling until now. I'm not sure what time it is, but I should get up
and start the coffee, maybe I can actually beat Pyper to the pot
for once. I yawn and begin lifting my arms over my head for a
nice full body stretch when I realize something is off. I feel a
weight pressed against me and I look to my side and see Luke.
He's lying with his back pressed against the back of the couch,
his arm stretched out under me and I'm using it as a pillow. His
other arm is stretched across my waist and his eyes are still
closed.

Once I recover from the fact I completely forgot where I am,
I just revel in my close proximity to him for a while. Looking at
him, I start at the top of his head and take in his dark, sleep

disheveled hair. His long eyelashes look even darker against his cheeks. My eyes trail down his straight nose to his full lips. I love how he seems to constantly be sporting a five o'clock shadow, even after he shaves. It's one of my favorite things about him, it's so damn sexy. The small dimple in his chin, his high cheekbones and strong jaw make me want to trace them with my fingers or tongue.

My eyes continue down the line of his neck, to his chest. Not for the first time, I long to see under his shirt. I want to trail my fingers down his muscled chest, see if he has the abs I'm certain are hidden under his shirt. In his sleep, his shirt has raised a bit and a strip of skin is exposed, revealing the hair on his belly. I want to touch it. Follow it down.

I jump when I hear, "It's a good thing you can't start fires with your eyes. Given the look in them right now, I'd be in flames."

I blush. Busted.

"Don't worry, angel," he says while touching the blush at my cheeks with his fingertips, "I watched you sleep for a long time last night too, the only difference is I spent a long – uninterrupted - time enjoying the view because you didn't know it." This only makes me blush more. "Besides, I'm glad that you like what you see." And now the cheeks are on fire, giving away just how much I like it. What, am I sixteen? Stupid cheeks.

I want to tell him that I'd like to do a whole lot more than just look at him, but I don't. Instead I say, "I was disoriented when I woke up. I don't even remember falling asleep."

"We were almost at the end of the movie and you fell asleep on my shoulder. I didn't want to wake you, so I just settled us on the couch together. I couldn't resist the chance to hold you."

I remember now. We had sat together and watched an old action film. I really wasn't up for a romantic comedy because I knew the kissing parts would make things a little heated. For me, at least. I would have wanted to recreate the scenes on the T.V., making them my reality, so I thought an action movie was the way to go. We ate popcorn, and since both of us had seen the movie before, we talked some during the film. It was a nice time and I enjoyed just hanging out with him. It was comfortable and felt like old times. The whole night, I kept waiting for him to finally ask me on a date, and surprised when the moment never came.

"That's okay. I slept really well, actually," Luke smiles at my admission, "Oh crap! Pyper! I bet she's worried."

"No she's not. I sent her a text from your phone letting her know you were sleeping with me."

"What?!" I laugh. I can't help it. I can't believe he did that. Pyper must have been in Team Luke heaven.

Luke smiles, "I just told her you were staying on the couch. I didn't want her to worry about you."

"Well I guess you thought of everything," I tease.

Luke smiles bigger. That sexy mouth of his starts descending towards mine. He's moving slow, I'm sure waiting to see if I invite him to continue. I want this so much. Heat floods my belly in anticipation and I start to move my mouth to his. I'm giving in to my desire, I'm so tired of overthinking everything. His lips barely brush mine when I realize this can't happen. Oh my god! "No!" I cover my mouth with my hand, freaking out. "I have morning breath!"

Luke leans back and sighs, "I don't care. Let me kiss you, I'm dying to kiss you."

I become a pile of Olivia goo at his words but I refuse to give in. "Sorry. I can't."

"I will go to the store right now and buy you a damn toothbrush, or use mine for the love of god. Just kiss me."

I laugh, "No, but I promise to make it up to you, okay?"

His eyes narrow, "I'm holding you to that."

I smile flirtatiously and then close my mouth because again, ew. "Please do." *Oh yeah. Go me, getting my flirt on*! "I need to get home. Thanks for letting me crash on your couch."

"Believe me love, the pleasure was all mine."

Yep. Goo.

"I want to see you tonight, do you have plans?"

Here it comes, I smile in anticipation. "No plans that I know of, why?"

"Will you go on a date with me angel? I would love for you to come to the club. I can send a driver to pick you up, we can have dinner together, and maybe dance a little if you say yes."

"I would love to." And I would. The thought of being on a date with him feels right and I want it. Desperately.

His grin is cocky now, "How about I have my driver pick you up around eight? Would that work for you?"

"Sounds perfect." I am reluctant to get off the couch and step away from the warmth of his body, but I do. "I'm looking forward to it."

"Me too." Luke stands up and pulls me into a hug. He places a tender kiss on my forehead.

I pull away from him and Luke reaches in his pocket and holds my keys out in his palm. "Oh! My car! We left it at the park. How is it here?"

"After you were asleep, I called a couple guys that work for me and had them take care of it."

"Thank you."

"No worries, love."

I smile at him then go to his dining room table to get my purse and make my way to his front door.

"Olivia, wait!" Luke calls.

I turn around and see him approaching me with a few pink roses in his hand. He hands them to me, "For you. Think of me. See you tonight."

"See you." I smile and turn back around and walk out the door.

When I arrive at the condo, I head straight to my room and into the bathroom so I can start getting ready for the day. I want to work on an article for Trend Magazine. They contacted me asking for another piece to publish in next month's magazine, so I need to get that done.

I also want to call my parents, go to the grocery store for a few things, and I've decided to join a gym today. It's time to do things like that for myself and who knows, maybe I will meet some people too!

Several hours later, I'm feeling quite accomplished since I completed everything I had hoped to on my to-do list. Standing in my closet, wrapped in nothing but a towel, I am once again pondering what I should wear to the club tonight. I want to make Luke sit up and take notice when I walk in. The thought of his bright blue eyes roving over my body taking in the outfit I wear just for him, lust evident on his face, makes a shiver of anticipation run through me straight to the center of my legs. Keeping my control around Luke is proving to be more and more difficult.

As my eyes trail one end of my closet to the other, I spot the perfect dress. I bought it a while back on a whim and haven't worn it, the tags are still attached. Taking the hanger with my dress off the rod I hold it in front of me giving it a once over. A black, sequined, strapless mini-dress. Perfect for a night at Luke's club and even more perfect to make Luke's jaw drop. I smile at the thought.

I walk out of my closet, dress in hand so I can get the perfect lingerie to go under the dress. Rooting around in my dresser, I find exactly the set I had in mind. A black strapless bra that has ruffles on the top of the cups with a black thong that has ruffles around the legs. It's perfect. I slip the panties on, put the bra on and walk to my floor length mirror. I have to admit, I look hot. *Not bad, Olivia, not bad.*

My phone chimes. I walk to where it's charging on my beside table, pick it up and see a text from Luke. "Can't wait to see you. Kevin, one of my staff will be there to pick you up in twenty minutes. Don't open the door unless he identifies himself. See you soon, angel."

I type a reply, "Can't wait to see you too. XO."

His reply is quick, "I think I will take that X and O in person, beautiful." I grin.

I set my phone down and turn, picking up the dress lying on my bed. I remove it from the hanger and take off the tags. I unzip the hidden zipper in the side and slip it on, zipping it in place. I walk to the mirror again and take a look. I curled my hair into soft waves and it looks shiny and pretty. My makeup is dramatic around the eyes and my lips a glossy, light pink. I just need some black stilettos and I'm good to go. I sort through the shoes in my closet picking out the perfect pair, then reach up to the shelf where I store my handbags and grab my hot pink clutch for my necessities.

I contemplate taking a picture of myself to send to Pyper. I know she would approve and will be sorry she missed it. She's working a late night, completing inventory at the spa. I guess she just got a new product line in.

Ten minutes later, there's a knock on my door. Looking through the peephole, I see a man dressed in a suit and tie. Without opening the door, I say, "May I help you?"

"Hello, Ms. Brooks. My name is Kevin and I am here to drive you to Mr. Easton's club, Zero Gravity." I open the door and smile at Kevin. He nods his head in acknowledgement and waits politely as I shut and lock the condo door. We walk to the elevator, enduring an awkward silence until we get to the parking garage. Kevin is driving Luke's car and he holds the passenger door open for me so I can get in, and closes it behind me. Once he gets in the car and starts it, we are on our way to the club. It is kind of strange being in Luke's car without him.

Before I can open my door, Kevin has gotten out of his side and holds the door open for me, offering his hand. I take it and am careful as I get out to keep my legs together in my short dress. "Follow me, Ms. Brooks," Kevin says. He offers his arm and I take it. He walks straight past the bouncer at the front door and takes me into the club.

The place is pretty empty, given the early dinner hour. I am once again amazed by how nice the club is, but this time, I also feel pride knowing Luke was the master behind the design. "Luke will be with you momentarily, Ms. Brooks."

"Thank you, and please call me Olivia." Kevin smiles, gives me another nod -which is obviously his chosen form of communication, and walks away. I stand there a moment and consider walking over to the bar to order a drink, but decide that since I'm pretty sure I know where Luke's office is, I will just start heading that way.

I walk the length of the room and go up the stairs on the left side. I remember seeing a door there and I assume it leads to staff rooms. If I'm wrong, no harm done, I will just keep searching until I find him.

As I approach the door, I notice it isn't closed all the way. I start to push it open further to peek inside, when I hear Luke's voice. "Rebecca, I don't know what else to say."

My heart starts to pound. Rebecca? As in the Rebecca that wanted a long-term commitment from Luke? Here? Now?

"Then don't say anything. Let your body do the talking. I know you want this, Luke, you can't deny it. I see it in your eyes. I knew the moment I let you leave without fighting for you, it was a mistake. I want you, Luke, and I know you want me too."

I hear Luke sigh and then say, "Rebecca..." I step closer to the door and peek in. Rebecca is standing in front of Luke so I can't see him. I see her reach behind her back and slowly start to unzip her dress.

I feel sick. I've seen enough. I start to back away, then turn and run as fast as I can down the stairs. I feel like I can't breathe. I hold in a sob and when I'm on the sidewalk outside the club, I put my hands on my knees and suck in breaths like I'm starving for air, my heart is pounding so hard I hear it in my ears. I was going to let my guard down and give Luke another chance. I started to trust him again. I'm so fucking stupid. Things were going to be different this time.

I stand up straight as the word different keeps replaying in my head. Different...different...things were going to be different. I start to feel angry. At myself. What the fuck am I doing? What is wrong with me that whenever things get hard, I run or let people tell me what to do? Why am I so quick to relinquish control of my own destiny?

This isn't seven years ago, I'm sure as hell not the same girl I was then. Luke isn't the same man. I believe Luke when he says he wants me, wants an "us," and that Rebecca was a thing of the past. Why am I so quick to assume the worst? That bitch up there is trying to take my man and my response is to just run away? No. NO! I don't think so.

I turn on my heel and march my ass back into the club. The bouncer gives me a strange look when I stalk by, but I just take a cue from Kevin and nod at him. I march all the way across the club, up the stairs, and I don't stop when I get to Luke's office. I barge through his door and looking out of the corner of my eye, I'm surprised to see that Ms. Hussy still has her clothes on, despite trying to rid herself of them. Luke's eyes widen when he takes in the complete fury on my face. He's standing an arm's length away from Rebecca and now that I can see his face, it brings me relief. He's happy that I'm here.

I stand next to him, link my arm through his and face Rebecca. I extend my other hand to her, "Hello, my name is Olivia, I'm Luke's girlfriend," oh yes, I'm going there, "and you are?" I'm not about to use her name.

Luke smiles and unlinks our arms so he can place his arm around my waist instead, pulling me even closer to his side. "Girlfriend?" Rebecca asks Luke, barely even acknowledging me.

I intervene before Luke can respond, "It's rude to look at him when I'm the one that addressed you." *Take that bitch.* "Yes, girlfriend, and you would be?"

She looks at me with eyes full of anger, "I'm Rebecca. Luke and I were in a relationship for a couple years and we lived together."

I look at Luke, "So this is the one you were telling me about?"

Luke only has eyes for me. If I had to guess, I would say he almost looks proud and somewhat smug at the moment. "Yes, this is Rebecca."

Looking like a proud peacock, Rebecca says, "Oh, so Luke talked about me huh? I'm not surprised, I know he still has feelings for me, so let's quit this game and get back to you and me, Luke. Go ahead and let her down easy, I'm sure she can handle it."

Luke's jaw tightens and he opens his mouth to say something but I beat him to it. "Yes, Rebecca. Luke told me all about you. I know you broke up before he moved back to Illinois. I know you wanted a commitment but he...what was it?

213

Oh right, he didn't. I also know he's spent the last seven years missing me as much as I missed him. Now I suggest you get the fuck out of my boyfriend's office and do not come back here, unless you want me to kick your ass all the way back to Miami." I know I'm being a bitch, and it feels fucking great. I feel liberated. It's amazing to finally get a backbone and not assume the worst. For once, I'm taking control instead of letting people try and take it from me.

Rebecca's mouth falls open at my comment, "Luke, are you going to let her talk to me like that?"

Luke's jaw ticks on the side indicating he's clenching his teeth. I turn towards him, reach up and smooth my hand down his jaw. His eyes meet mine in surprise, "Don't, baby, she's not worth it."

His eyes soften and something passes through them too fast for me to define. He kisses me briefly on the lips and as always, I warm in my belly at the contact and instantly want more. Returning his gaze to Rebecca he says, "Obviously, the nice approach doesn't work with you. I tried to ask you nicely to leave before, but you aren't listening." Luke turns to me again and pulls me up in front of his body. Looking down, his eyes only for me, he tells her, "I've moved on, Rebecca. I suggest you do the same." His gaze leaves mine and anger fills his eyes, focusing on Rebecca to once more drive his point home.

"You will regret this, Luke Easton, you and that little bitch. I changed everything to come and be here for you."

"I didn't ask you to."

"I wanted to, for you. I know you want me, and eventually you will get tired of your little whore and come crawling back, and then, I will make you beg."

"That's not going to happen. Stop making a fool of yourself and leave."

My mouth drops open when Rebecca stomps her foot like a baby before turning on her heel and stalking out of Luke's office, slamming the door behind her.

Stepping back from Luke, I place my hands on my hips and glare at him. "Luke Easton, you have some explaining to do."

Chapter Twenty-Two

"Fashion tip: When dressing formally for a night on the town or an evening at a trendy club, know what your best asset is and emphasize it! If you love your toned arms, wear a strapless or halter dress. If you love your legs, show them off in a mini dress. Got a great ass? Wear a longer but tighter skirt or dress and show it off. If you love your breasts, that's fine, just make sure you have the girls tightly secured!"

When Luke looks at me, I see humor twinkling in his eyes and a smirk on his sexy lips. God his lips are sexy, they just scream 'KISS ME'. "Girlfriend?" he asks.

"Oh, no you don't! Not until you explain yourself. What the hell was she doing here?" I hear the accusation in my tone, but I can't help it. Fury is still coursing through my body at the shock of seeing her. I feel my body shaking from the combination of an adrenaline rush and the shock of finally figuring out what I want.

"Angel, I was as surprised to see her as you were, trust me. She called to tell me she was in town for business. She's a physician's assistant, and I guess she's attending some training conference or something. She asked if she could see me for a few minutes to see how I'm doing and because she had some news to share." Luke runs his hand through his hair in exasperation. "I told her I would see her, but that she would have to meet me here. She wouldn't give me a firm time and there was no way I was going to risk her interfering on my dinner plans with you."

Luke gestures to the navy blue couch in his office and we take a seat. His office is really quite nice, painted in navy blue and cream, complementing the colors in the club below. Luke's desk is across the room, facing the door when you walk in. The glass wall to the left allows him a perfect view of the dance floor and bar area below. The glass is one way; he can keep an eye on what's going on in his club, but no one can see him doing so. The wall on the right has a long couch against it, which is where we are sitting to discuss Rebecca.

I sink into the couch, making myself comfortable, "What did she want?"

Luke sighs, "I'm sure it was obvious. She wants the two of us to get back together. I guess the company she works for is opening an office in the city and she applied for a transfer. She hoped that would mean the two of us could pick up where we left off, convinced that the real reason we broke up was only because I had to leave to take care of my mom. Forget the fact that I never once asked her to come with me or to give a long distance relationship a try."

"I don't understand why she would just assume something like that. Have you been talking to her since you've been back in Chicago?" I feel jealousy stir in my belly again. I don't like thinking about him carrying on any kind of relationship with a woman he lived with, even a friendship, when clearly she had other ideas.

"She's called once or twice, but I've never really given her the time of day. I have not encouraged her at all, but Rebecca is a woman that is used to getting what she wants."

"Well she can't have you," I blurt. My cheeks flush scarlet. "Well...er...I mean..."

Luke's eyes twinkle again when he looks at me, a smile playing on his lips again. "No. She can't. Apparently I'm taken. I have a *girlfriend*. Care to explain? Not that I minded that response from you one bit."

"I came to the top of the stairs and heard her talking to you. I couldn't see your face, but I heard her say that you wanted her. When she placed her hands behind her back to unzip her dress, I flew out of here. My automatic reaction was to run. I was down the stairs, across the club and outside so fast, I didn't even think it through, I just did it. I had to get away."

Luke's eyes widen and he starts to get a look of panic on his face, as though my retelling of what I did is going to change the outcome.

"I was standing in front of the club, gasping for air, and I started thinking that this was just like seven years ago all over again. I thought to myself that things were supposed to be different this time. Then, I remembered when I ran seven years ago. If I had just stayed and confronted you, things could have been very different."

Tears come easily to my eyes, but I don't let them fall. "Out of nowhere, I had clarity. I knew I could not allow myself to make the same mistake twice. I was not about to let that woman, any woman for that matter, walk in here and walk all over the progress we've made. I was furious. I stomped back in here, and when I saw the look of relief on your face when you saw me, it was like it gave me this amazing super power and suddenly I was confident and not willing to take Rebecca's shit."

"If I had come back here and you told me that you did want her back, well that would have sucked, but at least I didn't just run. At least I would have confronted the issue for once and known the complete truth." I purposefully look Luke in the eye, "No running. Not anymore."

Luke cups my face and his mouth starts to move towards mine. I lift my head in anticipation, my lips ready and waiting to meet his. We are interrupted when a knock sounds on the door. Luke sighs and drops his hand. I frown. "Who is it?" he bellows. I'm glad he is as unhappy about being interrupted as I am.

Kevin opens the door and peers around it, "Sorry to bother you sir, but your dinner has arrived."

Luke nods, "Thank you, Kevin."

Kevin nods in reply and exits the room.

Luke stands and holds his hand out to me. When I stand, he finally takes me in from head to toe. His eyes darken and become heated with lust, and I know in that moment he only has eyes for me. This dress was definitely the right choice. Luke always liked my legs and his eyes linger there for several moments before returning to mine with a smile.

Luke looks spectacular himself. Wearing black dress pants, a crisp, white shirt with no tie and a black jacket, I can't look away. His very presence encompasses the whole room and leaves me breathless. I can't see, smell, or hear anything but him.

"You look stunning." He takes my hand and holds it above his head and indicates with a finger on his other hand that he wants me to do a twirl. I indulge him and twirl for him. His eyes heat even more, if that's possible. "I'm going to have to keep a close eye on you tonight."

"Why is that?" I ask breathlessly in response to the blatant need and want I see in his eyes.

"Because I'm going to have to fight the other men off with a stick," he growls.

"What men?" I ask coyly.

"Good answer, angel. Come on, follow me."

Luke pulls me out of his office and we walk only a short distance to the room next to the office. I follow him in. It looks like a mini conference room. A large table, mini kitchen, TVs, couch, and chairs make up the room. The color scheme of the rest in the club continues in here too, but somehow manages to come off as more comfortable and relaxed.

The table is set up with a candlelit dinner for two. There are tall silver candlesticks on the table with lit white candles perched inside. In between the candles is a vase holding at least two dozen pink and red roses. Two table settings with flatware and wine glasses are set up across from one another, with salad plates on top already adorned with a tasty looking salad. Down a little ways on the table, out of the way of everything else is a large, silver domed top covering whatever Luke has chosen for dinner, as well as a bottle of wine chilling in an ice bucket. Music is playing softly, adding to the very romantic setting.

"This is lovely." I smile, looking at him.

"I'm glad you like it. I had food brought in from one of your favorite places," he says proudly.

I look at him curiously, "Where?" Luke holds my chair out for me, waiting for me to sit. I think I have a pretty good idea since even the covered dome can't completely contain the amazing smell permeating the air.

He takes the dome top off with a flourish and exposes my favorite pizza from Gino's East. I laugh, "Perfect!"

He replaces the top with a smile and grabs the wine bottle out of the bucket, opening it using the corkscrew strategically placed next to the bucket. After a loud pop from the air pressure, Luke fills our glasses and places the wine back in the bucket and takes his seat.

Luke has thought of everything and I love it. He even has my salad dressing on the side, just like he knows I like it. While my salad does not have tomatoes because I despise them, his does because he loves them. The fact that he remembers small details about me warms my heart and makes me fall a little bit deeper under his spell.

"Do you remember the day we met?" Luke asks, eyebrow raised.

I smile. "Of course. In health class."

He returns my smile, "Yes, in class. You came into class late that day and all the chairs were taken. They had more against the wall but as you walked in, taking in the filled seats, all I could think was..." he stops. "Well, maybe one day I will tell you what I thought."

"What?! No fair! You can't just tease me like that!"

"Oh yes I can, you have to earn those thoughts, love. Anyway, do you remember what I said to you?"

"How can I forget?" I ask, rolling my eyes.

Luke chuckles, "I told you that you were more than welcome to sit on my lap since there wasn't an available chair. Man, I was cocky."

I laugh, "Was?"

Luke narrows his eyes at me, but continues. "Your cheeks flushed a little and you rolled your eyes at me, stalking over to get your own chair from the stacked ones on the side of the room. I jumped up to help you, our hands touched when we reached for a chair at the same time, and your cheeks became fire."

"That's really embarrassing," I mumble.

"No, it's beautiful, *you're* beautiful," he says looking at me, "In that instant, I made myself a promise that you would be mine. I wanted to be the one to put that blush on your cheeks again and again. I wanted to see how far I could push you before your cheeks would become that color. Would it be a few sweet words, a slight touch, a whispered promise, or an inevitable compliment that would put it there? I wanted to find out. I was determined to find out," he whispers the last.

I feel my cheeks flush at his words and my heart flutters in my chest. "Just like that," he says, reaching across the table to touch my cheek. "Each day after that, I made sure I was sitting next to you in class."

"I remember. You were annoying. Asking me out on a daily basis."

"And you kept telling me no."

"Until I finally realized that I didn't know why I kept saying no. One day I decided when you asked me again, I would finally say yes. Only, you didn't ask me that day."

"I had given up," he admits, "for the time being. I was working on developing a new strategy."

I laugh. "I can't imagine what that would have entailed."

"If I remember correctly it involved baseball, ducks, and roses."

A loud laugh escapes me, "What?"

"Don't ask."

"Okay, but one of these days that is going to need explaining." I tell him.

"We'll see. I remember the day I actually beat you to class. I don't even remember why I was early for once. Normally, I would try to time my entry into class about the same time you arrived so I could snag the seat next to you. This time I beat you, so imagine my surprise when *you* sat next to *me,*" I smile at the memory and he smiles too, "and *you* asked *me* out."

"Now, wait a minute. I don't remember it that way!" I pretend to be serious when I know that is exactly what happened.

"Oh, don't even try and deny it, angel. I had finally worn you down. You wanted me."

"I'm not denying that, but I do believe what actually happened was that I asked you why you hadn't asked me out lately."

Luke smiles, "And I looked at you and smiled and said I didn't want to be shot down again."

"And I asked you if you would ask me again if you knew you weren't going to get shot down."

"I believe my exact words were 'hell yes'."

My smile is bigger now, "So I said, go ahead, ask me. And you did."

"We were inseparable after that. That was the best day."

"I was pretty happy too, if I remember correctly," I tease. That day is ingrained in my mind. No way could I ever forget it. .

"As much as I hate what ended up happening to us a couple years later, Olivia, I would go back to that moment with you again and again and again to hear you tell me yes again."

"A few weeks later you gave me your letterman's jacket to wear. I loved walking around and wearing that, even though it was way too big for me."

"I loved seeing you wear it too, but I loved seeing those gorgeous legs in your cheerleading uniform even more."

"You loved getting your hands under my cheerleading skirt even more than that."

Luke's grin is downright devilish, "Very true."

We both laugh, and I love this reminiscing. Luke takes the dome off the pizza and serves a piece to me and then one to him. I pick up my knife and fork and begin cutting pieces to eat, and it tastes divine.

I marvel at the realization that thinking about our past no longer feels painful. It's like a very important piece of my life has been missing. Those years with Luke helped shape the person I am today and those years were some of the best of my life. Sure, they were in high school and many would say I couldn't have known love then or that it's ridiculous to feel that way, given the fact high school is so juvenile. I personally believe that only those that didn't experience love at that intense and passionate age can say such a thing.

At the age of sixteen, I had barely experienced life. I had no idea that love could be painful or destructive. I think that lack of knowledge enabled me to love with a different level of intensity. There was no fear, no trepidation; just magic and beauty. That was the kind of love I had with Luke.

I smile and ask, "Do you remember our first date at Gino's?"

"Yes, I do. I thought I was super cool because I passed the waitress some extra cash in order to sit us in the corner booth."

"I didn't know that!"

"I can't divulge all my secrets, woman," he grumbles making me laugh.

"Wow, you are super smooth. I'm impressed."

"As you should be, angel."

Man, he is sexy when he grins and laughs at himself like this. I just want to eat him for dinner instead of my pizza.

"Well, I will always remember us signing our names on the wall." That is one of the things I love about Gino's East. Every square inch of the wall has graffiti all over it with the names of everyone that's visited or couples professing their love. I know that even my parents put their names on the wall too. It's very romantic.

"I remember that too. Speaking of our names being signed in places…" he trails off.

I know what he's going to say, "Our tree," I murmur.

"Yes, our tree. Have you been by? To see if our initials are still there?"

"No. I couldn't bring myself to think about it, or go back there," I confess.

"Well, if you are up for it, maybe we can check it out together some time. See if our initials are still there," he says softly.

"I would love that."

"Me too. It's a date. Girlfriend," he says and the wicked grin and gleam in his eye is back.

"Oh, no. I should have thought it through before I said that!"

"I'm glad you didn't. Now that it's over and I can look back on the confrontation I can see that," he pauses for dramatic effect, "it was totally hot! You, all feisty with your claws out fighting for me. Mmm mmm, angel, so sexy!"

"Oh please. Dream on."

"Oh I do, angel," he whispers.

Chapter Twenty-Three

"Fashion tip: "Did you know that you can save time in the shower by coating your legs with a thick hair conditioner in place of shaving cream? It softens the hair, making it easier to shave and leaves your legs feeling amazing. Your legs will not only look hot in that mini dress, but they will feel sexy too!"

After we finish our meal, I stand to clean up. Luke stops me immediately by taking the plates I have in my hands and sets them back on the table. "Someone will take care of it." I reluctantly leave everything where it is as Luke takes my hand and guides me, suggesting we head down to the dance floor.

"Let's stop in my office first so I can hang up my jacket before we head down."

I nod my head and follow him inside the door, closing it behind us. He walks to his desk and takes off his jacket. When he unbuttons his jacket and opens the front I step behind him intent on helping him pull it off his shoulders. The action of removing his clothes is a huge turn on. As I slide it down his arms, I intentionally trail my fingertips down the length of his arms, feeling his muscles ripple underneath.

Luke turns and faces me as I fold his jacket over my arm. "Thanks." His voice is husky and I feel its effect in my belly.

"You're welcome." We just stare into each other's eyes. Can he see the desire in mine? Can he tell that I am done with keeping him at a distance, that I want him? All of him? As I move toward him, head tilting up, intent on ensuring he knows how I feel, his phone rings. Luke looks at me, a question in his eyes. "Go ahead and take it, it's fine."

While I'm hanging up his jacket, Luke answers the phone behind me. "Luke Easton." Standing and staring at the crowd, my enjoyment of people watching is salved. "No, that's too much." Luke's tone is harsh, surprising me.

"No. I said, that's too much. No. I'm not willing to pay that much. Negotiate the price lower by at least twenty percent per case and then he has a deal; got it?" I turn to look at Luke and he winks and smiles at me. "That sounds like a you problem, Chuck, not a me problem. This is what I pay you to do, so get it done. Handle it." Luke abruptly hangs up the phone and walks around his desk toward me. "I should have just let it ring."

"Oh, well," I say shrugging my shoulders. Truthfully, hearing Luke be all business is hot. I turn back around to look through the window again and take in the colorful display of writhing bodies below me. They all look different from up here; intoxicating. Luke comes and stands behind me pressing his body against mine, and his very presence sends heat shooting up from my toes to the top of my head. I think I could be sizzling – is smoke rising?

Leaning his head down so that his mouth is right next to my ear, he whispers, "Let's go, I want to see you shake that sweet ass of yours in that dress." His voice sends goose bumps running up my arms. I'm electrified; alive. My legs are quivering in anticipation.

"Okay," I squeak and then wince at how ridiculous I sound.

I hear Luke chuckle softly, damn him. He knows the effect he's having on me. Oh well, he's playing with fire and I intend to drive him wild when we are dancing. He takes my hand and leads me out his office door and down the stairs to the club.

On the floor, a large number of people look Luke's way. Some women look him up and down with lust written on their faces, and guys nod their head in acknowledgement. Luke seems

225

oblivious to the women and nods in return to the men. He never let's go of my hand and in places where maneuvering through the crowd gets tight, he puts his hand on my back and guides me through, keeping me protected against the crowd.

"Would you like a drink from the bar?" he asks.

"Yes, please!"

We weave in and out of the crowd and head to the bar. Like magic, people seem to move out of the way when Luke approaches and the bartender immediately makes his way over. He's an attractive man, dirty blonde hair and hazel eyes, but it's his bulging biceps that grab my attention when he places his hands on the edge of the bar and leans toward Luke to say, "Hey, boss. What can I get ya?"

"Hello, Jimmy," Luke says then turns to me, "What would you like?"

"I'll take a jack and coke please," I tell Jimmy the bartender with a smile. Jimmy's lips form into a large smile while he looks me up and down.

A clearing of a throat catches my attention and I glance at Luke to see he is scowling at Jimmy. "And I will have the same as *my girl* please," Luke says as I try to hide a smile. I think it's cute that now he's the one a little jealous.

Jimmy quickly starts filling his boss' request, and in no time our drinks are ready. Luke hands me my glass, and taking my other hand, steers me to a corner where there is a high top table. We lean on the table, facing each other and take sips of our drinks.

The club's music is blaring. Leaning in towards me, Luke presses that luscious mouth of his to my ear again and says, "Have I told you how beautiful you look tonight, angel?" I shudder again at the contact. The way he makes me feel is unlike anything I've ever felt before. Well, two can play that game.

Standing on my tip toes, I press my lips to Luke's ear and say, "I do think I remember hearing that somewhere. Have I told you how mouthwateringly scrumptious *you* look?"

Luke's grin is downright devilish, "Mouthwatering, you say?"

The jack and coke combined with the wine I already drank makes me feel relaxed and bold. I lift my mouth back towards Luke's ear again, dragging my lips up his cheekbone as I go. Pressing my mouth to his ear, "I could eat you with a spoon," and then I flick my tongue and nibble gently on his ear lobe. A shudder wracks Luke's body in response, his grip on his glass tightening. My breath catches audibly. Trembling, he pulls away, takes my drink, sets it on the table, and leads me to the dance floor.

Luke doesn't stop until we are in the middle of the crowded floor. The DJ's current selection, a slow, sinful, steady rhythm resonates through the room. Luke pulls me against his body, hands caressing with enough pressure to make me tremble, before they land on my hips, gripping tightly. His legs are on either side of mine; my hands on his firm chest. I flatten my palms and slowly work them up his chest and over his shoulders, until I reach his nape and clutch handfuls of his hair. Placing my cheek against his chest, his fast thumping heart ignites me. We sway side to side, moving to the beat of the song, when I feel Luke's chest rise and fall under my cheek in a big breath.

I return the sigh. How amazing it is to be in Luke's arms again. I nestle closer, unable to remember when I have felt absolute contentment. I believe all of us have another half. Not that we aren't complete or enough as we are. But there's a desire to find that compatible someone to fall in love with, one's soul mate. I've always believed Luke was that person for me. I thought I had lost my soul mate forever, so it feels unreal that I am standing here again in his arms.

Before I realize what has happened, the slow paced song has been replaced by one with a significantly faster beat. The bodies around us pick up speed instantly. The change of beat makes the bodies press in on us. People brush against my back and sides, adding to the heat I already feel coursing through my veins. I drop my arms from around Luke's neck and move away from him, just a little, so I can dance faster. Luke doesn't let go of my hips and when he moves, his pelvis brushes against mine and as I move, my breasts brush against his chest. The barely there touches make the lust I'm feeling almost unbearable, my body is demanding something more. Luke sways his hips faster and I totally get lost in the music. I put my arms above my head, close my eyes, and just move. The beat resonates through my body, giving it a life of its own.

With effort, I open my eyes and see Luke's hooded gaze looking back at me. The tops of his cheeks are flushed and I see more of his exposed chest. He looks so hot, completely and totally edible. His eyes are on fire and I know mine are too.

The intensity is too much, I turn around and put my back to him, placing my ass right in his crotch. He lets out a groan, but I ignore it and start shaking my ass back and forth in his lap, purposefully rubbing against the hardness I feel there. I put my arms up, lock them around the back of his neck and keep dancing. Just to be a tease I let go from his neck and start a slow slide down his body to the floor, feeling my skirt come up my legs even more, and then I carefully, intently, work my way back up, feeling every inch of his form against my own.

Luke takes hold of my waist again and spins me around to face him. I'm breathing hard, my breath coming in pants. The other dancers close around us even more, causing me to feel warmer. The heat from dancing, combined with my raging hormones, makes it hard for me to breathe. The air feels charged, my body a bomb ready to detonate at the slightest touch. Luke's grip on my hips tightens and he pulls me against him so close there is no space between our bodies at all. One of his legs is wedged between both of mine and the friction is making me want to ride his leg until I feel the sweet pleasure of release.

I look up, put my hands on either side of his face, and pull him towards me. I want, no I need, to taste his lips. Recognizing my intent, Luke doesn't waste time. As soon as his lips meet mine, I open for him and he sucks my tongue into his mouth. We touch, seek, and explore one another's mouth. My hands can no longer stay still, I'm running them all over his back needing to stroke and caress him. I clutch handfuls of his shirt and try to bring him even closer. Luke's hands leave my waist and clutch my ass, driving me up higher on his leg. The friction, oh it feels so good.

I'm lost in him. I can't get enough. My hands move to the front of his body, I back up just enough so I can seize him.

228

Across his strong shoulders, down his broad chest, down his rippled abs, and over his tight belly, with a slight pause at his taut thighs. And just as I reach my destination and barely touch the front of his pants, Luke takes his lips from mine and looks down, entreating me. For a moment, my tunnel vision is interrupted and it's as though I am only now aware that others are in the room. Not sure that I care, I stare back into his eyes making my intent clear. I want him. Now.

Leaning towards my ear, Luke says, "Follow me."

I nod my head, and Luke hurriedly makes his way through the crowd of bodies back towards the stairs, we climb them, headed towards his office for seclusion. I'm barely through the door before Luke slams it shut and immediately puts his mouth on mine and nearly engulfs me. The passion that became out of control on the dance floor is now set free. His lips part from mine and start trailing down my neck, I arch my head, extending it to the side as far as possible, granting him access, wanting more. This is need, it's raw, desperate, and demanding.

Luke's body is pressed hard against mine. His hand eagerly, but purposefully trails down the side of my hip, my thigh and then grabs me behind the knee and places it onto his hip. Steadying myself by using his shoulders and the back of the door, I wrap my legs around his waist. I groan when I feel his hardness pressing against the ache at my core. A few thin layers of clothes is all that separates us, that awareness sends flames shooting through me and I gasp...I want him, and I want him to have me. I try to completely unbutton his shirt. I let out a soft groan of protest, unable, but resolved to complete my task, unwrap my legs from his waist and gently push him back.

Luke raises an eyebrow in question but grins when I smile at him and keep unbuttoning his shirt. He walks backwards towards his desk and I follow, thoroughly engrossed in my mission. When his shirt is finally hanging open in the front, exposing his ripped and defined chest, I let out a deep groan. My fantasy has turned to reality and it is not disappointing.

He's beautiful. I can't help but press a kiss to the center of his well-defined chest. I shimmer lower and place kisses on each of his six pack abs, ending at his hip bones, where I nibble for a bit on one and then trail my tongue across his stomach to the other side, where I obtain equal delight from the other. I feel my own tremble and tighten my now rubbery legs. Before I can proceed with my inventory, Luke interrupts, pulls me up, embraces me, and we lock lips. We kiss long and deep and then he abruptly steps away from me.

Luke walks to the front of his desk and to my shock swipes the top of it, knocking everything to the floor. A high-pitched, but weak gasp is expelled and I giggle. "I've always wanted to do that," he smiles mischievously. "Come here."

I go without hesitation. Whatever Luke's intentions are, I am a one hundred percent willing participant. When I reach Luke's side, he tugs on my dress with a question in his eyes. I lift up my arm and point to the zipper on the side. Luke unzips the dress, one unbearably slow inch at a time, drawing out the anticipation. When my side is fully exposed, he slides my dress down my body until it drops to the floor.

Standing there in my lingerie and high heels, Luke gasps as he lets his eyes slowly roam my body from head to toe, lingering on my breasts and at the tops of my thighs. I blush. "Oh my god, you are absolutely breathtaking. My imagination didn't even begin to do you justice."

I move closer, he puts his hands around my waist, and props me on the desk. Woah. How…erotic. He turns, grabs his desk chair and sits down, rolling it towards me. "I want to touch you and taste you angel. I want this to be about you. No buts, let me do this."

I look in his eyes and see the heat and raw desire there. I nod my head up and down. Well, if he insists, what kind of person would I be to deny him? *Yeah right, Olivia, you are such a giver.*

With him sitting in the desk chair, he is eye-to-eye with my breasts. He leans forward, keeping eye contact with me the whole time. I begin to pant in and out in anticipation of him reaching his destination. He closes his mouth around my nipple and teases it through the fabric of my bra. The feel of his mouth, the lace, and his tongue further arouse me; my head falls back and I let out a moan. He gently bites down before moving to the other breast and gives it the same attention.

His hands that were at my knees start climbing up my thighs and then they travel up my back to the clasp of my bra. Unfastening it, he slides the straps off my shoulders and down my arms. When he pulls the fabric away, I watch him take in the sight of my bare breasts. My nipples are hard, I'm beyond excited and ready to fall off the edge.

Luke's mouth is on me again and he circles his tongue around my nipples on each breast again and again, making me writhe in ecstasy. His hands slide to tease the inside of my thigh. He moves them up and comes close to my center, then moves them away again. He repeats this over and over, and every time I think he's finally going to touch me, he moves away, teasing me mercilessly. He pulls back and looks at me, and I know he sees the need and want in my eyes; I don't have to say a word. He leans in, his lips reaching for mine at the same time his hand moves up my inner thigh and finally, it doesn't stop and he touches me right where I'm aching for him.

He strokes me through my panties and I clench my teeth tight in an effort to keep myself from losing it. He moves my panties aside and strokes his long fingers up and down, teasing me before he starts moving a finger in and out, in and out. At the same time, his tongue is mirroring the same action in my mouth.

I'm so close to coming. Just when I think I can't take it anymore, Luke slides my panties down my hips and thighs. "Gorgeous. You're lovely, angel. I've never seen anything so beautiful in my life. I can't believe you are here. That I have you again."

I place my hand on the side of his face speechless, words are inadequate. "Lean back," he says. Reclining on my elbows Luke grabs my knees pushing them open, my heels on the edge of the desk .

When the warmth of his mouth touches my hot center, I nearly jolt off the desk raising my hips in excitement. Luke's tongue repeatedly strokes me up and down and concentrates on that one sweet spot. I can feel my orgasm building and building. I'm almost there. Almost there. "Oh God. Luke. Don't stop. Oh God."

When he sucks on the small nub that will take me to heaven, that's all it takes and the clouds part and the angels start to sing. White hot heat hits my belly, I open my mouth in a silent scream, my hips come off the desk and I pump my hips, using his tongue to ride it out. I feel like I'm having an out of body experience.

I dig my heels into the edge of the desk and on some level, I realize Luke has backed up, hooded eyes watching me, just enjoying the show. As I come down from my intense high, I push down hard with my heels raising my hips too high and suddenly I go tumbling off the desk and crash onto my head. "OUCH! FUCK!" I yell.

I pop up as fast as I can. "I'm okay, I'm okay. Show's over. Nothing to see here."

I look over at Luke and his eyes are wide and his mouth is hanging open. He chokes out, "Are you okay?"

"Yes," I manage through my embarrassment and the fact I'm still feeling the after effects of my orgasm.

Once Luke knows I'm fine and didn't give myself a concussion, he laughs so hard that tears stream down his face.

At first, I look at him completely mortified. A blush, that is already staining my cheeks starts moving its way down my body. He's laughing at me but then, as I look at my sexy man, I can't help but laugh right along with him.

Laughing at myself.

And it feels so good.

Chapter Twenty-Four

"Fashion tip: Crocs, anything requiring batteries, trucker hats, leggings being worn as pants and too short jorts are a few things that you should treat like a fashion virus. Just say no!"

The last few weeks with Luke have been amazing. We've gone everywhere – the aquarium, the zoo, the museum, the planetarium. My favorite date was when we went to Navy Pier. It was chilly that evening, but we still did everything and anything. We played games like children. We rode the ferris wheel and kissed at the very top. We even went on a skyline boat tour just for fun, it was beautiful. Luke held me close and we delighted in the sights as though it was our first time viewing any of it. The skyline at dusk will always take my breath away. Finally, we cuddled up and watched the colorful fireworks at the end of the night and shared several kisses between "oohs" and "aahs". It was a perfect evening.

After each date, Luke would drop me off at the condo and walk me to the door, like a perfect gentleman. Other than kissing, and a bit of groping through our clothes, we haven't been intimate since the night at his club. I'm ready for more, and I'm sure Luke is too. He may be trying to be considerate and hesitant to push me too fast, but the fact is that I have needs and may physically combust if I don't have some release for all this pent up sexual frustration.

Trying to regain self-discipline from my daydreaming, I am sitting at my computer and supposed to be typing out a blog post that that will also serve as an article for Got Style magazine. The title is '*10 Things People Should Never Wear. Ever.*' I expect some will disagree with my opinion but that's okay, the conversation my views stimulate is one of the reasons I love what I do. I'm putting the finishing touches on the article when there's a knock on my door.

"Hi Livvie, whatcha' doin'?"

"Hiya, love! Just finishing up a blog post and article, then I need to get ready for my date with Luke. Want to help me pick something to wear?"

"Sure," she smiles, "where are you two love birds going this time?"

I roll my eyes at the use of the words 'love birds'. "I don't know. That's why I want you to pick something out. I'm thinking about it too much, which is making the decision harder than it needs to be. He merely told me our destination is a surprise."

Pyper jumps up and down clapping her hands, "Oh yay! I love surprises! Did he give you any hints? Did he tell you how to dress or anything like that?"

"Not really, other than telling me to dress comfortably and to bring a jacket. And you do not love surprises; you can't keep a secret to save your life."

Pyper gasps and strikes a dramatic pose which entails one hip being cocked and her hands placed on her hips, "That is not true, Olivia Brooks! I am the best secret keeper ever." She holds her hand out and starts counting out on her fingers, "I never told your mom that time you broke her favorite vase from Italy. I never told Luke where to find you, even when he begged me. I never told anyone about that time you were in college and you sent me the pictures of you almost naked and…"

"NO! NO! Do not finish that sentence. The official story is that that never happened, remember? We do not speak of it," I reply in horror.

"I think I've proven my point," she says full of sass.

"I concede, you win. Good point. You are a master secret keeper and the bestest friend ever. Thank you for the reminder that as my best friend you can embarrass me and ruin me in seconds should you repeat half of what you know about me!" *Of course that goes both ways,* I think to myself, smiling wickedly.

"Damn straight," Pyper replies. "Now, let me go through your clothes and find you an outfit."

"Thanks, bestie," I say, still trying to kiss her ass. I'm no fool.

"Yeah, yeah." She winks at me and raises her eyebrows. She's no fool either.

While she's in my closet sliding hanger after hanger across the bar, looking through everything, she turns to me and says, "How are you doing, really? I mean, you know, how does it feel to be back with Luke?"

"I haven't been this happy in a long time," I confess, "but part of me still feels... I don't know. I guess the best word would be fear. Part of me still feels afraid. I guess I haven't completely overcome the fear yet?"

Pyper raises her eyebrows and a concerned look flashes across her face, "Afraid? Fear? What do you mean?"

"I know, without a doubt, that Luke is what I want. When I saw Rebecca in his office and ran out, as infuriating as that was, it gave me clarity. It made me realize I want to be with Luke. I think on some level, I'm waiting for the next ball to drop. I hate feeling like this. Like I'm just waiting for something bad to come and ruin it all."

"Why do you think you are feeling like that?" Pyper gives up her task for the moment and is leaning her hip against the doorframe of my closet door; her attention completely on me.

I click publish, my blog is done, then I shut my laptop so I can give her my full attention too. "I know that part of the reason is because I'm still learning to trust Luke again. While I understand why he told his mom what he did, it doesn't change the fact that he should never feel like he has to lie about how he feels about me."

"Olivia, you were just kids," Pyper reminds me.

"You took the words out of my mouth. I was going to say that I know we were young and he just wanted her off of his back. I get it, but the part of my heart that is still protecting itself says that isn't an excuse. I forgive him, but I haven't completely let it go yet."

"Just keep giving yourself some time. No one says you should be over it yet, or maybe you never do get over it completely Olivia."

"Yeah, maybe."

Pyper is about to turn back around when I blurt out, "His mom wants to see me."

Pyper's head snaps back around to me. "Woah. What did Luke say about that?"

I think back to a conversation Luke and I had last night on the phone. "He told me that he told his mom that we are seeing each other again. He says she is sorry for what happened and she wants to see me in person to apologize and make amends for what she said. She feels bad for how she treated me back then."

"Wow, Olivia. That's huge. What did you say?"

The heaviness of my heart with the weight of my decision makes me sigh, "I told him I would think about it. He was quick to assure me that I didn't have to, but I think I'd like to. Maybe it would help me let go of the last bit of bitterness I'm hanging on to. Plus, I think it would make Luke happy."

"I'm not telling you what to do..."

I smile because she and I both know she always tells me what to do, "But..."

"But, I think you should see her too. I think it would help like you said."

"Maybe. One thing I do know, the decision is mine to make, no one else's." I look at her a little pointedly.

"Right you are," Pyper smiles knowingly and turns back around to finish her task of finding my outfit.

I'm getting the hang of this being in control thing. Deacon made me so insecure. All of my choices and decisions felt suspect. After a while, it was just easier to give him complete control. Moreover, if without complete control, he was abhorrent and there was no way to deal with him. Since I've been away from him and taken control back of my life, I'm remembering more and more every day what a strong, independent, intelligent woman I am who is fully capable of deciding her own path in life. It doesn't hurt that I have the great support of Pyper, and now Luke.

Pyper walks out of the closet with clothes in her arms. "Okay, I've got it all figured out. Let me show you and feel free to tell me how awesome I am. I've got these black leggings with this long, gray, off the shoulder sweater and this black tank top to go underneath the sweater. Then, I grabbed this teal scarf which will look great with the gray and either these black ballet flats or these knee-high black boots." She holds everything up for me, as she talks about each one, for inspection.

"I like it. Comfortable and warm like Luke said, and I'm thinking I want the ballet flats. Can you also grab my black Coach bag with the long strap please?"

Pyper goes to the closet again, "Oh yes, perfect choice!"

"Why, thank you my dear!" I tease.

"Can I help you do your hair and makeup like we used to?" Pyper asks.

I laugh, "Sure! That would be fun! I want to throw my hair up in a braided bun anyway and you do them the best."

Pyper does a slight bow, "At your service, ma'am."

I giggle at her and head to my bathroom with Pyper following.

An hour later, I am standing against the wall, while Pyper takes a picture of my outfit so I can post it on my blog later. I have to admit, I do look really fashionable. I may be casual, but Pyper had fun with my makeup and gave me a very smoky eye with gray eyeshadow and put lots of pink on my cheeks and lips. With my hair in a bun with what looks like a huge braid wrapped around it, combined with my off the shoulder sweater and leggings, I look like I just stepped off of an old episode of The Hills. I look very casual chic. I like it.

"Thank for your help, Pyper."

"But of course! I'm going to go get something to drink. Want anything?"

"No, thanks."

I grab my leather jacket from my closet, and just as I finish changing out my purses, I hear a knock on the front door. Perfect timing. I grab my phone off the charger and head out of my bedroom, closing the door behind me.

Pyper must have let Luke in, because I hear voices coming from the kitchen. I pause in the hallway before completely revealing myself and listen to them banter back and forth. "All I'm saying is that you totally owe me, Easton. If it wasn't for my helping you out when she was going on those horrid dates, you wouldn't even be together now."

I hear Luke laugh, "Okay, well I will give you that. Your sleuthing was very helpful."

"Helpful? It was freaking gold and you know it. I was like a freaking double agent for you!" Pyper says, sounding very affronted that he wasn't kissing her feet.

"I wouldn't go that far. I mean you passed on some helpful information, but double agent sounds a bit...I don't know...dramatic," Luke says.

I hear Pyper snort and I have to smother a giggle, "Do you know me at all? Of course it sounds dramatic! Now, what are you going to get me as a present to thank me for my help?"

"Present? Are you serious? I already had to bribe you with two pairs of Christian Loubotin shoes. Do you know how much that set me back? Wait, what am I saying? Of course you know." Luke sounds exasperated. As much as I enjoy listening to him sweat, I decide he's had enough.

"I knew it was shoes, Pyper. I knew it! You are so predictable." I say.

Pyper turns to me with a sheepish look on her face, Luke turns to me with his signature sexy smirk as he looks me up and down. I have eyes only for him. He looks delectable in jeans, a blue button down shirt that is untucked and rolled up at the sleeves. His black boots finish the look. It's not the clothes – it's how he fills them out. He makes my mouth water. Walking over to me, he hands me a few pink roses. "You look gorgeous as always," he says, giving my heart wings and making me smile. I place a soft kiss on his lips in thanks.

"Thank you. For the compliment and the roses," I tell him with a smile.

"I'll put them in a vase for you, Olivia," Pyper takes them from my hand. "You guys go ahead. Have fun. Don't worry about me. Here. Alone."

"Oh, please. I don't buy that sad speech for a second," I tell her, "you could have your choice of the litter on Date Me, so why don't you take advantage."

"Date Me?" Asks Luke, a question in his voice.

"A dating site," Pyper tells him then turns to me. "My last date through them didn't go well and I'm just giving up. I'm just meant to be single, I think."

She's too much. "Oh, please. Is this the same girl that kept making me go out over and over and even go speed dating?"

"Speed dating?" Luke asks and is ignored when Pyper says, "I did that for you, not for me."

"Whatever, Pyper. Stop being a bore and go meet some people. Why don't you jump like you told me or is that advice only good one way? Or don't, because you know what I think?"

"Oh no. Do I want to know what you think?"

I choose to ignore that question, "I think you will meet someone when you are least expecting it."

"I can set you up with one of the guys from the club I bet," Luke offers.

"Ew. No thanks. I prefer my men to be tie-wearing professionals, thank you."

"Hey!" Luke and I both say at the same time in defense.

"I'm allowed to have a type, you know." Pyper says, sticking up for herself and I swear her nose is slightly raised in the air, but I won't call her out on it. This time.

"Of course you are. I love you no matter what. We are leaving. Bye." I tell her with a smile, putting this conversation away for later.

"Bye, Livvie. Have fun, and I love you too. Luke, take care of our girl." Pyper says.

"Always." He tells her, but he's looking at me when he responds.

We head out the door and close it behind us.

When we are in the elevator, Luke pushes the button for the parking garage and turns to me, pressing me against the wall.

"Remember when we rode down this elevator together for the first time when I convinced you to go to breakfast with me?"

"Yes, I remember," I tell him looking into his eyes, loving the feel of his body pressed against mine.

Luke leans in closer, his lips are almost touching mine and he says, "I wanted to kiss you so bad it was a physical ache in my stomach. I wanted to touch your hair," he says while putting a lock of my hair between his fingers. "I wanted to cup your face in my hand," he says and then does it. "I wanted to look deep into your eyes," My eyes couldn't look away from his if they wanted to. I'm in a trance listening to what he's saying, "and tell you that every second, minute, and year apart from you caused physical pain. I missed you, angel. I wanted to press my lips to yours and taste you, to see if you taste as good as I remembered."

My heart is racing, his words slamming need through every inch of me. "And do I?" I ask, my voice gravelly with lust.

"Even better," he whispers, and he puts his mouth on mine. I open immediately and he sucks my tongue in his mouth. He tastes better than I remember too. I pull back a little and nibble and suck on his bottom lip. He groans, then pulls me closer to his body, leaving no space between us. The tips of my fingers are digging into his back and his hands are tangled in my hair, clutching fistfuls. Nothing else matters but him and this moment.

I barely register the ding of the elevator as it arrives to the parking garage; I'm so caught up in the taste, smell and feel of the man in my arms.

We hear a throat clear and reluctantly pull apart. Luke turns around and I get on my tip toes to see over his shoulder. An older man using a cane is standing there waiting for us to vacate. Fortunately he has a smile playing on his lips. "Sorry, sir." Luke murmurs as he grabs my hand and leads me to the car.

Once we are both situated in the car, Luke opens the console between us and he pulls out black silk. "I want you to put this on please."

I look closer at his hands to see he has a black sleep mask. "Why do I have to wear that?"

"Because I want you to be surprised."

I hesitate.

"For me, angel?"

I can't say no to that, "Okay. I'll wear it."

He leans over and kisses me on the lips and lingers for a moment, "Thank you."

I will do anything this man asks me to do if he keeps kisses like that coming. I look at the mask warily, but take it and put it over my eyes. "Can you see anything?"

"Everything straight ahead is completely black. There is a little light coming from the bottom but I only see my lap."

"Okay that's fine, but no tilting your head back to try and see," Luke teases.

"Oh alright, I promise. Geesh, I'm not six-years-old, you know."

Luke laughs. "Alright, we are off to your surprise."

I grin to myself. I can't wait.

Chapter Twenty-Five

"Fashion tip: Weather can be unpredictable. Don't be caught with your mascara running! Fold up umbrellas come in all kinds of fashionable prints. They can complement your shoes and handbag, and give you your own sense of style."

We drive for a while and make small talk about how his mom is feeling, how it looks like it might rain, and Luke talks about a recent shipment of some dated scotch he was able to acquire that he's excited about.

I finally feel the car come to a stop. "Wait right here, I will come around and get you, okay?"

"Okay." I really have no idea where we are, and I feel a little anxious. I hope I like it.

The door next to me opens and I feel the heat from Luke's body as he reaches across me to take off my seatbelt. Taking my hand into his, he tugs, silently suggesting I step out, and places his hand on my head so I don't hit it on the door frame of the car. Once I'm out, he places both hands on my shoulders. "Just a second." I hear him shut my door, and a "pop" like that heard when a trunk opens. Standing there, trying to determine where we are, I hear leaves rustling, feel a slight wind in my hair and suddenly the sound of the trunk closing.

Taking my hand back in his again, he says, "Okay, I'll lead you."

We walk for a little while and based upon the soft ground I feel under my feet and the fact I can feel something brush against my legs occasionally, I start to have an idea of where we are and tears start to flood my eyes.

We stop and I hear some rustling again for a moment. "Okay, are you ready?" Luke asks after a few seconds, sounding a little breathless, like he's nervous.

"I'm ready," I respond, my throat full of emotion.

He lifts the mask off my head and it takes me a moment to orient myself to my surroundings. Once I do, I take in a long deep breath. We are exactly where I thought we might be. Standing in front of "our tree". Luke has spread a blanket on the ground underneath the tree, and I look at him before I can bring myself to look at the tree. He nods toward it and my eyes move to the large trunk of "our tree."

The tears in my eyes escape and fall down my face. I can't stop my tears when I see 'L loves O' carved in the tree right where he put it years ago. Except as I look closer, it appears as though it's freshly carved. I look at Luke with a question on my face.

His eyes look a little glassy too and he swallows a few times before he answers my unasked question, "I came here earlier today. Our carving was here, but a little faded, so I carved over the old one so it would stand out more."

I step to the tree and brush my hand over them. My tears are coming faster now. "I still remember the day you did this."

Luke steps behind me, enfolding me in his arms, "I remember too. We were having a picnic and I was looking at the tree and thinking about how it had become ours. It was our place to come and be with each other. I knew even then that our love would last forever. Today, like then, I wanted to declare it to the universe."

I smile at him, remembering his concentration as he worked hard to carve our initials into the hard, rough bark with his pocket knife. He had gotten some scratches and scrapes on his fingers for the effort but he was so proud when it was complete.

"I love it. Thank you for bringing me here. I never thought I would be back here again."

"Let's sit."

"Okay," I respond and walk over to the blanket a couple feet away and have a seat facing the tree so I can still see our initials. Luke sits down next to me.

Luke is quiet and I feel him staring at me. "What's wrong?"

I smile at him and Luke smiles softly and says, "I love you." He said it so quietly I almost didn't hear him.

I just stare at him in response, and Luke speaks again, louder this time, "I love you, Olivia."

I just look at him and feel my throat close up as it fills with emotion at his confession. I feel like I can't speak. My heart is ready to burst at his words and the butterflies are on steroids in my stomach. I feel a mixture of excitement and fear. It's the same feeling I was telling Pyper about. I know my eyes are displaying the panic I feel at his words, because his eyes widen in response. Then he straightens his back, lifts up his chin and looks at me with determination and purpose.

"Olivia. I have loved you every minute of every day since you left me. Every second I missed you, longed for you. I tried to move on, but I felt the loss of you not only in my heart, but in my soul. There were moments when I couldn't breathe because the pain of losing you was so strong, so brutal, that at times I lost all ability to even function. I could sit and stare at nothing for hours, just replaying our last moments together and the lie you heard me say over and over again in my mind. Sometimes I would daydream that there was a different outcome, and I even prayed to God for the chance to just talk to you, to explain. In my darkest times, I would beg him to just turn back time so I could fix everything, knowing there was no way that could happen, but wishing for it all the same."

His words make my panic begin to subside and the tears return to my eyes. I swallow back a sob.

"For a while, I didn't even know how it was possible to move on without you. Somehow I managed to, but I don't even know how, to be honest. Survival instinct, I guess. I searched for you, I begged and pleaded with family and friends to try and find you. I would have sold my soul to the devil for one more minute with you. Eventually, I lost hope and with that, a small piece of me died, and the other tried to move on, but was always keeping one eye open for you just in case."

"When I saw you that day at the restaurant, the very girl that still haunts my dreams, I didn't waste any time thanking God for bringing you back to me." Luke stops and swallows again. I need to move. I stand because I need a little space between us. I walk to the tree and stare at our initials until I feel Luke come up behind me and whirl me around placing his hands on my shoulders.

"Olivia, I will spend every day of the rest of my life begging you to forgive me. I will do anything you want. Anything. But please, all I'm asking is for your forgiveness and for you to just love me. Tell me there's a chance, tell me you can get there, tell me what I can do."

I just stand there and look at him, feeling scared but also a new feeling starts to run through my body. I had already forgiven him, but in a way I don't think I'd forgiven myself. I'm just as much to blame for what happened because I ran. I didn't trust Luke either.

"Luke, I've not only forgiven you, but I've forgiven myself too."

"Forgiven yourself? For what?"

"I realized something the night at the club when I almost ran away again, and right now while listening to you, it's even clearer. I had already forgiven you for what had happened, but in a way I don't think I'd forgiven myself." Luke opens his mouth to interrupt me, but I place my fingers against his lips quieting him. "I may not have been the one to tell a lie, but I'm just as guilty for what happened as a result of it. I ran, Luke. I assumed the worst and I ran. I've spent almost every day since running. I didn't trust you. I just made an assumption and based my actions on that assumption. I'm so tired of running. I want to stay in place, to trust again. I want to learn to trust myself again and I trust you. Can *you* ever forgive *me*?"

"Angel," he whispers, "there's nothing to forgive."

"But there is. I'm so sorry for not trusting in you, for not trusting in us. Please forgive me."

As I look at him and wait for his reply, I feel a few rain drops hit me on the scalp and nose. I look up into the sky, my eyes in a squint. The sky is darkening fast. Luke still hasn't responded, but I can feel him looking at me intently. I meet his stare, "What is it?"

"I forgave you years ago, so if you need to hear it then yes, I forgive you."

My eyes fill up with tears again and I feel relief run through my body like a river from head to toe. I didn't realize how much I needed to hear those words.

Four years it took me to snap out of the illusion my mind had created for me when I was married to Deacon. Years to finally get a clue and to confront the reality of what my marriage really was. One big giant lie that I had tried to make look pretty in my mind, but that's the thing…I didn't believe the lie because I had to; I believed it because I wanted to. I was still running. I didn't want to admit failure, I worried about what others would think, and I didn't want to be alone. I allowed myself to live a lie because I was afraid of those things, and that is so much worse than the very things I feared.

As I think those words, they take on a whole new meaning. It's like the clouds part and let the sunshine in, even though it is starting to rain harder – a light, but steady sprinkle. Everything inside of me is screaming for me to just admit to him that I love him too. Oh! I love him too! I need to trust my heart and let down my walls. I've been ignoring these emotions inside of me. And why? Because my dignity and proving a point is more important? Because I'm worried about people judging me? What people? There is no one in my life right now other than my parents and Pyper. Deacon made me ostracize everyone. So what am I so fearful of? When am I going to finally stop making excuses? That isn't me. Not anymore. Now, I'm a woman that finally stands up and takes control of what she wants. I'm a woman that needs to start listening to her heart and stop living in fear. It's time I jump again and trust my instincts. They've never been wrong – I knew deep inside marrying Deacon was a mistake – but I just pushed them aside and forgot to trust myself.

I already have far too many regrets at the young age of twenty-five. I don't want to add anymore to the already too long list.

Luke is watching me and waiting, instinctively knowing I needed to work some things out for myself before responding. My heart aches a little looking at him. He's wringing his hands in nervousness, his shoulders have slumped and he's biting his lip, but there is a glimmer of hope in his eyes while he watches me.

I step to him and raise up on my toes to kiss him. My lips just whisper against his at first. I trace the seam of his lips begging for entry, he gives it and I kiss him deeply. I take the lead and stroke my tongue against him, exploring his mouth and putting everything I'm feeling into it. Everything that I haven't yet said to him. My hands clutch his shirt in tight fists. His arms come around me and he presses our bodies together. I kiss him for another minute and then pull away, breathless. "Luke, I love you too. I never stopped. I want to be with you, I've missed you so very much. For the first time in a very long time, I feel complete again. I feel like I'm home when I'm with you and I don't ever want to lose you again. You don't have to ask me to love you, I already do."

The smile on Luke's face is brilliant. He responds by kissing me and this time, he's the one that takes the lead. He doesn't beg for entry, he takes it. I feel his love, relief and need in our kiss. It instantly gains heat and before I know it, he's backed me up against the tree. I lift my legs wrapping them around his waist. Luke's hands are flat on either side of my head and I pull apart from him.

I look into his eyes and the love and passion I see there takes my breath away. I hope he sees the same look in mine. Despite the sanctuary offered by our tree, the occasional drops of rain that started as a cold gentle caress demand more attention now as they gain strength and fall harder and more frequently against our skin. I couldn't care less, all I can think about is how much I want him. Now.

I start unbuttoning his shirt and when I reach the end I push it off his shoulders and down his arms and for the first time his whole upper body is completely bared to me, which is why I see the tattoo dusting his skin for the first time. On his upper arm a large circle with an interweaving pattern sits there. It's beautiful. I smile, "Wow. A tattoo? Aren't you full of surprises?"

Luke smiles, "Do you like it? It's called a Celtic tattoo. The tattoo tells a story."

"Yes, I like it. It's hot." Luke's grin widens. "Why a Celtic tattoo??"

"A Celtic knot is a design that has no beginning and no end. It represents repeatable cycles of rebirth and death. But most importantly to me, it also symbolizes love and personal growth. I got it…" Luke swallows, "I got it because it reminds me of you."

My mouth opens. Then closes again. "Of me? How?"

"Yes you, angel," he says as he brushes my hair out of my face, "Always you. It reminds me that I should always tell the truth, that my journey of personal growth is not something I should blow off. The knots have no beginning and no end, like my love for you. This knot design also means that all our paths are connected and I've always hoped mine would cross with yours again. I got it about a year ago."

I gasp, "A year ago? But…but I left seven years ago."

He smiles sadly, "I know."

My love for him flows through my body. This man is everything. I want him now, and every day from now on. "Luke, I love you. I'm so glad our paths crossed again. I need you. Now."

Luke looks at me with surprise, "Here? Now? It's raining."

"Here. Right now, like this, here. It should be here don't you think?"

"Olivia…"

"Luke. I love you. Now touch me. Don't make me beg."

"Never," he replies breathlessiy.

Luke lifts my sweater over my head. Then he lifts my tank top up exposing my sheer bra. He touches my breasts and moans. "You have the most beautiful breasts, Olivia." I groan.

I unwrap my legs from his waist and push him away from me a little, my back still against the tree. I reach for his pants and start unbuckling them. Pushing him away a little more, I stroke him and then drop to my knees and take him into my mouth. Luke's groan of pleasure makes heat enter my belly and flood between my legs. I run my tongue up and down his length again and again until I feel Luke tug on me pulling me back up. "I want you now."

We pull my leggings down, I slip one leg out leaving the other inside. Not perfect, yet at the same time, just right. Luke walks toward me and puts my back against the tree once again. He presses our hips together and I feel his erection between my legs. "Now, Luke."

The rain is pouring now and Luke and I are soaking wet, but I do not care. All I notice is him and how beautiful his skin looks with water pouring down it. He presses closer and I put my legs around his waist again and Luke starts easing himself into me and I've never felt more full. Complete.

We both groan together and Luke begins sliding in and out. I've never wanted anyone more. Our bodies are wet and each time we come together when he thrusts, our bodies make a loud slapping sound. He reaches down and starts stroking me and I throw my head back in pleasure, banging it against the trunk of the tree, but I barely notice.

A feeling unlike any other starts gathering in my belly. Like a constant ache that I can feel, but not quite reach, my orgasm approaches. "More, Luke." In response, Luke moves faster and he sets my nerve endings on fire. I'm lost to him, and before I know it, I'm tumbling over the edge, as I'm finally able to reach the ache and make it mine, leaving me to shudder uncontrollably. With a couple more thrusts and a whispered, "Angel," Luke soon follows me. He doesn't remove himself from me completely, just holds me to his body, both of us trying to get our breathing under control.

"I love you, Olivia," he whispers in my ear.

"I love you too, Luke."

I'm complete.

I'm whole.

I have the 'more' I've been searching for and deserve.

Chapter Twenty-Six

"Fashion tip: When meeting people for the first time, first impressions are very important. Wear something that is a reflection of who you really are! Don't be afraid to show your personality and taste."

I'm preparing to leave the restaurant where I just had a great oriental salad for lunch. Having decided that it was time for me to expand my world, meet some new people and make new friends, I joined a local writers group. While both Pyper and Luke have friends that would likely be glad to include me in their circle, it's important to me to do this on my own. I'm sure I'll eventually meet more of their friends, but going through this process, connecting and relating to people and selecting friends and acquaintances based on mutual enjoyments and opinions, is exciting.

Our first meeting was really great. I met three women that I felt like I could possibly have a great friend connection with over time. We'll see, but Lauren, Cindy, and Tami were all really nice girls and I'm already looking forward to getting to know them better. Not only do we share a love of reading, I enjoyed finding out that we have a lot in common, including fashion – especially a love for handbags. It's like they had a key to my heart.

Before I approach the turn style door, the maître d' stops me with "Miss?" Presenting me with a wrapped bouquet of red roses he states, "These were delivered here for you. I believe the card is inside. Have a wonderful day!"

Nearly skipping to my car, I remove my phone from my jeans pocket. I had it on vibrate while we lunched so we wouldn't be disturbed. Having felt a buzz earlier, I look at the screen. I smile seeing Luke's name. "I woke up wanting to kiss you. I can't wait to see you tonight. I love you, angel."

He makes me glow with happiness. When I looked at myself in the mirror the other day and saw this girl staring back at me, with eyes shining full of love, dark circles under her eyes gone and cheeks flushed in health, I barely recognized myself.

It's been a couple weeks since our date at our tree. I smile and blush, just thinking about it. To say Luke and I have been hot and heavy since then is a drastic understatement. We can't seem to spend enough time together or get enough of each other right now. We can't keep our hands to ourselves. I crave him like a drug and I hope to never get enough. I love him more than I ever thought it was possible to love someone.

I unlock the car and quickly take my seat, eager to look at the card that came with the flowers. I smile. I love that Luke surprises me like this. I hope he never stops. It makes me feel so special. I wonder if he gave me red roses now that we've declared our love for one another.

I pull the card out and before reading it place the roses to my nose. They smell exquisite. A beautiful deep blood red color, they have partially opened and are gorgeous. I open the card reading the note, "Come home as soon as you can. Have a surprise for you."

A surprise? I wonder what it is. I wasn't supposed to see him until tonight. I look at my text again and see it came in an hour ago. He must have changed his mind since he sent it. Tonight we have plans to go to his childhood home. I told Luke a few days ago that I decided to meet with his mother. I know it means a lot to him that I have agreed to see her. Luke asked me if I was sure and said again that I didn't have to do it if I didn't want to, but I think it's time to put that part of our life behind us. We are back together and happier than ever. It's time to move on, and I know part of that includes seeing and forgiving her.

Luke and I spoke recently about moving in together. I am conflicted. I don't want to bail on Pyper, I enjoy our time together and I know she is just as happy to have me there as I've been to be there. While I know she would be thrilled for me if I moved in with Luke, I'm just not sure I can leave just yet. However, the thought of waking up in Luke's arms every day fills me with warmth. I can't imagine anything more wonderful. I have been spending a lot of time with him at his place, so maybe I should think about it some more. It does make sense.

Pyper makes fun of us, saying we are too lovey dovey for her, that it makes her nauseated. I just laugh, because I see her smile secretly at us. When I told her what happened the night of our date at the tree she squealed and hugged me so hard. I started to cry when I was talking about it with her and she started to cry too, so then we laughed and shared ice cream and wine. I love that woman. Not for the first time, I acknowledge how lucky I am to have someone care for me and my happiness so much.

I pull into my designated parking space when I get to the parking garage and put the car in park, unbuckle my seatbelt and grab my phone. I text Luke a quick reply before exiting my car even though I know he must be here. In case he has a surprise, I suppose it would only be thoughtful of me to give him a heads up of my arrival.

"Thanks for the roses, handsome. I just pulled in. I love you too and can't wait to see you in a second."

I put my phone back in my jeans pocket, get out of the car after I grab my purse and roses then head to the elevator. I tap my foot impatiently, waiting for it to arrive.

DING. The sound of the elevator arriving makes me jump. Geesh what is wrong with me? I giggle a little at myself.

I enter the elevator and wait for it to ascend to my floor. I look up and around feeling impatient. I notice the camera in the corner of the elevator appears to be busted. The glass screen on the front of it looks smashed. Hmm. That's weird. I will have to report it.

The elevator arrives at my floor and I step out. I feel my phone vibrate in my pocket as I approach the front door. Ignoring it for a moment I reach in and take out my keys from my purse and put them in the lock, then I grab my phone and see Luke has texted me back.

"What roses? Where are you, angel?"

Huh? What does he mean what roses? I stare at his text in confusion. Oh well, I guess I will ask him in a second.

I turn the key in the lock and open the condo door. Stepping inside, I see red rose petals all over the floor. I smile. Now I know Luke was joking. What romantic encounter has he cooked up now? I place my keys in the bowl, put my phone back in my pocket and drop my purse by the front door too.

Looking up, I see Pyper's head. She's sitting on the couch that faces the view out the window so her back is to me. That's a bit surprising, given the rose petals and whatever Luke has cooked up. "Hi Pyper."

She doesn't turn to look at me in acknowledgement. "Pyper?" I wonder if she was hoping I wouldn't notice her and would just follow the rose trail, which looks like it may lead to my room. Or maybe she's on the phone. Luke won't mind if I check in with her for a second.

I approach the couch, "Hey, Pyper. I see you. Luke obviously has something cooked..." I stop because as I've rounded the end of the couch and reached Pyper's side, I realize she isn't speaking or moving because she can't. She is tied up from head to toe and has duct tape across her mouth. She looks at me with fear in her eyes. I drop the roses and run to her side, "Pyper! Oh my god! What happened? Are you okay? Did we get robbed?"

Fear engulfs me – I feel my eyes widen, the hair on the back of my neck stands up, and panic swells my throat. I want to untie her, but am unsure of where or how to actually begin. I may need a knife. She starts shaking her head back and forth over and over. I don't pay attention and reach for the tape at her mouth so she can talk to me and tell me what happened. Just then, I see movement out of the corner of my eye.

I look up and over to the right and the fear multiplies when I see Deacon standing there in my condo with blood red roses in one hand and a gun in the other.

"Hello, princess."

Author Jennifer Miller was born and raised in Chicago, Illinois but now calls Arizona home. Her love of reading began when she was a small child, and only continued to grow as she entered adulthood. Ever since winning a writing contest at the young age of nine, when she wrote a book about a girl with a pet unicorn, she's dreamed of writing a book of her own. The important lesson she learned about dreams is that they don't just fall into your lap – you have to chase them yourself. Most importantly, she is a wife and mother, and is very lucky to have a family that loves and supports her in all things. She also has an unhealthy addiction to handbags and chocolate covered strawberries, neither of which she cares to work on.

Bonus Material

Excerpt from Book 3 of the

Turn Towards the Sun

Series By Jennifer Domenico

I answer the ringing phone on my desk without checking the caller id. "Ava Milano speaking," I say.

"Ava Milano," the woman's voice repeats. I realize it sounds very familiar to me. "I have some information you might be interested in."

"Who is this?"

"Who is this? Come on, Ava, you know me. We go way back," she says.

A feeling of discontent settles over me. It can't be who I think it is. It just can't be. I stay silent, deciding my best bet is to wait for her to speak again.

"I think you should know that your darling husband Enzo has been quite the scoundrel. The minute you left him alone he couldn't wait to see me again. You think you've got him wrapped around your finger but I've got proof that you don't."

With a sinking feeling, I realize exactly who it is. Fucking Anna.

"How did you get this number?" I demand.

"It's a public number."

"You're not supposed to be contacting me or Enzo. I'll have you arrested for violating your parole."

She laughs bitterly into the phone. "How are you going to do that? You don't even know where I am. Did you hear what I said, *Mrs.* Milano?" she sneers. "I've already seen Enzo. It was divine too. You're so smug thinking you've got him. I thought you'd like to know he's not the faithful husband you think he is."

My whole body shakes with anger. "Oh please. Do you really expect me to believe that Enzo cheated on me with you? That's ludicrous, you insane bitch."

"Are you sure about that? Maybe you should ask him about me and the charity event he attended two months ago. You weren't with him, remember?"

My head spins. I'm smart enough to know this is some kind of ploy. There is no fucking way Enzo did anything with this whore. He hates her. We both do. To think I actually felt sorry for this pathetic bitch.

"I don't have time for your nonsense, Anna. You are completely insignificant to me and my life with Enzo. Whatever you're trying to do, you're wasting your time. I don't give a fuck about you."

She laughs again. "You will. I'm going to take everything you have. It's already started. You think things are so great but you have no idea I'm about to ruin your perfect little existence. You'll give a fuck by the time it's all over with."

Anna's words scare the shit out of me. I already know she's crazy enough to attempt murder, what else will she do? She's not even supposed to be near me much less calling me or seeing Enzo. If he did see her, why didn't he tell me?

I do my best to maintain my composure. "Are you done now? I have work to do, and I still don't give a fuck about you and your ridiculous threats. I will say this though, so you better listen." I take a deep breath. "You stay the fuck away from me and my husband. If I ever see your sorry face again or hear that you came anywhere near us, you won't have to worry about the police, Anna. I'll kill you with my bare hands. Believe it."

Sneak Peek of

Something Great

(July 24)
by author M. Clarke
(pen name for Bestselling author of the Crossroads Saga, Mary Ting)

I was just about to head in that direction when someone spoke to me from behind in a deep, manly voice that sent shivers down my back.

"I'm your prescription. Let me be your new addiction." His words glided like butter, smooth and cool.

Startled, I twitched, and turned my body to his voice. There he was, all six feet of him, peering down on me with that smile that could make me do just about anything. Though there was nothing to laugh about, especially seeing this hottie in front of me, I couldn't help but giggle from his words.

He wore beige casual pants and a black sweater that fit perfectly to the tone of his body. His hair was brushed to the side, showing his nice forehead. Whatever kind of cologne he had on made me want to dive right into his arms...maybe it wasn't the cologne, but just him.

"Pretty cheesy, huh?" he chuckled.

I shyly giggled as I stared down at my shoes. What is wrong with me? Answer him. "Umm...kind of," I smiled as I peered up, only to have him take my breath away again.

"Sorry. I just had to say that. You looked so lost and vulnerable. Did you need some help?"

Great! To him I was just a lost puppy...lost and vulnerable. "I actually found what I was looking for." I was staring into his eyes, melting, feeling myself sinking into him. Snap out of it!

"You certainly did," he said with a playful tone.

Arching my brows in confusion, I thought about what I'd said. From his perspective, my words had been about him.

"We meet again, for the third time."

He was counting?

"You left so abruptly at Café Express, I didn't get to ask you for your name."

"Umm...my name? Oh...my name is Jeanella Mefferd, but you can call me Jenna."

Extending his hand, he waited for me. "I'm Maxwell. But you can call me Max."

Nervously, I placed my hand in his to shake. It was strong, yet gentle...just right, and heat blazed through me from his touch.

"Are you here with someone?"

"Yes." I looked away shyly.

"Are you lost? Do you need some help?"

"Actually, I was looking for the restroom. Since I didn't know where it was I thought I'd ask the bartender, but I guess there isn't one, and I'm on my way to the restroom." I rambled nervously as I slowly pulled my hand back to point in the direction I meant to go. I had just realized we were holding hands during our short conversation. "So...I'd better go."

"I'll walk you there."

What? "Oh...no need. I'm sure I won't get lost." Feeling the heat on my face again, I turned before he could say another word, but it didn't matter what I had said. His hand was gently placed on my back, guiding me to the women's room. I turned my back to the bathroom door to thank him, but he spoke first.

"I think this is my stop," he muttered, looking straight at me. "I'm not wanted in there. What do you think?" He arched his brows, and his tone held a note of challenge.

Huh? He wants to go in with me? I gasped silently, as I was still lost in his eyes. "I think the women in there will throw themselves at you." I couldn't believe I'd said those words. I couldn't take it back. What was I doing, flirting with him?

He seemed to like what he heard. His arms reached out, his muscles flexing as he placed one on each side of me on the wall. With nowhere to go, I was trapped inside the bubble of his arms. He leaned down toward the left side of my face and brushed my hair with his cheek. "You smell...delicious," he whispered. His hot breath shot tingles to places I hadn't expected them.

Out of nervousness and habit, my left index finger flew inside my mouth. Max gave a crooked, naughty grin and slowly took my hand out of my mouth. "Did you know that biting one's finger is an indication one is sexually deprived?" His words came out slowly, playfully, but hot. "I can fix that for you, if you'd like."

He did not just say that to me! I parted my lips for a good comeback, but I couldn't find one. Feeling my chest rise and fall quickly, I tried to control the heated desire. Sure, he'd helped me once, but that didn't mean we were friends, or flirting buddies, or that I would allow him to fix my sexual deprivation. Oh God...can guys tell if you haven't done it in a very long time? This had to stop or else...oh dear...I wanted to take him with me into the restroom.

Needing to put a stop to the heat, I placed my hand on his chest... big mistake. Touching him made the heat worse, and tingles that were already intensifying burst through every inch of me. I had to push him away.

As if he knew what I meant to do, he pulled back, but his eyes did the talking instead. There was no need for words; I felt his hard stare on my body, as if he was undressing me with his gorgeous eyes. His gaze was powerful, as if his eyes were hands; I felt them all over me, completely unraveling me.

Just when I thought I was going to faint, his eyes shifted to mine again. "It was really nice to meet you, Jenna. I'm sure we'll see each other again, real soon. I better let you go. Your someone must be waiting for you. By the way...." There was a pause as he charmed me with his eyes again. "You...took my breath away. If I were your someone, I wouldn't let you out of my sight for even a second, because someone like me will surely try to whisk you away." He winked and left.

Chapter Two of

My Unexpected Forever

by *USA Today* Best Selling Author
Heidi McLaughlin

Katelyn

I SET THE PHONE DOWN, resting my head in my hands. I know I can do this. I just have to convince myself that Liam didn't make a mistake in hiring me. What was I thinking when I opened my mouth at Christmas saying I could be their manager? I fear I've bitten off more than I can chew, but Liam has confidence in me, even if I'm only booking 4225 West in small bars.

They laugh – the bar owners – when I call and book a gig. They ask if I'm joking and I assure them that I'm not. I tell them, repeatedly, that the band is trying a different angle, more family friendly and want to give back to the fans that have made them so popular. Still, I can hear the humor in their voices when they agree to a booking and the small fee is figured out. What they don't understand is with a bit of advertising they will clean house at the end of the night. 4225 West isn't asking for a large percentage; they just want to play and want to do it without the bright lights shining in their face.

My phone rings, startling me. I almost spill my coffee when I reach for the handset. My hand steadies the cup before there's a mess everywhere. I don't know where all these jitters are coming from… okay, yes I do. I know exactly what or who is setting me on edge. I just choose to ignore it. I can't focus on my children and career with the distractions that face me daily. I need to get through… I don't know what. He's my boss. That's what I keep telling myself, whether he's actually the one who signs my check or not. I work for him.

I pick up the phone on the fourth ring, clearing my throat and taking a deep breath before saying hello.

"Is this Katelyn Powell?"

"It is," I say, pulling my pad of paper closer to me to take notes.

"This is Christa Johnson and I represent an artist known as DeVon. He's an up-and-coming artist that we recently signed. His debut single releases next month and we're interested in getting him some attention. I'm calling to see if *4225 West* would be willing to work a small tour with him?"

"What type of music? He sounds more hip hop with a name like DeVon." I write down his name and scribble *research* next to it. I haven't heard of him, but that doesn't mean anything. When it comes to music, I'm pretty much in the clouds.

"You'd think, right? DeVon is actually blues with a rock vibe. It's very funky with a kick. We think that with the success of *4225 West*, DeVon will not only gain some fans, but will learn from the veterans and how they run a tour."

Veterans? I know I'm not a veteran when it comes to tours, but the guys are. Me? I'm just the person behind the desk trying to find places willing to pay them.

"Do you have venues set up?" This is important. How much work am I going to have to do?

"About fifteen, but we'd like thirty."

I can arrange the remaining venues. This will be good experience for me. "Where are you looking to tour?"

"Ideally, we'd like to hit the younger crowds, so Miami, New York City, Seattle."

"And when would you like to start?"

"We're hoping for August."

August? One month before school starts. Not that I need to be on tour with the guys, even though Liam will want me there. I'm sure Josie and Noah would go and Harrison would probably take Quinn as well. The guys have a new CD coming out and this would probably be a huge benefit for them. Thirty stops, is that enough?

"What about forty-five days?" I throw that number out there, hoping I'm doing the right thing. Liam has given me full reign to do whatever I see fit, but I still question everything. He rolls his eyes most of the time or tells me to ask Harrison and that's really not going to happen.

"We can do that."

"Great." Christa and I spend the next hour on the phone hashing out the details. I take copious notes and she promises to email the contacts from the venues she's already booked. We agree that I will take the lead as 4225 West will be the headliner.

I look out my window to see if the red studio light is still on. It's not. I gather my notepad and pen and head out to the studio. The guys are standing around Tyler, laughing. This is good. This means they've recorded something they like and are happy. I like happy.

Liam kisses me on the cheek when I walk up to him. He puts his arm around me, pulling me closer. He's been like this since he moved back. I'm not complaining. I love him like a brother and he's been there for us, helping out more than I could ever thank him for.

"Katelyn, did you meet Tyler?" Liam asks as he points to Tyler who nods.

"Yes, Jimmy brought him in to fill out his paperwork. Did you guys get something recorded?"

"No," Harrison says sharply. I look at him and immediately wish I didn't. He's staring at me, or Liam's hand. I'm not quite sure. Either way, his piercing green eyes are looking at me. His expression is stoic, almost hard.

"Well listen," I say. Liam drops his arms and moves so he's standing in front of me, leaving just enough space for the other guys to hear what I'm saying. We're talking business now; he's being serious. This Liam sometimes scares me. "I just got off the phone with a manager whose client is releasing a CD. His name is DeVon—"

"Is he a rapper?" Harrison asks, interrupting my spiel. I don't know why he does that, but it makes me want to slap my hand over his mouth.

I shake my head and continue. "DeVon is a blues artist with a bit of a rock kick. They're looking to build his fanbase and asked if we're interested in a tour. I figured with the CD about to come out, we could use the publicity so we're doing a forty-five-city tour starting in July. You guys will be back in time for the kids to start school."

"You guys?" Jimmy questions.

"Yes. I'll stay here."

"No, you'll be coming with us." Liam says. "Book a tour bus. Harrison can help. He has some connections and knows what we'll want. This will be fun."

Harrison and I stare at each other. The black beanie that he always wears is mocking my imagination of what his hair looks like. I've only seen him without his hat through pictures, never in person. I'm the first one to look away because I can't take the intense way he looks at me. Or maybe it's because I can't take the way I look at him. Or the way I want to know more about him.

Liam kisses me on the cheek before heading upstairs. He declares it's lunchtime before I have a chance to say anything. Jimmy and Tyler move faster than I've ever seen them before, leaving me with Harrison.

"Should we go into your office?"

I look up quickly, expecting him to smile or change his expression, but he doesn't. I remind myself that this is my job and he has the answers I need to get my job done; and as much as I don't want to sit in my office with him while he leans over me, it has to be done.

I nod and lead the way. I count the steps to my office and then to my desk; twenty, twenty-one, twenty-two. He pulls out my chair. I make the mistake of looking at him as I sit down. The slight turn of his lip tells me that he's happy to be here. He beat me into my office and I don't know how. Was I really walking that slowly?

He pushes in my chair slightly and leans over me. I try not to breathe in his cologne. I don't want to know what he wears, but he smells good. I lean away, closer to my screen and he leans in too. I wonder if he knows what he's doing to me. Doesn't he know I'm trying to avoid him? That we can never be anything?

Harrison tells me what site to bring up and I do. Except my

fingers aren't working and I have to type the web address repeatedly. He moves his fingers over mine. I pull them back instantly, afraid for him to touch me. My hands rest in my lap.

"Sorry, I was just trying to help."

I nod and realize how stupid I'm being. We can be friends, right?

He brings up the website and walks me through how to order a custom charter. He says that they've used this company before and to call and ask for Larry; he'll make sure we get what we need and in time. I write down what he tells me and he laughs. I turn slightly, but think twice and focus on my paper.

"I think I can take it from here."

"Katelyn?"

The sound of his voice, the way he says my name, low and sweet with just enough mystery, makes me look up at him causing me to mentally kick myself.

"It's lunchtime and Linda doesn't like to leave out food for too long."

He's right. I slide my chair back. He moves one-step back giving me some space. I was hoping I could follow him upstairs, but he doesn't move or lead the way. He waits for me.

I feel stupid for feeling like this, but it's too soon after Mason. In fact, nothing will ever happen with Harrison. I know how he feels, but it just can't. Not only because I love Mason, but because he's not my type. I would never date a man who is covered in tattoos, wears a beanie and shorts all the time. He's the quintessential rocker and doesn't fit my life.

I don't care that the way he looks at me makes me feel wanted.

I don't care that the way he looks at me makes me feel desired.

I don't care that the way he smells makes me want to crawl into his skin until I'm enveloped in his scent.

I don't care because he's not Mason.

Made in the USA
Charleston, SC
15 June 2013